Through the eyes of
*William*

# THE DISCOVERY

# MARK A. DOWLER

Extended Edition

Copyright © Mark A. Dowler 2022

All rights reserved. No part of this publication may be reproduced, distributed, or transmitted in any form or by any means, including photocopying, recording, or other electronic or mechanical methods, without the prior written permission of the author or publisher.

This book is a work of fiction. The names, characters, places, events, and incidents are either the product of the author's imagination or are used fictitiously.

The author and the publisher assume no responsibility for the direct or indirect consequences of the use of the information herein.

## About the Author

Throughout his lifetime, Mark has been dedicated to the personal and spiritual teachings he has received from Spirit and of life. His sensitivity has enabled him to help others through his ability to heal and teach. He has shared the knowledge through his empathy and his ability to channel Spirit.

Today you will find Mark following a new direction in his service, bringing the teachings through the medium of the word.

# Acknowledgements

I would like to acknowledge the spiritual influences, seen and unseen, that have been a light in my life and continue to do so.

-

I would like to thank those who have supported me in writing and editing this book.

## Introduction

The story was written to bring awareness into our lives. But unfortunately, it often takes another to show us the way and awaken us to a deeper spiritual understanding of the world we are exposed to. Even though the story is fictional, it encompasses a hidden truth of reality that we face in every waking moment of every day. It reveals to us that there is more to life and that we are all connected.

The story introduces William, who changes the lives of all those he meets while grasping the reality of emotions and insights into an understanding of a new world. He appears initially as a young child within the story, and as the story unfolds, they soon realise that his knowledge and understanding are far more worldly than his age would seem to appear. Adapting to his new environment with his new family, he soon realises that all is not well as they face a threat. With newfound abilities awakened during his stay, he becomes the catalyst for the many changes and phenomena in the lives he touches. Not only is William a mystery, but a greater one unfolds, as they all soon discover!

See the world through the eyes of William on his account of his journey into a new world.

# Contents

| | |
|---|---|
| A New Awakening | 11 |
| The Meeting | 16 |
| The Insightful Journey | 20 |
| My New Home | 26 |
| The City | 36 |
| Returning Home | 62 |
| The Discovery | 67 |
| The Unexpected Visitor | 80 |
| The Other Realm | 97 |
| A Village Suffering | 103 |
| A New Insight | 142 |
| An Unexpected Turn | 152 |
| The Village Fayre Encounter | 172 |
| The Enchanted | 195 |
| The Forbidding Contract | 211 |
| The Path to Deliverance – Part I | 233 |
| The Path to Deliverance – Part II | 246 |
| The Uncertainty | 264 |
| A Trodden Path | 266 |
| The Seeker | 272 |
| The Trial | 278 |
| The Vantage Point | 290 |
| Strange Encounter | 294 |

| | |
|---|---|
| The Chase | 307 |
| Within the Shadows | 317 |
| Finding the Way | 328 |
| The House of Hibahrous | 343 |
| Gulielmus | 359 |
| The Enchanted Isle of Emlkuyh | 365 |
| The Enchanted Isle of Emlkuyh – The Cavern Part I | 378 |
| The Enchanted Isle of Emlkuyh – The Cavern Part II | 398 |
| Camarierhn City | 406 |
| Home Sweet Home | 424 |

*Chapter I*

# A New Awakening

It was a sunrise like any other. As the darkness started to withdraw to welcome the new day, a gentle sea breeze could be felt as it embraced all in its path, dancing over the sea and across the sands. A flock of coastal birds flew swiftly over the coastline in search of food. As the tides made their way into the land, they embraced the sands and rocks in their path. All was in harmony, of peace and serenity as nature intended.

Suddenly, the flock of birds parading the sky started to react differently and soon left. It was as if their senses had alerted them that something was amiss. The coastline became void of all life, except those creatures burrowed deep within the sands and the marine life in the sea near the coastline shore.

A short, loud burst of sound resonated, causing an alteration in the vibration of energy within the coastal area where it appeared. The wind started to swirl, forming the outer ring in the creation of a phenomenon. A gust of wind began to brush the sands, the rocks, and the sea below. A light presently appeared at the centre of the ring, and soon there was silence. This was shortly followed by a sweet vibration of sound that hummed, and then as it quietened, a sphere of intense bright light appeared from the centre of the ring. The light shimmered multi-faceted colours within its core. The wind started to settle as the phenomenon began to withdraw and dissipate, leaving the sphere to gently hover. As the coastal sands lay still, and with the calming of the sea, it wasn't long before the birds and other coastal life returned to their natural state.

The sphere then lowered itself to where the sands lay, soft and calm. As it altered its structure, it then began to take human form. It became dense as its vibration changed, slowing down and altering to vibrate and harmonise within its new frequency.

Here, I came into being to a realm of emotions and consciousness. Being conscious of the sand beneath my feet, the waves of the sea and the birds in the sky, I soon found myself adapting to this new awareness of life. With a gentle cool breeze gently caressing my face, I had a sense of being present. As I walked the path along the sands, I felt more connected to the ground supporting me. With only a garment of clothing covering my body, I soon adjusted to the conditions of the environment. I knew that there was more to my being, a presence in the physical universe of life.

As I glanced down, I soon became more aware of my body, presented in its new physical form. The light shimmered, emanating from the skin of the body I had now inhabited. As the light faded, the reality of existing in the physical dimension became more apparent and real. My memories of my past dwindled and soon faded from the forefront of my consciousness. This, I understood, was part of the process of this new awakening.

As I looked around, and with no others present to share the view, I could see the beauty of the place I now occupied, accompanied by the bliss and stillness of how I felt. I also felt excited, knowing that a purpose was to be fulfilled in the understanding and what was to become of me. Little did I know that these emotions were to play an essential part in my journey. Everything was new to me in my understanding of what was, how this environment affected me, and how I felt stimulated by these newfound emotions. This presented many questions, and the foremost question was, who am I? I also noted that I wasn't quite sure where I was!

I became more alive at that moment by the stimulation of the senses that this new life granted me. It felt quite profound as the intensity of all the other senses came into play. I felt connected, a part of everything.

Looking around, I felt drawn to the sea. I could feel the stimulation of the unseen energy, the vibration of its pure state, carried by the breeze that embraced me. It gave me a sense of purity and of being naturally connected with the sea, the ocean, and the life sustained within it. As I started to walk towards the sea to a point where the tides caressed the sands, I began to reach down to touch the water. I could feel the coldness and the slight pressure of the water as the waves caressed my hand. Moving forward a few steps, I found myself standing on the wet sands, with my feet submerged in the cold water. I felt fully immersed in the experience. As if on cue, I seemed to gain an understanding to identify with what I had seen in the area I now found myself in. It made me wonder, what else was new to be discovered? I knew that there were gaps in my knowledge of this place, of this Gaia, but I knew I would soon come to learn of them.

I felt the urge to look down into the reflection of the water to see the form I now inhabited. A manifestation of a body that would allow me to interact with the world around me.

"So, this is what I look like", as the words became reflected in my thoughts.

My eyes were as blue as the sky reflecting on the ocean, as they glimmered and sparkled like the sun's reflection. My hair was full and slightly wavy, matched by the colour of the light sands of the beach. Bringing my hands to my face, I could feel how soft my skin felt with the sensitive touch of my fingers. I could see ears on either side of my head, partially hidden by hair. The more attention I placed on them, the more I could acutely hear the sounds around me. Looking at my nose, I noticed it was small. I was then aware of the scents that occupied the air and discovered that different scents caused different reactions. The most prominent feature was my mouth. Slightly full in size but seems to fit nicely in place. I soon found myself taking a breath through my nose, noticing my upper body rise and then breathing out my mouth, seeing my upper body fall. The more focus I placed on my new body, the more I realised I needed to learn more about the operation and the need to sustain it. Like all changes, it brought reflection on what was.

Even though I was experiencing a new emotion of wonderment, I felt something was missing within this new life that would complete it. I felt the need for an emotional connection with others like me.

Walking further back from the sea, I felt the sand's warmth and coarseness beneath my feet. I decided to see what this new body was capable of. As I walked, I noticed that not only were my feet creating footprints in the sand, but I was also making patterns. So I decided to pick up the pace, running in different directions. I found that manipulating this body enabled me to create various styles of patterns, some simple and some more complicated. Although my emotions were stimulated by this activity, I soon realised that this body was tiring. I was finding myself trying to catch my breath and decided to break from my activity. Having rested for a short period, I began to walk a slight distance away from the patterns, only then to turn back to look to see what I had created. I was impressed to witness the result. The simple patterns were more easily understood, as they were clear in their direction. I could see that the results brought more clarity. The more complicated they were, the more they required clarification and understanding. I preferred the simplest of patterns, like life in a way.

I decided to sit on a large rock to admire the scenery in front of me. It wasn't long before a young gull caught my attention. On further observation, it appeared to be injured, lying by a smaller rock just off to my left. As I reached down to hold it in my hands, my attention was drawn to one of its wings, which appeared to be damaged. As small as it was, I soon became captivated by the energy surrounding it. Shortly with more focus, a beautiful assortment of colours began to display itself. I could see the colours slightly change, blending as they started to expand. I noticed the accompaniment of dark patches within the area of its left wing. As I became mindful within the observation, I felt an emotional connection, finding myself sharing its emotions, feeling its sadness, its fear and its suffering. I could see the energy started to deplete, as its life force was leaving it.

As a feeling of emotional loss started to encroach, I could feel water seeping from my eyes.

It was such a young life that had barely impacted this world and would soon depart from it. Truly little was my knowledge of its life, but I knew I wanted to give it a chance to experience it to its fullest and to know love. I wanted to see this young gull alive and well. I looked to the ocean to find the focus and be mindful of the moment as I pondered this. Suddenly I felt movement in my hands. Wondering what this could be, I looked down. To my amazement and relief, the young gull was exercising both wings. I must have been a part of the healing in some way. I felt I had made my first emotional connection. To my joy and relief, the young gull was soon able to take flight and fly away.

I started to reflect on what I had discovered and learned so far. As I summarised my thoughts, I had the feeling I should head further inland.

*Chapter II*

# The Meeting

As I started to venture further inland, feeling connected with all I had seen and interacted with, two others approached me from a distance. I wondered if they were here for me!

As they approached, the younger, slightly smaller of the two softly spoke, offering words that appeared warm and loving. Although I couldn't quite make out the words, I felt they were concerned about my solitude in being here.

Listening intently, I knew from the reaction of their energy that they were trying to engage in a conversation with me. The more words that were spoken, I found it easier to adapt to the structure and formation of the sounds of their language. It wasn't long before the words became clear, enabling me to interpret them. I proceeded to open my mouth and started to utter some sounds. I initially struggled until I found the word I was looking for.

"Hello".

The taller of the two came closer. The sound of the voice seemed more intense and somewhat deeper than the other one.

"Where are your parents?"

Through an understanding of a sense of empathy towards them, I became aware of their genders and their emotional needs.

"What is your name?" the female asked.

I stood there, mindful of their attention on me. I noticed the energy of her aura, the light surrounding her body, and how it changed colour to varied shades of yellow, orange and red. I felt their openness and their encouragement in ensuring I was OK. As their questioning continued, I could see that their emotions and the colours within their auras were responding to my feedback.

Not remembering who I was, I wasn't sure how to answer their questions. I again opened my mouth to utter some sounds until I found myself replying, "Name".

I then proceeded to move my head from left to right in response to support what I was trying to convey. Talking got easier as more words were spoken. From my response to their questioning, I could see that they were pleased with my answers. I also noticed the energy of their auras became more vibrant in colour, reacting to their emotions.

"Where are your parents?" the male asked again.

"Parents", I replied.

It seemed that I found myself repeating what they were asking. I noticed that the couple's auras had altered, as their colours seemed to lose their vibrancy.

The female then knelt in front of me, gently took my hand and said in a sad, soft tone, "Where is your family?"

I felt an overwhelming feeling of emotion embrace me from the female. This filled me with warmth, love, and a sense of emotional security as her energy started to envelop me. I motioned my head from left to right to provide an answer.

As I observed them, the female stood up and approached the male.

"Henry, we can't leave him like this, as he is only a child – He must be only seven by the way he looks!"

The man responded, "Jane, I know... it's probably just a coincidence. His parents must be around here somewhere!"

I realised that the new form I had been presented with was that of a young male child. Yet I knew, somehow, that this new representation of self would be the catalyst that would help bring me an understanding of my new life. I now also knew both of their names.

"We must see if we can unite him with his family - his poor parents must be frantic with worry. I can only just imagine what they must be going through!"

"I will call Jacob to see if any child has been reported missing".

Jane went on to say, "Henry, I'm worried. What if something has happened to them!"

"I'm sure there's a plausible explanation for this! Until we can find and reunite him with his parents, maybe the best solution, for now, is for him to come home with us?"

"We don't even know his name", Henry went on further to say.

Looking at me, she softly asked me again, "What is your name?"

Not remembering who I was, all I could do was shrug my shoulders and then move my head from left to right in response to her question.

I could see that Jane was in thought as to how to respond.

"That's it! Shall we call him William?" I heard Jane then suggest.

"Are you sure you want to call him William? What with that being your brother's name".

"Yes – I know what I am doing!"

Turning again to face me, she asked, "Are you OK if we call you William?"

From the way Henry had responded to her request, her emotions had become heightened. It occurred to me then that the name she had chosen for me was the name I then used to identify myself and for others to recognise me. With my own emotions stimulated in intensity, I recognised the warmth of the love of the relationship of a family bond between us. I realised that our paths had met for a reason, that they were here for me. Realising this and acknowledging her plea, I looked up to Jane and called out the name that she had suggested. This response caused another emotional reaction in Jane, as a smile came to her face.

I noticed Henry retrieve a small device from his clothing. As he turned away from us, from what I could hear and understand, the conversation must have been about me. I wasn't sure who he was speaking to, as no one else was with him.

As I looked at the energy of Jane's aura, the colours started to alter as more yellows, reds and browns were introduced. I started to become aware of seeing a strand of whispery energy being created between us, connecting us emotionally.

At first, my vocabulary was limited by my understanding of the language. I knew somehow, given time and opportunity, I would soon learn to master it.

A cool breeze caused my body to shiver. As I glanced at Jane, I noticed her watching me.

"Henry, would you please get the blanket from the back seat of the jeep for William?"

I noticed that Henry had left us for a short while. On his return, the blanket that Jane had asked for was placed around me, leaving me to feel embraced by the warmth it offered. It felt cosy and comfortable as I was partially cocooned within it. We then made our way to the jeep with Jane holding my hand. I was soon fastened in securely by a strap for my safety on a seat to the left side, positioned on the back row. With Jane and Henry seated and fastened, we headed to a destination called home. It was a place that I felt sure I would soon become accustomed to.

*Chapter III*

## The Insightful Journey

It was at that time I realised that my view of this world, of this life, would influence two special people to whom I would soon become attached.

Gently, Jane and Henry asked more questions. One in particular, how had I arrived at the beach? From the point of my arrival, I gave as little response as I could, only referring to my time on the beach. I knew that given time, they would start to realise that there was more to who I was than a child of seven years.

The journey was quite fascinating to witness. As exciting as this new form was to me, so was this moving mechanical structure that was carrying us to our destination. I could see much beyond the jeep. To help with my understanding of what I had seen, Jane was very helpful in explaining everything that I had pointed out. As I relaxed further, I could start to see the energy of Jane's aura, as colours of yellow, orange, and various shades of blue started to become more evident. I could see she was reacting to the notion that I had an inquiring mind, and at the same time, she was trying to understand me. As time moved on, for a period, there was silence. Although my eyes were partially closed, I found that I could still glimpse the world outside of the jeep.

I felt Jane move forward in her seat.

"Thank you for supporting me today", I heard Jane say to Henry.

I focused on their conversation, listening to what they were saying.

"You have been through so much. I couldn't let you go through this by yourself", I heard Henry say.

"I hope it will all make sense soon, what with the dream and all. I am hoping to get some sleep tonight", Jane responded.

"I do hope so, as this past week you haven't been yourself. It must have been nice to see your brother Wil in your dream".

"I still miss him very much. Seeing him in my dream just brought it all back to me!"

I could feel the emotional connection that she had with her brother, for he was the subject of her conversation with Henry. I could feel her sadness, a feeling of being alone. It reminded me of how I had felt earlier on the beach whilst holding the young gull. I wanted to find out more about her brother and her dream but knew I needed to wait for an opportunity to reveal itself. It wasn't long before Jane settled back into her seat, and I could see that she was deep in thought. I smiled and left her to dwell within her mind. I thought about Jane and silently wished her well with her thoughts.

Closing my eyes, I soon found myself slowly shifting consciousness as Jane's thoughts began to enter my mind. I soon became aware of her memories. We must have connected in more ways than I initially thought.

I could see Jane as a child, smaller than me and a little younger. I was witnessing her last memories of her connection with her brother. I could see a young boy and realised this must be Wil. I could clearly see that they both had created the conditions for their play from their imaginations. He was dressed like a soldier, pretending to protect her and her baby, fighting off any enemies. Looking at Jane with the doll in her arms, she was like a little mother. Caring for her child, demonstrating her ability to love and care for another, especially one of her own. An attribute of who she was as a child that still resonated with her today.

We were then taken to another memory, as Jane's thoughts shifted to when she was at school. I noticed that Wil wasn't with her. I felt a change in her emotions of uncertainty with regard to her brother. This was reinforced when Jane was taken to the headmaster's office to meet up with her father. I noticed her father was wearing a military uniform, and from that point, I could see the reason why Wil had portrayed the role of a soldier within their play.

emories then took us to another place where others were
I see Jane standing with her mother.

she said gently, "Wil isn't well. The doctors have tried to make ..... better but what is wrong with him isn't something they can help with – Wil may have to go to heaven to be with the angels – to be with God. This may be the last time you will see him".

I could see that Jane was getting upset, but she remained quiet.

We were then taken to another memory, and this time we were in a private room. Looking around, I could see Jane's brother Wil, pale and very frail, lying on a bed. Jane was standing close to him.

I could see Jane's father and mother talking to the doctor by the entrance. Listening to the parent's conversation with the doctor, it seems they were talking about Wil and the deterioration of his condition. As they began to talk about the illness he was suffering from, I felt something shift within my body, which brought me back.

Although I missed out on the last part of her memories, I hoped that I would get the opportunity to experience them again, learning of her brother's illness and of their last moments together.

Opening my eyes, I could see Jane facing my way with tears flowing down her cheeks. I could see how the memories of that time, of her brother, had caused her so much sadness. I felt my own emotions stir from what I had witnessed in empathy with hers. I reached out my hand to hold Jane's. In a similar way, as I did with the young gull, I felt the need to convey emotional support and somehow lessen her suffering.

Closing my eyes, I started to drift into a light sleep, in the warmth of knowing that somehow, I was helping her. After a short while later, I found myself opening my eyes to Jane, who was speaking to Henry.

"Maybe the dream is a sign that we can start trying for a child again!"

"We can try, and if we encounter problems, then maybe we can adopt", I heard Henry respond.

From his response, I could see that Henry was emotionally supporting her, also adding supporting comments to her cause for motherhood.

I looked to Jane to try to understand her health situation and what could prevent her from bearing a child. I soon became aware of a defect, an area where dark energy resided within the lower part of her body, near the abdomen. As I tried to investigate, I had a feeling that, in some way, it had to do with Henry.

Bringing my focus back to Jane, I noticed that something else was lying heavily on her mind. As I started to monitor her thoughts, her mind was preoccupied. I wondered if she was thinking about the dream she often referred to.

Jane had soon drifted off to sleep. There was a passiveness about the way she had rested.

Closing my eyes, I started to drift once again. With Jane and Henry's conversation as the last thought on my mind, I found myself more rooted in the deeper states of her consciousness. It wasn't long before I then found myself viewing the visual imagery that was in the state of play. The visual experience was somewhat different from when I linked earlier with her memories. I felt as if I could interact with this one. As curiously as it presented itself to me, I ensured that I remained an observer of the unfoldment of the visual experience.

Sitting in a field with daisies, making bracelets and necklaces, Jane was a child again. Out of nowhere, I noticed that she could hear her brother's voice calling her. Not sure where it was coming from, Jane stood up and called out for him. There was no response, and Jane continued with her search. Every so often, Wil would appear to her at a distance, beckoning her. As soon as Jane got too close to where he was standing, he vanished from her sight. I could see her efforts sway her from reaching her goal as she became deflated by the notion of failing. Just as Jane was going to give up, a large tree appeared in the distance, illuminated by a bright light. Seeing her exhausted, as tears flowed from her eyes, rolling down her cheeks, Jane then rested by the tree. It wasn't until a little while after Wil appeared beside her. Seeing her brother had infused Jane with a new release of energy. Raising herself to her feet, she then rushed over to embrace him.

I listened more carefully to the dialogue that took place between them as Jane proceeded with the question that played heavily on her mind.

"Why did you leave me?"

"I'm sorry! I felt so tired and knew that I wasn't going to get better. I was pleased that we had the opportunity to say goodbye. I knew I'd see you again, as the angels told me that we would – I have never been far, as I have always been watching over you, like the games we used to play. Through your pains and your sorrows, I have been there, even when you had emotionally felt lost".

Wil went on to say that he came to tell her about a revelation. I could see him pointing to the ground just in front of him. Water started to appear out from the ground until a pool had formed. I noticed Jane looking down at the reflection of the water. Jane could only see herself and Wil. It wasn't long before other images appeared. From nothingness came something, and you could see all the suffering and loss in the world. Jane was shown the pain and the wars both in the world and those created in the homes. So much heartache, so much grief.

"Wil, why does God allow this to happen?"

To reassure her, Wil asked her to look again at the reflection on the surface of the water. Suddenly the reflection on the water showed the world in darkness. Then from this darkness, lights started to appear around the world. He then informed her that these are lightworkers, those who work from heaven to those who have incarnated on earth to do God's will. He then went on to tell her that the world was changing and that she would be a part of something great.

Being present within her thoughts, I was aware of the many questions that were based on what Wil had told Jane.

Wil then told Jane to go to the coast when the sun was about to rise.

I could see the place where I had arrived, as it was shown in the reflection on the water. Then I saw myself wandering, walking along the beach.

"Wil, I know this place! That's State Park near Portland, Oregon".

"It's time for me to go".

"You have just arrived! What about this child?"

I presumed she was talking about me.

"You will know what to do. Trust and follow the intelligence of your heart", and with those words, Wil soon faded from her sight.

I found myself returning to my own conscious state, and as my eyes started to open, I felt gratitude for being given an understanding of Jane's thoughts and her journey. It seemed that her dream wasn't only a message for her but a confirmation for me as to why I was here. I started to feel tired and then relaxed back, closing my eyes for the remainder of the journey.

I was suddenly awoken by an echo of a young male voice calling my name. Opening my eyes, I noticed Jane was looking through the window to her right. Henry was focused on taking us to our destination, as he was mindful of his task and the road ahead. I wondered where the voice had come from. I looked through the window to my left and noticed that what I could see was a light shining through the trees. As I focused on the light, I could see the outline of a boy. Suddenly I could hear Jane's voice calling me. As I opened my eyes, Jane was telling me that we had arrived. Had I been dreaming?

As I looked back at the trees within the forest that we had passed through, I couldn't see the light shining through the trees to then see the boy, as I had done in the dream. I was curious about my dream at first, and then I turned my focus to the front, looking through all windows of the jeep to see where our journey had taken us. We were in a secluded place in the countryside, on the outskirts of the city.

## Chapter IV

## My New Home

"Where are we?" I asked.

Jane responded with a loving smile and said, "We're home".

I looked around through the windows of the jeep to see what I could see. As before, I seemed to understand and identify with what was presented before me. I noticed we were parked near a building with an external raised wooden floor, with steps leading up to the entrance of the building. The building was constructed out of hardened materials. Some of the windows brought much light and warmth into this home from the sun. I could also see shutters at the windows, providing protection from the harsher weather conditions. There appeared to be much land surrounding the property. I could also see buildings that housed machinery and could possibly be a shelter for animals. There were also cattle that were kept outside on the land. Over time, I intuitively felt I would learn much about their estate and its history.

Jane assisted me in getting down from the jeep while Henry opened the door to their home.

As Henry opened the door, a light brown dog came running out. From what I could see, it was light on its feet, boisterous in nature and young in appearance. The dog first greeted Henry, then sprang over to us to welcome Jane. Not sure what its reaction to me would be or its intention, I hid behind her. Jane smiled and then asked Charlie to sit.

"It's OK, this is Charlie; he is young like you, William. Bella will be waiting inside; she is much older than Charlie".

She then turned to Charlie while patting him and stroking him around the back of his head and ears with one hand.

"Now Charlie, this is William. He is family, be a good boy and go and find Henry".

As Charlie ran back into the house, I stepped back out from behind Jane to then stand beside her. We then made our way to the steps, onto the porch and then into their home. As I walked in, I felt that we were being observed, other than those physically present. I felt another presence, curious about my state of being. It was semi-transparent to the eye, white and whispery in form. I could see it was observing me from the other end of the hall, and then it withdrew back and disappeared. As neither Jane nor Henry reacted, it occurred to me that they couldn't see it. My presence must have startled it as soon as I entered the home.

The hallway led to many rooms. At the far end of the hall, I could see stairs leading to the first floor. I soon learnt that the first floor had three bedrooms and a bathroom for the family. On the ground floor, the main space for living was through the first door on the left. Through the second door to the left was the main family room. On the right, through the first door, was a dining room. The following door gave access to a small room that housed a toilet and a washbasin. A kitchen with a pantry could be found through the last door on the right. An open archway connected both the kitchen and the dining room. A door at the far end of the hall provided access to the study. Just by the door next to the dining room stood a tall standing coat rack. I also noticed a small window at the main entrance of the home.

"William, we will need to get you dressed into something warm and more comfortable. I have some clothes that may fit you – Shall we go and see?"

Turning to face Jane, I replied, "OK".

Jane then took my hand, and we made our way up the stairs that led to one of the bedrooms. As we reached the top, I became aware of the presence of two others. I couldn't see them, but I felt as if they were observing me.

I turned to Jane and asked, "Who else lives here?"

"Only us - why?"

Not wanting to unsettle her, as this may be something I needed to understand first, I just shrugged and smiled.

Jane smiled at me and said, "We must find you some clothes".

I was taken into a bedroom, the second room on the left, on the opposite side of the hallway from where I was standing.

"William, this will be your room".

The room was fitted with a small bed to the right, accompanied by a fluffy teddy bear. I could see toys that were placed in a box at the bottom of the bed. I then noticed a luminous lamp of a winged angel that could be used to illuminate the room. A dressing table could also be seen, positioned under the window at the far end. On the left stood fitted wardrobes.

I turned to Jane and asked, "Whose room was this?"

"You see, we were planning to have a baby girl. We had started to decorate this room for her, but she didn't make it... I had lost her late into the pregnancy".

"I'm sorry!"

"Why are you sorry, William?"

"For your loss".

I could tell from the smile on her face that she appreciated my response.

"Over time, our little Joe, who is our nephew, would have slept in here. Joe is fifteen now and usually stays with his father. His mother is Henry's sister".

I noticed that Jane felt comfortable and at ease talking to me.

"Are Joe's mom and dad not together?"

"No, as with some parents, they couldn't get along with each other anymore. So they thought it would be best to live apart, as it was upsetting for Joe".

I soon felt sadness as my thoughts were drawn to Henry for some reason.

Jane then went on to tell me about Henry's other sister, who passed away just over four months ago".

Not wanting to pry further, I felt what I initially needed to know was revealed by learning about Henry's other sister. I left it open to see if anything else could be said about her; if not now, then maybe later.

"We can decorate the room and fill it with the toys you would like to play with. We also need to get you some clothes. For now, there should be something you can wear in the wardrobe".

I felt a feeling of sadness from Jane as I felt the emptiness of her loss in her life. I felt a change was waiting to occur for both Jane and Henry, but I couldn't explain it.

"These will do!"

I could see her retrieve items from the wardrobe, telling me what each item was.

"OK, let's see what we have managed to sort out for you. We have a blue t-shirt, a white sweater and a cream pair of chinos".

Jane then opened the top left drawer to retrieve some underwear for me. As she opened the drawer beneath, it seemed to contain accessories, like gloves to keep your hands warm and sunglasses to protect your eyes from the sun. Opening the drawer at the top right, I noticed that she had pulled out a pair of blue socks.

"These should do", I heard her comment.

Jane then waited for me to try the clothes on, being on hand to assist me where appropriate, if required.

"They look as if they were made for you. How do they feel?"

I nodded to agree with her comments.

Now that I was dressed in the appropriate clothing, we went back downstairs. As we reached the bottom, Henry was in the kitchen, preparing breakfast.

Jane took me into the family room, where Charlie and Bella were resting.

Both are beautiful in colour and graceful and friendly in temperament. Bella looked old for a Red Setter, and Jane had told me that she was twelve, nearly thirteen. Charlie was a young Labrador Retriever who had only just turned three within the past month. They both were lying quietly around the fireplace. I felt at ease with them, feeling accepted as a member of their family.

I heard Jane call out to Henry, asking him to join us.

As Henry and Jane discussed what to do with me, my focus went to Bella. As she lay in her bed resting, I became aware of the energy of her aura. The more I was mindful of her, I could see it expand. Her aura seemed to permeate with soft colours of brown, mild green, and pink, with a little blue and yellow. She looked relaxed and curious about my presence. I noticed a slight escape of energy from the location of the heart. As I focused on the area, there appeared to be small amounts of dark whispery energy forming around the main organ. Her heart seemed to be degrading in health, causing a whimper and shortness of her breath. Noticing Jane and Henry still talking, I felt the need to help Bella. I made my way over to her to kneel beside her. I then placed my left hand slightly above and away from her chest, near the location of the heart. Suddenly the palm of my hand started to glow. I felt an intensity of divine energy, of love flowing through me, through my palm to Bella. It was as though nothing else was of focus, and I became one with the energy flowing through me. I then started to see the affected area being healed by the light entering it. As the last of the dark energy diminished, I could see the heart's energy return to its full health. I felt the need to withdraw my hand, and as I did, the light in the palm of my hand settled.

I briefly turned to face Jane and Henry. I could see that they were still focused on each other, talking about the day and other matters.

I noticed that Bella had raised herself to turn her gaze in my direction. It was looking into her eyes, I could see that she was thankful. The energy of her aura looked vibrant.

I suddenly heard my name being called. It was Jane asking me to follow them into the dining room. Leaving Bella, I got up and walked over to Jane. As we entered the dining room, with a little assistance from her, I managed to climb onto a chair. Jane had seated herself to my left as I waited to try the food for the first time. After about five minutes, Henry brought breakfast to the table and what seemed to be an object containing water.

As the small flat object was placed in front of me, it hosted two items that were circular and flat in shape. I looked at Jane to try to understand what was in front of me. I soon learnt that the breakfast consisted of two small pancakes.

"We have maple syrup if you would like to try it? It is sweet to taste. We also have bananas to go with the syrup".

I nodded to Jane so I could try them both.

As Jane poured on the syrup, she then sliced one of the bananas using a flat silver object to cut it into smaller pieces. The slices of the banana were then shared between the two pancakes. Once this was done, she then reduced the pancakes into smaller pieces.

Using what Jane had referred to me as a fork, she was then able to demonstrate to me how to pick up the pieces, to then place them in my mouth.

My fork happened to be much smaller than Jane's and Henry's. It seemed to be made from a different material that was designed and created for children. As I placed a piece of the pancake into my mouth, I started to get a sweetness of sensation, tantalising the senses of my taste buds. With the pancake in my mouth, I watched Jane demonstrate as she chewed the food before swallowing it. Not having to eat food before was a new experience. As demonstrated by Jane, I started to move my jaw in the way it was shown to me. Once the pancake was into more manageable pieces in my mouth, I began to swallow.

My energy started to react to the food I was putting in my mouth. As I paused to see what would happen, I could feel the energy adapt and then settle.

"Let's see if you can eat the rest?" asked Jane.

I proceeded with the ritual of eating from the plate and drinking from the beaker.

"I need to go into the city, to pop into the police station and speak to Jacob about William. While I'm there, I can pick up the parcel from the post office", I heard Henry mention to Jane.

"We'll come with you, as I need to get William some more clothes for him to wear", Jane responded.

I looked at Jane as she was speaking and noticed that she seemed delighted at the prospect of acquiring some clothes for me.

Once we had all finished with our breakfast, Henry started to clear the table while I followed Jane into the family room.

"Who is Jacob?" I asked.

"He is a good friend of Henry's. Jacob is the Police Captain and is seen as the local hero. He has done a good job in keeping the city and surrounding areas safe".

Realising that I needed something to wear on my feet other than socks, Jane asked me to wait in the family room.

"I won't be long. I am just going to fetch you something to wear on your feet for our trip to the city".

While waiting, I soon felt a coldness that surrounded me. The spiritual energy I first encountered earlier was now appearing in the corner of the room. It seemed to be fluctuating in its spiritual form. Although it kept its distance from me, I thought it would be a good idea to try to understand it, so I focused on its appearance. Within a short time, it became more distinguishable, so I beckoned it to come closer. Curious, the spiritual energy in its current form remained where it was. I then started to walk towards it. Stopping halfway, I held out my hand and started to send out healing energy as I felt I needed to reassure it of my intention. It seemed to be responding to my help as its spiritual energy began to take spirit form, becoming more identifiable within its state. I could recognise a lady of mature years, much older than Jane, appearing before me. Her energy permeated the suffering and torment she endured while living. The old lady started to cry, and after a few short minutes, she disappeared. I was then aware of Jane returning to the room.

"William is everything OK? I thought I heard crying coming from this room".

Noticing her concerns and not to alarm her, I replied, "I am OK".

I could see she was looking to reassure me, as I had a feeling that she had my best interest at heart.

"Please come and sit down on the settee for me while I try to see if these old sneakers will fit you. I found them in the back of the wardrobe in your bedroom".

The sneakers were slightly a little big for my feet, but they seemed to go on. It felt strange to wear them, as images of Jane's nephew started to appear in my mind of when he was young. I could feel his excitement, his love for Jane and Henry. The relief from school. I soon felt my emotions changing as I began to feel emotionally despondent. On further enquiry, I felt his emotional need to please his parents. I became aware of his sadness at the breakup of their relationship and his needs as their son. I then had a rush of a feeling and flashbacks of his adventures as a child. He seemed to have had an overly complicated emotional childhood.

I began to walk around the family room floor to balance and get used to them. As I turned to face Jane, I could see her peering outside the window. The day appeared to be bright and sunny, as the warmth of the sun brought a smile to her face.

"Was Joe sad?" I asked as the emotions of the previous owner enveloped me.

"Why do you ask?"

"I just thought about what you had told me upstairs".

"He was upset over the separation of his parents, I would say".

I felt that there was more. I held the rest back from Jane so as not to worry her.

Jane took my hand, and we both walked to the door which led to the porch. As she opened the door and we walked out, I looked over at the jeep and noticed Henry was already there. He was checking to make sure that all was OK for the journey.

I could feel the warmth of the sun on my face. It was good to see nature surrounding me. The area was full of life and permeating energy. It was beautiful and breathtaking to behold. I looked up at Jane and could see Jane looking at me. The energy of her aura was radiant, displaying a vibrancy of colours of yellow, gold, oranges, green and magenta. From her enthusiasm, I could see that she loved the outdoors and being in nature. It seemed to captivate her. I noticed that her eyes glistened, sparkling with the light of the sun. Her smile added to her perfection. As Jane was lovingly watching me, I was intuitively aware of a profound inner peace about her. I could see her take a deep breath in and out, then noticed that she had closed her eyes as if to take in and seize the moment.

"Are you coming?" I could hear Henry call out.

On hearing Henry's voice, I could see Jane slowly open her eyes, to gradually allow the light in. While facing me, I could see that she soon became observant and then emotionally overwhelmed.

"What the... Oh my...".

I could see Jane getting emotional and losing her words to formulate a sentence.

"How is this so?" she continued to ask.

I am learning so much about Jane. From her observations and how my emotions had reacted while being around her.

"Jane, do you have what you need?" I could hear Henry call out.

As Jane was alerted by Henry's questioning, she turned to face him, and I could hear her reply, "Yes".

As she turned back to me, and from the puzzled expression on her face, whatever she was a witness to just a moment ago, appeared to have gone.

"We must go now as Henry is waiting. We need to go into town to get you some new clothes and some food for this evening".

I could see that she was trying to figure out in her mind what had just happened. As we were walking to the jeep, every so often, I could see Jane taking a brief glimpse look at me. I was helped into the jeep by Henry, seated in the same seat as before, next to her.

As we were leaving the farm, there appeared to be only one road leading into and out of their property that I could see. As we passed the trees in the forest, I looked to see if I could see the light that I had seen earlier, but there was no sign of it.

While Henry was driving us into the city, I started to relax and close my eyes. I thought about Jane and Henry, then my new home. I then began to drift into a deeper state of consciousness. For a moment, it went dark, and then suddenly, I was shown flashes of images, which came and went as soon as they appeared in my mind. First, I saw a little girl, then some items of clothing. Next, I could see people crowded in different spaces, followed by images of different flowers. I could then see Jane laughing and talking to another person. The last images were of Jane and I sitting at a table talking to a young woman. The flurry of images soon brought me back to a conscious state. Opening my eyes, I looked around to see if Jane and Henry were still there for reassurance. Seeing them, I took a deep breath, then relaxed and closed my eyes. I felt Jane take my right hand to then hold it tight to comfort me. I could feel her warmth, and as I opened my eyes, I was welcomed by her loving smile.

*Chapter V*

# The City

It wasn't long before we reached our destination. Henry parked the jeep in a parking lot close to the shopping centre.

Jane helped me out of the jeep, and as I looked around at the surrounding area, I could see buildings varying in size. The place seemed to be busy, as families and groups of people were milling about, walking, and talking to each other.

As I looked at Jane, I could see her talking to Henry about what their plans were while we were here. As I waited patiently, I could see the affection they had for each other as they embraced each other with a hug before saying goodbye.

After their embrace, Jane took my hand and then we left the parking lot. We soon reached a large building with revolving doors that looked menacing. I wondered whether it was a matter of timing to pass through them. I was unsure of how to proceed, so I decided to stay rooted to where I was, out of uncertainty of what could happen to us.

"Are you OK, William?"

I pointed to the revolving doors and expressed concern.

"It's OK! There is another entrance with a door to the left".

With Jane taking my hand, I felt a sigh of relief, and we entered the building using the other entrance. We were assisted by a man with a cap who was dressed in a theme that matched the colours of the store. Once we found ourselves inside, it was as if we had entered another world.

With the place being so vast, Jane had helped me to read the signs. I soon learnt that there were four floors, with each floor hosting a different department. The first floor hosted items for the home, with the second floor for outdoor activities. The third and fourth floors were for clothes; the third was for women and children, and the fourth was for men. The restaurant was also on the third floor.

I looked up at Jane and saw her smiling down at me. Holding my hand and keeping me close, we ventured onto the moving stairs. I was nervous at first, but with Jane beside me, we managed to work our way up to the third floor, where we needed to be.

As I looked around the area, and from what I could see, there were mainly women with their children and newborn babies.

Jane went to get a basket to put the items of clothing in. We then walked around to carefully collect different items of clothing that would be more suited to my size and gender. We spent a good couple of hours with me trying on different clothes and footwear until we were both happy that the selection we had, was right for me. With all the items in the basket, we headed for a queue to pay for them.

While we were queuing, I could hear crying. I looked around and couldn't initially see where it was coming from. Wanting to identify who it was, I placed the focus of my energy on the sounds of the cry. I started to become aware of thoughts other than my own, as well as the feelings that accompanied them. As I was able to establish the source of the crying, I then realised I was dealing with the unseen emotional presence of a young girl. It was then I began to feel changes within my body as I could feel the temperature had started to drop. As I breathed out, cold air began to escape with it. I felt drawn to a rack of young girls' sweaters. Knowing that I couldn't leave Jane's sight, I needed to somehow look to see what I could do to help the girl.

As the rack wasn't far from where we were, I made my way as close as I could.

"William, please stay close so that I can see you", I heard Jane say.

"I will be here".

As I moved closer to the rack of young girls' sweaters, I could see the start of an outline as the spiritual energy started to take form. The young girl, although translucent, became clearer to see. The more I focused on her, the more she became solid in form. I looked around to see if others could see what I could, but I seemed to be the only one.

Turning around to look at Jane, I noticed that she was standing in the same spot where she had entered the queue and did not appear to be moving forward. I also could see she was getting a little impatient.

As I turned my focus back to the girl, I could see she was seated with her arms and knees held close to her chest. Her forehead was resting on her knees. She was wearing a white dress, and I also noticed that her skin was pale. Her hair was long with blonde wavy locks. The temperature of my body started to rise a little, but my breath was still cold. Wanting to know more, I reached out to touch her. As my hand got close to her shoulders, she quickly looked up, then scurried slightly on her hands and knees to behind the rack. I called out to her quietly, trying not to draw any attention from anyone else.

"Please do not be afraid".

I turned to look at Jane to see where she was in the queue. I could see that she was observing me, seeing what I was up to. Seeing that I was OK and then smiling briefly at me, I could then see her engage in a conversation with another person in the line.

I looked back in the direction that the little girl had scurried. I tried to see if I could connect with her emotionally, this time closing my eyes. It felt as if she was trying to distance herself, and it was as though she was fighting to let me in. After what seemed several minutes, as I opened my eyes, I became startled and unnerved as she appeared within a couple of feet of where I stood, facing me. We were practically eye-to-eye with each other.

The colour of her eyes was an icy blue, and it was as though they were penetrating my very soul. A coldness came over me as I felt a cold shiver go through me.

This had startled and unsettled me a little. What also caught my attention was a small picture book that was held tightly in the little girl's hand. I couldn't make out what it was about but wondered if it was significant in some way.

"You can see me?" She whispered.

"What happened to you?" I asked.

She pointed to a lady who was about fourth behind Jane in the queue. The lady appeared to be harbouring a loss, and there was sadness within her emotional energy. She appeared to be a little out of focus than I could see of the others. As I observed the lady further, my body started to reflect a weakness within itself as fatigue started to settle in.

I turned back to face the girl, feeling slightly confused and beginning to feel emotional.

"I'm not sure how I can help!"

The girl started to extend her hand to me, and I felt I needed to respond. As I held her hand, my vision was immediately directed inwardly. Here I found myself consciously transported back in time. This was new to me, as I couldn't recall any memory of having experienced this before now.

I was shown the little girl playing in front of a house, on the lawn, and away from the main road. It felt so real, as I felt totally immersed in the experience. It was a beautiful sunny day. I could see some of the neighbours outside, in front of their houses, either maintaining their gardens or talking to one another. Voices of adults and children, as well as the sweet sound of birds, occupied my auditory senses. The sounds were often polluted by the vehicles that would pass by. It was as if I could see all that was going on, and no one else could see me. I wanted to get to know the girl so as to understand her. With that in mind, I soon found myself standing near her. I noticed that the girl was unaware of my presence. As I monitored her energy, I was aware of a problem with her heart. I could see small amounts of energy particles of darkness lingering around the region and briefly touching her lungs. I looked around to see what else I could learn about her. She was sitting down, reading the book that I had seen her holding in her hand before I had arrived here. There were also a couple of other books on the lawn near where she had sat. I tried to see if the books could tell me more about my purpose here, but there wasn't much I could learn other than that she would like to read.

I felt the need to go into the house. As I looked up, I could see her mother through the kitchen window. She seemed to be preparing lunch.

As my thoughts were placed upon her, I soon found myself standing near her in the kitchen. Her mother was wearing a silk scarf that was covering her neck, matching a flower-patterned dress. She was slim and beautiful, and her hair was wavy, shoulder-length in style. I couldn't see much here but an adoring mother. Notably, as I observed her as she was preparing lunch, the first and foremost on her mind that was shown to me were her children.

My observation was soon directed to a baby, probably her brother, seated and secured in a highchair. I looked around the kitchen and dining room to see what other details could help me to gather more information about the girl. The only noticeable emotional connection was pictures of the family and little creations of fabric, with 'My Mummy' or 'I Love you Mummy' knitted onto them. I could see the baby observe his mother as he waited in his highchair. I noticed that his energy was calm. As far as I could see, he appeared healthy. Suddenly I was aware of a time shift. The baby was in a different place, seated upright. He was kept in place by small cushions that were positioned beside him on the carpet in what I could assume was the main family room. Seated cross-legged in front of him, I could see his mother's attempt to make him laugh. Sweet, funny sounds through the manipulation of her mouth could be heard. It was good to see his delight and appreciation of the effort she was making with him. Every so often, I noticed her observing the time on her watch. Her energy and her emotions were reacting to something or someone. I looked to see if I could see the girl through the kitchen window, and I noticed that she had moved further to the centre on the lawn. Another little girl appeared to be sitting with her. It was good to see that she was still OK. I then made my way back to the family room. I could see more pictures, some of the baby and others of the girl. There wasn't anything I could see or learn about the circumstances that would help me to understand the reason behind all this.

A noise interrupted my thoughts. It reminded me of the sound of when either Henry or Jane closed the doors on the jeep. I headed over to the kitchen window to look outside to see who had arrived. A man, who was tall and slim with brown hair that had been swept back, had walked over to the little girl. They both seemed to know each other.

Another time shift occurred. This time I found myself in the kitchen, observing the mother and the man who I had seen outside. I could see the mother was preparing the evening meal. I soon realised that the visitor was indeed the father. As they engaged in conversation, I noticed their voices started to rise in tone as they started to argue.

Thoughts of the girl soon entered my mind as I was then shown a vision of her entering the home and making her way into the kitchen. With all the commotion that could be heard, I could see her appear to check to see if her parents were OK! It wasn't long before she started to react to their emotional outbursts by becoming emotionally distressed.

The mother started to wave a piece of paper in her right hand while raising her voice about a medical bill. I could see that she was questioning the father about his gambling habits and their money concerns.

I could then see the father's energy envelope the mother's as he tried to manipulate her reaction to his error of judgement over a gambling choice he made.

The arguments to support their cause went backwards and forwards, adjusting to add weight to leverage their position.

It was through their conversations that I learnt of their names.

Cassy paused briefly to gather her emotions and strength to continue her argument with Wayne.

"You've changed! What happened to the man I fell in love with, the man I married? Have you forgotten your responsibility to us?"

I turned my focus to Amelia, the young girl who brought me here. Amelia looked weak at this point, her face pale with fear. I started to notice a change in her breathing pattern. I could see the energy of her aura, and it wasn't looking healthy, as darker patches of energy appeared within it. The parents seemed unaware that Amelia was in the room while their arguing continued.

Cassy's questioning about his gambling and responsibilities rifled Wayne's energy. Feeling interrogated and needing to regain control over the conversation, Wayne forcibly grabbed Cassy by the left arm. As he continued to argue with her, his voice started to change in tone.

As her tears flowed, Cassy managed to pull her arm loose from Wayne's grip and then retaliated by slapping him across the face.

At this point, I could see that it was getting unbearable for Amelia. Unable to take any more, with difficulty, she managed to climb the stairs to hide in her room. I felt uneasy about what I had just seen with her. Closing my eyes, Amelia was shown to me. I could see she was still breathing but not in a healthy way, as her heart was causing her pain. Curled in a ball on her bed, with her sobbing, I felt helpless seeing her like this.

Opening my eyes and looking at the parents, I could see they were struggling with their emotions.

I wanted to be with Amelia but found myself being held back for some reason.

I could see that Wayne and Cassy were unaware that their constant fighting was also impacting the health and welfare of their children. It seemed to me that they were losing their way.

With Cassy's devotion to family and the neglect from Wayne, her insecurities and abandonment from the one person she thought she could depend on had caused her much heartache. She felt she was losing him and all she had dedicated her life to.

From what I could learn from Wayne, the pressure of life had affected him, his work, the demands of paying the bills and dealing with stress. Little did he know that his suffering wasn't just impacting him but also affecting his family. Watching him, I was aware that his breathing was erratic. His situation in dealing with these problems was affecting his health and state of mind. The means to find a way to better his situation soon backfired as it soon became a distraction into gambling, a newfound interest, an addiction. Gambling was becoming a way of life, one he thought he could manage. It would soon then get to the point where he wouldn't be able to live without it and would cause the loss of what he held dearly within his heart. If he continued, the desire would be for more, and the need would become greater. It would start to challenge his decisions and impose on his emotions. These selfish actions would escalate to an enforced separation or the likelihood of one of them getting hurt.

I felt for the whole family and wanted to embrace them all. But my focus had been directed to Wayne and Cassy. I felt there was still a connection between them. The one thing that they had in common was their children. Their love for the children kept them both together, which kept back the divide in their relationship. Their focus now needed to be on Amelia, who was in pain and needed their attention.

Wayne attempted to grab both of Cassy's arms to calm her down. To avoid this, Cassy stepped back and caught herself on the corner of the table, resulting in her falling backwards and hitting her head on the kitchen unit as she fell to the floor.

Wayne was relieved to see Cassy was still breathing but only barely. A swelling soon appeared on the upper right side of the back of her head. Seeing this, he retrieved a tea towel from one of the kitchen drawers and soaked it under the cold tap from the sink. Crouching near where Cassy lay, I could see him then applying slight pressure with the tea towel to the injured part of her head.

Realising what he had done, Wayne reached out for the phone and dialled the emergency services line. On reaching the operator, I could hear him report the accident. As he was trying to grasp the reality of the situation, I could hear him struggle to explain what had happened. His emotions caused confusion as panic settled in.

After the call to the emergency services, I heard him say, "Cassy, I'm sorry, I didn't mean to. Please stay with me .... I love you!"

As carefully as he could, he carried her to the living room, putting her on their settee to make her more comfortable. I could see the concern for her life on his face.

As Cassy's life force began to weaken, I knew I needed to help but did not know how to proceed. Moreover, I wasn't sure what I needed to do.

Suddenly the frequency of my energy started to react. I could feel the vibration of my energy alter as tingling sensations could be felt. I was becoming more present within my form as if I could interact with this new reality. Being here, standing in front of Wayne, I wondered if he could see me. It soon became apparent that he wasn't able to. I seemed to be existing outside of his normal visible spectrum for sight.

I noticed Wayne had turned his focus to his son. With the tea towel carefully balanced, supporting Cassy's head, he left Cassy's side to attend to his son Peter. This allowed me the opportunity to see if I could heal her.

Reaching out to place my left hand near the area of injury, the palm of my hand started to get hot as the light began to flow through me. I could see the light working, healing the wound and reducing the swelling. It wasn't long before I could see Cassy's life force strengthening. As the healing finished, the temperature of my palm, as well as the light, receded. Cassy, although treated, was still unconscious.

Wayne realised his son, in his distress, was trying to reach out to Cassy. So he did what he thought was best and moved the highchair nearer where she was lying.

Wayne went back over to check on Cassy and noticed the bleeding had stopped. Checking that she was OK, I could see him adjust her a little to ensure she was comfortable.

With the thoughts of Amelia entering his mind, Wayne then glanced up to see if he could see her. Not knowing where she was, he called out her name, but there was no response. With his emotions still heightened, he left Cassy and Peter to look for her. Checking the front lawn first, remembering when he had last seen her, further warranted his concerns for her whereabouts and wellbeing. Due to her difficulty in climbing the stairs, his focus was mainly placed on his efforts checking the rooms on the ground floor. In his desperation, I could see that he was trying to work out where she could be.

I noticed Wayne appeared to be having problems adjusting his breathing to a regular pattern. Seeing him reach into his pockets, he pulled out a small device. After placing it in his mouth and a couple of deep breaths later, it wasn't long before his breathing returned to normal.

I wondered if somehow Amelia's problems were inherited from her father. I needed to find out more about what he knew about his daughter's condition. As I focused on Wayne, trying to tap into his memories, the answer was soon revealed. From what I could understand, Amelia would have had trouble climbing the stairs due to her condition. The stress would have been too much for her heart. It was also revealed that her problem was indeed inherited.

As I turned to look at Wayne, I noticed that he was already on his way up the stairs to see if Amelia was in her room. Shortly after, I could see him returning with Amelia in his arms, placing her on the second settee. Reaching out for the phone on a small table in the living room, Wayne picked up the handset for the second time to ring the emergency services line. This time his emotions got the better of him, as he cried out for someone to send help for his child.

I could hear Wayne mention that Amelia had Cardiomyopathy, resulting from a heart defect when she was born. That her heart had developed complications, even after two operations. The conversation continued, with Wayne answering several questions about her physical state and the medicines she was taking.

I noticed how tired he looked. He appeared to be tense but, at the same time, weak. Although trying to be strong, the stress was causing him ill health and internal suffering.

I felt the need to walk over to him, to then place my right hand on his shoulder. As I did, I could feel his emotional pain. It wasn't long before my palm started to emit light and warmth. I could see the light flow into him as divine love entered his heart and populated his thoughts. Once it had achieved what it needed, the light started to recede.

As I moved away, I could see the tears flow from his eyes, and I noticed a change within him.

I knew I needed to help Amelia. I walked over to her, placing my hand over the region of her chest, on her energy. I knew I needed to try and help, but there was no light this time. The need to help her overwhelmed me. I tried again but without success. I could see that she was getting weaker. I felt helpless in light of her situation and wondered if I had failed in my mission.

It wasn't long before I could hear whirring sounds coming from the front of the house. This, I knew, sounded like help was on its way.

I soon felt the vibration of my energy alter, and my vision started to fade. Finding myself back in the department store, I noticed that the girl in front of me had disappeared. Wondering where she had gone, as I wanted to speak to her about what I had witnessed. I felt, somehow, I had missed out on an opportunity. I felt somehow that I had failed her. These thoughts were soon corrected as I became aware of a hand being placed on my right shoulder. My thoughts became entwined with one other as Amelia's thoughts entered my mind.

"Thank you, William. You have helped us, and it was never about me".

As I turned around, I couldn't see anyone. I looked for the lady in the queue, who I now knew as Cassy, but she had disappeared. I felt emotional as a result of what I had witnessed. With each emotion, there was a different reaction within my thoughts, triggering other emotions to have their say. Even though I received those thoughts from Amelia, including her gratitude, I still felt helpless for her. I wanted to reach out to the family, especially to Amelia. All I could do was pray for her and her family. Hopefully, at some point in the future, I will be able to connect with the family once again.

Turning to face Jane, I noticed that she had moved slightly forward from where she had stood previously. I could see her talking to the lady who stood behind her in the queue. I decided to walk to where she stood and wait until there was a conversation break to call her name.

Catching her attention, Jane looked over to me, checking to see if I was OK.

I knew somehow what seemed around fifteen to twenty minutes was only seconds within the vision. I wasn't sure at this time what Jane would have made of my vision and of my emotional experience resulting from it.

Jane looked to see who was left in front of her to be served by the cashier. She then realised that she was at the head of the queue. It seemed that for Jane, she had lost the minutes I had lived through within the vision. Puzzled, she moved forward to pay for the items in her basket.

It was time for us to leave the department store. As we left the building, I looked back and thought about the vision and how it had emotionally left an impression on me.

"Would you like a drink, William?" Jane asked.

Feeling thirsty, I replied, "Yes, please".

I felt excited by the possibility of what else we might encounter as we ventured further. It wasn't long before we came to a standstill. We appeared to be waiting at what was a dedicated crossing to reach the other side of one of the main busy streets of the city. Jane explained to me about some of the stores we had passed. How she would love to see what was new, especially what sparkled. I had also discovered from her that sometimes she would love to shop with her eyes, looking at the things she loved, and admired as she looked at the items on display. As we moved to the other side, I felt captivated by the emotions of others. Some seemed to come alive with the prospects of attaining something new. Others were delighted with the company they were keeping. It wasn't long before we continued down another street as we headed to our destination.

We soon came across one store which caught Jane's attention. As we stopped, I noticed her smiling, finding her wholly entranced by what was on display. It was a small bouquet shop full of beautiful flowers. As I monitored Jane's energy of her aura, it expanded and became more colourful. The colours danced to the reaction of an emotional response. In her heart and mind, she was experiencing a spiritual vision. After a little while, I knew I needed to bring her back. I started to project my thoughts to her telepathically, calling out her name. After a couple of minutes, Jane was back with me. I could see that she was elated.

I felt something was going to occur shortly but wasn't sure how it was going to present itself.

"Are you OK?" I asked.

Jane smiled, then reassured me that she was alright.

I asked her if she could tell me more about what had just happened. After a pause, Jane openly spoke about her experience with what she had seen.

"As I was looking at the flowers, I noticed a glimmer of light surrounding them. The light became more prominent and colourful. I felt myself consciously drift, finding myself in a field of flowers for a little while. Each of them was beautiful in design and just as radiant. I felt captivated by their fragrance and presence. It was as if they were trying to reach out to me, but then I could hear you calling my name. As I focused on your voice, I found myself drifting again until I found myself being back with you".

I could see that she was trying to recall her feelings and the wonderment of what she had seen.

"I am not sure why I am asking you this, but something inside is prompting me to. I feel I need to ask you a question. I know you are only a child, and as silly as it sounds, I have a feeling that you will know the answer".

I waited for her to ask the question.

"A lot has happened since we found you walking along the beach… William, it coincided with a dream that I had about you. When we first met, even back then, I felt something was different, that you were different – Looking back to the way you were able to heal me. Thinking about earlier, with the glow I saw around you, and now with the vision. I realise there is more to you than both Henry and I first understood. Can you please explain to me why I feel the way I do? Why am I having these experiences?"

A sense of wellness and knowing entered my thoughts as I was aware that my consciousness had shifted into an altered state. As words began to fill my mind, I started to relay them to Jane in response to her question.

"Life is experienced through the senses. With the abilities to see, hear, touch, smell, and taste, as all were gifted to you at birth. You were created out of love – You will experience the world through emotion and through love. You are all born with the ability to experience these senses in a heightened state, to experience an extrasensory perception of awareness. These heightened states will alter your reality as you become more sensitive to thoughts, feelings, and the energies around you. As you just did then, moving your reality to the inner worlds, to the more delicate vibrations of energy. Inclusive of thought and of emotions, which will lead you on a sensory journey. To the discovery of self and the greater reality beyond the physical. The instrument for your thoughts, which you call the mind, has many aspects and associations. When you relax, the aspect of the mind, referenced as the lower mind, will bring about chatter to occupy the silence. This is where the thoughts can draw upon your emotions. The body will react, causing a change in your energy system and causing a reaction to your health. The lower mind dwells in your thoughts. These thoughts, for instance, exist on the surface of your mind and would like to chatter about random events, people, activities of self and gossip of others. It can shift towards self, highlight issues, and even promote fear, stress or suffering to lower self-esteem. An aspect of the mind, referenced as the emotional mind, will react and stimulate an emotional response to the chatter. Someone who is very logical in approaching this chatter can get caught up in the lower mind's thought processes and find logic for answers. Their approach will always be active and not passive. For most, they will never find the peace they are searching for. As the emotional mind will react and stimulate response to the logic but can have less of an impact on the result, as the logic can and often supersede the chatter. Through the stillness of the mind, through mindfulness, in the control of the breath, the approach will be passive to allow the higher mind to silence the chatter. To allow yourself to experience this expansion in awareness, you will start to perceive energy and the subtler realms. You are then able to blend with the consciousness and emotions of the inner world around you. Your emotional mind will benefit, resulting in a reaction to the experience. I do hope that this has helped".

I soon found myself returning to a natural state of consciousness. Even though I was in an altered state, it was as though I was in a place of observation while the words were being conveyed to Jane's question.

"Wow – OK", Jane responded. "Where did that come from?"

Jane went quiet for a moment. I could see she was thinking about what had been conveyed to her. She knew I was somehow different and felt quite taken aback by the response she had just received.

"Thank you for answering my question. It's given me food for thought".

I could see Jane was trying to fathom out what had just happened. From her reaction, she somehow seemed to have accepted the notion of it. I had a feeling that more experiences for Jane were soon to follow. This made me realise that keeping my identity from Jane would be more challenging than I thought. I soon learnt that she could possibly be my only confidant and that through her, I would be able to reach out to others.

"Talking about food, let us make our way to the café, so I can get you that drink I promised you, William".

To get to the café, we had to walk over to another side of the city's main street, again using another dedicated crossing. As we approached, I could see others waiting patiently to cross.

My attention was drawn to another as we arrived. I became aware of a lady waiting to cross at the same time as us, waiting for the lights to change to green. On further observation, there was a familiarity with her. She had a little boy with her, around the age of eight.

Could they be Amelia's mother and brother, whom I had seen in the vision in the department store?

As the lights turned green, my attention switched to Jane as we started to walk across. As we reached the other side, I looked to see where the lady and the young boy were, only to notice they were further down the street. While observing them, I became aware of Amelia, as she appeared briefly within my thoughts, confirming that my thoughts of her family were indeed correct. It was also interesting to note that although not physically present, Amelia was here, that our paths had crossed and would undoubtedly cross again.

Turning to face Jane, I noticed she was conversing with another lady. From their emotional behaviour and conversations, they seemed to complement and uplift one another. I could see that their relationship was one of a close friendship. Waiting patiently in reflection, it wasn't long before Jane turned to face me.

"William, this is Suzy; she is my friend".

I turned to the lady in question, smiled and said, "Hello".

On observation, the first thing I noticed about her was her long wavy hair, which was brunette in colour. Her eyes were brown, and as they sparkled, there was a purity about them that you couldn't ignore. Wearing a lemon patterned coloured dress, she looked pretty. She was carrying a stylish peach handbag that hosted many items, especially a night crimson-coloured lipstick. While she was talking, I noticed her retrieving it from her bag and then rubbing it on her lips.

"Hello, William", she replied and then smiled.

Suzy then turned to Jane. I could hear her say with excitement, "I have great news!"

She looked radiant, and the energy of her aura was vibrant with colour, as a person who loved life and was contented with her life circumstances.

As I looked closer at Suzy's aura, I noticed a small conscious form of spirit energy was connected within her auric energy field. This revealed to me that a baby was to be born to enrich her life further. Interested by what I had seen, I looked further into her auric energy field. I could also see the remnants of another child's presence within it and felt that this revealed she had another child present in her daily life.

I heard Jane replying to Suzy, "Yes, we will look forward to it! Shall we say around six?"

They both pretended to kiss each other from cheek to cheek, and then we went our separate ways.

Jane motioned for us to head to the café to have a drink and maybe some lunch.

I looked around and noticed that more people had started to appear in sight. It was a lovely sunny afternoon, with a slight breeze caressing my face. I closed my eyes and could hear the voices carried by the slight wind of those a small distance away. I found myself listening to the different sounds of the engines of the passing vehicles. As I relaxed more into the inner silence, bypassing all the usual sounds I could hear, I became aware of the tiny creatures that roam the pavements. Then followed by the birds in the skies and the small animals that roam the streets. Everything came into clear focus. I became aware of receiving impressions of electrical energy, fuelling the operation of the mechanical devices surrounding me.

"Are you OK, William?" Jane asked.

Feeling myself brought back, I opened my eyes and responded with a nod.

Holding hands, we continued with our journey to the café. The café was only a short distance away, and as we entered the building, I noticed the place was half-filled with people. I followed Jane to a table that would seat four. Seeing that one of the seats was positioned next to the window on our left, I made my way around the table to get to it. Sitting in the seat, the view from the window had a lovely outlook of the grounds, and I could see the buildings from where we had just come. I noticed that Jane had sat opposite me.

A pretty, young, slim lady with blonde hair and emerald-green eyes walked up to our table and realising who was seated, I heard her say, "Auntie Jane!"

Jane turned around and couldn't believe who stood before her. Then, standing up, they both embraced each other in a hug. I could see that it was an emotional reunion as they both had tears in their eyes.

On releasing their hug, she went on to say, "Beth, when did you get back?"

Adjusting myself, with my back resting on the back of the seat, I observed and listened to what else was going to be said between them.

"Only a few weeks. I kept on thinking about you both and how I missed you. So, I decided to move to the outskirts of the city. I just hadn't had the chance to call you. Also, I wasn't sure how uncle was!"

"Where are you staying?" Jane asked.

"I am renting a room at the 'Old Inn Cottage'. It is about ten miles north of here".

As I observed Beth, there seemed to be a warmth about her. The energy of her aura was bright, permeating colours of yellow, orange, and pink, with supporting colours of gold and red. Interestingly I noticed something different. A white protective layer encased Beth's auric energy field that I felt revealed a sacredness to her being.

"We would love for you to stay with us. You are family Beth. I am sure Henry would love to see you".

"As long as you wouldn't mind, and it wouldn't be an inconvenience for the both of you!"

"We have a spare room back at the house".

"Thank you, Auntie".

"If you write me down your address and mobile number, I will get Henry to pick up your belongings and move them over to ours".

With that, Beth reached into her waitress's front pocket, pulled out a small notepad and pen, and then wrote her details down. The paper was soon handed to Jane to keep.

"Beth, do you still have my number?" Jane asked.

"Yes, I have it recorded on my mobile – So, Auntie, who is this young man with you?"

I looked at Jane to see how she would respond to Beth's question.

"This is William", to then looking my way, "William, this is Bethany, my Niece".

"Hi William, it's nice to meet you – You can call me Beth".

As her eyes were placed on me, I could see them sparkle. There was an inner depth to her soul that could be seen within them.

"William", I heard Jane call to catch my attention.

Turning to face Jane, I could see her smile, then nod her head in such a way as for me to respond to Beth.

Turning to face Beth, feeling embarrassed, I replied, "Hello, Beth".

Beth reached out to place her right hand on mine and said, "That's OK, William".

As soon as I felt her touch, I saw an image of the universal tree of life, in all its glory, appearing within my mind's eye.

Removing her hand, Beth then turned to face Jane. I could hear Jane tell her about her dream and how we met by the coast.

"Henry is speaking with the authorities to see if we can find his parents. He has asked me not to become too emotionally attached to him".

Observing Beth's reactions to Jane about me, I heard her ask, "Isn't William your brother's name?"

I listened to see how the conversation continued.

"Yes, but he couldn't remember his name or where he came from. So we gave him a name for now".

"I could see where uncle was coming from".

"It just occurred to me, how is the studying going?" I heard Jane ask Beth.

"I'm getting there… I was able to transfer my training and study, so I could continue from here. I have another nine months left of studying to complete my medical degree".

"So, what's next?"

"Foundation training – I just need to decide on the area I would like to specialise in".

"It's good to see that you are choosing a career close to your heart. Your mother would have been proud" Jane smiled.

I could see that the loss of Beth's mother was still affecting her, as her emotional energy reflected her loss as varied shades of pink and red were introduced into her aura.

Beth handed a tall slim card with writing and pictures on it to Jane.

"So, here is the menu", I heard Beth say.

I observed Jane as she looked at the menu.

"Has the menu changed? It's just that I noticed that there were tacos listed on the menu", I heard Jane ask Beth.

"We have a new chef who has joined the team for over a week now. They are looking to give the customers a different choice of food on the menu".

"Is he tall, dark, and handsome?" Jane asked, accompanied by a smile.

"Auntie!"

"Well, is he single?" Jane continued to ask. "We know he can cook".

"The 'he' is a 'she', plus I am not looking for a relationship at the moment, Auntie. I am leaving it up to destiny".

Jane responded with a smile, "Whoever you find to share your life with, know that you have our support".

"Thank you, Auntie".

Beth turned to me, "William, what would you like to have to eat and drink?"

I could see Jane was on hand to assist, "Shall we try you with an orange juice?"

I nodded in affirmation of what had a pleasant sound to it. Jane then motioned to me, pointing at the pictures on the menu she was holding.

"What would you like to eat, William?"

Not sure what I was looking at, I glanced over the menu at the pictures. I found myself pointing at one colourful image.

Jane looked at the choice I had made. Then turning to face Beth, I heard her say, "William will have the vegetarian tacos and an orange juice. I will have the chicken tacos for myself with an iced tea".

Beth noted our choices, "Excellent, I'll get this ordered now for you both". She then walked over to the counter to place the order. Once done, she then disappeared through another door.

I looked at Jane as she was looking in the direction of the door. "Who does Beth belong to?"

Jane smiled, "Do you remember that I mentioned that Henry had a sister that went to Heaven".

"Yes".

"She was Beth's mother. Her name was Emma".

"What happened to her?"

"She had a problem with her brain. No one knew, as there were no recognisable symptoms, until one day, she just collapsed. She was taken to the hospital and went into a deep sleep. Beth had been staying with her overnight in the hospital for about two weeks. One early morning she woke up at her mother's bedside by the monitor alarm. From what I had heard, the doctors tried to save Beth's mother, but they weren't successful. Emma soon joined the angels in Heaven – Beth and her mother were very close. Beth has two younger brothers and a younger sister".

"Beth has two brothers and a sister!"

"Yes, they live with Thomas, their father".

I could see Jane reflect on what she was about to say.

"Henry and his sister Emma were very close. He is still getting over the loss of Emma. I am missing her too".

I could see that Jane was getting emotional as a period of silence followed.

"Henry is also close to Charlotte, his other sister, who lives in England, not far from their parents".

"Where's England?"

"A small island to the east".

We both sat for a few minutes in reflection on the conversation that had taken place. I turned to look passively through the window. I didn't notice it before, as I was caught up in the moment with our discussions. I could hear an arrangement of sounds that was accompanied by voices.

I turned to Jane, "What is this sound?"

"This is music, songs being played on the radio".

I tried to understand the concept of what I could hear, "Why are they telling stories?"

"Some people tell a story or reflect on their life or emotion through words. Instead of saying them, they reveal them by harmonising their voice in tune with the music accompanying the words. Music can reflect and give volume and enhancement to the words being vocalised. This is often referred to as singing".

I could see Jane was doing her best to help me understand. As I looked at her, she could see that I was trying to comprehend what she was saying.

Although I was grasping this reality, all that I was experiencing was new to me. It was interesting to hear how Jane explained it.

Wanting to make it clearer and thought a demonstration would be helpful, Jane smiled and said, "Can I sing to you a song my mother would sing to me? It is called God's little creation. Do you feel this will help you understand?"

I nodded, then waited for her to continue.

Jane composed herself and, with emotion, harmonised her voice and started to sing. I was captivated by the harmony and beautiful tone of her voice. The words seemed to resonate with all those who were listening.

The singing soon turned to a tune as she started to produce musical sounds with the words she was harmonising with. I looked around and noticed that she had the attention of all those in the café. My attention was soon drawn to looking at the window as if someone were observing us from the outside. I could see no one. Returning my gaze to Jane, she continued to harmonise her voice with words. Every so often, expressing emotion through the way she composed herself, using the gesture of her hands and the features on her face. She had everyone moved with emotion. On finishing the song, a round of applause and cheers could be heard. She seemed to have captivated the hearts and the minds of those listening. Beth stood amongst those around the café. Proud of her auntie, I could see tears gently flow down her cheek.

I smiled at Jane and then reached over and embraced her, giving her a big hug. Jane held me tight and then gently expressed her thanks to me.

As I pulled away, I could see Beth returning to the table with our food and drink.

"Auntie Jane, It's my break now. May I sit and eat with you both?"

"Of course, you are always welcome".

Beth sat to my right, diagonally opposite Jane, and then they continued with their conversation.

I looked down at my drink and the food on my plate. Not sure what I was about to consume, I picked up my fork and started to move the items around on what looked like a small flat pancake. The energy of the food looked vibrant, even though it looked as if they had hit hard times.

I looked up and noticed Jane and Beth watching me. They both were smiling at how I tried to work out the food on my plate.

"Would you like some help?" Jane asked me.

I replied with a smile and then queried about the food on my plate.

Jane started to explain and identify the food. The tacos were used to contain the fillings that accompanied them, similar to the pancakes we had in the morning.

I looked up at Jane and smiled. I could see that Jane remembered the way I reacted at breakfast. Seeing how she was eating her taco lunch, I proceeded to eat the food on my plate with the fork. Remembering how earlier, I was shown how to chew and swallow the contents of the food. Every so often, I also took a sip from the beaker containing the orange juice.

I could hear a further conversation between Jane and Beth. As I became focused on what I was eating, their conversation faded into the background.

As I finished, I started to feel tired. My eyelids felt heavy as I tried to keep them open. It was as if consuming the food and the drink impacted my energy.

"William, we need to get you back home for some rest", I heard Jane say, as she seemed concerned for my wellbeing.

Looking up, I could see both Jane and Beth watching me.

As I looked at Jane, I nodded to confirm her suggestion.

Jane then turned to face Beth.

"Beth, can you please excuse us?"

"Yes, of course, Auntie, I should be getting back to work".

"I will get Henry to call you later this afternoon so that he can arrange a time with you to collect your stuff".

"Great, I'll look forward to catching up with him".

As I removed myself from the table, Beth then held my hand. While we walked to the entrance, Jane went to pay for lunch. I felt stimulated and energised by the energy that appeared to be coming from Beth. As I looked at her, I could see the energy as it was being directed toward me. I was soon greeted with a smile as I looked up at her. I could feel a connection to a deeper side of Beth's intuitive self and wondered if it had to do with the universal tree of life that I had seen with her.

We were soon joined by Jane, who thanked Beth for their conversation and for her company.

"Remember, I will get Henry to give you a call", as she hugged Beth goodbye.

"Goodbye, William. It was nice to meet you. I will see you later and hope you feel better soon", said Beth, then motioning with her hand to say goodbye.

Beth had left an impression on me. I smiled and waved my hand to return the gesture.

Jane reached out to take my hand and then opened the door. As we left the café, with the door closed behind us, we were ready to walk back to the jeep.

We started to walk back in the direction we had come from, back to the parking lot. As we got closer, we could see Henry waiting by the jeep. He seemed to have a smile on his face, as if he had some good news to share with us.

As soon as we arrived, I could see that Jane was intrigued, "Well, what is the good news?"

Henry then went on to tell Jane about his success with the Bank and the success with the mayor. From what I could understand, the mayor's name was Helena.

"I got the loan... Helena has authorised the go-ahead to make renovations on the barn and for the house extension, " he said with a smile.

I listened to the conversation between them. It was lovely to see Jane and Henry's connection, as threads of light had linked the energy of their thoughts and hearts.

I could see that Jane was curious about something.

"Did you get the parcel?"

"Yes, it's in the jeep, placed on the passenger seat in the front".

"Did you manage to speak to Jacob about William?"

"While I was talking to Helena, Jacob walked into the room. I told them both that we found him wandering by the coast. It has been agreed to keep him with us, in our care, until they can identify who he is and find his parents. Jacob mentioned that he would be sending a police officer around tomorrow with a social worker".

"That's good! Oh, by the way, guess who I met?" I heard Jane say.

"Suzy!"

"Wait! How did you know I met Suzy?"

"I met her at the mayor's office. She told me that she saw you and William, and I believe there is good news".

"I think I already know! Guess who else?" I heard Jane go on to ask.

"Give me a clue?" Henry teased.

"She is family, blonde, slim and has been away for three months".

Henry's face lit up, knowing it could only have been one person. I could see from the conversation, and the reaction expressed that Beth and Henry were close. Henry would be Beth's favourite uncle and be an authoritative figure in her life, someone she would look up to.

Jane handed the note to which Beth had put her current address and contact details to Henry.

"I have invited her to stay with us; I knew you wouldn't mind. Could you please help her move her stuff over to ours? Just give her a call to arrange a time".

I could see Jane was excited by the notion of Beth coming back to stay with us.

"Tonight, I am going to cook my speciality with grandma's meatloaf recipe", I heard Jane mention to Henry.

Jane then helped me into the jeep onto the back seat, behind Henry. As before, Jane then sat beside me. After everyone was safely strapped in, Henry drove out of the parking lot and began heading home.

Although tired, I felt the need to focus on seeing Jane well. With these thoughts alone, I soon became aware of the healing that was being given to her.

I started to feel my eyelids getting heavy, finding it difficult to keep my eyes open. As I closed my eyes, I drifted into a light sleep.

I was suddenly awoken by an echo of a young male voice calling my name. Opening my eyes, I looked around, only to find Jane looking through the window on her side, with Henry driving. I looked through the window to my left and noticed that what I could see was light shining through the trees. As I focused on the light, I could see the outline of a boy, again around my age. This time I could see an old ruin of a building with a light shining from it. I tried to see more but soon found myself awoken by Jane, whose sweet voice beckoned me.

"William... William, it's time".

It seemed that we had arrived home. It occurred to me that this had to be more than a dream, a message for what was to become. As I started to awaken to full consciousness, I could see Jane's loving eyes looking at me.

## Chapter VI

## Returning Home

I waited in the family room on the sofa while Jane and Henry were offloading the shopping from the jeep. As I started to relax, the furniture began to vibrate, along with everything else within the room. I could feel the vibration resonate through my body as my sensitivity increased. I soon was aware of light pulsating from my body. As the new energy restored me, I no longer felt tired. I wasn't sure what was happening, but I decided to go with it. I started to receive greater clarity in my understanding of thoughts and emotions. The language of spoken word and the language of emotion became clear. It wasn't long before the light receded, and my energy returned to its normal state of presence. The vibration of the furniture, along with everything else in the room, returned to its natural state.

Curious, I glanced around the room to see what may have changed. It was all in the details. Three maroon cushions kept me company on the large three-seater sofa that was cream in colour and set against the right wall. A large, thin, black TV was fitted on a bracket on the wall opposite. A cream recliner chair was also set just by the corner of the room near the patio doors that lead to the back garden. A small, white table was set slightly forward and to the left of the chair. On the table was a fantasy novel called 'Alice Through the Looking-Glass', with a pink leather bookmark inserted a third of the way through. Cream curtains were held back to allow the sun to shine into the room by a motorised cord and rail. The wooden floor was covered with a cream and maroon patterned rug in the centre of the room, supporting a large white wooden and toughened glass table. Lastly, the table, where a porcelain vase had been placed on a circular patterned lace of floral design. As one of the main focal points, the fireplace entertained a black wood burner protected by a brass metal surround. Set to the right of it stood a brass container containing wood. On top of the fireplace stood a family photo frame of Jane and Henry with Bella and Charlie. I could see every detail within it as the colours became enhanced. Near the fireplace for Charlie and Bella were soft circular beds, one for each of them. Currently, only Bella was lying comfortably in hers. I looked around for Charlie in the room, but he wasn't to be found.

Everywhere I looked, I was reminded of Jane and Henry. So far, everything showed me that Jane and Henry liked the comforts of the home. The room was tidy and tasteful in its décor. I liked the touch of the vase and the delicate floral design. What I could see personally revealed to me the sensitivity shown as well as the emotional strength of support of Jane and Henry's love and care for the family.

With my new lease on life, I decided to leave the settee and explore further. As I reached the door to the hallway, I could hear Henry call out to Jane.

"I've put the shopping in the hall, and the parcel is in the study, on the table. I'm off now to collect Beth. I'll give you a call when I get there".

"OK - have a safe journey. Give my love to Beth, and I will see you both later", I heard Jane reply.

An aroma of what was cooking in the oven drifted through to the hallway, and my senses became enriched with the scent. I closed my eyes to bring the other senses more into play. As I tuned in to the aroma, visual images started to populate my mind. I saw how the ingredients came into being, of the preparation of what would be used to create Jane's grandma's favourite recipe.

The visual image I saw of the beef from the cow unsettled me. I could see all the ingredients being placed into a large bowl, which consisted of oats, onions, parsley, garlic, eggs, milk, basil, salt, and black pepper, to create grandma's favourite recipe for meatloaf. I could see the ingredients were gently prepared, kneaded and thoroughly combined to the right consistency. The mixture was placed into a loaf pan and put into the preheated oven until firm and cooked inside. My eyes soon opened as the vision finished.

As I walked into the kitchen, Jane was preparing the vegetables to accompany the meatloaf.

"William, the meatloaf won't be ready for another thirty minutes. I just need to finish off the vegetables and the potatoes. I'll join you shortly in the family room".

As soon as Jane joined me, I asked if she could tell me more about her grandma.

"My grandma would love to bake for her family. She would often tell me stories about her past. Her strongest memories were of the times she would compete with Mrs Emmet at the village fayre. My grandma would always talk about the fond memories of that time. There was one thing that I wish I could have found out before she passed. She would tell me about a strange encounter with a young lady in her later years. As she began to recall her memories of the time, her thoughts would often drift - I never did get to find out about it".

Curious about the parcel, I asked, "Who is the parcel from?"

"The parcel... I forgot the parcel. Please stay here for me, William".

Jane then left to make her way to what I could assume to be the study to retrieve the parcel. Ten minutes then passed, and there was no sign of her. I waited for another ten minutes and then decided to go and look for her.

As I walked into the study, I could see it was much smaller than the family room. The walls were painted maroon. A colour that I felt direct the focus of my eyes to the contents of the room. To the wall, just to my right, as you came into the room, there were bookshelves and a two-seater cream settee. On the opposite side of the room, I could see a window that gave a view of the lake and grounds. A small cabinet set against the same wall had photographs of Henry and Jane in photo frames, placed in view of those sitting on the settee. To my left was a wooden desk with drawers that stood against the wall. In the centre was a small table. I could see the parcel was still on the table, where Henry had mentioned he had left it. I could see no sign of Jane.

Making my way back into the family room, I appeared to be the only one present in the house. I decided to go into the kitchen to check on the meatloaf in the oven. I noticed the oven was switched off, and as I looked through the glass, I saw the oven was empty.

Confused, I tried to figure out what was going on. As I returned to the study, the parcel remained on the table. It was the only other constancy that I could recognise. I walked over to the parcel and reached to pick it up. As I got closer to holding it, I felt the presence of another, one of familiarity, standing in front of me. It appeared as a light, shimmering with iridescent colours. As I tried to understand and sense who it could be, I was soon drawn to another's footsteps from behind, getting closer. I returned my focus to what was in front of me, and then the presence disappeared.

"William, what are you doing in the study? I thought I left you in the other room", I heard Jane call out.

Something was happening, and strange occurrences were manifesting. It was as if time had stopped, and I had entered another realm of reality

"You were gone for about twenty minutes. I was worried, so I came to find you", I explained as Jane entered the study.

Jane smiled, and I could see she was looking to reassure me, "I know you might find this all a little overwhelming, but honestly, both Henry and I have your best interest at heart".

Seeing various shades of colours of pink, yellow and brown permeate her aura not only reassured me but also uplifted my energy. I knew her intention was only one of emotional support. I reached out and gave her a hug to reciprocate my acceptance of her intentions. I needed to reassure her that I was OK and happy to be here. As we released from our embrace, I could feel the warmth of her smile

We both returned to the family room with Jane carrying the parcel. As Jane held it in her hands, I could see it was unsettling her, as if something were wrong.

"Why would a gift from an old friend of Henry's have this effect on me? Something doesn't feel right with it", I heard her say.

Moving closer to Jane and the parcel, I wondered what was inside. As I studied the parcel, I intuitively felt that there was something about the material's substance, its compound structure. A slight pitch could be heard as my auditory senses became attuned. I stepped away from the parcel until I knew what we were dealing with.

Not wanting to hold the parcel anymore and seeing how I responded to it, Jane returned the parcel to the small table from where it was retrieved. It wasn't long before she was back with me.

After a few minutes, I could see that Jane was deep in thought.

"Are you OK?" I asked.

"Sorry, William, I was thinking about a dream I had".

I could see she was getting emotional just by recalling her thoughts.

"William, I had a strange dream that led me to where we found you. I am not sure why, but I am glad we did. Since you've come into my life, a lot has been happening. I've been seeing and hearing things that aren't natural. I'm starting to question my sanity".

I started to observe Jane being aware of her thoughts and her logical way of thinking. I was aware she was trying to analyse her dream and the chance of our meeting.

Sometimes actions can speak more of the truth than words.

*Chapter VII*

# The Discovery

As I shifted my thoughts to focus on the bond that was being created between us, I reached out to hold Jane's hands. As she reciprocated, a light started to appear, encircling the space where we stood. I noticed that my vibration of energy started to alter, allowing more light to be present. I could feel my energy expand as the light intensified. As I began to focus on Jane, the light started to pour into her being and then began to raise her vibration, lifting her from the ground. There was a stillness about her. It wasn't long before I became aware of a picture show of the most prominent memories on her mind.

The memories began where they left off with seeing Jane's father and mother talking to the doctor by the entrance of the room in the hospital. From what I could learn, Wil had Leukaemia at the young age of eight.

As I focused on the young Jane within her memories, I felt an overwhelming sadness for her, witnessing her brother's loss at such a young age. I could see her brother trying to whisper something to her. Wanting to hear what was being said, I felt my eyes close and suddenly found myself within her memories, standing next to them both.

"I have been waiting for you, Jane. I am pleased you are here, as I need you to hear this".

I could see he was trying to gather his strength.

"I will always be your big brother, you know – Look after mom and dad for me".

Wil started to cough up a little blood, then went on to say, "I never wanted to leave you!"

I could feel his sadness, for her need for his presence in her life... As he would miss her too!

Tears began to appear coming from his eyes and then gently flowed. I then could see a little more blood spill out from his mouth as he started to cough.

"I love you, little sis".

I noticed Jane as she struggled to utter words.

With one last breath, I could hear him say, "One day, we will meet again!"

With little strength, I could see Wil slowly reach out to hold his sister's hand. As their hands clasped, Wil smiled and then gradually closed his eyes for the very last time.

I soon found myself leaving Jane's memories and being present within my own, feeling tears flowing down my cheeks. As I opened my eyes, I could see her eyes were sparkling with light.

The realisation of what she was now experiencing revealed a truth. One of acceptance and one that led her onto a path of the discovery of self.

As the energy withdrew, Jane lowered back to the ground.

"William, I was so caught up in myself, and I truly didn't see you for you".

I could see the experience had left Jane wanting answers.

We were soon distracted by the aroma of the meatloaf. Then, realising that it was still in the oven, Jane returned to the kitchen to check on it.

It wasn't long before Jane called out my name, and she sounded emotionally pleased by the sound of her voice. I can only presume that the meatloaf had turned out the way she intended it to be. I made my way into the kitchen, and as I entered, the aroma of the meatloaf was more potent than before. Images of the ingredients had again populated my mind. I could taste the texture of the food as if it were in my mouth, as my taste buds became overloaded with information.

I began to feel different, sluggish and tired. Returning to the family room, I soon found comfort on the cream recliner chair near the patio doors. My eyes started to feel heavy, and I soon found myself drifting off to sleep.

I woke to find myself standing, looking through the patio door window. The view of the land and the lake was picture-perfect. As time passed, from day to early evening, I started to reflect on what I had learned. I glanced around the room, noticing Bella was resting. My thoughts went back to reflect on this morning. I knew I needed to be mindful and pay attention to the details.

Looking through the patio door windows, I could see a glisten of light as a young boy appeared from the trees. This was similar to the dream I had experienced earlier while returning home in the jeep. I could see two other people making their way across the land towards what I understood to be an old ruin, reminiscent of a place of gathering. It seemed to keep company and synergy with the lake. As the other two entered the ruins, I soon became aware of a bright light surrounding the building, which sustained itself only for a short period of time before the building returned to its natural state. This piqued my curiosity, as I wondered what was going on. Walking over to the patio doors, I tried to open them to take a closer look, only to find them locked. I felt the need to investigate but felt limited from doing so. As I focused more on the building, curious to see who had entered, the effort of needing to see more soon caused a shift in me. I found myself opening my eyes, seated on the recliner chair.

I couldn't be sure if I was asleep or awake. I was starting to get confused with the reality of what I was seeing.

My thoughts went back to the kitchen and how the aroma of the food had made me feel. I knew I needed to reinforce my energy and repel the denseness of the energy that kept entering my system. With this thought, I imagined myself in a protective bubble.

Leaving the chair, I returned to the kitchen to find Jane. The aroma was still strong, but this time I knew the energy of the food wasn't going to have an impact on me. Having faith in the bubble and believing it to be as real as I was, my accomplishment of this had proved successful.

Looking at Jane, I had a feeling that she would look at me differently than when she first saw me. However, it was interesting to note that her emotions were reinforced, tightening our bond.

"William, can I get anything for you?"

"While it's still light outside, can we please go for a walk to explore more of the land?"

"Where would you like to go?"

"Could we go to see the lake? Maybe Charlie could come with us".

"That would be a good idea. Give me ten minutes to cover the food and set the table for tonight?"

While I was waiting for Jane, I went to look for Charlie. I knew he wasn't in the study or the family room. As I entered the hallway, I found myself at the bottom of the stairs. I could hear a slight whisper of my name being called out to me. Looking up, I felt a presence at the top of the stairs. I could feel the atmosphere and the energy around me alter as the temperature reduced slightly. A vapour of a mist started to appear, and as it built, I could make out the outline of a little girl observing me. I noticed she was pointing to the door that led to the front porch. Intrigued as to who she was, I motioned her to come to me with my hand. Seeing that there was no response to my request, I invited her along to join us on our adventure outside. There was what I believe to be a smile on her face, and then shortly afterwards, she faded from my sight.

I felt excited by the notion of another apparition in the house and wanted to share it with Jane. I went back into the kitchen, where I could see Jane was just finishing tidying up.

"Did you find Charlie?"

Even though she asked the question, I still thought of the young girl I had just seen at the top of the stairs. I felt the need to hold back on this information and informed her that I couldn't see Charlie in the house.

Jane retrieved a small flat item out of her pocket and started to briefly press on it several times with her finger. Curious, I asked what she was doing.

"Maybe he got locked out when Henry closed the door to leave, or perhaps, he took him with him to pick up Beth. I'm texting Henry to see how long they will be".

Jane went on to tell me that this was what they call a smartphone. That it was used to contact one another, either by message or a voice call. In this case, she used the smartphone to send Henry a message.

Hearing a noise from her smartphone, it seemed Henry had replied to her text. From what I could gather from Jane, it seemed that Henry and Beth wouldn't be with us for another couple of hours. I felt that there was other news in the text from Henry, as Jane appeared to be curious about something contained within it. Jane then sent another text to Henry with regards to Charlie. This time there was a slight delay in his response.

"Charlie isn't with him. We may find Charlie sitting out on the porch, waiting for Henry to return – We should have just enough time to explore the grounds".

The trees were swaying a little outside the kitchen window, indicating that the weather had picked up with a slight wind, even though it was a beautiful day.

I noticed Jane retrieve the gilet, the sleeveless padded garment from the new selection of clothes she still had in the shopping bag.

"William, let's get this on you. This should keep you warm".

As we left the house, we noticed Charlie was resting on the porch, soaking in the sun.

On hearing us, Charlie lifted his head.

Being attentive to his needs, Jane crouched down to comfort him. Then she began to stroke him around the back of the head and down his back.

Knowing that the time was getting on, Jane stood up and asked, "Where would you like to go first?"

I pointed over to the direction of the lake, and even though there was a little wind, the sun was still parading in the sky. The warmth of the sun was inviting. With Jane holding my hand, we started to make tracks. We could see Charlie following us. Every so often, we could see him checking the scent of the land, and it was good to see Charlie invigorated by his exercise.

I could see energy permeate the flowers and the trees and hear the echoes of life permeate my auditory senses. The birds, the insects and the wildlife were at play in rhythm and danced with each other. It was at this time that I noticed the little girl was following us. Slightly less translucent and more recognisable. She appeared to be keeping her distance as if not to alarm us of her presence. I smiled as my suggestion to her appeared to have piqued her curiosity back at the house.

As we moved further across the land, Jane showed me where Henry would work, preparing the wood for the burner to keep the home warm. I could see a small storage unit where the logs were kept. Just off to the left, a trodden path could be seen, indicating where they would go while riding the horses. Looking at her emotional energy, I could see it alter as it was responding to her thoughts as she shared her knowledge of the land.

"Can you tell me about your horses?"

"We have Toby, Hazel, and Basil. Basil was our first, then Hazel came a year later - Toby, the youngest, has been with us for about two years now".

"Will I get to see them?"

"I can show you them tomorrow if you would like?"

"So, where do you ride the horses?"

"There's a path that takes us through the forest. We discovered it shortly after we moved here. Apart from the wildlife, there is a small bridge that covers a small river and a couple of water springs".

I looked to see where Jane was pointing and noticed an entrance that led into the forest.

As we approached the lake, I could see large, broad animals, ranging from various shades of brown and white, roaming freely on the land.

Curious, I asked, "What are those?"

Jane smiled, "They are what we call cattle".

"Can we please go and see them?"

"We can but only briefly - there is something I would like to show you first before it gets dark".

As we made our way over to the cattle, they appeared to be passive and curious within their nature. I soon became aware of their mental prowess and of their intellect on various emotional levels.

Having seen the images that populated my mind earlier from the meatloaf, it became clear that they wanted me to protect them from the harm and the suffering inflicted upon cattle. I started to feel emotional and then looked at Jane.

"What will happen to them?"

"In time, they will be sold. For now, they are grazing the field and providing us with milk".

I felt relieved that their purpose was none other than what Jane had mentioned.

I noticed that some of the cattle were reacting to another presence other than us. Curious to see what was alarming them, I soon felt the young girl's presence, observing from a short distance away. It was interesting to note that even the cattle could feel the presence of the unseen.

We soon set off to the path that led us into the forest. As we walked through the trees, I felt a tingling sensation throughout my body. I was curious as to what Jane was going to show me. As we walked further, I felt my senses intensify. Closing my eyes, I could see multiple tiny lights. My auditory senses became aligned with the newfound vibration of thoughts. If the trees could talk, I was sure I would be able to hear them whispering. While my eyes were closed, I could see the path was clear as if my eyes were open. I felt a breeze caress my face, accompanied by a brief shiver in my body from the temperature drop and energy vibration of this place.

"We're nearly there", I heard Jane say.

On opening my eyes, I started to realise that there was something special about this place. We soon arrived at a large old tree. I could see its energy was extraordinarily strong and could see the light emitting from its core.

Suddenly I was aware that the girl who followed us was now standing near the tree, looking up at it. This time she appeared as real to me as I was to Jane.

"I often come here to relax, to gather my thoughts by this old tall oak tree", I heard Jane say.

"I can see why you have brought me here. I like it too. Thank you for sharing this with me".

I could see Jane smile but noticed that she did not seem to be able to see the girl.

"Was there anywhere else you would like to visit before we go home, William?"

As I looked in the girl's direction, I noticed that she was observing us.

"There was a building near the lake. Can we please have a look?"

"The old ruin – I haven't really paid much attention to it - I suppose it's always been there".

We started to walk back, with the girl not far behind us.

We headed closer to the building as we reached the clearing at the edge of the forest. On closer initial inspection of the structure, the building was rectangular. It had four stone walls that had partially worn away two-thirds of its structure from the top. The entrance leading into the building was missing its door. A small square window with corroded iron bars, positioned like a cross within the window, was situated on the left central upper wall. The roof that would have provided shelter and privacy was missing. I tugged on Jane's hand to move forward into the broken structure of the building that stood in front of us. Wanting to inspect it first, Jane motioned me to stay where I was and then stepped through to ensure it was safe. It took around six minutes before Jane returned to confirm it was OK to go in.

As I stepped inside, I noticed that it appeared bigger than I first initially thought. The first sense that became stimulated within the ruins was one of scent, as if from scented lit candles.

"I wonder who's been lighting candles here?" I heard Jane ask out loud.

I could see Jane's energy expand as she took in the scent. The building was fulfilling her other senses with the information stored within the energy archives of its history.

The floor was also created from stone. The building housed a small iron grate covering a well towards the opposite side of the entrance. Rotted wooden pews were positioned against the left and right walls. Faded paintings decorated the inner walls, portraying people worshipping a person surrounded by light. In addition, there were paintings portraying the healing of others and another depicting the ascension of a person. It appears as if they were conveying a story. Faded symbols and other patterns were positioned strategically on the ground. A small altar, a focal point, was positioned on a ledge protruding from the wall mid-way up from the ground. There was still evidence of melted wax on the shelf where candles had once been placed. In the centre of the altar, I could see six holes aligned like a hexagon, with a seventh hole in the centre. The painting on the back wall looked like a prism, held at a certain height and positioned at an angle.

"I never noticed... I mean... I have been here before, but the markings on the ground, the paintings... Where did this ledge and altar come from? Why now?" I heard Jane enquire out loud.

The altar had a purpose... Had this been why I had seen the others entering this place earlier?

I soon felt another presence. When I turned around to see who it was, I could see the girl. She seemed to resonate with a more substantial presence. On further observation, I noticed her pointing to the altar behind me.

When I glanced back, to my surprise, I could see the outline of the energy of a translucent being radiating a bright iridescent light. Although I couldn't determine the gender or the likeness to who it could be, they appeared taller than me. I was soon aware of chanting that initially appeared as a whisper and then soon increased in volume. Although I couldn't recognise the structure of the language spoken, it echoed within the confines of this place. Luminous geometrical shapes appeared on the walls. The atmosphere became charged with energy as a bright light started to fill the room. The whole building started to rebuild itself before me. I began to phase in and out of this dimension. Circling on the spot to see what was happening, I noticed Jane was motionless. Looking at the Altar. I started to radiate and pulsate with light, rising off the ground. Taking it all in, I closed my eyes for a moment. When I opened my eyes again, I found myself with my feet on the ground. Everything within the ruins of this place returned to the state it was initially in, as it was before we entered. The altar had disappeared, along with the paintings and symbols on the floor.

I felt different somehow but knew it had something to do with what had just happened. I wondered if I had gone through some sort of ascension, as shown within the paintings. I looked around and noticed Jane was lying on the ground; she must have passed out. I looked for the girl and noticed that she had gone also. Wanting to see if Jane was OK, I walked over and knelt beside her. Placing my hand on her shoulder, I gently rocked her backwards and forwards to wake her. On the first inspection, I couldn't see any injury. I tried to telepathically call her name to see if it would bring her back to awakening consciousness. It seemed that my efforts were not in vain as I noticed that she started to recover.

"Are you OK?" I asked.

"I still feel a little drowsy. I'm not sure what just happened", Jane replied.

As I got to my feet, I then assisted Jane to help her to stand upright.

"Let us go home", Jane suggested.

As we stepped outside the ruins, we were welcomed by Charlie, who appeared happy to see us.

We started to make our way back home. By the time we reached the front of the house, Henry was just pulling in and getting parked. I could see the arrival of Henry and Beth was perking Jane's spirits up.

As Henry started to take Beth's luggage and her boxes into the house, it wasn't long before Jane was with Beth to welcome her.

Standing a little distance away, I waited for them to make their way back into the house so that I could follow.

I soon noticed Beth had given me a little wave. My memories took me back to meeting Beth in the café and how she left a lasting impression on me.

It wasn't long before I noticed them walking toward me. I was soon greeted by Beth with a warm embrace. Then, with Jane and Beth, we made our way to the stairs of the porch, where we soon entered the home, with Charlie following shortly behind.

I wondered how much stuff one person could have, seeing all the boxes and the luggage in the hall. With the assistance of Jane and Beth, Henry was able to move all of Beth's boxes and luggage to her room, which happened to be opposite the room I was staying in on the first floor.

Jane was soon back in the kitchen, preparing the evening meal.

I decided to go into the family room and wait for the others. I thought about what had happened in the building, the girl and what I had seen and experienced.

My thoughts were soon interrupted.

"William, please, can you assist me in preparing the dining room table for the evening meal?" I could hear Jane call out.

As we set the table for the meatloaf, my mind was again populated with images, accompanied by feelings of emotions, as the scent of the meatloaf was still present in the kitchen. On this occasion, I seemed to be fine.

Henry soon returned to the kitchen.

"How are we getting on with the meatloaf? I am certainly looking forward to your grandma's recipe, as I'm famished".

I could see Henry rubbing his hands together back and forwards in motion.

Being present in their company, I had a feeling the conversation would soon somehow relate to me.

"Nearly there, dear. What were the papers for?" Jane asked.

"I got a call from Jacob. After some enquiries, it seems that no one has reported a child missing with William's description. I had mentioned that you were taking a liking to the young boy. For now, he is in our care. Mayor Helena has agreed that this would be the best course of action to take. This will ensure he gets the love and best care he needs at this time. Considering this, I picked up an adoption form. Who knows, maybe as the dream foretold, perhaps he is meant for us".

I could see Henry smiling at Jane, from his feelings that he knew deep down that this was what she wanted.

Jane appeared to be in deep thought. It wasn't long before I could see the expression on her face with the prospect of extending her family unit as it registered with her.

"Are you OK with this, William?"

As I nodded with affirmation, I could see Jane's face light up, conveying an emotion of joy.

"This is great news! We must tell Beth - William there's a possibility that you will be staying with us more permanently - maybe for good!"

I felt her love. Reciprocating, I sent the love back to Jane, and I could feel the warmth and the light increase within her.

It soon occurred to me that my stay could be short-lived. I knew, for now, I just needed to place my focus on the moment. To welcome, honour and appreciate the time we had together to share.

Thoughts of Beth soon entered my mind. I felt a sense of unease with her and felt the need to venture upstairs to the door that led into Beth's room.

"Jane, can I be excused?"

"Of course. Dinner will be ready shortly – Try and be back soon".

I left the kitchen and went to find Beth. As I got closer to the top of the stairs, I was aware of another presence. This time the energy was more divine in its nature. As it had taken form, I could start to see the outline of a boy. I could see he was pointing to Beth's bedroom door. There was a brilliance of light emanating from him, angelic of nature. I reciprocated by smiling and with a gesture of gratitude.

I could hear voices coming from Beth's room. Curious as the feeling got stronger, I quietly positioned myself as close as possible to the door. I pressed my left ear against the cold wooden surface as I needed to hear what was being said in the room. I could hear two voices on the other side of the door and recognised one as Beth, and the other appeared to be a lady of mature years.

I turned to face the boy, but he had gone.

As I closed my eyes to focus on the voices intently within Beth's bedroom, I found myself on the other side of the door in an ethereal light form. My energy form had shifted, vibrating to a faster frequency. I wondered if it had something to do with what had happened earlier. I felt lighter and not bound to the confinements of the physical universe as I did in the human form. I wasn't sure what was happening to me, but I knew there would be a reason, so I went with it.

*Chapter VIII*

## The Unexpected Visitor

B ethany stood talking to the presence of the same old lady I had spoken to in the family room earlier. I could see that she was upset and aware of a disturbance within her aura impacting her emotions and state of mind. I wanted to help her but knew I couldn't alert her to my presence. I needed to learn more about the lady, so I waited patiently and listened carefully.

"Why are you here?" asked Beth.

"My dear, I need your help?" the old lady replied with a frail voice.

"I can't help - please stop!" pleaded Beth.

I noticed a pause as Beth was trying to gather herself.

"I moved away to rid myself of this!"

"I need you to give my boy an important message".

I had wondered who she was referring to.

"Go away, please go away!" I heard Beth cry.

I noticed a weakness in Beth's energy as it started to withdraw inwardly and gradually dissipate, affecting her emotions and well-being. The questioning from the old lady appeared to be the cause of Beth's suffering.

I became aware of my emotions and how I felt a fondness for Beth. Strange, but somehow without cause, my feelings also extended to the old lady.

I suddenly became aware of another presence within the room. Before I could see or sense who it was, I noticed a decrease in my vibration of energy.

"What is happening?" the old lady asked.

It seems that the old lady was able to see me. Looking at Beth, she appeared motionless. I soon felt I was directed to apply reasoning to what was about to unfold here.

"First, what do you want with Beth?"

The old lady tried to leave but couldn't. It was as if something were keeping her here.

"Are you an Angel? I did not mean her any harm. I just need her to pass on a message from me to my boy", the old lady said.

I became aware of a strong presence encircling and encompassing me. I became assertive, overcome with inner strength.

"You say that you mean her no harm, but you are absorbing her energy by demanding answers. What is it that you truly ask?"

My words seemed to resonate, as I could feel every word of the power of authority overshadowing me.

"I am Mrs Mable. I used to live near these grounds. I just need to know where my boy is. I need to speak with him".

I could see she was unnerved by the effects of my questioning.

The lady answered, "I just need to know where my boy is. Do you know where my boy is?"

I found myself saying, "Maybe she is not the one you need to ask. Your boy has since passed over. He was involved in a motor vehicle accident as he was on his way to you. Although the weather conditions and the road did not help, his passing was quick, and he hadn't suffered any pain".

I paused to see her reaction to this news. The lady stood quiet, trying to assimilate my answer.

More words started to flow, "It is now time for you to move on. Your suffering must stop now. Please go and be with your boy as he has been waiting for you".

The old lady nodded in affirmation. Then, subdued with this new understanding, she drew back her energy. I could see an angel of light stand beside her to assist. I could feel her emotions become liberated and noticed that she started to fade from view. I somehow knew that she would find her peace and be with her son soon.

As soon as it came, the presence that encircled me had left.

As I looked at Beth, I could see that she no longer appeared motionless. With her energy and strength restored, I knew that there was a possibility that she would find me here, in her room. With that thought, I soon found myself transported back to the other side of the door, returning to my physical state. As soon as I was fully adjusted, the door opened. Standing in front of me was Beth.

"Strange, I had a feeling I should open the door, only to find you standing here. Why are you here?"

I needed to quickly redirect the focus back onto Beth and her situation.

"I was on my way to my room and heard raised voices coming from yours. You sounded upset. Who were you talking to? Is she still in your room?"

"I am not sure why I am telling you this, but I feel I can confide in you. I have this overwhelming notion of telling you something, and I am starting to realise why. It all began when I was a child. The lady would often appear to me, and no one would believe me as no one else could see her. It stopped when I moved away, and I thought it was all behind me in the past. Until tonight, only to find her appearing in my room".

"Appear?" I asked.

"I'm not sure quite what she is, possibly an apparition", Beth replied.

"An apparition?"

"Yes, an appearance of someone who has lived before and has since passed over to the afterlife", Beth explained.

Waiting to see my reaction, all I could do was nod in affirmation and continue to listen.

"There is something I must tell you. I had a vision that led me back here for a reason. The vision was of the old lady and Uncle Wil, auntie's brother. I can't remember the details of the vision, but I knew it was important. It wasn't until you both left the café that I remembered another part of the vision. It occurred to me that the vision was about you. Please do not say anything to Auntie and Uncle about this?"

"I promise. Just to let you know, I have a feeling the lady will not be visiting you anymore".

I could see Beth respond with a smile and then embrace me in a hug to demonstrate her appreciation.

It was interesting that she had a dream about me, but as she couldn't remember, it wasn't worth bringing it up with her, knowing that she had just been traumatised by the old lady.

I informed Beth that Jane was preparing the meal for tonight and it would be ready shortly. I then left her to be, to finish getting ready.

As I made my way back downstairs, on reflection, it was interesting to see where my journey was leading me to. I have already learnt so much from those who I have met.

As I entered the dining room, Jane helped me to a seat at the table. As we waited for Beth, my thoughts returned to what had just happened, raising a few questions about what I had witnessed. But, for now, I needed to put those questions aside as I needed to focus on the others. It wasn't long before the presence of Beth was felt as she entered the dining room. The energy of her aura captured my attention, as it appeared radiant and rich in colours.

Sitting next to my left, she whispered in my ear, "Thank you, William; I have a feeling that you helped somehow. I feel lighter as if the whole world has been lifted from me".

It was interesting to hear these words from her mouth as I felt a similar feeling for being around her. A feeling that everything would be OK!

The four of us were seated for grandma's meatloaf. While Henry was sitting opposite me, Jane was sitting opposite Beth. The day was turning into the evening as the night was coming upon us.

As Jane started to dish out the meatloaf, she turned to Beth and asked, "Have you managed to finish unpacking?"

"Not fully. Still some boxes to go".

I waited to see if their conversation had finished, as I needed to inform Jane that I wanted to pass on the meatloaf.

"Please, can I have something else?"

"What's the matter, William?"

"I am not sure if I can eat the meatloaf?"

"Can you please try some for me - Just a little?"

Before I could respond, a knock sounded at the front door.

Jane and Henry appeared to be emotionally startled. They seemed to be on edge for some reason.

"Who could that be at this time of night?" I heard Jane say.

"I'll check to see who it is", responded Henry.

With that, there was a second knock on the front door. I noticed Henry had left the table and made his way to the hallway, shortly followed by Jane.

Looking into the hallway from the dining room, we focused on the door, curious to see who our visitor may be. I noticed that Jane had also kept her distance. As we observed Henry, he was peering through the small window that looked out onto the porch. From his observations, there was little he could see, as the porch light wasn't lit.

"What is going on here?" I could hear Henry mutter the words under his breath.

Turning to Jane, I could hear him say to her, "There's no one there. I am not sure if the bulb has gone or there is a fault with the wiring".

As I was watching them both, I felt that there was more to be known about Jane and Henry and what they were keeping from us.

A third knock came, followed by a few more. I could see Henry reaching for the handle to slowly open the door to see who was waiting on the other side. At first, we couldn't see anyone, then shortly as our eyesight adjusted, we could make out the appearance of a young girl. She stood waiting a couple of feet away from the entrance. Initially, we couldn't hear or see any response from our visitor.

"Hello", Henry called out.

Still, the young girl stood before him, sheltered from view, mostly by the darkness from where she stood.

It felt a bit eerie.

"Hello, can I help you?" Henry called out.

We noticed the young girl had turned her head to look behind her.

Soon she was accompanied by two others, as a lady appeared from behind her, accompanied by a tall man. The man was slightly taller than Henry but similar in build. As our visitors moved closer, further forward into the light that came from the hallway, they were recognised by Jane, much to our relief.

"Suzy, it's good to see you. We weren't expecting you until tomorrow".

Jane motioned the family forward to enter the house. As they walked in, Henry closed the door behind them.

As an observer of the gathering, I continued to listen to the exchange of words expressed between them.

"Suzy, it is good to see you. Please... Please come into the dining room. Have you eaten? We were just sitting down for our meal, and you are most welcome to join us".

"I hope you didn't mind! We were just preparing the meal when we heard a noise outside, and then the lights went out. Tom went to have a look at the fuse box, only to find that a fuse had blown. I tried to find the matches for the candles, but we couldn't find them. As I then started to panic, the thought of you popped into my mind. I then started to calm down as I knew that everything would be fine if we came to you".

"That's OK! You are most welcome to stay with us tonight", suggested Jane.

"Rachel can stay in my room, as I can make room for her", Beth commented.

"If it is not too much trouble?" replied Suzy.

I was still waiting by the dining room entrance, listening, observing, and in a state of curiosity. I then noticed that Jane had looked my way.

"William, please come forward and say hello to Suzy, Tom and Rachel. They will be staying with us tonight".

With all eyes then focused on me, I could see Suzy, Tom and Rachel waiting for me to greet them. I held myself upright and walked over to Suzy.

"Hello, William", she said with a smile. "It is good to meet you again. This is my beautiful daughter Rachel and my wonderful husband, Tom".

Rachel's hair had a similar colouring to her mother's. She was wearing a brown leather jacket, blue jeans, a maroon blouse, pink sneakers, and a fluffy pink scarf which was wrapped loosely around her neck.

I smiled at Rachel and said, "Hello".

I was soon drawn to the energy of her aura, as colours of maroon, magenta, and varied shades of pink, yellow and brown filtered the other colours already present. I became aware of a feeling of disinterest, as it was as though it was an inconvenience for her to be here. Her response was short and to the point, almost closing the conversation before it had started.

"Hello William, it's good to finally meet you", Tom spoke in a self-assured voice.

I raised my head to reach his gaze. I noticed his hair was brown and swept back. He was slim with facial hair, had large hands and a sturdy frame. His eyes contoured the lighter shades of blue, highlighting the features of his face. I had a feeling to glance over to Suzy and noticed that she was lovingly gazing at him.

Turning my focus back to Tom, "Hello, it's good to meet you too".

"Let us get you out of those coats", I heard Jane say to our guests.

As they took off their coats, Jane collected them to place on the tall standing coat rack by the door.

"Now, let's get you fed and watered", I heard Jane say.

Playing the caring host, Jane, then led our guests into the dining room. I followed last, just behind Beth.

Beth assisted Jane in setting the table with additional cutlery and plates, along with napkins, to accommodate the visitors. As Beth and Jane set the table, I turned my focus to our guests.

"Are you OK, William? You seem a little distant", Suzy asked.

"A little tired".

"You look a little tired".

Leaving the others as Jane and Beth finished setting the table, I made my way into the family room. As I climbed onto the sofa, I then laid across the seats, with one of the cushions to support my head. As I closed my eyes, I could hear movement. On opening them, I could see Jane was checking on me to ensure that I was OK. Jane then left the room to attend to her guests in the dining room.

After a short while, my eyes gently began to close. My body started to relax, causing my senses to be heightened. I was soon awoken by a presence which stood beside the settee. As I opened my eyes, Rachel was standing in front of me, observing me as I slept. She wasn't wearing the same clothes she had arrived in. I sat up and turned my head towards the entrance leading into the hall and could hear laughter coming from the dining room. As I turned back, Rachel was still staring at me and seemed curious.

"What are you doing?" I asked her.

"Just observing".

"Why aren't you with your parents in the dining room? What happened to the clothes you were wearing?"

"William, there is so much to be revealed here that you need to pay close attention to, as tonight, the lives of those here in this house will change forever".

Wanting to find out more, "How do you know?"

I then had an overwhelming feeling of looking to the entrance leading into the hallway. It was as if we were being observed, but I couldn't see anyone. When I turned my head back to face Rachel, she had gone. Startled by what had happened, I felt another shift within. I found myself opening my eyes and then wondered how much of what I had just witnessed was experienced through a dream state. Curious, I climbed down from the sofa and walked to the dining room entrance.

Rachel was still seated, wearing the same clothes she had arrived in and eating what looked like tasty pancakes. Jane appeared to be in conversation with Suzy about her news of Suzy's expectancy. Knowing that the life of everyone here is going to change tonight, I felt I needed to be more attentive to the emotions of the others.

Seeing where my chair was at the table and still empty, I made my way into the kitchen and managed to climb onto the seat with a little effort of upper body strength and some leg work. With Beth realising I needed some help, she then assisted in moving the chair forward, so I could sit close to the table.

"Are you feeling better now, William?" Jane asked.

I nodded in affirmation and then asked, "Can I please have some pancakes?"

"What would you like with your pancakes?"

Remembering what I had this morning, I reminded her of my choice from earlier. The pancakes were just as tasty as they were this morning. I enjoyed every mouthful.

Once everyone had finished, we went into the family room apart from Henry and Beth. They remained to clear up the table before joining us a little later.

I was still yet to know Henry. From what I had learnt, he came from a small island called England and had two sisters, but who was he as a person?

A short time passed, and we were all settled in the family room. The adults were in conversation, which brought about reminiscing and laughing about the past. I could see their energies react and blend to encourage, support, and uplift each other. It was like a dance, invigorated by their emotions, as the colours were altered by their responses to each other, reflected in their perceptions.

My initial observations were on Rachel as she stroked Bella while seated on the rug. It would be interesting to get to know her, especially knowing the dream I had earlier involved her. I was waiting for the right time before I felt comfortable speaking to her. I wanted to ask Rachel the question before everyone retired for the night.

Finding a comfortable place to sit, I sat as close to her as I could.

"Rachel, can I ask you a question?"

"What would you like to ask?"

I knew I must not read too much into this, as learning more about the forthcoming events and how integral my part was to play in the lives of those within this room, would be. However, it was good to see Rachel still smiling, encouraging me to ask the initial question more.

"From our discussion earlier, are you able to tell me more?"

"Sorry, I am not sure what you are referring to!"

"Rachel, is there something you would like to tell me?"

"No, why do you ask?"

"No worries .... It's OK".

I thought about what had happened and felt slightly puzzled.

I turned around to continue to observe the conversations between the adults. As I was still learning the language, I continued to take in what was being discussed.

I started to close my eyes, listening to the inner silence. It wasn't long before I started to receive an intuitive feeling, an awareness that something was about to happen. I looked around as I opened my eyes and noticed Rachel observing me. Surely this wasn't another dream. Seeing her wearing the same clothes, I knew I couldn't have been dreaming. She soon got up and walked over to where her mother sat. I felt the need to observe the others, to listen to what they had to say.

We could hear the wind as it started to howl outside. I could see the moon was full and bright in the night sky through the patio door windows from where I was seated. Suddenly the lights in the house went out, and we were in total darkness.

"This is what happened at our house!" I heard Suzy exclaim.

I was aware of movement and could just about see Henry as he went to investigate.

"I'd best go and check the fuse box".

As he passed us by and went into the hall, the lights came back on. The main door of the house started to rattle. The motion got more erratic as time went on. After a few minutes, suddenly, a loud knock was heard coming once again from the front door. I could see Jane looking unsettled as she turned to face Henry.

"Who could be here this time of night?" I could hear Henry say,

I noticed the others were unsettled by the knocking. I wondered if this was going to be the start of the change that was mentioned earlier. Two more knocks were then heard, coming from the same place. I stood up and walked into the hall, facing the main door. I could hear Jane call me to return to the family room and be by her side. A breeze could be felt as I entered the hallway. A gush of wind was heard circling and howling behind the main door leading onto the porch. It felt as if something or someone was eager to come in.

"Tom, can you please give me a hand, as I am going to need your help".

"Sure, Henry".

As Tom joined Henry, I peered into the family room and saw Jane, Beth, Suzy, and Rachel standing, concerned and worried about what was going to happen. Their emotions became heightened as fear started to overcome them.

"William, please come into the family room. I need to know you are safe!" I heard Jane call out.

"I'm coming!"

Suddenly the lights went out again. I turned to face Henry and Tom, and my attention was drawn to their conversations.

"I can't see anyone", I heard Henry say to Tom while trying to see who was outside the door on the porch through the small window.

Suddenly the noise of the wind stopped, and an eeriness filled the hall. Both Henry and Tom looked at each other. They then heard a clicking sound. As Henry looked towards the lock on the door, it seemed that some unknown force was rotating the handle to the door, backwards and forwards erratically. I could just about see Tom, with his body weight pressed against the door, preventing it from opening. I felt his anxiety!

"William, get the others upstairs, into the main bedroom and lock the door!" Henry exclaimed.

"I need your help Henry, as whatever this is, my weight isn't strong enough", Tom gasped with the effort of trying to keep the door shut.

I could feel Henry's heart pound while he helped Tom hold the door in place.

Looking into the family room, I noticed Bella and Charlie sitting up and watching me. They did not appear to be reacting to or trying to ward off the presence on the other side of the door. As I watched them, I noticed I felt calm.

"William, please ask Jane to take the others upstairs?" Henry's voice was slightly raised in a concerned tone this time.

On hearing Henry's words from the family room, Jane gathered the others and asked them to follow her to the main bedroom. As she made her way upstairs, she asked me to follow. A wave of peace appeared to come over me as Jane and the others hurried upstairs, with me trailing behind. As the others before me entered the main bedroom, the door closed shut before I could enter. I could hear Jane call out to me as she tried to open the door, but it seemed to be sealed somehow. Her voice became muffled, then silent. Curious to see what was happening downstairs, I slowly made my way back down the stairs. Halfway down, I noticed the main door to the house was open. Curious, I decided to take a closer look and continued to the bottom step.

I could see Tom lying on the floor, a little distance from the main entrance. He appeared to be unconscious, with a gash on his head. Looking over at Henry, I could see him on one knee, trying to get back onto his feet near the dining room entrance. Both appeared motionless as time seemed to have stopped still for them both. I could also see the main door to the house, held in mid-air as if it were hurtling towards the direction of the study.

Intrigued, I wondered what this unknown presence was that blended into the darkness.

Seeing Tom needing help, I headed over to him. As I knelt beside him, I placed my hand on his shoulder with the intention of healing him. I noticed there was no light - no heat. I wondered what was preventing me from healing him.

I looked in the direction of Henry, only to notice that he appeared to be OK, somehow.

I called out for Bella and Charlie. There was no response from them either.

Looking towards the main entrance, I could see that something was manifesting, building into form. The energy of the phenomena seemed to fluctuate. Sparks of light appeared and disappeared randomly for about three minutes. Then, an intense light appeared at the entrance. I could make out a silhouette of a tall person.

I could feel thoughts entering my mind, which somehow stimulated the need to understand the consciousness, the driving force behind what was happening. As I started to initiate my questioning, the silhouette vanished, as iridescent light filled the space and then lit up the hallway. Before me, I could see a tunnel of light, a portal appearing at the main entrance to the home.

A voice soon entered my thoughts, "Bring the others from the room upstairs with you".

Again, the voice seemed familiar. I felt an emotional sensation that was divine, fulfilling me. With this, bringing myself back to my feet, I made my way back up the stairs. As I reached the first step, I glanced into the family room and noticed that both Charlie and Bella were motionless.

"Hurry, as there is not much time", came a voice from the portal.

I made my way upstairs to the main bedroom. Initially, the door was closed and seemed to be locked. I tried the handle again, and on the second attempt, the door slowly opened.

At first sight, I noticed that Jane, Beth, Suzy and Rachel stood motionless.

"How can I get them to follow me?" I voiced out to whoever was communicating with me.

It wasn't long before I received a response back, "Touch each of them on the shoulder".

Curious, I responded, "What do you want with them?"

I soon received a response asking me to trust.

Wanting to know more, I replied, "I do trust, but can you give me any more information?"

"I was with you when you first arrived in the place you called 'City'. I was also with you in Beth's room. I have always been with you, especially on the journey into this life. William, you are here for those in the lives you touch".

Accepting the answer and what with the message earlier, I went into the bedroom. I first reached out to Jane first and touched her shoulder.

"William, what is happening? Why are the others not moving?"

"It's all connected! The flower shop, the old ruins, and the large tree in the forest. Especially the exchange of energy that we both witnessed together in the family room earlier. It all has something to do with this, for what comes next".

I could see she was still slightly apprehensive but wanted to understand more.

I then touched Beth's shoulder, then Suzy and lastly, Rachel's.

I could see that they were unsettled with fear by what was happening. They all appeared to be huddling around Jane as their emotions reacted to the situation. With a little help from Jane, I noticed they started to relax as I heard her reassure them of the circumstances.

While trying to listen to her words, I received an insight which highlighted our situation, so I shared this with the others.

"It is time. I feel that more will be explained later".

"Will it be safe?" Jane asked.

"Yes, we just need to trust".

"Trust who? Who or what do we need to trust?" Suzy responded.

I could see that they were all looking at me.

I placed my hand on my heart and said, "Here, we need to trust ourselves and know that a greater power is at work".

Still overwhelmed, Suzy, although hesitant at first, looked to Jane for further assurance and guidance.

Needing to make a move, I started to make my way into the upstairs hallway, hoping the others would follow. Looking back into the bedroom, I could see Jane reassuring the others again. It wasn't long before I could see her look my way. Then, seeing me, she nodded, confirming they were ready to follow.

With Jane leaving the room first, the others followed her shortly after. We then started to head down the stairs. As we reached the ground floor, I noticed that both Henry and Tom were still motionless.

"What has happened to them?" Jane asked as she appeared uneasy with the situation.

"Both are still alive. Time has just temporarily stopped for them.

"How do we know you're telling the truth!" I heard Suzy exclaim.

"I am asking you to trust me". I could feel the anguish of Suzy's emotions, of her concern for Tom.

"Is it safe? We don't know what is on the other side", I heard Beth ask.

"Yes", I replied.

I had a feeling it was time for us to leave. Making my way, I started to walk towards the entrance. As I got closer, I found myself standing just before it. Turning to face the others, I looked to see if they were coming. The others seemed reluctant as they did not want to leave Tom and Henry in the state they had found them in. I knew that I couldn't force them to come with me. I could understand their reasoning for this. I looked at Jane and could see her looking my way. Closing my eyes, I then relaxed and could feel the pull from the portal. The light started to surround my body, as it did earlier, altering its vibration. To my surprise, I could see the light extend out to the two men. I could see healing light enter their bodies, restoring all cuts and bruises their bodies had inflicted earlier. I looked at Jane, then smiled. It wasn't long before my vibration of frequency was beyond their normal visible spectrum for sight, disappearing in front of their eyes.

Interestingly, I was still present, observing them. There must have been a reason why I had not passed through the portal. Somehow, I knew that they were needed for what was to come. I soon was drawn to Jane, the feeling of her emotions and the awareness of her thoughts.

I could feel a strong deep emotional pull manifest within her. As Jane tried to understand these newfound emotions, she soon became aware of memories surfacing within the mind of her dream of Wil. Realising the answer she had been searching for was on the other side of the portal, Jane instinctively knew it was the right decision to make. As Jane got closer, Beth reacted and pleaded with her to stop. Tears could then be seen rolling down Jane's cheeks. Turning to face Beth, she explained why she had to go and then reassured her that everything would be well. Extending her hand to her, I could see Beth react cautiously and reluctantly, finally accepting her invitation.

Jane turned to the other two. I heard her reassure Suzy again, telling her she needed her help. Although hesitant at first, with her daughter in hand, Suzy moved closer to stand next to Jane and Beth.

Jane then entered the portal with Beth, with Suzy and Rachel following shortly behind them.

After they went through, I soon felt a shift within me, finding myself travelling through the portal, wondering what would await me on the other side.

*Chapter IX*

# The Other Realm

B eautiful flowers with scented aromas surrounded me as I found myself in a field, rich with colour and full of life. As I took in a circular view of my surroundings, I could feel a mother's warmth bathe me and caress my face from a source of brightness in the sky. I could hear the whispers of soft voices that came and went as if they were carried by a gentle breeze.

My thoughts soon turned to the others, as concerns for their safety and comfort of a new awareness brought upon them.

As time passed, I started to be aware of more than one presence, and although semi-transparent, they started to shift in and out of view in the environment. Curious to investigate, and with that intention alone, I could consciously see myself witnessing the moments of events in time, in history, in the present and glimpses of the possible futures of others. As visions began to appear, my mind was transported within them, for a short moment of time, within the consciousness of the individual's life. For my first glimpse into a vision, I found myself in the year of eighteen forty-eight. Observing a young lady training to become a medical practitioner - who will one day change the view of others to make a way in the medical field for women. After what seemed minutes, I found my mind transported back to where I was, in the field. I soon caught a glimpse of another, a few years later than the vision I had earlier. I found myself in Paris, observing a man in his late forties who would embark on a journey that would bring a realisation and understanding to help change the view of the world and make others re-assess their place in the universe. As before, within minutes, my mind was transported back. I seemed to be dipping in and out of lives, some known and some not, each having an impact on the world and the lives of others. This went on for a little while.

It wasn't long before I became aware of another presence. Barely visible to the naked eye, it was different but familiar, located not far from where I stood. The presence changed its direction, heading towards me. I could hear a language whispering in my thoughts. As I focused on the words, they soon became clear to me.

"Hi William, it is good to see you", the words appeared in my thoughts.

Appearing in front of me stood Jane's brother Wil. I had recognised him from Jane's dream.

"Hello, Wil. It's good to meet you".

"We are sorry we had to pull you and the others here in the way we did. We realised how the others must have felt – it is just that we urgently need your help!" exclaimed Wil.

"I notice that there appear to be others here. Where are we?"

"This is a place between other dimensions. It has many names and many references, with many facets to its nature. It is more than just about earthly beliefs and cultures. What you are seeing are souls. Each soul is unified and linked with others through lifetimes, within their ancestry and the events that have occurred. Each soul is defined through the many actions and thoughts of others as well as their own. Cause and effect, some will say. Each soul that ever lived has changed history. More some than others, and each soul's lifetime is recorded in history, on earth and within our records".

"What about free will?"

"The souls that you have seen are not their true representation of their self, of their totality. Their purpose is for truth on an understanding of their spiritual growth. The initial understanding of their identity provides them with a starting point. Earth is unique, with many possibilities to provide great learnings, especially that of free will and the overcoming of limitation, amongst other lessons".

"Can you elaborate?"

"There are those who may find themselves with less opportunity. For those who may experience a limit to their abilities, or a disability in one form or another, it does not mean they will not have the same spiritual growth as a person who has all their abilities. They are each on a spiritual path that leads them to where their goals require them to be. No one is further on their path than any other, as each soul has its truth. Each has gained in their learnings, and no one is separate or indifferent. They are co-creators of their lessons to be learnt and the path that unfolds in front of them".

"So how does it begin for them? I know that when I arrived on earth, I was welcomed to an emotional, sensory ride".

"The birth process into the human life cycle is sacred. The spiritual growth begins just before taking that first breath. All their emotional, mental, and physical sensations come into play. Once they are born, they are introduced to parents, to families and later to new friends. The unfolding of their relationships will help define them. They will become familiar with and identify with new faces, new personalities and characters as their lives unfold. Each relationship will teach them about self".

"Could some get confused with placing the importance of self with ego?"

"This is part of their lessons, to unravel the complexity of their emotions. It is in the acceptance of the absolute truth and not the truth they are conditioned to believe, is how they will be defined".

"Interesting, the ones that I have observed have very complex emotional lives".

"Their lives can be complicated. It is by their free will. They do not realise they have help available to them, that they are never alone. They just need to realise".

"Is there a reason why you brought us here?"

"William, there is more to you than you know, more than you realise. Everything that has been happening to you and the others on earth is happening the way it should be. When your memory fully returns, you will then see why".

"Who do you know me to be?"

"For now, all you need to know is that you were given the name William. Trust me, your instincts will kick in when you require them.

You will receive a knowing of what to do, as you are not alone in your efforts. I would like to show you something".

In front of us, over a small area, water started to seep up from the ground. I felt the need to look at the reflection of the water. At first, I could see a mist appearing over the surface for a short moment. Then as it cleared, I was shown a small village sheltered in darkness. As I started to question what I had seen, the images started to change, with Wil narrating what had taken place as it was reflected in the water.

"The box was discovered by two young sisters, Catriona and Jean. The sisters had found a small opening to a cave in Scotland, in a remote part of the country. They started to explore. Not realising what was waiting for them and finding themselves guided by an unknown force, the girls found a wooden box wrapped in a cloth. Excited, they managed to retrieve the wooden box and took it back to where they were staying to show their parents. The parents told the girls not to say anything about this to anyone. The father took the box to another room that was off-limits from the girls in order to study it further. Not understanding the inscriptions and symbols on the box had just increased his curiosity. On the family's return from their vacation, the box seemed at times to start to change his perceptions and his emotional reactions in response to those around him. He knew it was changing him, so he decided to keep the box locked away, hidden in plain view, where no one would have thought to look".

The vision faded on the reflection of the water.

"What happened to the box?" I asked.

"The last known location was the church".

"Is it still there?"

"We have lost sight of it, as it seemed to have vanished".

"How is the father now?"

"The father was never the same after the arrival of the item".

"Is the father still in the village?"

"Yes, he has kept out of the way in hiding out of fear of what the villagers might do".

"What had started all this?"

"It started with the mysterious disappearance of one of his daughters. It wasn't long before a neighbouring boy child went missing, which then led to a misunderstanding and a witch hunt for the father. We have been trying to help by sending a lightworker, but the circumstances are getting out of control".

"So, we have a missing daughter, a missing boy, a father who has gone into hiding out of fear and a mysterious box that has gone missing".

"You just need to find the box, and then the location of the others will be known to us".

"Surely you know where it is. Can you just not retrieve it yourselves?"

"It is not for us to get involved. You will be taking Jane and Suzy with you. It is for lessons to be learnt and understood".

"What have you done already to seek out the box?"

"We have sent a lightworker – he is going by the name of Father James, and he will be your contact. He has received word that his family is coming to help him. It seems that whatever has taken place within the village has affected his mind. Apart from the darkness affecting those who live in the village, we have identified another energy source just outside of it".

"Is this why we have been brought here?"

"One of the reasons. The other is about Jane!"

"Jane?"

"We feel that she will not be strong enough for what's to come".

"Are you able to provide some insight?" I asked.

"It is to do with our earthly father. Henry is involved. There is history to his past, the history that will catch up with Henry soon".

"History. Can you please elaborate? Does Jane know about her father's history? What does it have to do with Henry?"

"No, she is not fully aware of our earthly father's history, certainly not this part of his life. With regards to Henry, he was connected to an event that took place that linked with her father. I cannot say at this moment how and when this will take place. I have been informed we must ensure that Jane is emotionally prepared".

With concerns about his sister seeming to play heavily on his mind as we talked, I felt that Will was keeping something from me. His vibration of energy seemed to be affected by his earthly father's past actions.

"I will be with her, by her side, to assist her in whatever may confront her".

"Thank you, William, as there is not much I can do from here to assist. Please do not say anything to her, as she has a hard-emotional decision to make!"

"You have my word".

As my thoughts went back to the others, I was shown a vision of the four of them. They seem to be sitting by a bank by a river, having fun and laughing with others. I could see much colour and beauty in nature surrounding them. As the vision faded, I felt my energy shift and become light in form.

"It seems it is time for you to go, and please be safe!" advised Wil.

The light within me intensified within and around me. I thought about my conversation with Wil. I could see that he was affected by the events that had to do with his sister. I expressed a deep sense of compassion for him. My perceptions started to alter, changing my reality, causing Wil and the place that I was standing in - to fade. The light became the dominant visual factor.

*Chapter X*
# A Village Suffering

As the light started to fade, I noticed the village wasn't far from where I stood. To have any idea of what was happening, I needed to get a closer look. As time went on, the morning became the early afternoon. With still no sign of the others, I decided to get a little closer to see what else I could see.

A small river was separating me from the village. As I made my way to the river, I noticed a narrow bridge that would help me get to the other side. The bridge was made of wood, sturdy enough to support half a dozen people travelling across. With only a few people in sight, I took the opportunity to cross to the other side.

As I entered the village, I started to hear raised voices. The commotion appeared to come from a direction not far from where I stood. As I walked through a few smaller streets, I could see the village church.

A crowd had gathered around a young woman near the entrance.

As I moved closer, I could see the young woman was defenceless against the crowd harassing her.

Suddenly I felt a light touch of a hand on my shoulder from behind.

"Hello, William!"

I recognised the voice to be Jane. Turning around, I could see both Jane and Suzy.

"I wasn't sure you both were coming".

Jane crouched down to embrace me with a hug.

"We had heard raised voices and decided to see what was happening. That's when we saw you".

As Jane stood, I could see that the distress emanating from the young woman was unsettling her.

"We should help her, shouldn't we?" Jane asked.

"We will, but on this occasion, we need to wait as help is on its way", I replied.

"What are we to do here?" Suzy asked.

"We are to meet Father James, and according to Wil, he will be expecting us and will know us to be family", I replied.

While observing the crowd's energy, I noticed that they had succumbed to a dark force of influence. It appeared to be manipulating their thoughts and their emotions, feeding their anger.

The young woman appeared wounded, holding herself in fear of what was happening to her. Her right hand covered her stomach as if to lessen her pain. The palm of her left hand extended out towards those who wished her harm. As I observed her energy further, I noticed small amounts of dark energy had started to appear within it.

A man soon appeared at the entrance of the church door as it opened. He seemed to be smartly dressed, supporting a religious attire.

"Stop", he commanded, his tone assertive.

The crowd's attention was drawn to the figure who stood before them.

"Now go home and be with your families and leave this poor girl alone", the man commanded them.

He appeared to have a different accent from the locals. As I observed the crowd, they seemed to respect the man standing before them. There were a few mumblings about his reasoning.

I was soon alerted to a couple who raised their voices with their concerns about this young woman's nature. They seemed to indicate that she was cursed. Continuing with their argument, they called that she was a thief.

I heard the voice of an elderly lady from the crowd shouting, "Seathan will bring us justice".

I then heard the voice of a man repeating what had been said by the elderly lady.

Again, with an assertive and commanding voice, the man from the church responded, "Leave her to me. Go home and be with your families".

Suddenly, I could see the light of his aura, supporting his passion and the strength of his cause. It appeared to be extending from him to those of the crowd. As it encompassed them, the light started to transmute the darkness within those in conflict.

"Can you see what I am seeing?" I heard Jane commenting.

"I can see it, too", Suzy replied.

One by one, I could see the crowd depart in different directions.

The young woman was soon assisted to her feet.

"Catriona, please come with me", I heard the man calmly voice to her.

Supporting her arm and some of her weight, he then assisted her into the church. The door was soon closed behind them.

"Who was that man?" asked Suzy.

I smiled, then replied, "That was Father James".

I could see Jane react to Suzy's response with a smile, knowing probably what was going through Suzy's mind had something to do with a pleasurable outcome.

It was time for us to meet Father James. With Jane knocking on the door of the church, we then waited to see who would answer. We heard the release of the door latch and saw the doorknob start to turn. As the door opened, it revealed a figure of a man standing before us. His hair was fine, receding and slightly tainted by grey, carrying more weight and slightly fuller in build than Father James.

"Hello, please come in. I am Father Lachlan".

Father Lachlan then motioned with his hand for us to enter.

As Jane was taking our lead, she enquired, "Where is Father James?"

"Father James is busy at the moment, attending to another. He will be with you shortly – Is he expecting you?"

"We are here to surprise him", replied Jane.

"Can I ask who has come to visit?" Father Lachlan enquired.

Jane looked at me and remembered what I had mentioned earlier.

"We are his family".

Father Lachlan smiled and then closed the door as the last of us entered through. We were led into a small waiting room that hosted half a dozen chairs and a small table with a vase hosting flowers.

"Why do some of the other villages speak in a different language?" asked Suzy.

"Gaelic is the mother language here", Father Lachlan replied.

"Do you speak Gaelic?" asked Suzy.

"Inquisitive Mind a th' agad", replied Father Lachlan with a smile.

Father Lachlan then left through a door at the far end to let Father James know that we were here. As pleasant as he had seemed, something did not sit right with him. I felt that he was hiding something.

"What did he say?" Suzy enquired.

Listening to Suzy, I felt I needed to help her.

"He thought you had an inquisitive mind", I replied.

"Oh, OK, I just couldn't understand his broad accent".

We sat waiting for what seemed about ten minutes before Father Lachlan returned.

"Father James will be with you shortly. Can I get you lovely people a drink? What about the little one?"

"William, would you like a drink?" asked Jane.

"Yes, please".

Overhearing our conversation and taking note of my response, Father Lachlan then disappeared through another door. After around fifteen minutes, he soon returned to pour out some warm milk for us in what looked like three brass drinking containers.

"Thank you, Father Lachlan", I heard Jane respond.

"You are welcome, my dear. I shall keep you company until Father James appears".

"Where is he?" Suzy asked.

"He is in the sanctuary where we keep those who need healing of the mind, body and soul. Father James is currently in prayer".

We started to drink the milk that had been kindly given to us.

"Where are you from?" Father Lachlan asked.

Jane had to quickly think and then replied, "We are from the southern parts of the western isles. It has been a long journey to get here".

"What are your names?"

"Oh, my apologies, please forgive me. My name is Jane. This is my dear friend Suzy and my son William".

"I can see you are wearing a bridle band on your finger. Is your husband not joining you?"

"He is not far, as he has taken a different journey for business. We plan to meet later when our visit here is finished", Jane improvised.

"Where will you be staying?"

"We have yet to decide".

"How long have you known Father James?" Suzy asked Lachlan.

"A couple of years now. The church was too much for me as one person to handle. Enquiries were made, and Father James answered the call. He has been the village saviour and has gained much respect and admiration from his followers. He has made such a difference. Although I can see of recent, the suffering, the fighting and the constant victimisation has taken a heavy toll on his health".

"How has it been affecting you?" asked Jane.

"It has been tough, but Father James has been the light where darkness falls. I do my best where I can".

While listening to the conversations, my focus soon turned to the energy of his aura. I could see it permeate and fluctuate with colour. Dark energy patches in small amounts had clustered around the energy of his kidneys. I knew that this would need to be addressed at some point, as I could see he was getting tired. With the intention to heal him, I allowed myself to succumb to the divine. It wasn't long before the healing was passed through to his auric energy field and into his energy system. I could see the healing energy intelligently direct itself to the organs affected and to the dark areas that had formed. Seeing the dark energy within him diminish, the kidneys started to heal. I could see Father Lachlan's body shift to relax even more, as well as a peaceful expression return to his face, producing a welcoming smile.

We heard the door open from the sanctuary. A man appeared through the doorway to see who had come to visit him. As he stood, I could see that the time spent in this village had caused more infliction to his soul, that the fight for the cause was gradually weakening him.

Before he addressed us, he asked Father Lachlan to go to the market to get some lunch.

"Of course", replied Father Lachlan.

This confirmed that the man who now stood in front of us was indeed Father James. Father Lachlan departed by the entrance where we entered to fetch some food. Observing the others, Father James went on to acknowledge the identity of both Jane and Suzy.

Jane asked Father James, "How do you know who we are?"

"I asked in prayer for help. I was soon made aware of your arrival – It is good that family has arrived to help me with the burden that I have taken on", Father James replied and then smiled.

Father James then looked at me and looked puzzled.

"I wasn't made aware that a small child would accompany you both".

"This is William", I heard Jane respond.

I walked over to Jane to stand by her.

"Well, William, it is nice to meet you. So why has the father sent me young William?"

I heard Jane respond, "God works in mysterious ways", and then she smiled.

"As my family, you will all be staying with me in the church. We have a guest room you can stay in".

"Thank you, that's very kind of you to offer", Jane replied.

"That's settled then. I will get Father Lachlan to prepare the guest room for you when he returns".

Father James left us to prepare the table in the main feast area for eating, leaving us alone for a short while.

As we waited, I felt the need to say to the others, "With faith and religion, it is all about unity - a common understanding and coming together as a family. It is through our beliefs and our actions, in our support for each other, that we can get the best from ourselves. Therefore, you have references such as brother or sister. Even though we are not, as you would say, a blood relative, we see ourselves connected as a family. This is to show a form of respect for one another".

"So, what are you saying, are we related?" asked Suzy.

"We are all related. Do you see the flowers in that container on the table?"

"Yes".

"We're not separate from them. We are universally connected to all of life, to each other. What you see outside of yourself and what is witnessed within are related on one level or another. There is no separation. Look at the flowers for me, and please tell me what you see?"

"I see flowers".

"Look again, look at the flowers and tell me about them? This time, put your emotion into it".

"The flowers are varied in colour but weary".

"Allow yourself to become one with the flowers. Allow yourself to feel the connection. Try not to force it, just let the process envelop you naturally".

I could see Suzy relax, and she became more aware of the connection with a soft focus. As her awareness grew, a warmth came about her, and her sensitivity increased. I could see her energy expand and radiate as it blended with the flowers she was observing, adding to and enhancing the already-established colours of yellow, orange and gold within her aura.

I could see Jane was also observing Suzy and could also witness her energy expand as Suzy became mindful of the exercise at hand.

Between them, they appeared to have a unique emotional connection.

"You are doing well, Suzy", I commented.

"Wow", Suzy replied.

Her energy had expanded further than before and within minutes, finding herself entranced on a conscious roller coaster ride. I could see Jane was expressing her happiness for Suzy as her smile widened. After a short while, Suzy was back with us.

"What did you see?" I heard Jane ask Suzy.

"I was looking at the flowers, then suddenly the colours became enriched and vibrant... I could see the energy around them and feel the life force of the flower, with my heartbeat as one with the universe. I felt alive!" she said wonderingly.

"Did anything else happen?" I could hear Jane inquire further.

"I could see us as we are now, but I was outside of my body looking down from above. I could see the energy that surrounded us. I then found myself travelling beyond this room, this church and beyond this planet. It was amazing. I started to go further, but my emotions started to get the better of me. I became anxious about being away from my body, and I soon found myself returning".

I could see Suzy pause to catch her breath.

"Wow, that was amazing!" Suzy continued to reflect.

I could see the tears appear as they then rolled down her cheeks. This left her in deep thought, leaving the room in a state of silence and reflection.

A few minutes later, Father James returned and noticed the ambience of the room.

"Has Father Lachlan not returned as of yet?" asked Father James.

"No, did he have far to go?" Jane asked.

"The church is pretty central within the village and is not far from the market. I will see what the delay is".

"Be careful!" Jane responded.

Father James collected his coat and left the church premises to search for Father Lachlan.

"Are we OK?" Jane asked me as she started to be concerned about our safety.

"We need to find the young woman, Catriona", I responded.

"Are we in danger?" Jane asked.

"Given the circumstances, I felt that we would be OK".

Leaving the room and exiting through the door to where Father James had initially entered led us into a hallway. There were two doors on the right, one on the left and another at the other end. We noticed that all the doors had a written sign to identify the room's function. Looking at the first door on the right, we could see it was the washroom. Opposite the washroom was the sanctuary. Thinking that this would be a good place to start, we entered the sanctuary to look for Catriona.

We were welcomed into a large room, with another small room partitioned off on the far left. The room appeared to be dedicated to those who required healing. There were also prayer stools for those who sought private prayer and sanctuary for their wellbeing. The stools were accompanied by a church font towards the far right. At the front, positioned next to the wall, stood a wooden cabinet decorated like a shrine. A bronze cross was positioned on top. A painting of Mary and Jesus could be seen just above the cross on the wall.

There was a certain feeling about the sanctuary, one that I felt I would surely discover later.

"She may be in the inner room", I heard Jane say.

Jane soon left our side to investigate.

I could see Suzy was getting restless.

Jane returned a short while later, only to inform me that the room was empty.

An unsettling feeling started to come over me, but I knew we needed to continue.

"She must be here", Suzy commented.

"Let's check the other rooms", Jane asked.

Back in the hall, Jane headed towards the far room at the other end. Suzy headed towards the second room on the right. I decided to check the Washroom. We agreed to meet up in the hallway by the sanctuary door.

As I walked through the door into the Washroom, the room appeared to contain the essentials. It was good to see that it was clean.

Not seeing Catriona, I returned to the hall. I was shortly joined by Jane and Suzy to inform me that Catriona wasn't in those rooms either.

"William, I am not sure if this is significant, but I could hear a humming sound within the room at the far end. I have a feeling that the room is possibly where Father James could be sleeping", said Jane.

"That's interesting!"

Deciding to investigate Jane's findings, I went into the room at the far end. A basic room with little in the way of comforts other than the bed and a side cabinet. As Jane had mentioned, I could also hear humming coming from the wall where the sanctuary room would be, located on the other side.

Needing to see the 'Guest' room, I made my way there. It was another room that hosted a bed, a table, and a chair with a smaller table. I wasn't quite sure how the three of us would sleep in this room. There wasn't much I could feel or sense here. I joined the other two back in the hallway.

As we ventured back into the private sanctuary, I felt the need to place greater attention on the shrine while both Jane and Suzy walked to the inner room.

Upon closer inspection, I noticed that the symbols and the writings were like those seen in the small building I encountered back on Jane and Henry's land. My energy started to react as I got closer to the cabinet. I soon felt a tingling sensation throughout my body. I knew the object must be close. Seeing the cabinet doors, as I tried to open them, they appeared to be locked. I even tried to apply a little pressure and weight which had proven unsuccessful. There was no way that I was going to get them opened. A key would certainly be required to investigate inside.

Being focused on the shrine, I didn't notice that Suzy had returned from the inner room as I heard her call out to me, "William, we found Catriona. She was resting on one of the two beds in the inner room".

"How is she?"

"Recovering slowly".

"Can you please bring her to me?"

Suzy went off to assist Jane. When they returned, it occurred to me that the young lady could be one of the sisters who found the box and whose father had brought it back to the village. I could see that Catriona looked weak and seemed confused about what was happening. I asked Jane to find a seat for Catriona.

Jane soon returned with a small chair that she retrieved from the inner room. Helping Catriona, we were able to get her to sit down, taking the weight off her feet while she was recovering. Needing to see her safe and in good health, I asked Suzy if she could fetch a glass of water or milk from the table in the reception room.

I soon felt a further sense of unease, as if darkness would soon be upon us. Of the feelings I was receiving, I wasn't sure if there was enough time to get to see what was in the cabinet of the shrine. My thoughts went to the others of concern for their safety. With no sign of Suzy, I hoped that she was well and safe.

"Shall I go and check on Suzy?" Jane asked.

"We should give her a few more minutes".

A short time passed, and there was still no sign of her.

"Jane, I am going to check to see what has happened to Suzy. Could you please see if there is a way out of here? Maybe there is a window that leads onto the garden of the church".

"I'll look now, William".

As I was about to leave the sanctuary, Suzy walked through the door, trembling.

"There are men in the main church, in the other rooms searching for Catriona and for us".

"Did they see you?" Jane asked.

"No, I don't think so. I did manage to get some milk".

"If I help Catriona with her drink, can you both please see if you can find something to blockade the door to prevent them from coming through?"

Suzy handed me the milk while she and Jane started moving items of furniture, placing them against the door. Several minutes had passed before they managed to complete the task.

It started with the handle to the door rotating backwards and forwards and was soon followed by shouting from the hallway.

Somehow being close to the box containing the object was affecting our perception of reality. We could hear intense humming coming from the shrine's cabinet.

My focus was soon directed back to the door. I could hear the noise of the force being applied by the men who were trying to get through the door as each attempt gradually weakened the barrier.

I noticed that Catriona still looked pale and weak. Holding both her hands, I could feel the warmth and love build within me. As the light intensified within, I could see healing energy enter Catriona and start to replenish her energy, healing the wounds and the marks on her body. I soon had her full attention as she became consciously alert.

"Where am I?" she asked.

"What do you remember?"

"Being chased by a crowd, then seeing Father James".

"Catriona, I know you don't know me, but can I ask you to trust me?"

Catriona seemed to be in deep thought. I wasn't sure if she had heard me.

Calling Jane and Suzy over to me, I asked, "We need to amplify our energies, focusing on giving the energy to each other, with the intention to try and raise each other's vibration".

As they both joined us, I could see that Catriona was a bit reluctant, having trust issues. This I could understand, given her past.

"Please listen to him. He is only trying to help you", I heard Suzy say.

Catriona rose to her feet and replied, "You don't understand! I am not sure that he can... I'm sorry!"

She then left us, making her way to the inner room to hide from the men.

"Shall we go after her?" asked Suzy.

A reassurance of thought from a voice soon appeared in my mind to leave her be.

"I have a feeling that Catriona will be fine. We need to bring the light forward. Let's focus on sending energy to each other, letting the light manifest".

As we did, a light started to appear within each of us. As it intensified, our vibration started to shift and fluctuate. We continued to raise the vibration of each other and the space we found ourselves in. Selflessly sending love with the intention of supporting each other. I started to notice an increase in each of our energies, to a new frequency of vibration, shifting to a new frequency within the room. As we started to achieve this, I noticed that I was struggling to keep the frequency. Something was holding me back. It wasn't until I lost sight of the others that I felt the presence of the object.

The door to the sanctuary finally broke down. Five unruly men barged their way into the sanctuary, with another man following straight after. He was tall, stern, broad, sporting a beard and dressed in black. His energy was as dark as the clothes on his back.

Shortly after, Father James entered. He looked harassed and was accompanied by another man, who stood broader and taller than him, also with a beard. I could see Father James was being hurried along by the man who accompanied him.

"Where are the visitors? Where is Catriona?" asked the man who accompanied Father James.

I wondered if they couldn't see me.

With the five men inflicting damage to the furniture within the sanctuary as they carried out their searches, the results of their findings were short-lived and unsuccessful.

"Where is the box, Father?" asked the man with Father James.

"It is in the cabinet under the shrine".

"What cabinet? What have you done with the shrine?"

Father James looked to the location where the shrine should be. All that remained was the mural painting.

"It's gone... I swear it was there!" as he pointed to the place where it stood.

The five men were ordered to leave and search for us outside. Father James was then thrown to the ground, depleted of energy.

I found their comments strange as I could see the shrine and the cabinet in place against the wall.

My emotional concerns went to the well-being of Father James, who was lying on the floor of the sanctuary, injured and weak.

"Don't forget who is in charge here", said the man who had brought Father James to the room.

I considered the name of Seathan, as I'd heard from the crowd earlier on. Along with what I could believe to be his brother, they had left the church to search the village with the other five men for Catriona and us.

Standing, observing the destruction that had taken place, I could see Father James was still lying on the floor, and I felt helpless in the time of his need.

It wasn't long before I could see Father Lachlan coming into the sanctuary and kneeling beside Father James. He first raised Father James' head and then lifted his upper body to a seated position.

I knew that there wasn't much I could do to help Father James, but with Father Lachlan by his side, I felt he would be the best person to help him recover and help him heal.

With regards to Jane and Suzy, I wondered if they were back with Wil.

As I focused on my situation as a child, I will have to be careful as understanding my age will influence the local's opinions of me. I must try to figure out what is happening here and see if I can resolve the problem.

As time passed, I observed my surroundings, trying to gain an understanding of the sensations that I was feeling in this state.

I felt enriched and energetic, but I knew that I couldn't interact with what I could see at the frequency I was observing. Tingling sensations were soon felt throughout my body as a response to the awareness and full activation of all my energy centres. The colour in the room was vibrant to the frequency of each item represented.

I decided to walk to the cabinet that hosted the shrine as it stood, supporting a glow of bright light. As I examined the shrine, the Cross seemed to glimmer with golden light, and the cabinet doors were open. I began to investigate the contents of the cabinet and noticed that it was empty. I wondered where the box was! - I looked underneath and behind the shrine. I decided to examine the Cross. As I picked it up to hold it in my hands, I could see symbols engraved on it. The longer I held the Cross, the more I could see its energy was reacting to mine. Light started to manifest, first encompassing my hands to then expanding to the rest of my body.

A voice came into my mind, "Trust, for the light is within. For what you seek is only your reflection".

After a couple of minutes, the light started to recede. I could see that time, in its essence, was being reversed. I soon found myself returning to the normal state of the frequency of the sanctuary. I noticed that everything had returned to its original state. As I looked through the windows, it seemed early in the day and just after sunrise. I could feel the temperature as it started to rise.

I began to hear the voices of two men. The voices seemed to be heading in my direction. Not wanting to be detected, I found myself hiding in the inner room. It was Father James and Father Lachlan discussing a recent argument between the congregation during the service in the church hall the previous night. The door to the sanctuary opened, and Father James and Father Lachlan entered the room.

"Young Catriona will need to be careful. You can't save them all the time", said Father Lachlan.

"I feel responsible for her. We must keep the box hidden, as it was entrusted to us by her father".

"There is a connection between her and the box. Have you seen the way the box responds to her?"

I could see Father James as he proceeded to unlock the cabinet to retrieve the box with a key. The key was pulled from an inner pocket located under his cassock. As he opened the cabinet, it was empty; the box was no longer where he had kept it.

"Where has the box gone?"

"I have not touched it. You are the only one with the key".

I started to hear a buzzing sound, causing a tingling sensation in my ears. Unaware of what was happening, I closed my eyes to focus to see where my attention needed to be. It wasn't long before I began to hear a voice.

"William, we have what we need. It is time for you to take your leave. Suzy will join you shortly and will be waiting by the bridge".

As I heard these words, I knew I had to remove myself from this place, to continue dealing with the darkness within the village.

"What about Father James?" I replied in thought to the voice.

As I looked over by Father James and Father Lachlan, I was aware of a light appearing around Father James's head, like a halo. It seemed to be interacting with his thoughts as he entered an entranced state. As my focus went to Father Lachlan, I could hear him call out to Father James in concern for his wellbeing. After a few attempts, he soon got his response as the light receded from Father James's head.

"The box is safe", replied Father James.

Voices were heard coming from the reception room.

"'That must be young Mr Brogran Dùghallach and his young lady Fildema to discuss their ceremony – Can you please see to them?" I heard Father James say.

I could see Father Lachlan leave the sanctuary to attend to the young couple.

Father James started to walk in my direction and stopped just before the entrance leading into the inner room.

"William, you can come out now".

I soon joined him outside of the inner room, standing just beyond the doorway.

"Hello, Father James".

"William, please know that you are safe with me. I was made aware of your presence – I know you were sent here to help me, but I am not sure how. Yet I feel there is more to you than your appearance tells me".

It occurred to me that most people look upon a child as a weakness. They do not realise that some of the greatest minds and talents in the world are children.

I smiled and then said, "It was time for me to go".

"Are you in a hurry to be somewhere?" Father James asked.

"There is another who is waiting for me – maybe there will be another opportunity for us to meet again", I replied.

"I do have some questions that I would like to ask you. I suppose we can discuss them at another time. Until then, William, please stay safe".

Leaving the church, I continued walking through the streets, tracing my steps back to where I could remember seeing the bridge just outside the village.

With the bridge within my sight, I looked to see if I could see Suzy. As I couldn't see her, I decided to approach the bridge to cross to the other side to see if she might be waiting there.

I noticed that it was occupied by a lady and four children: a daughter and three sons. I could just about see the boys playing at the other end of the bridge. The girl who was separated from her brothers was playing on the side closest to where I was approaching. The mother could be seen occupying the middle space of the bridge between them. I could also see that her observation was shared between the children.

My focus of attention was soon redirected as I caught sight of Suzy approaching the bridge from the other side, taking refuge and comfort beside a tree.

Approaching the bridge, I was getting closer to the little girl. There seemed to be something different about her energy. It was as if there were two of her. An eerie sense of a presence filled the atmosphere – it felt most unsettling and unnerving.

Trying not to alert the girl to my presence, as she appeared to be mindful in playing with her doll, I wondered if I could carefully pass her by. After a few steps across the bridge, I felt a shift of energy within her. Continuing to walk across the bridge, thoughts of the girl entered my mind. I decided to stop and glance back to see if she was OK. I noticed that the girl had not moved from her position. I felt a little concerned. I thought about continuing with my walk across the bridge, but my feelings wavered back to the girl. My concerns began to get the better of me, so I decided to go to her to see if I could help in any way with her situation. With that thought in mind, an apparition appeared in front of me. Her eyes were black and appeared menacing. Her skin was pale, and she was wearing an off-white-coloured gown. I became aware of her hold on the girl and wasn't prepared to give her up at any cost. I could feel the negativity emanating from her, causing my energy to alter as it began to react to her presence. It was as if she was trying to instil fear into my thoughts and emotions.

Thoughts soon appeared in my mind from the apparition, "Go away, leave now, leave us alone".

I turned to face the girl who was seated to see if she was aware of what was happening. I could see no response from her. As I turned to look back at the apparition, it was gone. Suddenly I was aware that something had changed in this situation. The girl stood up to face me with her head facing down. Seeing this, I started to walk back in the direction of where she was.

As I reached a short distance from where she stood, I asked, "Are you all right?"

At first, there was no response. It wasn't long before the girl raised her head to face me. I noticed that her eyes were closed.

"Are you alright?" I asked again.

My feelings soon indicated that the young girl who I thought I was addressing was, in fact, someone or something else, manipulated and controlled by another consciousness. The girl's eyes slowly opened to reveal a presence that was cold and dark. With an eerie two-toned voice, she warned me to leave them alone. Raising her hand, I felt a powerful blow hit my stomach and chest from a strong harsh wind that forcefully pressed itself against me. Within seconds I had been repelled backwards some feet away in the air, to the ground.

Feeling my breath briefly taken away, I felt bruised, with most of my strength taken from me. Feeling the pain surrounding my heart, I placed my right hand on my chest and imagined being whole, believing the light could heal me. After a couple of minutes, I was able to get to my feet, wiping off the dirt. I then headed back over to where I had stood.

Seeing what had happened, the lady on the bridge approached me. I could see she was concerned and checked to see if I were OK.

"A little out of breath and a little bruised, but I will be fine", I replied.

Moving a little closer, standing up to the opposing force that stood before me, overshadowing the girl, I commanded, "This needs to stop. Remove yourself from her now!"

The little girl again raised her hand.

I felt my body starting to shudder, causing a disturbance and weakness in my energy. I soon found myself losing strength in my legs, unable to support my upper body. With both my hands and knees on the ground, I knew I needed to gain strength to face the presence before me. Raising my upper body, allowing my knees to support me, I extended my right hand towards the girl and placed my left hand over the area of my heart. With my will focused and aligned with my attention, the power of my energy increased. I soon was able to get to my feet, one foot at a time. As the divine light flowed to and increased within me, I was able then to direct it to the girl.

The girl started to rise from the ground. As the divine energy intensified, I could see the presence of the apparition grow weaker. Within minutes, it was expelled backwards from the girl, breaking their connection. The girl then dropped to the ground, collapsing to the floor.

The apparition infused with anger soon appeared between the girl and me.

Directing the light towards it, this time, the apparition was held in place, encased within the light. It wasn't long before it was defeated and then dispelled from our sight.

As I looked at the girl on the floor, I noticed that her mother had joined her. The girl was held in her mother's arms in an attempt to comfort and reassure her daughter that all would be well. I could see the girl was shivering but could feel within her the relief of knowing that she was free from the torment of her uninvited guest. It wasn't long before the mother turned to face me and thanked me for saving her daughter.

I knew I needed to somehow relieve the suffering that they both endured. Placing my hand on the mother's shoulder, I could feel my hands get warm as the healing was given. I could see the healing taking effect as both of their faces became radiant, sensing an inner peace within them both. Once the healing had finished, I wished them well and safekeeping for the future. I had a feeling that all would be well for them.

I was aware that something was alerting me that there was more to the history of this place, where this bridge had stood, and the area of the river it covered.

I knew it was time for me to go to meet Suzy on the other side of the bridge. As I caught up with her, she appeared to be concerned and worried about me. Suzy informed me that Wil, Jane's brother, had arranged to transport them back to be with him in the other realm. From there, they were able to watch me deal with the incident in the church.

I went on to tell her about what I had received while crossing the bridge. I was aware of something that needed to be investigated, needing to find a possible cause of what was going on here.

Seeing that Suzy was unsettled, I asked, "Is everything OK?"

"It feels different, somehow", Suzy commented as her emotions became more sensitive and heightened.

"I feel something drawing me to the river", she went on to say.

"Be strong, Suzy. Remember, there is more to you now. You will start to see and feel more than you would normally. As I mentioned earlier, there is more to investigate in this area".

"I will do my best, William. I do hope that we will be safe".

I could feel her anxiety about our safety. I started to walk back to the bridge, and Suzy started to follow, soon catching up with me, walking by my side.

"What are you looking for, William?"

"I need to tap into the source of this presence to find out what it is and how to remove it?"

"I can feel it, William", Suzy confirmed.

It was just a matter of finding a secluded patch of grass near the bridge to sit on. We soon managed to locate a spot obscured by bushes and closer to the lake. Holding hands and seated comfortably, we sat facing each other.

"Are you ready?" I asked her.

"Will this have an impact on my unborn child?"

"The child is protected, Suzy", I replied to reassure her.

"I am ready", she confirmed.

I looked around to check to see if anyone was watching us or was in sight who might try to disrupt what we were trying to achieve. There appeared to be no one around.

Firstly, I asked Suzy to close her eyes and then started to take her through a mental exercise, initially reassuring her that I would be with her all the way.

"What are you seeing, Suzy?"

"I am in a field surrounded by daisies, wearing my favourite dress. I can feel the grass beneath my feet. There is a slight breeze caressing my face, accompanied by the warmth of the summer sun. It is so nice here. So peaceful".

"That's good! What are you doing now?"

"I'm swirling around. Max is with me. We are playing with the scarf".

"Who is Max?"

"Max was my best friend when I was a child. We had so much fun and great times together".

I noticed that she started to get emotional from her memories of her companion.

"It's good to hold on to those memories. As good memories keep you alive inside".

"It feels so real", as tears rolled down her cheeks.

"Please hold on to these emotions, Suzy, as they will assist us with this task. The sun is your reflection; allow yourself to shine".

"I can feel the warmth, and it feels good", Suzy commented on her observations of self as she took in the scenery.

Again, I asked for more clarification on Max.

"He is still with me, encircling me. He seems happy we are together again. It is as if I can read his thoughts".

I was pleased with her progress so far.

"Suzy, you are both connected - there is no separation. When did you first meet Max?"

"When I was three".

"Why do you think he has come to be with you at this time?"

"I am not sure".

I needed her to identify the reason why Max had appeared to her. Was it connected to her past?

"We need to find out why? It is important for you to understand".

"Where has he gone?" Suzy asked with an anxious voice.

I could feel Suzy's emotional energy fluctuate as the visitation within her vision from Max had stimulated her emotions.

"Oh, I can see him now".

"Where is he?"

"At a distance on top of a small hill. He is barking to catch my attention. He seems to be calling to me".

"What is Max?" I asked to seek further clarification.

"Max is a dog. Why?"

I smiled, realising my error, thinking Max was a human. I was pleased I was able to clarify this now, or else it could have led to confusion further into the conversation.

I felt that we were closer to our answer and replied, "It seems he wants to take you somewhere".

"As I am moving nearer to him, he seems to be getting further away".

"What does this tell you, Suzy?"

"I am losing him again!" she cried.

I felt at this stage, I was able to link into Suzy's vision, monitoring her emotional and mental state. Appearing in her vision, I could see that not only was she emotionally exhausted, but she also looked depleted of love. I could feel her loss of the one companion she could rely on when she was a child. As the vision became her reality and she succumbed to the emotions of her dilemma, she was now appearing as a child of four years. I needed to let her know that I was close and, at this point, decided to place the image of myself in her vision, standing before her.

"Suzy, I have found Max".

"Where?"

Max then appeared by my side so that Suzy could see him. In her response, she seemed to be pleased with his return.

Needing to see what the connection would lead us to, "Suzy, why do you think he has come to be with you?"

"I'm not sure".

I could see her focus diminish as her thoughts dwindled to the time of her childhood.

"Suzy, please look at me, as this is important. What happened when you were four? What can you remember? Has it something to do with Max?"

As Suzy looked up to face me with her childlike face, looking bewildered, I could see she was in deep thought. With time against us, I prayed for her to receive guidance.

Suddenly, the voice of someone she knew from her past could be heard coming from a short distance from us. The sounds were carried by a gentle breeze, caressing Suzy's little ears. With recognition of the voice, she lifted her head to see where it was coming from.

"Grandma, is that you?"

An elderly lady then started to appear, standing a short distance from Suzy.

"Grandma, it's you!"

I could see Suzy's excitement as she ran over to be with her, reaching out with her arms to briefly embrace her grandmother in a hug.

I walked over to where they were standing and stepped to one side to let the conversation continue between them, hoping the answer would be revealed.

"Now, Suzy, my dear, what have you been up to?" Suzy's grandmother had asked her.

"I have missed you so much! There is so much I need to tell you. Is grandpa with you?"

"No, dear! Suzy, do you remember the day when we last saw each other?"

"I remember you were in the hospital .... Mama had told me that you went to meet grandpa in heaven".

"Do you remember what happened with Max?"

As Suzy looked down, I noticed Max was no longer with us. I could see her look around to see where he had gone.

Responding to her grandmother, she replied, "When we arrived home, Max wasn't there. Somehow he escaped .... Papa went looking for him".

I could see that Suzy was getting upset.

"Now, dear, try not to get upset; let's dry those tears", Suzy's grandmother said gently as she handed her a handkerchief.

"Papa found him. He was hurt and weak, barely alive. Papa had brought him home in a blanket".

"How did he find him?"

"Papa said while he was driving slowly, peering down alleys. A lady dressed in white caught his attention. He referred to her as an angel. She would appear to him frequently, pointing in a direction as if guiding him. At first, he thought it was strange, but he knew the angel was helping him. Then, just as he was giving up hope, she again appeared, pointing to the ruins of an old building. Papa turned to face the old building from within his car to see where he needed to be, but as he turned to face the angel to give thanks, she had again disappeared. Parking the car in a safe area not far from the old building, papa ventured into the grounds. He looked around, looking everywhere he could, but Max couldn't be seen.

Papa was about to leave as it was late in the afternoon. The temperature appeared to be getting colder, and then from nowhere, he heard his name being called. Startled by what he had heard, he turned around and suddenly, instead of finding himself in the ruins of an old building, he was transported to another place and time. He found himself standing in a cathedral in its full glory. He went on to say the décor was beautiful and breathtaking. There were stained glass windows with a brilliant light appearing through them, with pictures that seemed to tell a story of creation. Then came an awareness of not being alone, a feeling of being accompanied by more than one presence sharing the hall he was occupying. There were people of light encircling him. A beautiful harmony of voices was echoing within the hall of the large room he was standing in. His heart was filled with pure emotion. He felt a love that surpassed any he had felt before in his life. While taking in the surroundings presented before him, papa informed me that as he looked around, he was mesmerised by what he had seen.

He soon set his eyes on a golden statue holding a golden Sceptre. The main feature of the Sceptre was a beautiful iridescent ornament. He heard his name being called once again. As he turned around to face the direction of where the voice came from, he saw a figure of a woman of light – it was the angel standing before him. In her hand was a crystal pendant, iridescent in colour, and she offered it to him. Papa took the crystal pendant and thanked her. The angel nodded in affirmation and informed him that the pendant was for me, his daughter. The angel then pointed behind him. As papa turned around, another angel was holding Max in his arms. Relieved, papa retrieved Max from the arms of the angel and thanked him. Papa then suddenly found himself back in the ruins of the old building. The angels were no longer to be seen".

"Where is the crystal pendant now?"

"I am not sure! When papa gave it to me, I held it in my hand close to my chest while I slept. The next morning, it had gone. Max had also miraculously recovered from his injuries that night".

There was silence for a moment.

"We must go now, my dear", I heard Suzy's grandma say.

"Why? Can't you stay?"

Suzy's grandma pulled her tight into her arms to give her a strong hug. As she released her embrace, she started to fade along with Max.

"Will I see you again?" Suzy asked.

A faint whisper of her grandma's voice replied, "Yes".

As they faded, Suzy looked sad. I reassured her that she would have another opportunity to see them again. I then started to bring myself back out of the vision.

"Suzy, it is time for you to open your eyes and tell me what you have learnt?"

We both found ourselves back on the grass near the bridge over the river. I could see Suzy was starting to remember, recollecting her memories of when she was a child.

"The Sceptre, my father had mentioned. Do you feel it has something to do with the box and what is happening here?"

"It is a possibility".

"The pendant was beautiful. It was a shame that I lost it".

I smiled and then pointed to her chest.

"It was never lost and has always been with you. It seems you have been chosen, Suzy".

"What do you mean?"

"Sitting next to the river will help establish your connection with the Source. I believe it to be the crystal that will guide you and alert you to the Source's presence".

I looked around and could see that we were still very much alone.

"Before we continue with the next part of the journey, I need you to hold on to what you have learnt about your vision and the gift bestowed upon you. Remember, you have been chosen. The source, which you are reacting to, is somehow connected to the suffering being caused in this village".

"How are we going to find it?"

"I have a feeling that we will not be able to find it here".

"What do you mean?"

"I have a strong feeling that we will need to shift our frequency of energy to enter the realm of where it is located".

I started to glimpse images within my mind of a cave near the riverbed, just near the bridge.

"I am confused".

"I can feel a dark portal converging within one of the tunnels of a cave that is somehow connected with this location. The cave is located near the riverbed at the bottom of the river, near the bridge. It is the energy of the Source that you are connected with, which is keeping the dark portal open".

"I am not comfortable with this! Do I have to do this?"

I realised that Suzy was connected to the Source. It seemed to be the only possible route linking the dark energy through to her, entering her energy field and affecting her thoughts and emotions.

I knew I had to act quickly. Facing Suzy, I took both of her hands and focused on the divine energy entering her being. After about six minutes, the intensity of the light fought back the darkness, returning colour and peace to Suzy's emotions and thoughts.

"Are you OK, Suzy?"

"Yes, sorry, William. I let my guard down then and let the situation get to me".

"When we shift into the other realm, the water will not be there. Instead, the cave entrance will appear in front of us. So what you see now will be different from how it will be in the other realm. Are you ready?"

"What would you like me to do, William?"

"As I have mentioned, the place we need to go is not of this realm. We will have to mentally shift our consciousness from this realm of reality into another. We need to break the connection that binds that realm with this one".

"What do you mean?"

"Our reality is based on the focus we give to it. Our minds provide our consciousness the vehicles it needs to operate in this realm's reality. If we attune our minds to focus on another frequency, to another point in time, then anything is possible. Our mind allows us to see vibrations of conscious frequencies into other dimensions or realities. Through the window of our mind, through the imagery of thought, we can perceive it as it is shown. Once we become more immersed in the new reality shown to us, this becomes our new reality. Adapting to new feelings and thoughts. Everything is connected, seen and unseen".

"Will my body still be here?"

"Yes, there is no need to worry. Our bodies will be temporarily shifted out of the visual range of others until we return".

"Will you help me?"

"I will be with you all the way".

"Close your eyes," I instructed, "Relax and take a deep breath for me. Focus on the Source, the vibrational energy of your crystal will help you with this. Feel the crystal pulsate within, allowing the rhythm of your breath and your body to sync. Let the new sensations enrich your mind, and then focus on the cave. Set your intentions to focus on finding the object of the Source. You will then start to see the entrance to the cave appear in front of you. Can you see it?"

"Not at the moment. Am I doing something wrong? Oh, wait! Something is happening. Yes, the cave seems to be coming into view within my mind".

"The crystal will assist you. Your imagination is a powerful tool; allow your emotions to help bring validation to your imagination. Imagine standing near the entrance, then accept this as your new reality".

"I can see it now".

"Now, let this be your new reality. I am going to now join you".

Closing my eyes, I soon shifted consciousness and focused on joining Suzy in the other realm. From what I could estimate, we stood about twelve metres from the cave entrance. The environment was bare and rocky.

"I am so pleased you have made this conscious leap. Are you ready?"

Suzy smiled and then nodded in confirmation. I advised her that we needed to keep alert for any unwelcome surprises as we started to make our way closer to the cave.

It wasn't long before we were standing in front of the entrance. Asking Suzy to hold back a moment, I moved closer, from the outside to just a short distance within. There wasn't much I could see due to the little light available to me from the daylight that had bathed us from outside. It was the darkness that kept me from seeing further into the cave.

Waving to Suzy, I beckoned her to come in and join me. Looking at her, I could see by her energy that there was an element of apprehensiveness about the idea. As we moved further into the cave, we seemed to be entering an energy field that felt tangible. I felt the temperature had dropped considerably. As we exhaled, our breath became like smoke. Our goal was to find the Source from within the cave as quickly as possible.

"It is so dark in here", I heard Suzy comment.

Realising we would need a way to see, I called out for assistance in my thoughts to find our way through the cave tunnels. It wasn't long before I received my answer. I was reminded to use the inner light of the spectral mind. Using the technique, I was then able to see clearly the path ahead. I then assisted Suzy. It took a little time to master, but she managed to achieve it.

"How do you know these things?" asked Suzy.

"I seemed to be guided when needed. We are never alone, especially in times of need. Please keep close to me".

I started to move further into the cave with Suzy close behind me. It wasn't without uncertainty. We were soon faced with a decision as the cave led to a crossroad of four tunnels.

Turning to Suzy, "We have no time to search all the tunnels. We need to allow a greater power to guide us".

"How do we do this?"

"I need you to focus on the direction ahead, as we need to find the Source. Your mind may play tricks, but I need you to relax and, with the greatest of intention, focus on the path to its location".

"I will do my best".

I could see Suzy relax and close her eyes. All the time, letting her know that I was close. I could see her energy started to expand as she placed more focus on the location. Finally, I felt a pulse of sonic energy leave Suzy to explore all four tunnels.

"What did you see, Suzy?"

"I saw glimpses of images in my mind, along with voices. There were many."

"Are you able to tell me more? Are you able to identify to whom these voices may belong?"

"I was aware of the two brothers, and they appeared to be lost – There were others, but I wasn't sure who they were. I could sense their fear and their suffering. It was as if I was amidst all the suffering in the world, and I felt it was hard to be a part of!"

I could see that Suzy was getting emotional from what she had just experienced.

"I felt the darkness was calling me, but I knew I was safe because I had you, William".

I felt emotional upon hearing her comment – this was new to me. It established my realisation of my connection with Suzy and the others. Confirming what she had voiced, I held her hand to reassure her.

"Are you able to tell me anything else about the brothers?"

"It is the darkness influencing them and driving them forward. Clouding their judgement and manipulating their emotions".

"Are you able to tell me why they are here?"

"They seem to be searching for something".

There was a pause as Suzy caught her breath.

"The Source is shifting from one location to another. I can feel it. It knows we are here".

I smiled. "It is connected to you, Suzy. Look at your chest - it is glowing".

Suzy smiled. "I can hear it calling me".

As Suzy moved forward, I started to follow. As we started to walk through the second tunnel, I could start to feel the presence of Seathan and his brother.

"Be careful, Suzy", I advised.

I couldn't be sure if she could hear me as I became aware that Suzy was becoming unresponsive to my voice.

As we were making our way through another tunnel, I could hear the two brothers' voices in the distance. They appeared to be arguing as their search was becoming too long and tedious.

Moving my focus back to Suzy, I could feel I was losing her to the Source. Trying to catch her attention, I quietly called out to her, but again she did not respond. I noticed that her energy became iridescent, similar to the crystal. A short while later, Suzy started to fade out of sight until I could no longer see her. In one way, I knew deep down she was safe, protected by the Source.

Shortly after, I could feel a disturbance within the foundations of the cave. Something was happening, as I could see walls starting to crumble around me. I knew, at this point, I needed to make haste and get out of the cave as soon as I possibly could.

As my thoughts turned back to Suzy, I could hear a whisper, "We have them, William. Please return to the church to meet up with Father James".

It all made sense when listening to Suzy's story of her father earlier. I was pleased to hear that Suzy was safe.

Now I needed to get out of here, but I knew it wasn't going to be easy. I hid behind a rock to ensure the brothers couldn't see me. As far as I could ascertain, the brothers were unaware of my presence. I could hear them getting closer as their voices became louder. I looked in the direction we had come from and could see it was blocked by fallen rocks. Something was preventing me from leaving, as the only Source of power in the cave was the darkness. A particular aroma settled around me, with an element of pungency. It started to affect my sensitivity. I knew I had to get out of here, somehow. As I heard the brother's voices passing by, I managed to sneak past them, back through the tunnel from the direction they had come from. I was careful not to alert them. Being small and nimble had played to my advantage.

As I made my way through the tunnel, I would often be confronted by choices that led me further into others. I knew I had to choose wisely, as some tunnels led into open caverns, while others were small and often narrow. Whilst rushing to find the light, I had to pause every so often to catch my breath.

As time passed, I soon had a feeling that I was being observed, but I was not sure by what. I caught glimpses of shadows, as some appeared to be still while others were shifting. I knew I had to keep on moving, even though I was getting tired. Eerie whispery sounds echoed through the tunnels behind me and seemed to be getting closer. Trying not to let fear enter my mind and my emotions, I focused on attaining my goal, on getting out of here. I would often see structures carved within the shadows of the walls of the tunnels of possible places I may have known. Some had brought a sense of familiarity to draw me in and then trap me. I started to move forward to avoid them, walking tightly to the other side of the tunnel wall. I soon became aware of hearing the voices of men echoing through the tunnel, arguing as if they were trying to find someone. As I focused on seeing what direction they were coming from, they appeared to be the one I was heading to. I had to be careful as I ventured forward.

I needed to take a break as I started to feel tired. For a brief moment, I felt the gentle thoughts of Jane and the others appear in my mind.

The voices of the men started to get louder. Moving a little further forward, I soon noticed a rock protruding from the tunnel, not that far in front of me. I quickly hurried to hide behind it to evade confrontation with the men. I couldn't see them, but their shadowy figures were felt as they passed me by, along with the voices they carried with them.

After a short period of moving further down the tunnel, I started to get a glimpse of possible light. As I ventured further forward, I found my path opening into a large cavern. The path shortened to a ledge, a foot in width. I paused to take a breath and found myself looking down into a void of nothingness.

I could feel the air as it was starting to get thinner. I soon became aware of shadowy figures. Not only could I feel them, but it was as if they were breathing down my neck. Although I couldn't see them, I could feel them draining my energy. It wasn't long before I felt their presence from above and on the other side of the cavern, as if I were entertaining an audience.

I started to become breathless. I knew I had to take the chance to move forward along the narrow ledge. Being careful, I started to make my way, pressing myself as tight against the wall as I possibly could. As I reached the other side, I continued with my journey. Although the tunnel seemed never-ending, I still had the notion of proceeding forward. I was hoping that it would lead me to an opening. I was starting to tire. It felt as if I was pulling the weight of my body twice over. The darkness began to overshadow me.

In my mind, I was praying for help to reveal itself and be my saviour. As time passed, I started to feel weaker as the darkness began to permeate the air that I breathed and manipulate the thoughts that entered my mind. The walls felt like they were closing in. I started to suffocate, choking on truly little oxygen. Breathless, I knew I had to keep on and try to focus. Taking in whatever air I could, helped me to gain some strength. I started to cough to clear my throat. My emotions were conflicting within me. Conflicting voices came upon me as despair, depression, anger, suffering, and neglect plagued my mind. I felt alone, losing control of my thoughts as the darkness continued to settle in. Holding on to an ounce of self and taking more deep breaths, I started to struggle as I felt my windpipe tighten. My eyes began to close, and possibly for the last time.

I was just about to give way to the darkness when something changed inside me; clarity of thoughts entered my mind. It was as though I was given a choice to either allow the despair, depression and suffering to continue and be my lifelong companion or to let the light of the divine that I know and love be my saviour.

With one last effort, I focused on the light entering my being. Within an instance, a glimpse of light appeared within my mind's eye. This gave me hope and kept me focused on what was presented to me. I started to feel the love empower me with divinity. I began to breathe it in, tapping into an unlimited source of energy. I found it to bring further clarity to my thoughts. In this state of understanding, the dilemma of letting the darkness consume me prevented me from knowing the truth. As I started to breathe in more oxygen, I was gaining strength. As I held on to the love, I could see the darkness retreat to a short distance away.

Images of Jane, Beth and Suzy soon entered my mind as if they were trying to reach out to me. I could feel the connection of their love. Knowing this helped me with this conscious decision to allow myself to be free from that which I am not. To accept the love that was being offered.

I realised, as if the answer became clear to me, that I had entered this realm through my thoughts. I just needed to make a conscious decision right now, and that was to change my thought processes and start living.

I soon found my eyes opening with a residue of light, awakening me from this slumber. Realising that I was still seated on a patch of grass by the bridge. As I looked for Suzy, I noticed that she was no longer sitting on the grass next to me.

I felt so grateful and humbled to have this understanding, which I am a part of. Having this experience highlighted an understanding in me which was shared some time ago. This reiterated within my mind, "To achieve an overcoming of suffering, it is to first acknowledge and realise that you are suffering foremost and, more importantly, you have a choice".

Feeling a freshness within my mind, I could feel the clarity return, and the suffering that I had experienced had all gone. I felt different.

The portal was now closed. It was good to see the changes within the environment that surrounded me. The area was vibrant with life. I could see a young couple walk by, laughing as they were enjoying each other's company, as well as seeing children playing not far from where I was seated – This felt good.

Walking over the bridge to the other side and back into the village, I heard a voice call my name. I turned around and saw Suzy running towards me.

It was good to see her! As she caught up to me, she lowered herself to embrace me in a hug. I could feel the strength in her arms as she tightly wrapped them around me.

"We thought we lost you!"

After our embrace, Suzy stood up. I could tell she was eager to tell me something.

"So, what do you have to tell me?"

"The Sceptre is now whole and is safe".

"The Sceptre?"

"Yes, the ornament from the church and the rod that I retrieved from the cave formed part of a holy Sceptre. It was dismantled into two parts. Each part was hidden in two different realms. It was the same Sceptre my father had seen in the cathedral from the vision".

"Suzy, I am so pleased, as you did us all proud".

"Wil informed us there is another part of the puzzle to solve. He mentioned that you were involved in it someway".

It was interesting to see that there was more to come, although I felt I needed a short break from this one first. Out of curiosity, I enquired after the others.

"They are fine", she said with a smile. "We were with you all the way, even though you couldn't see us".

It was interesting to learn of Suzy's last words. Holding Suzy's hand, we made our way into the village to the church. The energy of the atmosphere felt different as we entered the village. We soon arrived at the door of the church. As the pressure of her grip lessened, I felt Suzy let go of my hand.

Suzy knocked on the door of the church, and as there was no response at first, Suzy knocked again. As we waited, it wasn't long before the church door started to open. To my surprise, Jane was standing before us, with Beth by her side. With an emotion of love, they both lowered themselves to embrace me in a group hug. It was good to have such a feeling. Both Jane and Beth then released their embrace to then give Suzy a welcoming hug.

After the hugs were finished, I turned to Jane with a lovingly smile and said, "I love you". I could see tears starting to appear, reacting out of emotion. Hearing those words coming from me, she embraced me again.

"I love you too!"

As she pulled away, I could see the light of her aura expand.

"We have been enlightening Father James about you. He is ready to speak with you".

Both Suzy and I followed Jane to the room where we had waited before while Beth closed the church door to follow us from behind. As we entered the small reception room, I noticed that Father James was waiting for me.

"Please take a seat, William".

I looked at Jane for a reaction, and she responded by nodding her head in affirmation.

I sat down to listen to what Father James had to say.

"Your presence has certainly made a difference here. It appears that Seathan and his brother Tamhas will not be causing any more problems. From what I have learnt, they have both passed away in their sleep".

I now knew the name of Seathan's brother, Tamhas.

"So, what are you to do now?"

"My time here has now come to an end. Thanks to you, to all you fine people, it is time for me to move on, maybe to return home. Father Lachlan will continue my work here".

"Where is Father Lachlan?"

"He is in the sanctuary, preparing for his duties for today".

"May I visit the sanctuary one last time?"

"Sure".

As we entered the sanctuary, Father Lachlan was placing the hymn books on a small table, ready for the parishioners to collect when they arrived. Interested to see the shrine one last time, I made my way to the other end of the sanctuary to examine it. As I placed more focus on the shrine, I was soon aware of a protective barrier encompassing the whole church and its grounds.

"Are you OK, William?" Jane asked.

"Yes, just reflecting... It is time for us to go now".

"Will I see you again, William?" Father James asked.

"I have a feeling our paths will meet again".

I said my goodbyes to Father Lachlan and Father James. I wished them well as they continued in their service. I then mentioned to the others that it was time to go.

As they said their goodbyes, I took one last look around. As soon as they were ready, a brilliant light soon appeared, encompassing us within it. Then all we could see was light.

*Chapter XI*

# A New Insight

As I opened my eyes, I was welcomed by a familiarity. I recognised the room in which I found myself. Dressed in pyjamas, I sat up to take in the view of the bedroom. The sun was welcoming as a ray of light lit up my newly appointed bedroom through the windows. Even though the recent past events seemed to be a dream, I knew that they had happened.

I was starting to become more aware. There was still more to learn as the identity of self unravels in mystery.

I wondered if the others were back at home. Being comfortable in the bed, I relaxed and rested a little while longer before deciding to go and check.

A short time had passed. Removing the bed covers from my body to one side, I then made an effort to climb out of bed. Standing on the carpet floor in bare feet, feeling the texture of the carpet on the soles of my feet and the threads between my toes, gave me a sense of emotional grounding. My body and mind felt recuperated and refreshed, ready to start the morning of the day that welcomed me.

As Henry's name appeared in my thoughts, I began to feel uneasy. I knew I had to investigate. As I made that decision, the feeling of unease left me.

I opened the door quietly to see if I could find anyone else up. Not seeing anyone, I began to quietly walk to the top of the stairs. Not being sure who was downstairs, I listened carefully to see if I could hear any voices. As I adjusted my focus, I could just about hear a conversation between two female voices. The voices seemed familiar and appeared to be coming from the direction of the kitchen.

I started to make my way down the stairs. As I reached the kitchen entrance, Beth was sitting down on a stool, talking to Jane. I could see

Jane was preparing lunch. Once I had established who was talking, I then moved closer into the kitchen to be with them both.

"How are you feeling?" asked Jane.

In truth, I was feeling recuperated, refreshed and alert. To find myself awakening in such comfort of a bed. Then to arrive downstairs to be greeted by the love and smiles of two beautiful people; I felt blessed.

"I am feeling good... a little hungry".

"William, please come and join us at the table in the dining room", Beth requested as they made their way there, leaving the kitchen.

As I walked over to the table, Beth helped me to get onto the chair.

"You have been asleep for a couple of days. After lunchtime the following day, when you didn't wake up, we started to worry. Auntie had to call out Dr Harrison. She couldn't find anything wrong and suggested that we keep an eye on you and contact her if your condition had worsened".

"A couple of days...".

"Yes", Jane replied.

"When I awoke, I was so excited, I wondered if it was true or just a dream. I quickly ran out of my room to see if Auntie Jane was up. I knocked on the door and called out to her. We both could still remember what had happened, as clear as day", I heard Beth as she continued the conversation.

"What happened to Suzy and Rachel?" I asked.

"Interestingly, they awoke in their own homes", Jane replied.

"Do they remember?"

"Suzy, more than Rachel", Beth replied.

"Now that you are awake, I will let Suzy know, as she would like to talk to you about her experience in the village", said Jane.

Jane prepared the pancakes, placing them on a plate in front of me. The pancakes were topped with a sliced banana, with syrup poured over them, accompanied by fresh orange juice that was hosted in a container. As usual, the pancakes were delicious. They went down a treat with the juice.

Henry's name popped into my thoughts again. This time the feeling felt stronger.

"Where is Henry?" I asked.

"I spoke with him earlier. Uncle informed me that he was going to gather some more firewood. He is probably at the wood yard".

"May I be excused from the table?"

As soon as I had the go-ahead from Jane, I felt intuitively drawn to the family room. The feeling was soon accompanied by an image of seeing myself by the patio door windows, looking at the view of the grounds and the ruins.

By the time I reached the hallway, time had started to slow down. As I entered the family room, I could see both Charlie and Bella relaxing on their beds, resting. I found myself paying more attention to detail as I started to look around the room. I soon felt the need to gently close my eyes as time became still. My body started to relax, altering in frequency, fluctuating in and out of this dimension. I began to hear music that seemed to resonate with my being. The more I focused on the sounds, the less of my energy body resonated with this dimension. I felt myself gravitate as if hovering from the floor. I could then feel the warmth of the sun, and its rays were welcoming me. As I opened my eyes, I could see a change in the energy of my body as it shimmered into a bright iridescent light. I also noticed that I was no longer where I thought I was, as I appeared to be near the patio doors, facing out towards the land.

As I started to focus on what was presented before me, my attention was soon drawn to a young boy looking in. I soon recognised the boy to be the angel with whom I had met on top of the stairs. This time he was standing outside the house, watching me through the patio door windows. Once he had my full attention, I could see others, represented in light, that stood around him.

I started to feel a warmth of love build within me. Newfound sensations had given birth to new feelings. I was also receiving clarity within my thoughts as I found myself having a review of this new life from my arrival to this moment now.

During my reflection, it was good to know, during those darkest times, that there were those in my life who had supported me with their love. I realised how it gave me the strength to cope and to see through the illusion that was presented to me. I could feel the tears as they rolled down my cheeks, as I became more emotional with the thoughts of what had taken place.

I soon became aware and felt the need to harmonise my spiritual body, as the recent emotional reflection on what was happening was causing a disruption to the layers of energy that were protecting me. I could start to see the angels encircle me, and with their help, I was able to contain them. It took a little while before it was completed. I was soon lowered to the floor before the light had diminished, returning to its natural physical state. I could see it was harmonising and resonating with this dimension. I looked to the angels and thanked them for their help. Once I was stabilised, the angels who surrounded me vanished, and time returned to normal.

I noticed that the boy I saw outside was no longer there.

It wasn't long before I felt an urge to go for a walk, to look for Henry. Walking back into the dining room, I could see Jane was busy clearing the dining room and preparing the table for later.

Noticing my presence within the room, Jane turned around to face me.

"William, have you been crying?"

"A little", I replied.

Jane came over to me, crouched down to embrace me in a hug, to comfort me.

"We will always be here for you!" she responded with heartfelt emotion.

I reciprocated the embrace with Jane but then thought about the time I may have left to spend with those who I had come to love and call family. Beth must have heard our conversation as our embrace was shared, extending to a group hug.

As we parted our embrace with each other, the feeling of unease was felt again.

Sharing my concerns with them both only increased the intensity of finding him. I knew I needed Jane to understand what I was trying to share with her, so I reached over to hold her hand. I was then able to transmit images of my connection and awareness of Henry's situation to her mind. Initially, there was no reaction. I then increased my intention and concern about what I had been made aware of. As I started to observe her, I noticed the expression of an emotion of fear appeared on her face. What she was seeing was unsettling her. I could see Beth stand quietly as she monitored Jane, trying to understand what was going on.

"Auntie, what are you seeing?"

"I can see a couple of men talking to Henry. They seemed to be interrogating him".

Releasing my hand, I could see Jane pause as she was trying to understand within her mind what she was seeing.

"We need to get you dressed first, William. Beth, we need to go and find Uncle Henry. While I am assisting William in getting him dressed, can you please finish tidying up here for me?"

As soon as Beth agreed, with Jane holding my hand, we both started to walk up the stairs to my bedroom. I soon was aware of the presence of the boy who I had witnessed observing me earlier.

Jane waited while I got dressed. As I was putting a sweater on, I wondered where the boy was, as I could still feel his presence. Observing the room, I tried to see if there was anything that might stand out. It felt as if the boy had something to reveal to me.

"Let's get you on the bed, so I can put your shoes on", said Jane.

As I sat on the bed, I turned to face the window to look to see what I could see outside. Within minutes, I heard my name being called. I turned around to face Jane and noticed that the time had stood still. The boy, who made himself aware to me through his presence, was as solid in form and standing next to Jane.

"I noticed you earlier. What is your name?" I asked.

"My name is Peter".

"I felt that you needed to be settled first before I introduced myself. I have always been with Jane since she was a child. I am one of her guardian angels. I thought it was best to introduce myself to you now.

It occurred to me that when we last met, there was an angelic persona about him. It made sense now.

"Why are you in the form of a child?" I asked.

"I can ask the same question of you, William. Jane is a delicate soul and finds it hard to allow others in. She has an affinity for children. Jane is not fully aware of us, but she knows that someone is looking down from heaven, looking after her".

"Downstairs, there were others with you - were they also here for Jane?"

"Some of them. Most had come to help harness your energy".

"Can I ask you why I see you the way I do?" I asked.

"It is how we choose to show you. It is time for me to take my leave. Please remember we are always near and watching over her".

With that thought, time had returned to normal. Peter was no longer with us. Unaware of my conversation with the angel, Jane proceeded to place the shoes on my feet. Once I was suitably dressed, we continued downstairs. We collected my gilet in case the temperature had dropped outside before meeting Beth by the front door. After assisting me in putting the gilet on, Jane then checked with Beth to ensure she was OK and was ready to leave. As the door opened and we started to make our way outside onto the porch, I heard Jane call out to Charlie to assist us in our search for Henry. Within moments Charlie was by our side.

Sensitised to the electricity in the air, I started to sense a change in the weather. I looked up and noticed the sudden appearance of clouds gathering in the sky.

"That's strange! It looks like a storm is brewing", Beth commented.

"We'd best hurry", Jane replied.

We walked in the direction of where Jane knew Henry would be, as indicated by the vision she had seen of him. Heading over to the logging area where Henry would normally chop the wood, Henry was nowhere in sight. A small wind started to form. We walked into the forest to see if we could pick up a trail. As we ventured further, it wasn't long before we could hear Charlie barking. When we caught up with him, he was facing in one direction as if he were trying to let us know where Henry could be located. With Charlie picking up a scent, I heard Jane instruct him to go and find Henry. It wasn't long before Charlie had set off further into the woods. We tried to follow him, but our pursuit proved unsuccessful.

"Auntie, this doesn't feel right! We should start to make our way back home. Looking at the sky, it looks like it is going to rain", Beth mentioned to Jane as the clouds started to darken.

I could see that Jane was holding her stomach with her right hand. As I looked at her face, she seemed upset and distressed. As I looked to see what I could observe about Jane's discomfort, I was aware of dark energy converging at the base of her lower body. The energy of her aura started to alter as darker shades were introduced, tainting the already established colours, and causing them to decrease in vibrancy. I was slightly confused by the return of this energy.

The rain soon distracted my thoughts, which started to lightly fall upon us. As we were partly sheltered by the trees, we managed to avoid most of the rain. We could feel the temperature drop as the cold started to settle in. I could hear Jane and Beth as they began to call out for Henry and Charlie.

With Jane starting to feel sick, I could see Beth couple her arm with her auntie, trying to shift some of her weight onto herself. I wasn't sure where Beth's state of mind was focused, but I am sure it was in the welfare of us all as I overheard Beth repeat her suggestion that we return home.

Suddenly I was aware we were surrounded by many tiny lights, the lights that had appeared to Jane and me earlier. As if on cue, we found ourselves soon totally sheltered from the rain. As I looked up, I noticed that the lights were gathered to form a shelter over us.

I noticed Jane had slumped a little, causing more weight to fall onto Beth. It looked like Jane was losing strength in her legs. I wanted to help Beth, but I wasn't sure how! My thoughts were soon filled with the notion of moving forward to the old tree that Jane had shown me earlier. As I focused on the journey ahead, I made them both aware of what I had been shown. I then prayed for strength for Beth to assist her in carrying Jane forward further to where we needed to be.

Observing Beth, it was interesting to see as her energy expanded to encompass Jane, supporting her emotionally and, with the best of intentions, seeing her well. I could see beautiful colours of orange, red, pink, brown, and blue as they blended in line with the colours in Jane's aura.

We soon found ourselves by the tree. I could see Beth's relief to know we had arrived. She could now relieve herself of the weight she was carrying. I could see her focus was on ensuring her auntie was resting as well as she could. Assisting Beth, we managed to place Jane in a seated position, with her back against the tree.

We both took a good couple of steps away from where she rested, being mindful of where we had placed our feet so as to not trip or cause a fall.

"This is where your auntie brought me earlier", I informed Beth.

Taking a breather and needing rest, I sat down next to Jane with also my back against the tree.

I soon felt I needed to look up at Beth. Her facial expression was one of amazement and excitement at what she was witnessing. I could see an acceptance and openness of her positioning on the phenomenon that was taking place. The tree, as grand as it was, was emitting light as it had earlier. As I turned to face Jane, I could see her aura becoming more vibrant and pulsating with a multitude of vibrant colours. They were mainly supported by various shades of blue and green. I could see the healing from the tree restore the energy she had lost, as well as diminishing the dark energy that resided within her. After a short while, the small lights that surrounded us and the light emanating from the tree soon diminished and everything returned to its natural state.

Jane started to open her eyes – It was a gradual awakening on her part. Seeing the tree gave her clarity and a sense of grounding. Jane then stood up from the ground and walked towards us.

"We need to continue to find Henry".

Hearing what Jane had to say, we soon heard a rustling noise. We could see a clearing of a path open before us through the thick shrubbery of the forest. It was as though we were being listened to.

"Shall we follow the path to see where it goes?" Beth asked.

We all felt we should investigate, as this had been offered to us. So, as we ventured onto the newfound path, we were curious and a little apprehensive about what we may find. As we moved further away from the tree, the air started to change. The light rain fell as we began to approach a clearing from the forest.

As we got closer to the clearing, we could hear men's voices coming from the open space that awaited us. I could see that Jane wasn't happy or content, knowing that there were trespassers on her land. I was aware that Jane's energy started to react, indicating emotional dissatisfaction with what she saw as an invasion of her property. It wasn't long before we could hear more voices, this time accompanied by the sounds of heavy vehicles. Still discontented and without thinking, Jane entered the clearing to investigate and interrogate the intruders on her land. The rain began to recede as she did, and a mysterious mist settled in.

I could hear Beth call out to her auntie to be careful, but by this time, it was too late, as we could see Jane disappearing into the mist.

"We must follow her!"

Seeing Beth's concern, I could understand her feelings, but we did not know what awaited us on the other side.

My thoughts were soon directed from her as I heard a feminine, soft whisper of words enter my thoughts, "The path that unfolds before you will be yours to claim soon".

I then had the feeling that we were to stay where we were until we were told otherwise.

I informed Beth of the thoughts and feelings I had received. Although she was reluctant at first due to her emotional need to support and help her aunt, she soon accepted the decision to wait.

## Chapter XII
## An Unexpected Turn

I could see Beth's emotional energy reacting as she became more agitated whilst the minutes passed us by.

It wasn't long before a slight wind encircled me.

Another soft whisper of words could be heard, "It is time for you both to enter".

I informed Beth about the thoughts I had received and that we needed to be careful.

We began to move forward into the clearing in pursuit of Jane. As we stood within the mist that surrounded us both, there wasn't much else that we could see. Our views only reached out just beyond each other.

"Where are we?" Beth asked.

There was silence at first, followed by a slight vibration of energy that we both felt.

"I'm not sure about this!" exclaimed Beth.

I could understand where Beth was coming from, as there was an unknowingness about the mist and the place that we found ourselves in.

"I am sure that we will find a way to where we will need to be", I replied.

We could hear the echoes of voices surrounding us. As we looked back to where we had come from, all we could see was the mist. Feeling uncertain, our focus needed to remain on Jane.

"Beth, we need clarity within our thoughts – they can be clouded by our emotions and by the circumstances we are faced with. Take a couple of deep breaths, as this will allow you to relax and to place focus on our goal".

I could see Beth relax as she took in a few deep breaths.

"How do you feel now?" I asked her.

"Much better, thanks", she replied.

As Beth started to relax further, I noticed that she had closed her eyes.

"William, I can see the path we need to follow. I'm seeing images appearing in my mind, revealing the path through the mist".

"What else do you see?"

"I could see glimpses of auntie".

"That's good! Are you able to lead the way?"

Beth opened her eyes and replied, "Yes, I will show you".

I put my trust in Beth to guide us. As we started to move forward, some of the voices that we could hear were getting louder. We seemed to be walking in different directions, still limited by our vision of the path ahead by the mist that surrounded us.

We soon found ourselves near an old building. I could hear Beth talking about a military camp. By this time, the mist had started to clear a little. So as not to be seen, we hid behind a collection of what Beth referred to as oil metal drums.

As Beth was much taller, she was able to peer over the metal drums. She went on to describe to me the details of the activity on the land that she was able to observe. As she continued to look, I could see her being mindful of her task, stimulating her mental prowess. I noticed that her gaze was directed to a location just over to her left. Something had caught her attention, as I could see that she was lifting her body to try and get a better look.

Interested to see what she was looking at, I looked around to see if there was something I could stand on to give me height. Unfortunately, I had no luck.

I noticed Beth lowering herself quickly to hide behind the metal drum as the voice of a soldier soon passed us by.

"What could you see?" I asked.

"As the mist was clearing, I could see a large building, possibly a warehouse with offices attached".

I wondered if both Henry and Jane were in the large building Beth had mentioned.

As the day was still young here, we waited a little longer for the right opportunity to make our move. We found a secluded area to sit and wait. As time passed, the grounds became less occupied.

As the temperature began to drop, my attention was drawn to Beth. The energy of her mind appeared to be active, heavy with thought. I could tell that she was becoming restless.

Deciding to take another look, Beth stood up and walked over to the metal drums, scouting the area with her eyes once more.

"I suppose we could take a closer look at the building William. Although it's not going to be easy".

With Beth briefly lifting me to get a better view of the area, we looked for the best route to get to the building without being detected.

As I was lowered back to the ground, I soon became aware of a vision of Jane appearing in my mind. She was held captive in an office guarded by two men. They appeared to be waiting for someone. I couldn't see Henry or Charlie in the images shown to me.

I informed Beth of my vision.

"What else do you see?" she asked.

I closed my eyes to see if the vision would return and relay any more information about Jane's situation. As I did, I was shown more of the office and where it was located. An older man, tall with white facial hair and wearing a dark navy suit, was shown to be sitting opposite Jane. I was aware that he was directing questions at her. Even though there wasn't much that I could gather from the conversation, I did hear Henry's name being mentioned.

I went on to tell Beth about what I had seen and what I could understand from the conversation.

"How are we going to get past the guards?" Beth asked.

"Have faith, as I am sure there is help on hand for us".

Avoiding the soldiers and places that would leave us exposed, keeping as quiet as we possibly could and trying not to alert others of our presence, we made our way to the side of the main building.

I noticed Beth was peering through one of the lower windows on the ground floor.

"What can you see?" I asked.

"The windows need a clean if you ask me", Beth replied with a witty remark.

It was good to see Beth's humour making the situation a little more light-hearted.

"With very little light, there is not much I could see from here", Beth responded.

Suddenly we heard shouting. We looked around and could see one of the soldiers on patrol with a dog heading toward us. We headed for the trees as the best possible direction to run. Every so often, we looked back, avoiding those who were in pursuit of us. I heard a loud, sharp noise coming from the air, and I felt this was to warn us. Shortly another similar sound was heard, and this time it sounded louder than before. We continued to keep our distance, taking advantage of the shelter from the trees. Our only weakness was our stamina and the obstacles we found in our way. As we headed deeper into the forest, we were able to lose our pursuers.

"That was close! We'll have to be more vigilant now that they know we are here", Beth exclaimed while trying to capture her breath.

As I looked at Beth and apart from her clothing being slightly torn whilst running from the soldiers, she also appeared to have grazes and cuts to her arms and lower right abdomen.

As my adrenaline started to quieten, I started to feel a cold, sharp pain in my upper right leg, just off to the side. As I looked down to check where I felt the pain, I noticed that my pants were torn. There was a lot of blood seeping from the area.

"William, you have been shot!" Beth exclaimed.

Apart from the trail of blood that was created from my wound, I could see that she was looking for something on the ground.

Beth started to wipe her face of the tears with her hands. She knew she had to keep calm and focused whilst trying to fight back her fears of the predicament we now found ourselves in.

After finding a suitable place for me to rest, I was carefully assisted and lowered into place by Beth. I appeared to be seated against a large tree.

I could feel the tiredness envelop me. I was also aware of Beth's voice becoming more distant as time passed by. I soon felt the need to close my eyes.

It wasn't long before her voice became a faint echo – I could hear her begging me to stay, continuously talking to me, calling my name. It helped me to remain present for a short while until I felt myself drift as my life force energy began to escape this body of mine. I suddenly became aware of hearing Beth sobbing. Briefly opening my eyes, I could see that Beth had tightly wrapped my leg with some of the material torn from her own clothing. As Beth sat down to my left, I could feel her warm embrace, holding me tight in her arms. I could feel the dampness of her tears as they trickled onto my face. It wasn't long before the warmth within me receded, and I began to lose the sensation within my body, feeling it become limp.

I soon found myself looking down on my body, one that had given me shelter on earth. I was of pure energy again, in a spiritual energy body, free of pain and the emotional suffering that accompanied it. The curiosity about what was next occupied my thoughts. I felt peace, free of the life that I once knew. I could see Beth holding my body tightly, not giving up, hearing her still calling my name. Once colourful and exuberant, the colours of Beth's aura soon started to change as varied shades of magenta, brown, red, and indigo were introduced, taming the vibrancy of the colours that were already resident. I could only imagine the emotional pain she must be feeling as I could see Beth gently rock me backwards and forwards. I noticed then Beth started to scout for help with her eyes but without success, with no hero to save the day. I became aware of a silver cord of energy connecting me to the body below. It seems that I was still, in one way, present within my body.

I soon became aware of her thoughts, and I was troubled by what I had learned. Suffering from emotional exhaustion, Beth was contemplating giving up, as she saw this as the only way to release her despair. I felt helpless to respond to her cry for help. I felt an enormous amount of compassion for her, and before long, she began to close her eyes. Knowing that she felt helpless and distant within herself, I could see her resting her head near mine. I felt emotional, a sense of sadness for a beautiful soul. With her life force starting to dwindle, her soul started to prepare before its departure. I didn't want Beth to give up, as she still had so much to live for.

It wasn't long before angels started to appear and gather around us. Bringing an iridescent healing light with them, I knew somehow that they were here to help. I was soon also witnessing a beautiful display of colourful energy in dance, permeating both of us. It was emotionally overwhelming.

Observing my body, I could see the light build within it. It wasn't long before I felt a warmth, a feeling of sensitivity, as my consciousness was drawn back into my body.

Opening my eyes, and as the light receded, it took me a couple of minutes to adjust. Gathering my strength, I positioned myself sitting up, gently releasing myself from Beth's arms. I felt guided to place my hand on her forehead. As I did, a light appeared and started to flow from the palm of my hand. It wasn't long before I had the feeling to remove it, the light receded, and the heat diminished. Slowly to my great delight, Beth opened her eyes.

Turning to face me, she asked, "Are we in heaven?"

I smiled at her question and then replied, "Thank you for saving me!"

I reached over to give her a warm embrace of a hug.

Gathering herself, Beth responded, "So, we are not in heaven?"

On releasing my embrace, smiling, I replied, "No".

I could see that Beth was trying to comprehend what had happened.

"But you died in my arms!"

I went on to explain to Beth what I witnessed and what happened to us both.

"William, please try not to die on me again!"

I could feel her emotional relief and felt intrigued to know why she had given up. I put the question to her.

"Since we met William, I have grown emotionally close to you – When you died, I felt a part of me had died with you. That's the only way I can explain it", Beth replied.

It made me realise that it wouldn't only be Jane who was the one to define me and shape my experiences here but now also Beth.

After a little rest, we both soon got back on our feet, with a little help from each other.

"William, will you be OK?"

"Knowing that you are here with me, I am sure that I will be".

I noticed that all her cuts and grazes had been healed, and they could no longer be seen. I could see Beth was taken back emotionally by what she had just witnessed. On querying this with her further, she went on to tell me that she felt blessed by the notion that she was a part of something that would be defined as a miracle in its essence. Her face seemed to have a glow to its complexion. From what I had learnt from her and knowing that we were both still alive, I could feel her thoughts turn to hope.

Shortly afterwards, I received another vision. This time it was about Henry. He was sitting in another office within the same building, talking to three others. I found myself listening to the conversation. The only words that I could overhear that seemed of importance were about the land that they owned, the location of the boy and something about Henry. They seemed to be more concerned about the latter.

I mentioned to Beth about the vision.

"Was there anything else about Uncle?" Beth asked.

"I will try again to see if any more will come".

Looking in the direction of the large building, I thought about how I was going to proceed with helping Henry and Jane. It wasn't long before another vision came to mind. I saw myself walking into the building and noticing that the entrance wasn't guarded. It was as if the route to Jane was free from interception. As I reached the office where Jane was located, and as if on cue, the guards were called away to attend to an incident elsewhere in the building.

I shared the vision with Beth. I could see she was concerned for my well-being.

Shortly afterwards, I soon became aware of another consciousness other than our own. I knew somehow that this presence had something to do with the vision I had seen. I soon was aware that we were being observed. A vibration of energy could be felt throughout my body, igniting my senses. Invigorated by the newfound sensations, I felt more alive and creative. I was sure that Beth was feeling it too. I decided to ask her the question and then waited for her to respond.

"What do you think it is?" Beth responded.

"I am not sure. It may be an answer to our request for help".

The sentient being became visible to our senses in a colourful form of tangible translucent energy encircling us.

"It looks beautiful! Do you feel it will protect us and keep us from harm?" asked Beth.

Suddenly, the sentient being had split into two; one had encircled Beth, and the other encircled me.

"It seems that way", I replied.

"Where did they come from?" Beth wondered.

"I am not sure".

Thoughts soon appeared in our minds that they were here to help us. Sent from the future, acting on a request I had made from another reference point in my timeline.

Reaching out, I telepathically asked them who they were.

Patiently waiting, we both then received thoughts from them as we heard, "Reihasiem - We are not known through identity but through the presence of our entirety".

"What do you know of me, of my future self?" I asked.

There was no response, so I asked another question, "What can you tell us about our situation?"

"You stand now, not on the land you entered from but at a vibrational frequency beyond the fourth dimension, a reality created by the thoughts of another".

"How long do we have?" I felt I had to ask the Reihasiem.

"There is not much time. We will help as much as we can, but you will need to hurry", replied the Reihasiem in unison.

"Beth, I need to make a move to find Jane".

"I'm not sure about this!" Beth was concerned for my safety.

"I will be careful. If I see or hear anything that could compromise me, I promise that I will turn around and come straight back".

I could see that Beth knew deep down that this was something that I needed to do. With the Reihasiem helping us, she felt more reassured, putting her more at ease with the situation.

"Just be careful, please, William!"

"I promise".

The Reihasiem started to fade from sight, and the sensations started to settle. Although they appeared to be gone, we both still felt them.

Leaving Beth, I made my way through the forest, leading back into the grounds of the camp. It wasn't long before I was in front of the building. As I entered, I used the stairs to the first floor. It wasn't long before I could hear voices, possibly two or three men. They seemed to be raised and agitated. So as not to be seen, I quickly hid behind a cabinet nearby. It wasn't long before soldiers had rushed past me, down to the other end of the corridor, where they soon disappeared through a door.

In one of the visions that were shown to me, I remember seeing Henry seated in an office with three other men. Recognising the corridor before me, as in the vision, I decided to see if Henry was indeed here. As the corridor appeared to be clear, with no other soldiers in sight, and as quietly as I could, I made my way towards the office. As I reached my destination, being small once again had an advantage. I was able to fit between a gap behind a cabinet near the room. As I attentively tried to listen to what I could hear from Henry and the men who kept him company, the voices seemed to be sheltered by a soundproof containment within the room. Closing my eyes, I knew I needed to focus to see if, somehow, I could project my consciousness within the room to pick up the sounds of the conversation taking place. As I attempted to try, I soon felt a shift in my body as I focused on Henry. I found myself in my spiritual body beside Henry.

I could see the energy that surrounded Henry and the energy of the three men with him. Henry's energy seemed to withdraw as they continued with their interrogation. Even though Henry was strong, having to deal with three of them, he started to begin to struggle. The men, in turn, knew what they were doing, putting various questions to him. I needed to find out what they were asking him. I needed to hear any information that could shed light on what was happening here. The man in the middle of the three seemed to be asking most of the questions, while the other two were directing questions related to a different matter. As I listened intently, I felt the main topic of the conversation was to do with the land which Henry and Jane owned. There were questions related to his family. Interestingly what caught more of my attention was their questions about me.

I could hear them talk about a sudden energy spike over the coastline and Jane's relationship with me. It appeared that they had been observing us. I could see by the reaction of his emotional energy that Henry was opposed to them spying on his family. As I listened further, I could hear them talk to him about his past connection with their organisation. I wondered if Jane was aware. I then became aware as my attention was directed to an inner feeling as I felt something or someone was trying to direct my attention to Henry. I was suddenly made aware of a dark energy building within Henry. I felt a little confused as it seemed it wasn't Henry's well-being I needed to be concerned about, but concern for the men who were interrogating him.

I soon found myself back in my body, behind the cabinet. As I peeked out from behind the cabinet, there appeared to be soldiers running down the corridor to reach the stairs. Something had stirred, causing them to react. Thoughts of Jane came into my mind.

Although I wanted to help Henry, I had a feeling that all would be well with him. As I looked at him, it did not seem that he was being held totally against his will.

When the coast was clear, I manoeuvred out of the gap behind the cabinet and carefully made my way back along the corridor. Knowing that I needed to find Jane, I turned the corner and headed down toward the location I had seen in my vision. I soon found myself a short distance away from the office where Jane was currently. To avoid being seen, I managed to position myself in a nearby empty office, where the window gave me a good view of the office, and I could see Jane.

Not knowing who the man was, my focus was solely on Jane. I just needed to work out how I was going to get her out of there.

It wasn't long before I could see Jane leaving the office, slamming the office door behind her. Jane did not appear to be happy as she made her way along the corridor toward me. Not wishing to be seen by anyone else, I kept my head below the window to listen to their conversations.

"Jane, there is nothing you can do about it. The land is being confiscated for further study, and that is the end of it", I heard the man say.

Unaware I was near her, I heard her shout back, "It is my land! Does mother know what you're up to?"

There was an exchange of other words, but I couldn't make them out.

In conclusion, by how they referenced each other, I understood they were father and daughter.

Raising my head to look out of the office window, I could only see Jane standing near the door to the office I was in. As I looked back to see if I could see her father, I noticed that he seemed to have disappeared. Turning my focus back to Jane, I could see that she seemed upset.

I made my way out of the office to the corridor where Jane was standing.

"William, what are you doing here?"

"We followed you into the mist".

"Where is Beth?"

"Waiting for us on the other side of the camp".

A thought soon entered my mind urging us to leave the place.

"We need to leave this place!"

Jane looked back to her father, only to notice he had gone. "Where did he go?"

"People are disappearing, and it is not safe for us to be here".

I noticed Jane was partially preoccupied with thoughts of her argument with her father.

"Jane, we need to go, as Beth is waiting for us!"

I could see finally I was able to get Jane to understand the dilemma we were in.

"OK, William, please take me to Beth".

Making our way down the stairs, we left the building. Once we were out, we started to make our way to where Beth was waiting for us. Just as we cleared the grounds of the camp, I felt I needed to turn around. A mist started to appear, encompassing everything we could initially see in the camp. As the mist started to build, we could start to see the outline of soldiers. We could hear voices, some louder and more assertive than others. To ensure we didn't alert them to our position, we managed to keep low and safely weave our way past them.

It wasn't long before we met up with Beth. I could see that she was relieved to see us both, especially her auntie, as they both welcomed each other with an emotional hug.

Leaving them to their embrace, I thought I had better check to see where the path we were on was leading us. Passing them both, I walked further down the path. As I ventured further, the mist started to clear. Looking back at Jane and Beth, I could see them in deep conversation. As I started to walk further ahead, I felt that something wasn't right. I felt I was being observed, being followed. The observation was coming from a distance not far from where I was, to my left, and a little further into the forest. I knew I couldn't let my observer know that I knew. I wasn't sure whether the observer was a friend or foe. I waited a short while to see if I could see any movement, especially one that was headed in my direction.

While I was waiting, I still was aware of the Reihasiem close by.

As there was no other activity within the forest, I started to walk back to Jane and Beth. I could feel an eerie presence checking my every move. It felt that there were many gathering, hiding to pounce. I felt more like prey on its way to being slaughtered. I continued back on the track of the path, waiting until I got closer to Jane and Beth before making them aware of our situation.

I could see Jane looking my way, and I surmised that Beth had shared with her the incident of my passing. So as not to approach the subject, I took the opportunity to softly whisper to Jane, as I approached her, that we were being observed.

"What should we do?" Jane quietly whispered back.

"If we walk down the path I have just been down, but keeping alert, then I feel we will be OK. Please let Beth know. It is important not to make eye contact with them", I replied.

Jane gave me a quick hug so as not to raise suspicion that we knew that they were there. She then walked over to Beth and whispered what she was now aware of. I could see Beth cast her eyes in my direction.

We started to make our way down the path to find our way back home. Although we could hear rustling amongst the trees, we remained cautious of the prying eyes and the observations made of us. Our pace increased as we moved further in. Surprisingly, even though it seemed as if it was getting late and the time was passing us by, the sun was still brightly shining through the trees.

"Are we lost?" I heard Beth ask.

"I am not sure. I could do with having a rest though", I heard Jane reply.

"Are we still being followed, William?" Beth asked.

"We may be OK. We will still need to be careful".

We soon entered a little clearing. There was something familiar I felt about this place. I couldn't at this time recollect if I had been here before.

I could see Beth looking for a place to sit down. Finding a broken tree that was suitable, both took the opportunity to rest, relieving the discomfort endured from the walk and enabling them to recover and replenish their energies. After finding a position that would support their upper body, I noticed Jane and Beth had closed their eyes.

My focus of thought was soon redirected as many questions entered my mind. Two stood out: the first is how we got here, and the second is what brought us to this moment. As I observed my location, I noticed a branch from a tree that I could climb upon. It provided me with a prime position to watch over Jane and Beth as they slept. It would also provide me with the opportunity to continue to dwell on the answers to those two questions. With a little effort, I was able to reach the branch and had time to reflect. I remembered some old sayings that were reflected in time that rested within my consciousness. A conversation I once overheard from memories past that could be related to the circumstances we now face and could perhaps provide the answers to the questions most prominent in my thoughts.

"Is the pursuit of one's own agenda a selfish or selfless cause?"

The thoughts went back to Jane and her father, remembering the conversation they had between them.

Another saying was, "The eyes and the ears that follow me. The gossipers, the influencers who pursue me. What is the sense that gives them validity? Only myself".

It is the ego of the self that draws attention. With all that has been happening around us, sometimes we can create an illusion that draws others to us. Was there an observer watching me? Or was it my self-conscious, drawing into the perception of self? I did know that we were where we were supposed to be, in this time, within this moment, sharing in this experience together.

As the day got shorter and the evening drew near. I heard a rustling in the trees behind me and then turned around to see who could be there. Although I couldn't see anyone, the rustling continued.

Climbing down, I quickly ran over to Jane and Beth, gently rocking their shoulders back and forth to wake them up.

"Beth, Jane, we need to go, as we have company...".

"What is the matter?" Jane asked as she was trying to bring herself around.

A further rustling could be heard, and this time by Jane and Beth as well, as the sounds seemed to be all around us. As the rustling noise got louder, we looked at each other. I could see Beth huddle up with Jane.

I knew I needed to do something. Within my thoughts, I called out for help. I soon felt the Reihasiem surround us.

The rustling in the trees started again but only for a short while.

My focus was soon drawn to the ground just behind Jane. As I focused my attention on the area, I could see the leaves and twigs on the ground being swept away by a gentle breeze as if to reveal a path for us to follow.

"We need to follow the path that was laid out for us. I have a feeling it will take us where we need to be", I suggested to the others.

"I am with you, William", responded Beth.

"Me too", responded Jane.

I soon received thoughts from the Reihasiem to assure me that all would be well and that it was their time to depart. I made them aware that we were grateful for their help.

As we made our way onto the path, we could only hope it would lead us home.

We soon came upon the old oak tree. As I stood near it, I felt bathed by the brilliance of its splendour and grace.

With the others wishing urgently to return home, we made our way back to the edge of the forest. We were not far from the place where we wanted to be at this moment in time. As we started to head back to the house, it began to get dark. It soon became pitch black in the light of day, making it difficult to follow the path to travel back home.

Needing a place of shelter, I felt a pull in the direction of the old ruins as though some force was guiding me. Being there before and knowing what had taken place, I thought it would be the safest place to be at this time.

The rain started to increase in mass and pour down heavier. Our eyes became blurred by the downpour, and as the darkness settled in around us.

"What's happening with this weather, and what's happened to the daylight?" Beth asked out loud, as to be heard.

"William, we need to get you out of this rain and get you dry. You will catch a cold – even pneumonia!" Jane raised her voice out of concern.

"We need to find shelter now and then head towards the house, Auntie", I heard Beth say.

As the visibility reduced, we started to hear voices. The voices' owners seemed to be lurking in the darkness, and they appeared to be searching for us.

This brought my memory back to the cave and the similarity with what was occurring now. We could see shadows take the form of men, with others altering their form back to their initial shadowy state.

"Beth, we need to get to the old ruins, your auntie and I had noticed it earlier", I strongly suggested, without alarming the men to our location.

"There are ruins here, on this land?" Beth queried.

"Yes, old ruins that would have been a place of worship for pilgrimages", I replied.

"Why have you not said, Auntie? You haven't mentioned this before!"

"It didn't cross my mind, Beth. Why?" I heard Jane reply.

Beth continued, "It all makes sense now – I was volunteering for a local shelter for the homeless, back where I used to live before coming here. I got speaking with an old man, a traveller. His clothes appeared worn, and his skin was partially flushed. He turned up one evening from the streets. Out of the other volunteers, he seemed to gravitate towards me. I became a friendly face and company for him. He thanked me for my company and for the kindness I had shown to him. He started to tell me about a place of pilgrimage that held great power. The man went on to say that the path to this sacred place had been lost in time. It was supposed to be centuries old. He informed me that one day it would be discovered again, revealing a great mystery, a higher truth to our existence. He went on to say more about it, but there was only so much I could retain in my memory. I thanked him for his story. Maybe more of the conversation will come to me a little later".

"Would you say that the place mentioned to you and these ruins are one and the same?" I asked.

"There is a possibility".

"Did he say where?" Jane asked.

As I stood listening to Beth, I could see her energy react to her emotions.

"No, only that I will know when the time is right. I am sorry for reacting the way I did. My emotions had gotten the better of me – Just as he was leaving, he mentioned a key. I did run out after him to find out more about the key, but he had disappeared".

It was interesting to hear Beth's story about the old ruins. I still felt the pull and knew it would be our safest option.

"William, where do we need to go now?" Beth asked.

The path was still being shown to me. Seeing it within my mind's eye and allowing my senses to guide me, we set off to make our way to the ruins, trying to avoid contact with the men in the shadows.

The path wasn't easy and seemed long, made more difficult by the rain and the muddy wet ground. Approaching the old ruins, we could see a couple of men dressed in military uniforms and carrying weapons. They appeared to be guarding the entrance of the building. Keeping low and hidden from sight, we were able to get as close as we could.

We were sheltering behind a large tree, out of sight of those we could hear shouting in the distance and those who stood guard over the old ruins.

I looked at Jane and Beth as to their reaction to what was happening. I noticed they looked emotionally and physically worn, finding themselves in this situation. Yet, I kept strong through the flood of adrenaline and my determination for us to get somewhere safe.

"What do we do now?" Beth exclaimed.

As I carefully appeared in the direction of the old ruins from where we hid, I knew that we needed to draw the attention of the men away from the building. So I sent out for help within my mind for higher guidance. My attention was soon drawn to the little girl who had accompanied us many times before. I could see her spirit as it started to manifest and appear thirty metres from the two men guarding the entrance. The young girl seemed to be drawing the attention of the men by calling out to them, drawing them away from the old ruins. Noticing her and not realising that she was a manifestation of conscious energy, they called out to her and started to head in her direction. Despite their efforts, the little girl kept her distance. This allowed us to make our move.

Both Jane and Beth looked over in the direction of the old ruin, and although hesitant at first, they made their way as quickly as they could, with me leading the way to the entrance.

On entering, we were soaked to the bone with the rain. I prayed that a miracle would be upon us at this time. I thought about my conversation with Beth and what had manifested the last time I was here with Jane. With time against us and surely with the men returning, they would be sure to capture us. As we stood in the old ruins, I looked to the altar and then at Jane and Beth. They both seemed to be shivering from the coldness, embracing each other to keep each other warm. It occurred to me that even though there was no roof to this structure, the rain did not seem to enter. As I turned my focus back to Jane and Beth, I noticed a warm glow set about them.

My attention was soon drawn to voices outside the ruins. The men had returned, but it appeared that they couldn't see us hiding within. It was as if they were looking straight through us.

Bringing my attention back to the others and to the inner space of the ruins, I could see the light starting to fill the space we were housed in. The ruins became whole as they did before. Revealing itself to be a sacred place, a place of ritual, for those who sought sanctuary. This time the internal space seemed to grow and expand, larger than before. The darkness soon left, welcoming the day's sunlight as it appeared through the windows. I glanced back at Jane and Beth. They both seemed to be glowing with radiant energy, as was I.

Love was soon permeating our being.

"Where are we?" Beth asked.

"In theory, we should be in the old ruins, but it has changed. It now appears we are in a sanctuary", I replied.

I could see that Beth was taken in by the transformation. Facing Jane and Beth with my back to the entrance, all was quiet for a short while as they appeared to be reflecting on recent events. I then began observing and listening to Jane and Beth as they were seated, trying to make sense of everything. It wasn't long before I felt a change in the room. I could see the others had also felt it as they turned to face me. I soon became aware of a presence behind me. My attention stayed focused on Jane and Beth, even more so as I could see both Jane and Beth's reaction as something or someone caught their attention. I could see them looking towards the door to the entrance. Wondering who it could be and feeling the presence getting closer, I felt the urge to face whoever or whatever it was. I took a deep breath and then turned around.

*Chapter XIII*

# The Village Fayre Encounter

S tanding in front of me was the girl. Surrounding her was a brilliant light, which lit up the entrance. It was the girl from the house who had accompanied us to the sanctuary last time. I had noticed her helping us a moment ago, drawing the men away from the entrance of the sanctuary.

"What is your name?" I heard Jane ask.

I could see her look at me, then at Beth and finally, her eyes were fixed on Jane.

"I am Alice", she replied,

"Alice, It is nice to meet you", I heard Jane reply

Curious, I watched Alice as she then walked past me to be with Jane. I listened to their conversation attentively.

"It wasn't your fault", I heard Alice say.

I looked at Jane and could see her crying.

Beth was looking at Jane in amazement.

"Alice was my grandma's name. I was going to name her – I had lost her during pregnancy because of an internal complication!"

Jane then embraced Alice with a hug, and with heartfelt emotion, she asked, "Why now?"

"I can't say!"

"How long are you allowed to stay?"

"Until it is time for me to go".

I could see Beth look at me and then turn to face Jane.

After their embrace, Jane then attempted to stand. The energy of the place was a little overwhelming for her and had caused her to slightly lose her balance. I could see Alice take Jane by the hand to help steady her.

"It is time for us to leave", Alice suggested to Jane.

"Leave! To go where?"

The doors to the entrance started to slowly open to reveal rays of beautiful sunshine entering the sanctuary. I felt a calling for us to walk through, and I was sure the others did as well. I could see energy threads of light, like a web connecting us all, shimmering within the space surrounding us. A cool breeze was soon felt entering the sanctuary from the outside as if to welcome us.

With Jane holding Alice's hand, they both made their way through the door, leaving the sanctuary.

Beth stood up to follow them.

Observing the hieroglyphics, symbols and scriptures displayed in light, written on the walls and on the ceiling of the sanctuary, questions soon populated my thoughts. I had never felt more of a connection, of an association, than I did now since my arrival on earth.

It wasn't long before I could hear Beth calling me from outside of the sanctuary.

"William, come quick - you have got to see this!"

I turned to the entrance and called out, "I'm on my way".

I could feel a change in my energy as I walked through the entrance to join the others. On glancing back, I saw there was no return as the portal started to fade. When the time was right, I felt the portal leading back to the sanctuary would reveal itself to us.

Looking around, I noticed we were no longer on Jane and Henry's land – we appeared to be in another time and place in history.

I was welcomed by the warmth of the sun in the sky. I felt refreshed and uplifted. My energy felt invigorated, feeling connected to the life force of nature that surrounded me.

Looking over at Jane, she appeared to be excited by her recognition of the place.

"Where are we, Auntie?" I heard Beth ask.

"This is the village where my grandma grew up. I can remember some of the buildings from when I was a child".

Alice soon beckoned us forward with the motioning of her hand to follow her.

Taking my hand, both Beth and I continued to follow Jane with Alice deeper into the village.

I could hear Jane as she was reminiscing about her childhood visits to her grandparents.

"I wonder where all the people are?" I heard Beth ask.

As we moved further into the village, our ears became attuned and accustomed to the sound of music and voices carried by a gentle breeze.

Jane paused and then said, "It seems to be coming from the village green. If I can remember, we just need to go down 'Cedar Street'". She pointed to the street a little further ahead.

The music and voices appeared to be getting louder as we were getting closer.

I started to receive an overwhelming feeling, followed by a strong intuition to hold back. I looked at Alice, who was watching Jane and wondered if it had something to do with them both. Turning to Beth, I gently tugged on her hands.

Beth turned to look at me and asked, "Are you OK, William?"

"Beth, we need to hold back. The next step is for your auntie".

"What is going to happen, William?"

"Do you trust me?"

"Yes, wholeheartedly".

With that, Beth called out to Jane, "Auntie".

Jane paused and then turned around to face Beth.

"Auntie, we just need to rest for a moment. We will catch you up in a little while".

Jane turned to face me with a concerned look on her face.

Not wanting to cause her to worry, I smiled and gave her a little wave.

Unsure of how to take my response, Jane then turned to face Beth and said, "With everything that we've been through of late, both of you should take it easy. We will see you both soon".

Jane then continued with Alice to the village green.

"Are you able to tell me anything else?" Beth asked.

"Grandma".

"Auntie's grandma is here!" Beth responded with a little excitement in her voice.

"Yes".

"Do we get to meet her?"

"I have a feeling that we will".

I could see Beth was curious and excited about the prospects of this chance meeting.

We continued forward, following the route Jane and Alice had taken before us. As we reached the village green, we realised that the village was hosting a fayre.

I noticed that Beth was taking in the view and the atmosphere as she looked around.

"Why is that man watching Auntie Jane?" I heard Beth say as she pointed him out to me.

By this time, I was trying to silence the many voices in my head as I became sensitive to the thoughts of others. I could also feel their excitement, their laughter, and their joy as they were immersed in the fun of the fayre.

I decided to try and see what the man's intentions were. Observing his energy proved to be difficult. We decided to take a closer look without alerting him to our presence, but as soon as we came within a short distance from where he stood, he disappeared.

"Where did he go? He can't have just vanished into thin air", I heard Beth question.

We walked through the entrance that led into the fayre to see if we could see Jane and Alice. With so many crowds, we had difficulty locating them. We could see a small outhouse hosting many tables, with people selling food and drinks. We could see stalls selling crafts and ornamental jewellery. An open raised platform with a couple of tables, just in front to one side, stood to the left of the village fayre grounds. The tables were decorated with prized entries, consisting of cakes and meatloaves. We could hear a brass band playing music at the opposite end. We could see all sorts of activities and games for the children.

The clothing was fitting for the period, not too different from the style we wore. The locals didn't seem to notice anything amiss.

I looked up at Beth and could see she was excited and wanted to participate in the activities.

"What do you see?" I asked her.

"Looks like fun".

"Look again and this time, relax", I advised.

I then focused on raising Beth's energy, helping her to fine-tune her senses.

"I can see energy everywhere I look. With some of the people, the energy is brighter and more colourful", she said wonderingly.

"Now, I would like you to focus on your auntie?"

"I can't see her?"

"You do not need to see her. Just focus on your auntie, and then a greater power, a guiding force, will show you what you need to see and feel. Be aware of what is being shown and feel how it stimulates your feelings and intuition".

I could see Beth relax to help her focus. I saw light appearing, blending with the energy of her thoughts, as she became mindful of the exercise at hand.

"I can see them. There is an older woman with her. Is this auntie's grandma?"

"A possibility Beth. Is there a man with her?"

"No, not that I can see", she replied.

Beth's focus soon returned, finding herself back with me.

"Wow, William, that was interesting! As I became more aware of auntie, I could see her energy. I then could feel her emotions!"

"As we place our focus, we connect in more ways than we realise, Beth. Sometimes it is about being mindful within our connection with each other, in paying attention to the details being revealed to us".

We started to walk around the fayre, taking in the atmosphere. It wasn't long before I had a feeling that Beth wanted to participate further in the activities of the fayre.

"What do we do now?" asked Beth.

"Let's have fun", I replied.

Beth walked over to the craft stalls, keeping me close to her. The first stall we encountered was selling scarves and gloves. I could see that Beth had fun trying them on. The next stall was selling blankets of various patterns and sizes. Although the interest was there, I could tell that there was something else on Beth's mind.

"There are so many different types of stalls with so much to buy. It's such a shame that we don't have any money to buy any of these to take back with us", Beth commented.

"Who knows, an opportunity may present itself to us. We will have to wait and see".

Suddenly, I could hear children playing nearby. As I focused more, I was aware of two boys and three girls. Thoughts of one of the boys came to my mind. I could see him coughing while holding his chest. A feeling of unease came over me.

I looked at Beth and noticed her watching me. I intuitively felt that Beth seemed to feel the same uneasy feeling I was experiencing. Beth, with some medical training, felt she needed to help.

"Let's see if we can help the boy", she suggested.

Unsure where to go, we allowed our inner intuition to guide us in the direction of where the children were. They seemed to be playing away from the crowds.

I noticed that the man we had seen earlier was observing the children from a distance.

The boy seemed to have caught a fever, and even though he was trying to hide it, the condition seemed to be getting worse. I could see his energy was weakening.

The other children were now exhibiting concern.

I noticed that one of the girls seemed to show more concern about his health than the others. I soon became aware of the emotional energy connecting them. The sense of a sister intuitively came to mind.

Looking more closely, I could see the boy's energy had started to withdraw as he became weaker. Dark energy could be seen within the energy surrounding his lungs and chest region, weakening his immune system.

As my attention was drawn to Beth, I could sense she seemed to recognise the symptoms.

"William, the boy has Tuberculosis. If he is not treated soon, he is going to die!" Beth exclaimed.

I looked over to the man who was observing the child. He stood there patiently as if waiting for something. I tried to see what else his energy could tell me about him, but as I delved deeper, there was something about a displacement of energy within him which prevented me from seeing clearly. As I turned to face the boy to place my focus on healing him. I soon felt a cold breeze shiver over me, as if the man's presence had just walked through me, even though I was aware that the man hadn't moved.

I began to hear crying and shouting from the boy's sister as her brother lay on the floor.

With Beth being as caring and as loving as she was, she made her way over to see if she could help.

I looked over at the man and noticed he was still facing me. With a nod, he then turned and vanished.

It wasn't long before the presence of the spirit of the young boy was standing to my right.

"Are you an angel?" asked the boy.

I knew I had to help him. Reassuring him, I replied, "I am here to help you. It is time for you to return to your body".

"Can I not come with you?"

"Not this time", I said gently.

I walked over to where the body of the boy was lying and stood beside it. I soon noticed that the boy's spirit had followed me, standing again at my side.

I could see his sister crying as she sat by his body, pleading for him to wake up.

I noticed the other children had left to find help.

I could see Beth first look at me and then look to my right as if she were aware of the presence of the spirit boy with me. Beth then crouched down to embrace his sister, to comfort her.

While no one was looking, I crouched down by the body and placed my hand gently on his forehead. The palm of my hand started to get warm, and I could start to see the light emit, entering above his brow. It wasn't long before I could then see the young boy's life force, his spirit, return to his body. I felt the healing light then flow through to his throat and then to his chest region, strengthening his immune system. Soon, the colour and the warmth began to return to his face and hands. After a few minutes, the healing was complete.

Removing my hand from his forehead and returning to my feet, I stepped away from the boy and made my way back to the stalls a short distance away.

The boy soon recovered. Opening his eyes, he sat up and called out his sister's name. To his sister's amazement, she removed herself from Beth to embrace her brother.

Realising that she was no longer needed, Beth stood up and made her way over to me.

As the boy and his sister recovered from their ordeal, they were soon joined by their parents. All they could get from the boy was that an angel saved and healed him. Both he and his sister, though caught up in the emotion of the situation, couldn't remember us. Their memories were weakened by the sister's sorrow and the boy's awakening back into life.

My thoughts went back to the man I had seen earlier. I wondered who he was, as he did not appear to be from this realm. I had a feeling that I would see him again.

We continued to look around at other craft stalls.

"I love trinkets", Beth commented as we came upon a stall that sold them.

I could see Beth's eyes glisten as she held some in her hand. I noticed that one trinket bracelet had caught her eye. It was as if she had a calling to it. As Beth briefly held it, I could see how the trinket bracelet brought a certain vibrancy to her energy.

Examining the bracelet, I noticed that the central piece was a green crystal that seemed to vibrate and harmonise on an emotional frequency. I could see the crystal shimmering with speckles of pink, green and gold light. There were other crystals carved in geometry-shaped designs that also had little flat stones and a small chain that linked them. I could see some of the stones had symbols on them, like the ones I had seen in the sanctuary. I somehow knew that this was meant for Beth.

As I handed the bracelet back to the lady who was managing the craft stall, the lady smiled at me and winked. Curious, I smiled back, feeling that somehow the bracelet would come to Beth.

We continued looking at other craft stalls, admiring what was on display.

Eventually, needing to rest and with hunger settling in, we sat down by the bandstand to gather our strength and to wait for Jane.

"Are you OK, Beth?"

"A little tired and a little hungry. I just need to eat some food".

I could see Beth closing her eyes and taking in a deep breath. As she started to relax, I could see her energy expand as she became more connected with the moment and the village fayre. A smile appeared, illuminating the beauty of her face as it radiated, creating youthfulness in the persona of her being.

As we rested, I could hear the laughter of children and adults alike as they were carried on the vehicle of the gentle breeze. Closing my eyes briefly, it wasn't long before I felt someone else had joined us.

"Hello, my dears. I do hope you don't mind, but I noticed that you both looked a little hungry. I brought some food and juice for you both".

Opening our eyes, we noticed the lady from the trinket stall standing in front of us.

The lady handed the food basket and juices over to Beth.

"My dears, can I ask your names?" asked the lady.

"My name is Beth, and this is William. Thank you for the food. May we ask for yours?"

"I do apologise, and where are my manners. My name is Mrs Emmet – I hope you don't mind. Beth, I have brought you a shawl to cover yourself with and to keep you warm".

Mrs Emmet handed the shawl over to Beth.

"Thank you", Beth responded.

Realising that this was the lady that Jane's grandma would compete against in the competition for the best meatloaf, I smiled.

First placing her shawl over her shoulders, Beth then briefly looked into the basket.

"I love meatloaf", Beth commented.

"I am so pleased you like meatloaf. You know, I make the best in the village", Mrs Emmet commented.

I smiled as I knew another that would claim the same.

"Are you entering the competition?" asked Beth.

"Yes... the competition looks good this year, but they will have to go some to beat my meatloaf", Mrs Emmet commented and smiled, her eyes twinkling.

"Didn't we see you managing the trinket craft stall?" asked Beth.

"That, my dear, is my niece's craft stall. I was only helping her out for a couple of hours".

"You have some nice bracelets on display", Beth commented.

"Thank you, I will let my niece know you liked them".

"I need to go and see what's happening in the competition and to see if there are any late entries. Would you both like to come?" asked Mrs Emmet.

"If it's OK with you, we will have a little rest first and then pop over afterwards?" asked Beth.

"Of course, my dear – Just before I leave you both, can I say, Beth, that you look so much like my nephew - he should be here later. Will you be around? I would very much like you to meet him".

"We hope so! Just need to let my aunt know, as she is very protective of me", Beth replied.

"It will be good to see you both again. Please bring your aunt, as it would be nice to meet her".

Mrs Emmet turned to face me, winked with her left eye, and then whispered to me, "I saw how you helped that young boy earlier. It will be our little secret!"

This closing of one eye to acknowledge or confirm an understanding intrigued me. There seemed to be more to this meeting than we could possibly have known at this time.

I smiled in response, having an appreciation of her awareness of the situation that had occurred earlier.

Mrs Emmet soon left us, making her way to the table hosting the competition entries.

Seeing Beth watching me, I could see she was trying to understand what had just happened. I could see that she was emotionally taken aback by the relief that someone, a stranger, had shown us kindness.

"You see, Beth. We will be fine".

Placing the basket next to her, she started to retrieve the meatloaf and other items from it. The contents of the basket consisted of one meatloaf, two apples, two cakes, two small bread rolls and some homemade jam.

"This should last us all day. Maybe we can share with auntie".

"Are you sure that you have everything from the basket?"

Bethany further examined the contents, only to find a paper bag under the cloth.

"How did you know?" asked Beth.

"I just had a feeling".

As Beth pulled out the small paper bag, I could see her assess the weight. Peeking into the bag, her face lightened with emotion. Seeing what was contained within, she took out a trinket bracelet.

It was the same bracelet she admired at the trinket craft stall.

"How is this possible?" Beth commented with emotion.

I could see that she had cried a tear as she placed the trinket bracelet onto her wrist to wear for the first time.

The main crystal and the symbols on the other stones of the trinket bracelet were beautiful, with varied shades of orange, yellow and green. Observing Beth, looking at the way she was looking at the bracelet, I could see her strength return as she adored the intricate design and how it felt on her wrist. It was good to see Beth's energy as it started to expand and become more vibrant.

I felt the need to place my hand over her wrist to feel the energy that was being emitted from the bracelet. I could feel the vibration permeate between my fingers, causing a tingling sensation within my hand.

Seeing Beth's eyes slightly glazed, I was slightly curious about the reaction she had to it.

"It is a part of you now". I commented and then smiled.

"I love it", Beth responded, confirmed by the expansion of her aura.

"Beth, shall we eat?"

"Of course, please let's tuck in".

Beth then started to break the meatloaf in half to share. Knowing how the scent of the meatloaf had made me feel, I declined and asked if I could have some of the fruit and bread instead.

As she started to eat the meatloaf, I could see that it was having an impact on Beth's energy system. I also noticed that Beth began to look unwell.

Although I enjoyed some of the fruit, the remainder of the food was kept in the basket.

"You may have to be careful about the choice of foods that you decide to eat", I suggested to Beth.

Seeing her unwell, I assisted Beth with restoring her energy system by showing her how to bring in healing energy. With a little guidance, this was achieved.

We sat, reflecting on the day for a little while, gathering energy and strength. With what seemed a short time that passed, my attention was soon back to Beth, as I noticed she looked emotional.

"What are you thinking about Beth? if you don't mind me asking".

"Just the last couple of days. What with Mrs Mable, the camp, the sanctuary and here. It's all been a little overwhelming".

As I observed Beth, the reflection of her thoughts appeared to me as a short film of extracts of her emotional times, her connections and her moments spent with her aunt, her uncle and meeting me.

My thoughts soon went to Jane. It wasn't long before I received words within my mind to wait by the games stall, where the adults were throwing balls to knock down tin cans.

I shared this new information with Beth. As soon as she was ready, we made our way, bringing the basket with us.

I felt the presence of Jane and Alice approaching, and I had a feeling that she was nearby and would be with us soon. Beth started to keep a lookout. It wasn't long before she was able to see Jane and Alice within her sight.

"Auntie", I heard Beth call out as she then ran over to Jane and Alice to bring them back to me.

As they made their way over to me, I noticed that Jane was out of breath. Looking at her aura, I could see some small dark patches clouding the energy of her mind as well as down towards the right side of her body. I knew I needed to act fast to cleanse her, so I reached out my hand to hold hers. I took a deep breath and opened myself to the healing energy. The palm of my hands started to produce heat and emit light. I felt connected to everything in the universe as if the universal energy of divine light flowed like a gentle river through me into Jane. It was no longer about me - it was as if I had become the river. The healing started to work as the dark patches in her energy field began to diminish. It wasn't long before the healing was complete.

"Thank you, William", responded Jane.

Jane went on to tell us what had happened earlier.

"While I was talking to grandma, I felt someone was watching me. I thought I would just take a quick glance to see who it could be, but no one stood out. It felt as if someone was trying to manipulate my mind – I began to lose my thoughts, and I soon found it difficult to express my words. It was only then I kept on seeing images of the both of you in my mind, and this worried me".

I could see the situation had caused her mind to reflect on the memories of the military camp and the time before we reached the sanctuary. It was like watching a video.

"Auntie, how are you feeling now?" Beth asked, with a concern for the woman she loved, lived up to and respected.

"Much better now. I had to make my apologies to Grandma, and then Alice was able to lead us to you both".

I closed my eyes and sent out a prayer of protection for us. Setting my intention helped seal the request for what I was asking. I could see Jane was starting to relax. I could then feel the warmth from the love of the protection that encircled us as the vibration of our energy altered.

"So, what did you two get up to?" Jane inquired.

"We had a good look around the fayre - we checked out the craft stalls - we also met Mrs Emmet", Beth replied.

I could see that Jane was curious as she asked, "What is she like?"

"She was kind and giving. She brought us food and some juice and then gave me this shawl", Beth replied.

"I would very much like to meet Mrs Emmet. I have heard so much about her from grandma", Jane commented.

"Have you eaten, Auntie?"

"I was offered a meatloaf and a cup of juice from Grandma. It was so lovely to meet her again. The meatloaf was just how I remembered it. We agreed to meet up later, and then I can introduce you both to her".

I noticed that Beth had not mentioned her trinket bracelet during this conversation. I thought that maybe she would mention it later.

It was time to see what else awaited us, as I had a feeling that we needed to move on. I suggested to Beth that we return the basket to Mrs Emmet.

With Beth leading the four of us, we made our way through the crowds to the tables hosting the cakes and meatloaves competition entries. When we arrived, we appeared to be early for the announcement of the winners. It was good to see the last of the entries being put into place, ready to be assessed by the judges.

Looking around, Mrs Emmet couldn't be seen. Then it occurred to me that she mentioned her nephew. Closing my eyes, I placed my focus on Mrs Emmet. It wasn't long before I received an awareness of where she was.

I could see that Beth was preoccupied with the cake tasting. Needing to catch her attention, I gently tugged her blouse.

"William, is everything OK?"

"I thought I saw Mrs Emmet talking to a couple near a drink stall".

"Which direction did you see them?"

I pointed to my left, then replied, "Just pass the hat, and the scarves stall".

"William, can you please let Auntie know that I am just going to return the basket and thank Mrs Emmet for the food she kindly provided us?"

I nodded to confirm her request.

Beth then made her way in the direction of the drinks stall. I could tell she was living in the moment, feeling alive and excited by the notion of the chance to meet with Mrs Emmet's nephew.

As it was getting a little crowded and preventing me from getting trampled, I moved back to an area slightly away from the others, still having a good line of sight of Jane.

A vision soon appeared in my mind's eye. I was shown three young men watching Beth from a short distance away, admiring how she looked. I wasn't sure of their intentions towards her, as the feelings I received felt unsettling.

When the vision ended, I looked around to see if I could see any of the men, but no one matched or came close to the likeness of those in my vision.

Alice would be what Beth needed at this time. Needing to keep an eye on Jane, I turned to find Alice and noticed she was sampling some of the cakes. I called out her name, and within a blink of an eye, she stood in front of me. Although translucent, it seemed that only I could see her. I could see she was holding a half-eaten cake in one hand and another in her mouth while trying to smile. While she was finishing off the cake, I explained to her what I had seen and told her my concern.

Alice seemed to understand and agreed to help, then soon vanished before me.

I happened to glimpse Jane and noticed that she appeared to be searching around for someone. As she came over to me, she asked, "Did you see where Alice went?" Then, realising that Beth wasn't with me, she also asked, "Where is Beth?"

"Beth and Alice have gone to look for Mrs Emmet to return the basket. I am sure they will be back soon".

I could see that Jane was unsettled, not knowing where they both were. I felt Jane needed a distraction, as I felt, for some reason, she needed to remain here.

"Jane, my dear", a lady called out to her while approaching us.

It was as if my thoughts were being answered. I noticed the lady was holding a container in her hands containing a meatloaf.

"Now, I had best get this into place before the judges come around. Jane, would you mind helping me?" the lady asked.

I could see Jane take one last look around to see if she could see Beth within the crowd.

"I would love to – Oh Alice, this is William, the young boy I was telling you about".

"Hello William. May I say you look familiar. I cannot say where I have seen you. I am sure it will come to me".

"Hello", I responded with a smile.

"What is the matter, dear?" Grandma Alice asked Jane.

"It's probably nothing. My niece has gone to return a basket to someone. I would just be more comfortable and have peace of mind if she were here with us".

"I am sure there is nothing to worry about, my dear. Let her be. She is probably having a good time".

Jane then went with her grandma to help her with the meatloaf.

Seeing a vacant chair near the table, I mentioned to Jane that I needed to rest and showed her the chair where I was going to sit. I could see she was happy to agree to this, as she could see me from where she was, to keep an eye on me. I walked over to the chair, and with a little effort, I was able to sit comfortably on the chair.

Crowds started to gather for the announcement of the winners.

Closing my eyes, I could hear those that gathered as they expressed their voices, championing the event.

As I became mindful in placing my focus on Beth, the sounds seemed to blend as one until all I could hear was the rhythm of my breath. In my mind, it wasn't long before I could see her. I could see that she was aware of Alice being close by.

The vision of Beth started to fade as thoughts of the young men entered my mind again. It was as if Beth's encounter with them was going to happen soon.

I sent out prayers for Beth to receive all the extra support she needed, to get through this.

It wasn't long before I found myself standing outside of my body, looking back at myself - I looked peaceful. I became aware of many thoughts as many voices entered my mind. Some were audible, while others presented themselves to me as thoughts.

I needed to make my way to Beth, but a higher power was preventing me. Words soon appeared in my thoughts, informing me that I could only observe from a distance.

I soon found myself watching Beth from a position above her. I noticed that I wasn't the only one, as I was joined by angels. As I looked to the ground, I could see dark shadows moving along the ground and entering the vicinity of the area near where Beth was standing.

I could see Beth talking to Mrs Emmet and a young couple with a young infant. I could see the emotional energy connecting them.

Focusing on the nephew, I could start to see a young man in his mid to late twenties. I could now see why Mrs Emmet had mentioned earlier the family likeness between him and Beth.

I soon became aware of how the infant child and Beth were connected. I could feel the emotional connection of a genetic bond between them. It was clear to see with the information presented before me that the relationship would be of a daughter and her father.

From the activity of her thoughts, Beth was working towards a definitive answer within her questioning without giving the game away of who she was. It wasn't long after their discussions that she was able to confirm and validate the connection of her relationship and understand who she was to each of them.

From further conversations they had between them, I learnt that Mrs Emmet's nephew was called Dr Walter Emmet, and his wife was called Kathleen. I could see that Beth's interest in medicine seemed to have been inherited from her grandfather.

I could see by her thoughts that she had many more questions to put forward to them if given the opportunity.

It wasn't long before the insight I received earlier about the three young men was to manifest, as I could hear shouting coming from a direction not far from where Beth had stood.

I noticed that Beth could hear them too. As I looked at her emotional energy, I could see various shades of pink, magenta and brown being introduced into her aura. I could tell that she felt uncomfortable with what she could hear.

As the shouting continued, I could see three young men pushing their way through the crowd, causing a disruption within the area. From the heavy consumption of alcohol, their actions were driven by their emotional desires and their selfish need to be in control.

Placing my focus back on Beth, I could see her pleading with Mrs Emmet and the others to go and find help. I could see Dr Emmet trying to reason with Beth but as strong and determined as she was, he was fighting a losing battle with her. With Beth placing her hand on Dr Emmet's shoulder, I could see calming energy being transmitted from her to Dr Emmet.

"It will be OK", said Beth as she was trying to reassure him.

My attention was soon drawn to the energy of the bracelet on Beth's wrist. I could first hear it humming, and then I noticed it started to glow. I was aware of a slight change in Beth's energy. Shortly after, the bracelets' energy soon receded, returning to a passive state. I wasn't sure if Beth had noticed it, as her focus was mainly on the young men.

With Beth's emotional energy being on a high, I noticed her grow in confidence and in strength, ready to take on any confrontation that awaited her. I could see her step away from the Emmet family, walking further into the crowd to steer the men away from her newfound family.

Looking for Alice, I could see that she was no longer at Beth's side. I wondered where she had disappeared to.

As Beth made her way through the crowds of the fayre, I could see she was trying to lose the three men who were in pursuit of her. Carefully choosing the best route to remove herself from the main crowds, away from open areas to avoid being seen. It wasn't long before the three men soon caught up with her.

"Hello beautiful, so you thought you could avoid us", came from one of the men.

"Are you trying to make it harder for us?" said the younger of the three.

"Why don't you want to be in our company?" asked what I could gather to be the leader of the three men, as he appeared to be spurring on the other two.

Trying to keep her composure, "May I ask your names?" Beth asked calmly.

I could see her trying to get to know her perpetrators and looking to defuse the situation as the three men were closing in on her.

Observing what was happening, I felt helpless.

"Why do you want to know our names? We are here to offer you more than our names. Just play nicely", the leader responded.

"Please, I want to help you!" Beth exclaimed.

"I know what I want!" the leader of the three men replied.

Beth turned to the other two men.

"You know this is wrong, right? I am sure you are better than this. Let me help you!"

"Don't listen to her. We are fed up with others dictating what we say and do", dictated the leader of the three men.

The younger of the men replied, "Maybe she is right".

"Are you with me or against me?" the leader responded.

"Come on, she is not worth it. Let's go", the younger man replied.

"If you don't want a piece of the action, then I suggest you leave now", the leader responded.

I could see the young man look to Beth, then look to the other men. "I'm going... I am not having any part of this!"

Before leaving, the young man turned to the other man who was with them.

"Surely, you can see this isn't right... right?"

The other man with them replied, "I suggest you go now".

The young man soon left.

Beth somehow knew that there was still an ounce of goodness within them, but it was the young man who chose to listen at this time. I then noticed Beth again tried to plead with the other two to appeal to their better nature.

As the leader turned to the other man, who decided to stay to join in the hunt, "So it is just us two now. The coward has gone. I will be having words with him later".

"I am sorry that you feel that way. I am only trying to save you. Please let me help you!" Beth exclaimed as she realised her fear of the situation would soon manifest.

As Beth walked backwards a little more to try to keep the distance from them, the men shortened the space between them, moving in closer. Beth soon found herself trapped behind one of the temporary housings that held some of the stands, with nowhere to go. The two men seemed to surround the space that she occupied, cornering her.

"Please!" Beth exclaimed.

Tears started to appear, rolling down her cheeks, and I could feel her heart rate and her blood pressure increase.

I felt helpless to protect her. All I could do was pray for Beth.

At this point, the young men seemed to be driven by their impulses, their self-directed lower emotions of desire. As they approached her, Beth turned and crouched down in fear.

The leader soon grabbed her arm, forcibly bringing her to her feet while the other man held her still.

My attention was drawn back to the bracelet, as I could see it react to her emotions. The bracelet then began to vibrate, altering its frequency to blend into her skin, leaving markings on her wrist as if the bracelet had been sketched in full colour. The bracelet then started to emanate light as her emotions increased, as did the intensity of the power of the bracelet, changing the frequency of Beth's energy vibration. It was amazing to see, as we could see it changing her on a molecular level.

I could see Beth turn her head as the leader tried to forcibly kiss her. As he continued with his advances, with Beth retaliating, I was pleased to see his attempt was proven to be more of an effort than he initially thought.

I knew she had the strength within her, but I prayed that she would win them over or keep them at bay until help arrived. Although feeling the pain of her suffering, of the situation she was enduring, I felt powerless to assist her and hoped that this would end soon, that Beth would be safe.

*Chapter XIV*

# The Enchanted

Suddenly a powerful pulse of light burst forth from Beth. As it propelled itself forward like a gust of wind, the two men were thrown off their feet a short distance from where they had stood. I noticed that anything electrical caught within the blast had been short-circuited.

Realising now, I could see that there was more to the trinket bracelet than I originally had thought. The bracelet was indeed enchanted, and now she was too.

Beth fell to her knees, with her hands covering her eyes as she became overwhelmed by emotion and started to cry.

Not entirely understanding what had just happened, the leader was trying to get to his feet. Being weak and confused, I could see he was trying to find his bearings. Sadly, this was short-lived as he soon collapsed into an untimely death as most of the blast had been directed toward him.

While the other man lay unconscious on the ground, I could see healing energy encompassing him. An angel of light stood by him as they waited for earthly doctors to attend.

I noticed Beth was still unaware of what had just happened.

I felt my attention was drawn back to the leader. Curious, I waited to see what was to occur next with him. There was still no sign of his spirit leaving his body.

My thoughts were taken back to the man who had appeared earlier with the young boy who had tuberculosis. A feeling of an acknowledgement of his identity and his role soon came to me. With that thought alone, both the angel and the spirit of the young man appeared to me, looking my way before shortly disappearing.

I turned to face Beth and noticed Alice appearing by her side.

I could see that Beth was overwhelmed by the exposure of the incident, and being directly affected, she had gone into shock. A sense of withdrawal had overcome her. She looked disconnected from the outside world, feeling numb and distant from her external self.

It was so difficult for me to not be able to get involved, to comfort and protect her. All I could do, along with the others with me, was to observe and wait.

A short time later, the younger man of the three arrived, bringing the police with him. I could hear the young man describe what he remembered of the time, pointing out the location where they stood. I also learned of his name: Stephen, and the other two young men's names: Scott and Richie. From what I could now understand that Richie was the dominant one, leading the others.

I could see one of the policewomen approach Beth to assist her in getting to her feet and finding her a place to sit down.

Alice, who was unseen by the others, followed Beth and kept her by her side.

Dr Emmet arrived shortly after and, seeing Beth in an emotional state, went over to her, checking her for any discomfort and pain.

With tears still gently flowing down her cheeks, feeling numb as her emotions were still in a state of shock, Beth gently shook her head from left to right in response to the question being put forward to her.

By this time, three ambulances had arrived, and Dr Emmet had to take his leave to assist the police with the injured young man. Leaving the policewoman all alone with Beth.

"My name is Officer Sarah Matthews; you can call me Sarah. I am here to help! First, let's get you to the ambulance to get you examined by the nurse", suggested the policewoman.

The policewoman then carefully and gently led Beth over to the ambulance.

"While the nurse is attending to you, are you able to help me with some information?" I heard Officer Sarah Matthews ask Beth.

Beth nodded.

"Can you tell me your name?"

Given the circumstances, I could hear Beth respond as best as she could.

"What do you remember?"

I could see Beth trying to compose herself. Having Alice by her side, even though others couldn't see her, helped.

I noticed Officer Sarah had registered her state of being by responding, "In your own time Beth".

With Alice providing a little energy and strength to her voice, helping to encourage her to speak out, Beth was able to respond.

"I felt threatened but tried to keep calm, as I knew that they had only one thing on their mind – I tried to reason, but they wouldn't listen – I just felt helpless and afraid!"

I could see that the questioning wasn't helping Beth with her emotions, as I could feel unease with her discomfort in answering.

"Beth, I have to ask you this question, did they harm you in any way?"

Looking at Beth as she tried to recall the incident, she had become subdued due to a lack of feeling of self.

With a cut on her bottom lip, accompanied by bruises on her arms and parts of her body, I could see the nurse recording Beth's injuries. The information was then given to Officer Sarah.

The questioning became more sensitive as Officer Sarah went on to ask her a couple more questions about their sexual advances toward her.

I could see Beth was trying to answer as best as she could with the motion of her head, finding it hard to voice her response.

In the meantime, I became aware of the presence of Mrs Emmet. I could see her talking to her nephew. It wasn't long before she made her way over to be with Beth. Seeing Beth in her current state, she delicately placed her arms around her to assure her that all would be well. Mrs Emmet stayed with her, keeping her company while the questioning continued.

I soon noticed that Alice was nowhere to be seen and wondered if she was back with Jane.

"I am sorry, Beth, but I have to ask these questions. Did you see what happened to those two men?" Office Sarah Matthews asked.

Beth shook her head from left to right.

I could see that she was still physically hurting from the attack.

"Now, this needs to stop… Stop with the questioning! Can't you see that this poor girl is shaken from her ordeal!" Mrs Emmet expressed and voiced her concern for Beth.

"Where are you staying, Beth? Just in case we have any additional questions we may need to ask you", Officer Sarah asked.

Mrs Emmet reacted by replying, "Beth will be staying with me".

With the thought of Jane appearing in my mind, I knew I had to let her know. As I acknowledged what I needed to do, I soon found myself back in my body.

As the Judging was soon to commence, needing to catch her attention, I called out to Jane.

Hearing my voice, I could see her turn around to then walk over to me, "Is everything OK, William?"

I reached out my hand to hold Jane's. I placed images in her mind of the ordeal Beth had just gone through.

With concern and fear for Beth's well-being, Jane was keen to get to Beth. When we arrived, we saw Beth was still being treated by the nurse.

I could see Mrs Emmet and Officer Sarah Matthews standing just off to one side, having a conversation.

Jane soon left my side to be with Beth.

"I am sorry, and I should have been there for you!" Jane exclaimed as tears started to flow down her cheeks.

I could then see Officer Sarah Matthews approach Beth to ask, "Beth, thank you for your help. If you remember anything, any additional details about what has happened here, please give me a call".

Before leaving, Officer Sarah made her way back to Mrs Emmet to provide her contact details.

I made my way over to sit next to Beth and waited patiently for when she was ready to talk.

With myself present at Beth's side, Jane went over to speak to Mrs Emmet to see if she could find out anything.

Although I was going to wait, I soon felt the need to speak to Beth, "I am sorry, Beth! I wasn't here when you needed me to be!"

"I knew you were close, and that's what gave me the strength to not give up!"

"I thought you were brave! Especially the way you stood up to them".

"I knew I couldn't give in to them, and all I could do was to fight them off for as long as possible. At one point, I was in fear for my life!"

I could feel her fragility as she tried to compose herself.

It was interesting that Beth hadn't acknowledged the bracelet and what it had done for her!

I had the feeling of holding Beth's hand, and as I did, I soon felt a warmth manifest within me. It was as though someone had turned up the heat. As I looked at Beth, I could see light manifest and appear within and around her. Looking around, I noticed that no one else could see it. As I turned back to face Beth, I noticed that her eyes were closed while she was receiving the healing. The cut on the lip had gone, as well as the bruising that was on her arms.

"Know that you are never alone, Beth – You could always fall back on the love we all have for you".

"Thank you, William!"

Looking over at Jane, I could hear her reflect on the day. It seems Mrs Emmet was able to share with Jane a lot about her grandma that she did not know.

An announcement from the village fayre speaker was soon heard informing us that the competition winner was about to be announced.

I noticed that Beth, although still slightly shaken, had started to calm down within her emotions and gained strength from the healing given to her.

I could see her bracelet was slightly aglow with the light on her skin, as it was still working on Beth.

Mrs Emmet and her family made their way over to the judging stand.

It would have been nice to stay to see who won the competition, but we knew it was time for us to go. We made our way to the entrance of the fayre to where we had entered. Looking back, we were still able to hear the results of the competition winner from where we were. As we stood to wait for the portal to open, it was announced that the best winner for the baked meatloaf would be announced last.

I could see Jane cheering as each winner of the other categories was announced. Alice could be seen standing close to her.

With Beth standing by my right side, I could feel her eyes observing me. Turning around to face her, I went on to share further observations I had witnessed earlier.

"Beth, I had felt so much of the love and the compassion that had encircled you earlier. Yet, witnessing and observing from the position I was placed in was humbling. I felt I was one of a greater consciousness that surrounded you. I saw a glimpse of your true power today!"

"I like the way the bracelet has represented itself as a tattoo. Thank you, William, for the opportunity to meet my family. I often knew auntie would speak off her grandma and her competition with Mrs Emmet. I just couldn't have imagined that Mrs Emmet was related to me. It was also good to see my father when he was young".

Beth lowered herself and embraced me in a hug.

As I felt her love and appreciation, I reciprocated in return. Beth released her embrace, smiled, and then stood up. I knew from this day we would see a new Beth.

Just before finishing our conversation, I commented, "When a new life is created and presented to this world, they are introduced to parents, families and new friends. I am so pleased I got to meet you. You got to meet the family you had no knowledge of – You showed tremendous courage earlier and compassion for the young men who threatened you. We can be influenced or can influence each other, leading to how we adapt and change to a new way of thinking and being. Since knowing you and the journey we have been on, today you have inspired me – Thank you for trusting in me and, more importantly, in yourself".

I could see Beth smile in reaction to my words.

It wasn't then long after that I could feel our frequency of energy had started to shift, as if the portal were starting to reveal itself to us.

Seeing Alice standing close to Jane, I thought about their time together, and now it was coming to an end.

"Thank you for helping us and for giving Jane and Beth the opportunity to meet their family".

Alice smiled and then looked at Jane – I could feel their connection.

Jane crouched down to embrace Alice, and I heard her say, "Even though you are not physically present in my life, I will know that you are close by. If we get the opportunity again, I shall certainly look forward to it".

Jane kissed her on her forehead before returning to a standing position.

I could then see the pain that Jane had harboured within her had started to heal.

"Did you manage to say goodbye to your grandma?" I asked Jane.

"I decided to spend what time I had left with my daughter", she replied with a smile.

As the results of the winner of the meatloaves were being announced, the vibration of our energy started to shift. We soon found ourselves back in the sanctuary.

"We never did get to find out who won?" Beth commented.

"I guess we will never know", Jane responded.

I could see that Beth was in deep thought, reflecting on her time in the village fayre.

"Beth, are you OK?" I asked.

"I am coping... a little fragile, given the circumstances".

"Remember, we are here for you!"

"I can't explain it, and even though you are only a child, I feel a sense of security with you, William. Also, knowing that I get to stay with my Auntie and Uncle, who I know will look after me, I feel blessed – It makes what had happened to me a little easier to cope with!"

The sanctuary became filled with light, our bodies translucent within it.

Alice was only with us temporarily. When the time came, she turned to Jane, nodded in affirmation, and then faded from our sight. I could feel Jane's sadness as she saw her daughter fade from her view.

Shortly as the light dimmed, we found ourselves in the light of day back in the old ruins. It was time to go home.

I could feel Henry and Charlie close by. This was confirmed as we heard barking. Peering out of the old ruins, I could see Charlie heading in our direction, with Henry following behind.

As I walked out of the old ruins, I was met by Henry and Charlie.

"William, where is Jane?" Henry asked.

"She is in the old ruins".

While Henry entered the old ruins, Charlie stayed with me, waiting outside. It wasn't long before Henry appeared with Jane, with Beth following behind.

Looking back at the sanctuary made me wonder about the secrets that this land held within its grasp.

I could see Jane and Beth weren't satisfied with what had happened with the recent events. It was as though they needed answers to what we had gone through, to what we had witnessed. The only person that could tell us was Henry. We needed to get everyone home first before we set about discovering the truth. Seeing Henry had brought back memories of the camp and the room where questions were being asked of him. We needed to find out why Henry was there and what was the commitment that Henry had made so long ago. There seemed to be more than just the mere appearance of the setting but also the interrogation.

We soon arrived home to be welcomed by Bella. It was good to be home and to be comforted by familiar surroundings. It had passed the time of lunch when we arrived. Once we had all quickly adjusted ourselves with a wash and with putting on clean clothes, it was time for Jane to have the conversation with Henry.

As I looked at Henry, I noticed that he was passive to the expectant questioning of the recent events. Even though his posture was relaxed, I could see the energy of his thoughts performing a merry dance. I could see he was trying to assimilate different responses to the truth of his past.

With Jane preparing a late lunch, I had now been accustomed to the energy of the food. On the table were sandwiches cut into triangles and filled with soft cheese or ham. The sandwiches were accompanied by a side setting of chips, a little salad and some raw vegetables cut into small-sized portions. Orange juice was supplied to me for a drink, while the adults had soft drinks more accustomed to their individual tastes. A practice or some would say a ritual that I had not seen Henry or Jane perform before, had occurred when Jane said a prayer for a blessing. A blessing of the food, of our health, for others, for the day and for the land.

Looking back at Henry, I noticed that he kept company with his own thoughts and wasn't always responsive to the others at the table. I see that Jane was concerned for his mental well-being.

"Henry", Jane called out to get his attention.

Still, his attention was focused elsewhere as if reflective of his thoughts. I could see Jane showing concern, reaching out to Henry's hand with her own. The touch of her hand brought his focus back to the room, to Jane and us.

"What's going on? You haven't been with us for some time, and your mind seems to be elsewhere", I heard her ask.

"There has been a lot on my mind recently, and I'm sorry that you had to go through what you did over the past couple of days", I heard Henry say.

I had a feeling to look at Beth and noticed she was looking at me. I could see her gesture with her head that we move ourselves to another room to give Jane and Henry some privacy.

"We are going to leave you both to it. If you need us, we will be in the family room", I heard Beth inform Jane and Henry.

"Thank you, Beth", Jane replied.

Looking at Jane's energy, I could see her emotional energy was starting to react to Henry's.

We left the table and headed toward the family room.

On route, I noticed the study door was ajar. I left Beth to continue into the family room while I quickly popped my head in to look to see if the parcel was still on the small table.

"I just need to check on something", I gently voiced to Beth just before I left her.

As I quietly opened the door to avoid making a noise, I glanced in the direction of the table. I noticed that parcel was still placed on the small table. I gently pushed the door closed as it had been before and then headed to the family room to join Beth.

On entering the family room, I noticed Beth standing by the patio door windows, looking over to the sanctuary in the distance. I could see Beth was deep in thought as she was looking at her wrist and the design of the bracelet. I noticed that as the bracelet glistened, so did her eyes. I began to move closer to Beth, and as I did, I could see that she was not responding to me as I called out to her. It appeared that she was unaware of my presence. Her energy made me mesmerised, and her consciousness seemed to be attuned to the bracelet. It occurred to me that we take many things in life for granted as part of our normality, but it isn't until we are used to its presence that we lose sight of it. For Beth, the design on the wrist was a permanent reminder of the fayre, the gift of the bracelet and how precious she was. She knew she was different but made more so by the recognition of the bracelet, which brought it to light. Looking at Beth, I was aware that her brain activity seemed to be balanced across both the left and right hemispheres of the brain. It was also interesting to see that every aspect of her energies was aligned and enriched with cosmic and universal energies. After a short time had passed, I needed to bring Beth around from the altered state she was in. Reaching out, I touched her wrist gently with my hand.

"Beth, it is time to return", I beckoned her gently.

I noticed that Beth had reacted to my touch as she returned to her normal awakening state and then turned to face me.

"What just happened?" she asked.

"It is the bracelet; you seemed to be enchanted with it".

"Is it a good thing?"

"Yes, it seems that it is certainly a part of you now, and we will have to monitor the changes within you".

We soon could hear a knock on the door. We both looked to the hallway to see if either Jane or Henry would appear, to then answer it. After a short time, another knock was heard. There appeared to be no sign of Henry or Jane. Deciding to see who it was, we both walked into the hallway, with Beth taking the lead towards the main door of the house. As Beth went to open the door, I stayed next to the entrance of the dining room.

Looking into the dining room, I couldn't see Jane or Henry. As I shifted my focus, I could hear movement from above us and a fragment of their voices upstairs. It seemed that they had moved their conversation to a more secluded area.

Looking at Beth observing me, I could see her trying to figure out what I was doing.

"I have a feeling they are upstairs", I informed Beth.

Beth looked through the small window and noticed Suzy standing behind the door. Opening the door, she welcomed her in.

Needing to hear what was said between them, I listened carefully.

"Suzy, are you OK?" Beth asked.

"I had a dream last night, and it frightened me. Where is Jane?"

"She is upstairs with Uncle", Beth replied.

Suzy threw her arms around Beth, holding her in a tight embrace. I could see tears starting to flow down her cheeks. She appeared emotional and upset by what had been revealed to her.

"I need to tell your aunt what I saw in my dream".

Seeing me, Suzy walked over and crouched down and embraced me tightly. I didn't realise she had so much strength. She almost squeezed the breath out of me.

"It is so good to see you, William. So much has happened since I saw you last!"

I could see she was still crying.

"It's OK, Suzy. They are upstairs having a private chat – What can you tell us about your dream?"

As Suzy stood up, Beth joined us and offered Suzy a drink.

Suzy nodded in affirmation.

"Suzy, was the dream about Jane?" I asked.

I saw Suzy look at Beth and then back to me.

"You were all in the dream".

Beth made Suzy a coffee and then handed it to her.

"So, what can you tell us about the dream?" asked Beth.

Suzy started to shake as fear began to settle in within her emotions and her thoughts.

"I could only remember glimpses of the dream. Jane and yourselves were surrounded by darkness - It was consuming everything. I could see you were all trying to find your way through the woods - I felt something lurking within it, waiting for an opportunity. I could then see Jane was in an old building, encircled with doubt and confusion, questioning herself. What I found more upsetting was when I then saw you both die, and there was darkness. From within that darkness, I soon caught a glimpse of Henry's face - this had really startled me, so much I woke up distressed".

In response, I tried to reassure her, "We are all here, alive and well".

Suzy appeared terribly upset. I could see Beth reach out to her to give her an emotional hug. Interestingly, I noticed that Beth's bracelet started to glow, and at the same time, the centre of Suzy's chest started to also glow. It was as though they were in perfect sync.

The hug seemed to help as Suzy began to feel better about our situation. As they pulled away from each other, Suzy caught a glimpse of Beth's wrist.

"Is the bracelet tattoo new?"

Beth went on to tell Suzy about our time at the village fayre. Then, she proceeded to tell her about the incident.

I could see that Suzy was taken back from what she had learnt and could feel that she became more empathic to Beth's needs.

"I'm sorry, Beth. No one should have had to go through what you went through. But please know that I will be there for you if you need a sister!" Suzy exclaimed.

I could see Beth had remained strong with her emotions as she turned to face me. I could see that she was taken aback by Suzy's reaction.

With the focus on Beth, Suzy's emotions became one of empathy, compassion and slight anger toward the men that had attacked her. I could see Suzy's heart region glow even more.

Aware of the light around her heart region, Beth asked Suzy about her story and how it came to be.

Thinking of Jane and Henry, with the thoughts of going upstairs and with Suzy's dream, I felt the person that I needed to work with was Henry. Leaving the girls to talk, I started to walk up the stairs. At the top of the stairs, I was met by Peter, Jane's guardian angel.

"How is the conversation going between Jane and Henry?" I asked Peter.

"They are in the bedroom having a heart-to-heart conversation".

Remembering our conversation from the last time we met, I relayed my thoughts in response. "I can see what you meant by an emotional heartbreak for Jane. Can I ask what is to follow from this point forward?"

"This time, it will be Henry that you need to place your focus on".

"So, what will happen next?"

Peter pointed to the door to Jane and Henry's bedroom. I noticed the handle on the door move.

"Have they finished their conversation?"

As the door opened, I turned to Peter and noticed that he was no longer there.

Turning back to face the room, I could see both Jane and Henry seated on the bed through the open doorway. I noticed both Jane and Henry were looking in my direction to see who had opened the door.

Although hesitant at first, I noticed Henry beckoned me into the room. As I moved slowly in, I could see Jane was crying.

Henry appeared upset by the notion of not only what he had learnt about me from Jane but also ashamed for keeping something from her.

I could see Henry was observing me as to what he could expect or conclude from what Jane had told him about me.

Beckoning me forward, Henry then asked, "William, I do know one thing, and that is that Jane's happiness is everything to me. What is it that you want from us?"

"I don't want or desire anything. I am here only to open your eyes and your hearts to the possibilities that are around you – The decisions you have made in your past have consequences, especially for those who have something to hide – We have a choice, do we let the past govern our future or do we allow ourselves to have a voice, and make that choice to change the course of our paths to better our futures".

"Sorry... I just... I just need to know... irrespective of what you have just said... I just need to know your intentions?"

I could see that Henry was a little apprehensive. As he asked the question, it was as if there was a slight hesitancy in his voice.

I felt the need to walk closer to Henry. Acting on this intuition, I was soon standing in front of him.

"You see, your love for Jane is strong, more than the love for yourself. Although Jane will forgive you, will you forgive yourself. It's time to let her know the truth".

I could then see him look at Jane to get a reaction from her.

"It's OK! Listen to what he has to say", I heard Jane respond to Henry.

Turning to face me, Henry then asked me to continue.

Feeling a presence of love from the divine encircle and flow through me, I reached out my hand to touch the region of his chest with my fingers. I felt an energy surge of divine love flow through me, through to Henry. The fingers of my hand were tingling as energy flowed through to him. I could see his energy react as his emotional energy responded to my touch.

"Feel the Love, Henry. Give yourself permission to forgive and love yourself. Let go of your suffering and your pain".

As I removed my hand, I could see Jane was watching and somehow understood what was happening. I felt the need to touch Henry's forehead. As I was just about to do this, Henry grabbed my hand, as he wasn't sure what I was about to do.

"Henry, it will be fine! Let William continue", Jane went on to say to Henry.

As he released my hand, I continued to touch his forehead. At that point, we found ourselves within his memories, to the point in time where it all began.

## Chapter XV

## The Forbidding Contract

Standing beside a desk in a large open office, both Henry and I stood. We appeared as unseen observers within his memories. All we could do was watch as the memories unfolded.

"Do you remember this time in your life?" I asked.

"Yes, why are we here?"

"Was this not your first post, working in this storage facility for the Military?"

"What does this have to do with my decisions?"

"We will get there. We need to look at the beginning; the answer may be here".

"I was nineteen, and I was transferred here as a young recruit", Henry recalled.

We noticed the clock on the wall had shown the time to be just before nine am. The 'young Henry', as I referenced him, entered the room through one of the doors.

As we observed him on this particular day, he was asked to assist in preparing some paperwork for items that were due to arrive later that afternoon.

"I remember this! I wasn't sure what all the fuss was. The items in question were found in an old storage facility and were brought here. There were no signs of any markers or any indications of what was contained within them. Therefore, there wasn't any danger that could be identified with what was presented to us".

Both Henry and I could see the paperwork that was laid out on the table. Typed on the paperwork was, 'Artifacts retrieved from an old storage facility, as they were examined, had shown no energy emissions. The contents contained an unknown metal with no scripture of any type. Found during an excavation of old ruins in Mexico'.

"I was responsible for ensuring that the items were initially categorised and marked up for further analysis before any final classification was given".

Young Henry appeared to be mindful of everything he was doing.

We soon found ourselves moved further on within this memory. We were no longer in the same room - now we were in a small office. We could see the young Henry sitting at his desk with paperwork, and he appeared to be in deep thought.

"What were you thinking about?" I asked.

"My career! I enjoyed what I was doing and got on with those I was working with, but the role wasn't fulfilling enough for me. I was also thinking about my family back at home, those here and those back in England".

"Do you regret your family ever leaving England to emigrate to America?"

"In a way, I do, but my father was transferred over here. I can remember just wanting to be like him".

The phone on the desk rang. On answering the call, truly little was said on the call from what we could hear. Once the call had finished, young Henry gathered the paperwork and then left the office.

We soon found ourselves standing near young Henry. He was standing next to an officer who was signing for items that had just been delivered.

"This was the process. We would sign for the items and then move them to a secure location to be analysed".

"So why do we see this particular part of your memory?"

"Thinking back to this time, if my recollection serves me correctly, this was when a fire incident occurred in the storage facility".

As I was just about to ask what had happened, we found ourselves in another memory, standing in a laboratory. We could see young Henry standing just off to one side as men dressed in military hazmat uniforms examined the artefacts.

"I was never allowed near the artefacts. On most occasions, I wasn't allowed in the laboratory. On this occasion, they allowed me to watch from afar, as they did not deem the items to be important or dangerous".

"Did the incident begin within this room?" I asked as we were brought to this particular memory.

I could see Henry trying to recall his memory of what had happened. We decided to observe this memory to see for ourselves. Walking around the men, my attention was drawn to the table. Four objects were being examined. One appeared to be different from the other three.

As I got closer, I noticed markings on the item. They appeared to be of ancient Mayan scripture. The markings seemed familiar somehow.

"Can you see Henry what I am seeing?"

Henry came closer, confirmed that he could see the scriptures, and then asked me if I could see anything else.

"Sometimes, it is all in the details. We can often see objects without actually seeing them for what they truly are. By paying attention to the details is when we can learn more about them. The same goes for people".

"Do you know what the scriptures are saying, what the symbols represent?" asked Henry.

On closure inspection, I found I could partially read some of them.

"It mentions a warning to the bearer. There is also a reference regarding the sacrificing of the soul and about great power at a cost".

"So why can I not remember this moment of my life?"

"I am not sure. We will have to see what happens next".

We waited, observing the examination taking place.

We noticed one of the men started to cough, followed by the shallowness of his breath.

Henry looked at me and then back to the three men.

We could see a black smoky substance leave each of the artefacts, passing through the protective clothing into each of the three men.

I looked at young Henry and noticed he had stepped back.

The three men soon fell to the ground. Looking back at the table, one artefact had remained.

We could see that young Henry was speechless. Usually, someone in his situation would be heading straight for the door. Instead, we could see him walk towards the table and the artefact.

An alarm began to sound and could be heard echoing throughout the laboratory.

"What were you thinking, Henry? You seemed to be conscious at this time", I asked.

"I don't know, I can't remember this. It hurts for me to try".

We watched young Henry reach for the last remaining artefact on the table. He seemed to be in a trance-like state.

"I certainly do not remember this", responded Henry.

As young Henry held the object in his hand, a voice was heard coming from a speaker located high up towards the corner of the room.

"Henry, put the artefact back on the table, then please step away".

We could see that young Henry was far too gone to respond to whatever request or commands were voiced through the speaker. The request was made again, but there was still no response from the young Henry.

We noticed gas entering the room from tubes fed into the laboratory.

"Will this be harmful to those who breathe it in?" I asked Henry.

"It will only put them to sleep", he responded.

Looking at the young Henry, it took a little while before he reacted to the gas, and then he collapsed to the floor.

"What happened to the artefact he... I mean me, was holding?" Henry asked. He sounded worried, as was himself from fifteen years ago.

We could see no sign of the remaining artefact – In fact, it seemed to have vanished.

The door to the room opened. Four men rushed in wearing military hazmat suits. Stretchers were brought in to carry the three men, and young Henry to what we could understand from the directions given was a quarantined area.

We soon found ourselves back with young Henry in a quarantined room. He appeared to be resting.

I looked at Henry for any recollection of any memories regarding the quarantine period.

"Sorry, William, again, this is new to me".

"Henry, what we are seeing must be buried deep within your subconscious, hidden away within your memories".

We watched the doctors as they undertook tests.

Shortly we found ourselves stepping forward into another memory. We could see young Henry was waking up.

"Do you remember waking up?" I asked Henry.

"Vaguely, it was all confusing, as I couldn't be sure where I was! Now that I think about it, I am only just remembering glimpses of my time in quarantine".

We were interrupted as a heart monitor within the quarantine room started to sound a loud constant audible beep. Followed by one of the nurses shouting, "Another one has flatlined!"

"Henry, can you please stay with your younger self? I need to check and see what all the commotion is about?"

Henry nodded to confirm he understood.

This allowed me to find more clues. As I listened for the details of the commotion, I soon found out that all the men, apart from young Henry, had died.

My focus was soon directed back to Henry.

"How are you coping with all this?"

I could see from the uncertainty that what had taken place when he was nineteen had caused him much concern and trepidation about the possibility of this outcome. I could see that he was getting nervous and had something heavy-laden on his mind.

"I have been having episodes of consciously losing time. Sometimes I would find myself in places with no idea how I got there".

I could see Henry becoming a little emotional as he said, "I didn't know how to tell her without concerning her".

"I feel there is more to learn from your memories".

As I turned to face young Henry, we found ourselves in another memory.

Young Henry was partially awake, only grasping certain words. He wasn't alone, as beside his bed stood military personnel and a couple of doctors.

Young Henry was the sole survivor of the incident. As we picked up from their conversations, the cause of the deaths of the other three was unknown. The only person that could answer their questions was indeed young Henry. Laying there, not fully coherent with those around him or the conversations being discussed.

One of the military men looked familiar. Recalling my memories from earlier, I recognised him from the camp. It was Jane's father.

As I turned to face Henry, I could see him looking at his younger self. He seemed unaware of the others in the room. I called out to him to bring him out of the state of mind he was dwelling in. Hearing my voice, Henry turned to face me.

"Sorry, William, trying to recall and understand what had happened during this time".

I knew I needed to slow down his thoughts and bring reason to his understanding.

"We always try to find reasoning to everything that defies our logic of understanding what we know. The more we learn, the more we want to learn to clarify our understanding. This is the mystery of life. There are things we just cannot explain. Therefore, we soul search. To put answers to the unknown or uncertainty of our unfamiliarity. We either dismiss the reality of it and put it back in the subconscious of our minds, or we try to face it straight on. We do not always like the answers we find, but it helps us identify more with who we are and what is hidden in life. It is usually through dreams that hidden messages are revealed. Whatever happens to you, this part of you is a mystery of self. Embrace it and take control of it".

"What if I do not like the person I have become or what has changed in me?"

"You have a responsibility to make the right choices – Do not let others dictate who you should be or how you should embrace the changes that await in you".

Henry turned to face his younger self again. Our conversation seemed to place him in deeper thought than he was previously.

The other men appeared to be discussing the future of young Henry. I could see that they wanted to observe him further and talked of transferring him to another facility for further examinations and tests.

I turned to Henry and noticed that he was also listening.

"They told me they had an exciting new opportunity for me, but first, they needed to run some tests to ensure I was OK. I should have known. I started to have the blackouts during my time at the new facility".

"It seems they were manipulating you. With all the experiments, they needed to see how you would react to the tests".

We then found ourselves in a memory located in a secure test facility. Young Henry was in a room that seemed to have cameras observing him, monitoring his every move. In addition, there were security personnel guarding the doors.

"What is happening here?" I asked Henry.

"I have little recollection. I do remember having nightmares, dark dreams. The doctors prescribed medication for them, but they never worked".

We were brought to this memory for a reason. We could see young Henry sitting at a desk with his forehead resting on his hands, supported by his elbows. But, looking around the room, there wasn't much we could see other than some test equipment.

Suddenly we could see whispers of dark energy fill the room. Interestingly young Henry did not seem to react to them.

I looked at Henry and could see he was uncomfortable with what he was witnessing.

A voice came from a speaker in the upper corner of the room.

"Henry, this is General Hammond. As we have discussed before, we would like you to pull back the energy so we can enter. We have a proposition for you".

I looked at Henry, "Are you aware of this?"

"I am not sure what is going on! I must have somehow been out of it".

"It sounds like the medication they were administering you was somehow putting you into some form of altered state. It allowed them to manipulate your mind through suggestion".

Young Henry had not responded at first, then lifted his head from his hands after a few minutes. We could see that his eyes were black.

"I didn't expect that", I thought to myself.

Looking at Henry, I could see him step back, reacting to what he had just witnessed.

The dark energy was pulled back as the door to the room opened. Jane's father and a couple of doctors had entered the room.

As we observed, the General had young Henry carry out various tests in the controlled state of several exercises.

"Were you aware of this agreement that had taken place between yourself and Jane's father?"

"No!" Henry exclaimed.

The emotions in his voice said it all. I could feel his anger build within him as he felt violated and used. Now knowing he had been manipulated for so many years caused so much anguish within him.

I had to ensure that his emotions were retained and encapsulated within this memory. I didn't want the power of what we just witnessed to be unleashed onto Jane. I needed to help direct his focus.

"Henry, there is nothing you can do as this was in the past! Realise that you have a choice about what to do with this information. You have seen the power you now have at your fingertips – Focus on your love for Jane. She is your light to the darkness held within you. Let her be your torch, your anchor of light".

"There are so many things I would like to do to him right now!" Henry exclaimed as I could see his anger build.

"For Jane's sake, he is not worth it. You will only be fighting fire with fire, and t will only worsen things. Jane will get hurt from the repercussion of your fighting. She needs your strength, not your weakness".

"I can see your wisdom, William!"

"Henry, if it helps, take long, deep breaths. This will help you focus".

I could then see Henry try to attempt to diffuse the anger that was building up within him. By focusing on his love for Jane, Henry started to feel at ease with his emotions, which soon helped lessen his anger.

We then found ourselves in an earlier memory, just after young Henry's recovery from the incident. We appeared to be in a large office. General Hammond was seated at a large brown varnished oak desk, talking to young Henry.... A doctor could be seen sitting on a wooden chair just off to his left in the room, listening to their conversation.

"You see, Henry, I would like to make you a proposal. I would like for you to work here as part of my team. We would still like to carry out tests, but you are free to come and go as you please. You can stay at the barracks on the base. I have spoken to your father, and he feels it would be a great idea. What do you say?" I heard General Hammond ask young Henry.

"What will I be doing?"

"We could start you with what you know, cataloguing the artefacts. There will be some fieldwork, which we will discuss later".

"It sounds interesting".

"Great".

General Hammond picked up the telephone receiver on his desk and dialled a number.

"Can you please ship Henry's belongings over?"

The phone receiver was replaced back onto the telephone hook.

"We will see you for eighteen hundred hours in the observation lounge, and Henry, please be punctual".

"I thought this would get me where I longed to be within my career. Little did I know that there was a hidden agenda. It seemed I was where the General wanted me to be, like a pawn on a chessboard! - Playing right into his hands", Henry commented.

I could feel Henry's emotions react slightly to the notion of General Hammond's intentions.

Suddenly the phone rang. General Hammond picked up the receiver once again.

"Send her in".

We could see by his emotional response that this was a meeting that General Hammond was looking forward to, as he was happy to receive this visitor.

"Close the door behind you, doctor, as you leave", instructed General Hammond.

We watched them leave the office, closing the door behind them.

Within minutes a young lady had entered.

"Hello, father".

I could see the delight on Henry's face as he recognised the young lady.

We noticed the door to the office was still open. We could see young Henry looking back towards the office, having caught sight of her from the hallway.

Removing the scarf that was protecting her face from the cold stood a noticeably young Jane. Taking one last look at her admirer from the hallway, she then closed the door.

We then found ourselves in another memory.

"That was the first time I glimpsed her eyes as she passed me by before she entered her father's office. The way she looked at me – my heart was a flutter. She took my breath away", Henry remembered.

Seeing how he embraced that memory of her confirmed that she was certainly the right person for him, especially now that we knew that was the case.

The next memory was initially distorted, and then it became clear. We found ourselves in an observation lounge. Young Henry was talking to the doctor, the one we had seen in the last memory. Looking at the clock on the wall, I saw the time was nearing six o'clock. Young Henry was drinking iced green tea, accompanied by a slice of cake.

"I can remember this, but my recollection of this time was a bit vague", Henry commented.

The door opened, and General Hammond, with a couple of senior command military personnel, had stepped through.

"We are just going to give you a sedative to help you relax", said the doctor.

"I don't need a sedative… I feel fine", we heard young Henry respond.

"This will help you and help with our tests", the doctor replied.

"That's some needle! Could I not just have a tablet instead?"

"This will not hurt", the doctor replied.

Pulling up his sleeve, the sedative was administered to young Henry. However, instead of relaxing him, the medication put young Henry into an induced state of consciousness. The doctor then proceeded to influence the mind further with hypnotic suggestions.

"Henry, can you hear me? Nod your head if you can?" the doctor asked.

Seeing the young Henry acknowledge the doctor's request, we paid close attention to the dialogue conversation between them.

"I need you to go back to the day of the incident, back to the laboratory. Can you do that for me?" asked the doctor.

"Yes".

"You are in the laboratory with the other three men. They are examining the artefacts. Something went wrong. Can you see what is happening?"

"Yes".

"Can you tell us what happened?"

"I stood back while the others were examining the artefacts when suddenly a whisper of black mist started to appear from them. It was as though the artefacts were dissipating into dust and transmuting into vapour form. It seemed to somehow disappear into them. I noticed something was wrong as they began to cough and then start choking. It wasn't long before they were all on the floor".

"What happened next?"

"I started to panic, but something kept me calm. I felt as if I was being pulled to the table. The last artefact looked bright and felt welcoming. I felt the need to hold it in my hands".

"Is there any more information you can tell us, Henry?"

"That is all I can remember".

Young Henry's body began to shake a little as if experiencing an epileptic spasm. As his bodily movement slowed down, he opened his eyes. They could see his eyes were black, causing fear to the men near where he sat.

The military men retreated to a short distance away from where young Henry was seated as they were unsettled by what they saw.

We could then see the doctor turn to face the General for direction.

"Bring him back?" ordered the General.

"Henry, can you hear me?" the doctor asked.

"Yes".

"Can you please close your eyes for me?"

Young Henry closed his eyes. The doctor proceeded to bring young Henry out of the induced state.

We noticed that the doctor had set some trigger words before finishing. As they might be needed moving forward, I noted them in memory.

"They had told me that I had fallen asleep", I heard Henry comment.

"I now can understand how they were able to control you, and that was because they induced you into a hypnotic state", I responded.

Henry vocalised some words I had not heard of before this time to express his emotions and his thoughts.

"At least we can address this!" I informed Henry.

"What they had done in the past to me... The experiments... This was a violation of my free will!"

Armed with this information from Henry's past, we soon found ourselves back in the bedroom of Henry and Jane's home.

There was only Jane in the room. Removing my hand from Henry's forehead and turning to face Jane, I asked her, "How long have we been?"

"Minutes, that is all – How did it go?"

"I felt it went well!"

Turning to Henry, I could see he was deep in thought about what he had witnessed within his memories.

"Henry, we need to remove those subconscious triggers that have been planted".

Henry nodded for me to continue.

Placing my hand on Henry's forehead, I proceeded to say with positive affirmation and good intentions, "Great Divine, heavenly spirit, utilise me as your humble instrument to heal Henry of his inflicted thoughts. Let him be free of any instructions or programming of triggers within his subconscious, hidden or known. To allow his free will to not be hindered or manipulated. Place a protected barrier of light around his inner mind and outer mind from external influences. I also ask that only good come of his thoughts and actions. Help him become enlightened through the love of others, his love for Jane and his newfound love for self".

I noticed that the palm of my hand had begun to emit heat and light. The light started passing through to Henry's forehead, pacifying his thoughts. I could see the energy of the healing being instrumental in clearing any blocks, any triggers and suggestions that were set within his subconscious. Once the healing had been completed, I felt the need to remove my hand. The heat then receded along with the light.

"How are you feeling, Henry?"

Henry looked at Jane, smiled and then turned back to me.

"Since the incident, I haven't always felt quite myself, as if I was a guest within my own body. Now it feels different!"

With this new release of emotions and realisation of self, I could see the change within him.

I felt I needed to turn towards the door. Unseen by the other two, I could see the angel Peter holding all four artefacts in the palm of his hands. There were other angels around him.

"William, thank you. The artefacts will be taken to a safe place. Please watch over Henry. Even though the artefacts have been removed from him, his senses will have been heightened. There may be some latent abilities that may have been awakened as a result of this".

As Peter and the angels started to fade from visual sight, I received one last piece of advice from Peter.

"There is one other who will require your help".

In my mind, I acknowledged to Peter these last thoughts I had received.

I turned to Jane and Henry. I could see the love they had for each other was strong.

"Henry, may I ask what time we were expecting Jane's father?"

Checking his watch, "Not until five, as we have a couple of hours yet – Why?"

"You both have a lot to discuss. I shall go downstairs to be with the others".

Leaving the love birds to themselves, I then made my way out of their bedroom and down the stairs to where Suzy and Beth were gossiping.

"Where did you go to?" Beth asked.

"To help Henry and Jane with something. They just need a little privacy at the moment".

It was as if Beth and Suzy could read my thoughts as they started to giggle. Then, Beth and Suzy made their way into the family room while I went into the study.

On arrival, I noticed that the parcel had gone. I couldn't see it anywhere in the room.

Deciding to catch up with Beth and Suzy in the family room, I could see they were still chatting. A conversation it was best I leave them to.

It wasn't long before I received words appearing in my mind informing me that the parcel was with Peter. Although I was curious about the contents within, I wasn't able to find out if it was actually a threat to anyone.

Leaving Beth and Suzy to continue with their topic of discussion, I proceeded to sit on the comfortable chair by the patio door. I could see the energy of Beth and Suzy's auras from a short distance away. It gave me a better angle to observe them.

As they reflected on their interests, their emotions became stimulated. Every stimulation of thought triggered an adjustment of their body. I noticed that they became more conscious of themselves by the moment.

In reflection, as I studied their energies, the colours within each of their auras were slightly different but vibrant. It was good to see the ebb and flow of the colours as they blended and expanded at times in reaction to a common understanding. All the time adapting to the topic of conversations being discussed. It was interesting to gain an understanding of Beth and Suzy through the colours of the energy reflected in their aura. Supported by my other senses, which gave me a more in-depth insight into the colours I was seeing or sensing.

Both had newfound abilities, which were not so identifiable within the lower aspect of their auras but could be seen if someone were to tune into the finer frequencies of their auras.

As an experiment, I prayed for divine love to enter their auric fields to see how they would react. It wasn't long before I could see their auras expand further. I noticed by their reaction that their conversations started to flow more easily as they became more relaxed. They became more focused on their attention to others in a selfless way. I noticed they started to reflect on the teachings they had received. I continued to send more energy their way to see what direction it would take them. From what I saw, I was pleased they were adapting well as their sensitivity increased.

It wasn't long before they both turned to me and, in unison, said, "William!"

I smiled at them as I could see the bond between them was getting stronger.

"William, come over and sit with us?" Beth asked.

I moved closer to sit with them, positioning myself so I had a clear view of the hallway and the stairs.

Just over an hour had passed, and I heard Jane and Henry return from upstairs. From where I sat, I could see Jane head towards the kitchen while Henry went into the study.

Hearing Jane as she entered the kitchen, Suzy and Beth left the family room to meet up with Jane.

I could hear giggling coming from the kitchen.

I walked to the hallway to see what was going on.

I could see Jane, Beth, and Suzy huddled together. They soon moved from the kitchen to enter the dining room.

To continue to listen, I walked further into the hallway to the dining room entrance. It was good to see the three of them laughing.

Henry soon appeared out of the study, walking past me into the dining room.

"Jane, have you seen my parcel? It appears to have gone from the table. I know I left it there".

"Sorry, Henry, I haven't touched it".

I then noticed Henry looking at Beth and Suzy.

"Not us either", Beth and Suzy replied in unison to Henry.

"William, have you moved my parcel?" Henry asked.

Suddenly there was a knock at the door. I remembered Peter's words, asking me to watch over Henry.

I could see Henry look at the time on his watch that was strapped around his wrist.

Henry turned to Jane, and then I could hear him say, "It is only four-twenty. He is not due until five!"

I noticed that his emotions were reacting to the misplacement of the parcel.

"Henry, this is between my father and me", Jane responded.

"We are doing this together".

"If only one of us is here, he can't force the contract to be signed. It requires two signatures".

"Why don't you go and leave me to your father?"

Another knock was heard at the door.

"Should we see who it is first?" Beth asked.

An overwhelming feeling came over me. As I closed my eyes, I could see trucks and jeeps entering the property. I informed the others of what I had been shown.

"It looks like my father has arrived with an entourage. What else can you see, William?" Jane asked.

"Men are surveying the grounds, and there is a woman with your father waiting outside".

"William, you must hide! I am sure that they are here for you as well. Beth, Suzy, can you please take William with you and go as far as you can away from here? We will let you know when it is safe. Leave through the back entrance. You best make a move now!" Henry urged anxiously.

Another knock was heard, and this time they were persistent. The knock was deliberate and made heavier and louder by someone strong and determined to gain access.

"Please hurry!" Jane exclaimed.

Beth grabbed my hand, and along with Suzy, we headed into the family room. We could see soldiers guarding the back door, preventing anyone from leaving.

"How are we going to leave?" asked Suzy.

"We need to distract the two soldiers somehow", Beth replied.

Images soon appeared in my mind with guidance on what to do next. I first needed to get Beth and Suzy to go along with what I was going to suggest.

"Beth, Suzy, do you trust me?"

"Why! What are you planning to do?" Beth asked.

"Suzy, we do not have much time. Can you focus on the mind of the soldiers to passively put them to sleep?"

"How do I do that?"

"You have the power and the ability to achieve this. Within your mind, see the soldiers relax. Allow tiredness to encompass them, inducing a change in consciousness to an altered state. Your last thought needs to be of them being asleep – Please try for me?"

"I will do my best!"

It wasn't long before the soldiers were asleep on the ground, literally where they had stood.

"I didn't realise I could do that!" voiced Suzy.

I briefly turned to face the direction of the hallway, where I heard Jane's voice. I couldn't quite make out what she was saying, but I could hear the dissatisfaction within her voice.

It wasn't long before the patio doors were opened.

"William, we need to go", prompted Beth.

Once we were out, we closed the door behind us.

"We need to get to the sanctuary without being seen", I suggested.

We could see more soldiers parading the grounds at this time, as three other soldiers were guarding the sanctuary entrance.

"We need to hide", I heard Beth say.

My eyes seemed to be directed to an area of the grounds that gave good shelter and a better view.

"Follow me", I asked them.

We found refuge behind bushes near some trees, a short distance from where we stood.

"What about Henry and Jane?" Suzy inquired.

"They should be fine. I am going to distract the three soldiers when the opportunity arises. I want you both to run to the sanctuary. I have a feeling you will be safe in there".

"We're not going without you, William!" exclaimed Beth.

"You both are taller than me. I'll have a better chance of hiding and losing them".

I could see that Beth wasn't prepared to lose me again. Instead, I could feel her emotional energies increase, feeling something was about to change within her.

"William, I have a feeling I know what to do".

As I turned to face Suzy, I noticed that she was glowing.

Turning back to Beth, I noticed she had left us, heading towards the sanctuary.

I soon heard men shouting. As I turned to face the direction of the noise, I could see Beth being confronted by the three soldiers.

I heard a noise behind us as two soldiers were searching not far from where we were hiding.

As I turned to Suzy, I could see anxiety was settling in.

"Suzy breathe - remember the exercise I asked you to do at the river by the village".

I could see Suzy starting to relax as she started to control her state with her breath.

My focus was soon directed back to the soldiers behind us. As I turned, I noticed that they had gone.

Turning back to face Suzy to see how she was doing and to let her know that the soldiers were no longer with us, I was surprised that she was no longer where I thought she was. I wondered if the men's disappearance had something to do with Suzy.

Looking over at Beth, I noticed that the three soldiers who had confronted her were lying on the ground.

To my surprise, I could see Suzy standing next to Beth. I wondered how she had gotten there so quickly. It must have been one of the new abilities that she had attained recently.

Driven by their emotions and intention to protect the land, Beth and Suzy's abilities were utilised as they became more aware of them. I could sense that they were getting stronger.

Not only did I pray for their safety as they started to scout the grounds, but I also prayed for the soldiers as they were only following orders.

Looking back at the house, I knew my focus needed to be on Jane and Henry.

I took another look in the direction of where Beth and Suzy were heading but noticed they had gone. It wasn't long before I could hear loud noises as guns were being fired, shortly followed by a loud explosion.

Ensuring the girls were OK, I went as close as possible to the action.

With a wave of her hand, the men in Beth's path were thrown off their feet. I could also see pulses of energy directed in the path of vehicles, causing much damage.

I couldn't see Suzy until I noticed her walking from behind a truck. She appeared to be controlling the mind of the soldiers, as they seemed to be turning on each other.

I was pleased to see that there wasn't any death being caused by their actions with their newfound abilities.

I was aware that they could sense me nearby. This was confirmed as I noticed Beth looked quickly in my direction.

Suddenly I felt a stronger calling to return to the family room, with the thoughts of Jane and Henry returning to my mind. I knew I needed to assist them. I hoped that I wasn't too late.

I started to turn back and head towards the Patio doors to enter the family room. Peering through the patio windows, I could see a glimpse of Henry with Jane's father walking past the family room entrance and heading towards the study.

Quietly opening the door, I was able to softly tread and make my way into the family room. Even though I could see no one, something did not feel right. As I closed the patio door behind me, the atmosphere seemed dense, supported by a drop in temperature. Looking towards the hallway, an eeriness pervaded the place. I started to question the validity of where I was and whether I was alone. I knew I needed to bring about a resolution to this situation. For those caught up in this cruel twist of fate would bring about a high cost, the full extent of which I was about to discover.

*Chapter XVI*

# The Path to Deliverance – Part I

I needed to learn as much as I could about what was going on.

Noticing earlier, seeing Henry and Jane's father heading towards the study, I made my way into the hallway. As I looked to my left, I could see the door to the study was open. It appeared to be a little too quiet for two adults having a dispute over the house and the land.

Trying not to be seen, I carefully peered into the room to see what they were up to.

Where were they? I was sure I had seen them head towards the study.

As I turned to face the main door, I listened out for any voices. Although none could be heard, I felt a pull to the dining room.

Curious, I peered in. Sitting motionless, I could see Jane holding a cup of coffee, with her mother opposite. I decided to get a closer look.

Questions started to populate my mind about the circumstances I was being faced with. I could feel my emotions stir as I began to feel and hear not just only my heartbeat but also the quickening of my breath.

I soon had the feeling that I was being observed. As my mind dwelled on this possibility, I felt cold shivers running down my spine. I took a deep breath to settle my nerves and to help me focus. Although this helped, something still did not feel right.

Looking for clues, I was soon standing next to Jane, observing her from her right side.

What was I missing?

I soon felt the need to briefly place my hand on her shoulder. As I did, suddenly Jane and her mother became re-animated. It was as if I were an observer looking in, as I noticed that they both couldn't see me.

I could see that Jane was pleased to see her mother. As I listened to their conversation, it appeared to be just two women talking, catching up on each other's lives.

I tried to see if I could see the energy of their auras, to see if they could reveal more about what was happening, but my efforts were limited by the denseness of the situation.

As I circled the table, I felt the need to observe Jane's mother. I noticed the way she held herself to compensate for a weakness. As I took a further look, I was drawn towards the lower left of her body, within the region of her stomach. I decided to briefly touch the shoulder of Jane's mother to see what impressions would appear. Suddenly they were both motionless again.

As it went quiet, I could hear a noise coming from the hallway, as if someone were moving in my direction. Turning around to see what or who it could be, I could see nothing. I moved slightly into the hallway, but again, I could see nothing.

Turning my focus back to them both, I could see a shadow behind Jane's mother. I became aware of dark energy surrounding the lower part of her body, passing around the stomach region. I then received an awareness that she had Stage three Cancer, and it had spread to her lower organs, moving on up to her upper chest.

On hearing this, my thoughts went to Jane, and I wondered if she had known of her mother's illness.

I soon felt the need to turn to face the study. As I did, I soon caught a glimpse from the corner of my left eye of shadowy figures entering the family room. As I turned back to face Jane and her mother, I saw that both were gone.

Were these the shadows of times past or of recent events? I wondered as thoughts went through my mind to try and understand what was really happening here.

Curious, I then turned back towards the family room to see if there were any more of an activity of the same nature that I had seen a moment ago, as it reminded me of my time in the cave. I noticed that the light was on in the study. Hesitantly, I decided to take another look.

As I walked past the family room, glimpsing in, to my surprise, I could see Beth, Suzy, and myself motionless, caught in the time before we left the house, escaping through the patio doors.

I could feel my emotions stir again as my thoughts became more sensitive to the events unfolding in front of me. Taking in a deep breath to help bring clarity and focus, I was soon alerted to a movement behind me. Turning around, I couldn't see anything.

As I placed my focus back into the family room, I was no longer looking at us. I could see Jane's father as he stood with his back to me, facing the patio. I noticed he appeared to be watching us back when we were discussing where to go next. Noticing that he appeared to be motionless, I decided to take a closer look. I entered the room and stood in front of him when my eyes were suddenly drawn to a black stone. It was shaped to fit as a ring ornament, which he wore on the index finger of his right hand. It seemed to resonate with a specific type of energy, similar to the artefacts we retrieved from young Henry.

As my thoughts went to Henry, my attention was drawn to the study. Leaving Jane's father where he was, I left the family room. As I entered the study, I could see Henry and Jane's father standing motionless. They appeared as if they were talking to one another.

I decided to take a quick peek back into the family room – now I could see Jane standing, facing her mother. Henry and Jane's father were sitting down.

It felt as if I were losing my grip on reality as I viewed these snippets of moments within time, each of them as still as they could be. I began to feel a discomfort in my head and shallowness in my breath as confusion settled in. I knew I needed to breathe to ease the discomfort and to focus on getting through this. Closing my eyes, I took a couple of deep breaths.

As I opened my eyes, I was drawn to look at Jane's father. I could now see him holding some paperwork that was clutched in his right hand. I wondered if it was the contract that he wanted them to sign.

Turning to face Jane, I could see she wasn't happy. It looked as if she was relaying her words of emotions through her hands. I wasn't sure how, but I needed to see if I could reach out to her.

As I was about to walk over to her, I heard my name being called from behind. Turning myself around to see who it could be, I could see no one.

I started to question the validity of what I was hearing. I knew it was a male voice.

Turning my head to face the others in the room, my name was called again. This time I recognised it to be Henry.

"Henry, is that you?" I turned and asked.

There was no response.

As I glanced back into the family room, I saw the room was now empty.

I heard my name being called again, and this time I recognised the voice to be Jane's. It appeared to be coming from the far end of the hallway, near the main door.

I decided to step out further into the hallway to try and understand what was happening. Whatever was here was trying to play with my mind. It was as if the memories of the past and present were being echoed throughout the house as if they were ghosts in the night.

Turning to face the study, I noticed that the light that was once on was now off.

I decided to make my way to the main door, where I heard Jane's voice to see where it would lead me.

After a few steps, a noise could be heard coming from the living room. Normally the door to the room would be closed, but as I turned to face it, I noticed that the door was now ajar.

My spine tingled with anticipation as to what may be waiting on the other side. I could feel my heart rate increase.

As I took a couple of steps towards the door, I paused and then opened it gradually, and I felt a cold breeze encircle me. I was welcomed by a sudden drop in temperature.

It was as if my heart had lost a beat, pounding in response to what may lay beyond – I wasn't sure what I was dealing with. I tried to delicately diffuse the tension within my mind and any fear that may have arisen.

Suddenly I heard a loud noise behind me from the hallway. I stepped back slightly, holding my hand on my chest. Taking a quick glance around, I noticed that the family room door was closed.

I started to question even more the validity of my state of mind, feeling the space that I occupied was shared. I knew I needed to be strong. Although I couldn't explain it, I felt as if someone was trying to show me something.

I looked back into the living room and decided to enter. Keeping calm, I knew that I had to be patient. The room certainly felt different from the others. With the uncertainty and unease of my surroundings, I thought about leaving the room. At that point, the door slammed shut in front of me.

It was as though the air around me had changed. I found myself struggling to breathe. The air appeared to be thinner, with a slight odour accompanying it.

I could feel something move around me, near the space I occupied. Not sure who or what it was, it gave me a feeling of being judged, of feeling criticised for who I was, feeding my mind with doubt and fear. Stirring with unsettling thoughts, I started to pray for liberation. I knew I needed to surpass any fear that presented itself within my thoughts and my emotions.

Closing my eyes, I soon felt something had changed. On opening them, it was as if I was in a different room. The theme of the décor was different, matching the style of furniture that accompanied it.

It wasn't long before I could hear laughter and conversations just outside, in the hallway. I noticed that the door was slightly opened, giving me an opportunity to see who or what was out there and hoping to shed some light on the situation. I noticed that the voices became more recognisable as the door further opened without intervention. I knew the voices to be those of Jane and Henry.

Leaving the living room, I was pleased to see the daylight lighting up the hallway, which I found refreshing and reassuring. I decided to continue to walk to the main door, where I had heard Jane's voice previously. As I got closer, I could see it gradually open by itself, inviting me to exit through it. Stepping through the doorway, I was welcomed by the warmth of the Sun and a slight breeze. My senses became more alive, enabling me to feel the energy and the presence of life in nature.

I soon felt a presence behind me. Turning around to face whoever it was, I noticed it was a young Jane. She appeared to be slightly fuller in size, as there appeared to be a bulge extending out from her front. Feeling the presence of a young life within her, I then realised that she was pregnant.

Without any warning and infused with emotion, Jane started to panic. As she rushed past, I noticed that she couldn't see me. Uncertain of what was concerning her, all I could hear was Jane calling out Henry's name.

"Am I just seeing into the past, or am I really here?" The questions went through my mind.

I decided to follow Jane to see where this would lead me. We were soon at the lake, located near a little fishing area that I had not noticed before. Sitting with Henry were three others. I recognised one of the gentlemen to be Jane's father, and the other two were unknown to me. All I could do was listen and observe.

As I observed, I heard Jane call out to Henry for help. Seeing the way Jane was, Henry soon left the others and made his way to her.

Curious, I turned to face the men he left behind to see if I could learn more about them. There wasn't much going on that I could initially see from where I was standing. I did, though, happen to see one of them turn to face the water as the others were focused on what was happening on land with Jane. He appeared to be dropping something into the lake.

Turning to face Henry and Jane, I listened to see what was troubling her.

"There is something wrong with the baby!" I heard Jane exclaim.

"We need to get you to the hospital!"

As they started to make their way back to the house, they were shortly joined and assisted by Jane's father.

I was curious to see what had been dropped in the lake. I tried to make my way over to the two men waiting there, but I felt a pullback to the house. Looking towards the house to see if I could see Jane and Henry, I realised I had lost sight of them. They must have entered the house. Returning my focus to the lake, I noticed that the two men had disappeared.

I made my way back to the front of the house and noticed the door was open. As I entered, I felt guided to go to the family room. Moving along the hallway, I could suddenly hear Jane crying out from one of the rooms upstairs.

On reaching the family room, I could see Henry and Jane's father. Looking at them both, I felt they were waiting to hear the results on the health of Jane and the baby.

Even though I felt the urge to be with Jane, I felt that it was more important at this time to stay where I was.

I was still the observer looking in as I noticed they could still not see me and weren't aware of my presence.

With Jane's father sitting patiently, I could see Henry pacing the room.

It wasn't long before I noticed a man in a suit walk down the stairs and wait by the entrance of the family room for Henry.

I decided at this time to leave Henry with what I could assume to be the doctor as they started to discuss the health of Jane and the baby.

Making my way into the family room, I waited near Jane's father to see if I could learn any more about who he was as a person. This was a man who kept his conversations short and to the point. As I started to analyse his energy, I could see that there was something not quite right about it. I felt my intuition was trying to tell me something.

Henry soon returned to the family room, and I could see he wasn't himself.

"Henry, Is Jane OK? How is the baby?" asked Jane's father.

"The doctor has done all he can from here. There's been a problem with the baby – The doctor is arranging for an ambulance to take Jane to the hospital – Please excuse me, as I need to be with her!"

"I understand", Jane's father replied.

Henry left to be with Jane, to comfort her while waiting for the ambulance.

With Jane's father now unobserved, it wasn't long before I noticed a change occur within him. It soon became apparent that there was more than one being that was present before me. Not of one dimension but existing between them. As its true nature and form were being revealed to me, I realised that the real occupant of the body was indeed a group consciousness rather than the consciousness of the man I thought was solely Jane's father. I could still feel the residual energy of her father's presence in there somewhere, his memories and his soul essence.

"Is this what you needed me to see?" I asked whoever may be listening as the mystery unravelled in front of my eyes.

With all the darkness that surrounded Jane, I could understand why she had health problems, and maybe this was the reason why she had lost the baby.

I soon received thoughts entering my mind of the man at the fishing spot by the lake.

"What did he drop in the water!" I wondered.

With that thought, I felt another presence from within the hallway. As I left the room and entered the hallway to investigate, I could see no one.

Looking back in the family room, Jane's father or whatever it was, had gone. I was alone again.

I soon felt a pull to the main door. As I started to walk towards it, it began to open by itself and somehow, I felt as if I was missing an opportunity. On looking back, trying to figure it out, I wondered what it could be.

One last attempt – I closed my eyes and took a deep breath, and started to relax. As I opened my eyes, I softened my focus. Looking around the hallway, there wasn't much I could see. I wondered if I was trying too hard.

"Is anyone there?" I asked.

"Why do you ask?" a voice replied.

"Have you been here the whole time?"

"I am never far away".

I started to feel emotional, as a feeling of love encompassed me.

"Who are you?"

"What do you feel inside, William? Who do you say that I am?"

"Are you God?"

"There are many references that can be found. Written in scripture, spoken in word, felt of the heart. Who do you say that I am?"

I wasn't quite sure how to answer that one.

"How am I doing?"

"Only you can answer that question".

"Are you able to elaborate?"

"Tell me, William, what do you know?"

"About me or about the path I am on?"

"Tell me?"

"Tell you?"

"Yes. Where is the clarity to the question you ask? I am unable to reply as I need to understand the reasoning behind what you are asking. Who is the question for? What is the purpose of this question?"

"I just need to do what is required of me on this path!"

"William, may I ask you, what is it that you have learnt?

"I have learnt about love: through my relationships with others, of self, and the way we express ourselves in this understanding. That there is strength in love and that we just need to recognise this. For love can be the light, where darkness falls".

"What have you learnt about relationships?"

"They can be as complex as we choose to make them. I feel without mutual recognition, it could cause a disharmony and imbalance in the lives that are connected through them".

"So, I ask you, what do you know?"

"The relationship between them is the key!"

"William, you are nearing the answer you seek. Break down the illusion and see the truth that presents itself to you. Be truly a witness through all your senses and not just the one".

The more engaged I was in the conversation, the more intrigued I was, leading to more questions I wanted to ask.

"Where do I go now?"

"Allow love to be your light on your path. You have been given all that you need – Be that which has driven you and guided you all your life, whether seen or unseen, it is that which defines you – It is your power and your life force essence, one that sustains you".

"Can I ask, is Jane's father's spirit lost in the presence that has encapsulated him?"

"No one is ever lost, William".

"I am concerned about Jane".

"Jane will be fine".

I thought about the conversation I was having and the way it was being received through the spoken word.

"Why are you hiding?"

"Surely, for what you choose to see is a mere perception of your mind that is trying to understand the concept of what you are now reacting to".

Feeling emotional and humble in the light of who I may have an audience with, I responded, "I am sorry".

"There is no need to be sorry, for you were given an enquiring mind to ascertain the truth. Always discern what you have been presented with. Not just on your sight but through the full awakening of all your senses".

With that, a light appeared in the same space as the voice seemed to be coming from.

As I looked to the corner, I could see myself.

"Why am I seeing me?"

"This form, I thought you would be most comfortable with".

A short time passed as further points were discussed with regard to my visit here. It was as if I could ask many questions, knowing that the answers would not only just be heard but would also be felt.

I soon felt our conversation was coming to an end.

"I am always listening. Just because you have not heard from me, it does not mean that I have not responded".

I then found myself temporarily embellished by tiny lights carried within the vehicle of a light breeze that greeted me and then went. As I looked at the presence who stood before me, it was no longer there.

I started to walk through the doorway onto the porch in reflection of the words I had heard and wondered in which direction I needed to go. The memories of the fishing spot where the men were populated my mind. Following my thoughts, I made my way there.

As I took in the view of the beauty of the land, of the life of nature that was presented to me, I realised that there was little I could experience. I couldn't see the energy on this occasion, but I felt an emotional sensitivity that permeated my senses.

As I reached the fishing spot, I looked in the area where I thought I saw the man drop the item, only to find that I couldn't see anything beyond the surface of the water. Finding a safe and comfortable place to sit, with my eyes closed and solely relying on my other senses, I knew I had to try another way. Allowing my breath to be in rhythm with the beat of my heart, I started to focus on one sense at a time. Bringing each of the senses I could work with into alignment, I could soon feel myself drift as a sense of displacement came over me. It wasn't of the body but of the mind.

Allowing myself to be intuitively guided, I felt myself drawing close to the location of what I was seeking. It wasn't long before the item was revealed to me. Located on the bottom, near some rocks, was what could possibly be a key. I soon received impressions within my mind that could possibly lead to answers. On opening my eyes, as I uncurled my right hand, the key was lying across my palm. I wasn't sure how it got there, but I was relieved that I didn't have to go diving for it.

I knew I had to place the key somewhere safe on my person. The only pocket that I had, which would be suitable, would be the one on the right-hand side of my pants.

With the key safe, I had the feeling it was time to move on. Standing up and considering my options, I thought about the key and the possibilities of what it would reveal to me. It wasn't long before these thoughts were interrupted by the reminder of the situation of Jane and Henry's dilemma, especially now knowing what or who they were facing.

As I stood between the lake and the door leading to the house, my intuition directed me to the sanctuary, but logic directed me to the house. I decided to go with my intuition.

Curious about the destination I was headed for, I wondered if it had something to do with the key. It wasn't long before I was in front of the entrance of the old ruins, and looking in, it appeared empty.

Being here triggered thoughts of Suzy and Beth. I wondered if they were OK.

Just as I was about to go inside, I felt someone pull me back. Turning around to see who it was, I could see Alice.

"What are you doing here?" I asked her.

Alice turned to face the back of the house, lifting her arm to point something out to me.

Turning to see where she was indicating, I noticed a black cloud had gathered.

"Please help them, William?" Alice's voice could be heard in my mind.

I suddenly heard Suzy's voice. As I tried to focus on the direction it was coming from, I soon realised that I was back in the present time. I turned to face Alice and noticed that she had disappeared.

A thought appeared in my mind of the importance of the key, and I knew that I had been given it for a reason.

As more men appeared on the land, I became aware and could see Beth and Suzy still trying to defend the property.

I had to find an answer to the dilemma we were now facing and knew I had to make the right choice. As thoughts of potential answers entered my mind, I started to question my next course of action. Then it occurred to me that the answer had, in fact, been revealed to me back in the house. How could I not have seen it?

## Chapter XVII

# The Path to Deliverance – Part II

I now had an inkling of what I needed to do. The key wasn't what I thought it would be, as in this case, it represented itself in more ways than one. As it all started to make sense, my immediate response was to initiate a chain of events that would later support the outcome.

As I turned to look for the others. I could see Beth but not Suzy. I wondered where she was and prayed that she would be OK.

Suddenly I was shown a vision within my mind's eye of Suzy resting behind a tree. I could see that she had been wounded and was trying to attend to the wound by holding her side and applying pressure to it. I was also shown Alice, as she was distracting the men away from Suzy's current location.

Great, this has created an opportunity for me to save her, so I started to make my way to where I was shown she was resting. I was only a few steps forward when I suddenly felt something guiding me back toward the sanctuary. The more I tried to head back to Suzy, the more I noticed the pull. Methodically, I went through every step, every decision of every choice that I had made. Still, I felt helpless to assist Suzy and prayed for healing to keep her strong and alive.

My concerns were soon masked by a female voice which echoed within my mind, bringing clarity.

"The most obvious action might not be the correct action to surrender to. As allowing the lower of emotions to guide you, the simplest of choices to act and to surrender could take you further from the path that grants you the outcome of success and onto the path of truth".

I had to put my faith in God to save Suzy. I prayed for both her and her unborn child. I could see that Beth seemed to have the strength to continue. I did not want to let Alice down as she had asked me to help the others. At the same time, I knew I had to follow the guidance. I hoped that Alice would understand.

The voice returned, echoing in my mind, "sanctuary, the answer you seek awaits you there".

I took one last look around the area before heading to the sanctuary.

Standing at the entrance, I took a deep breath in. Looking into the structure of the old ruins and reminiscing about what it truly stood for gave me a little hope. On reflection, the real presence of this place was hidden from those whose intention wasn't for the greater good.

Walking to the central point where the altar would have been, I waited to see if anything would occur. I couldn't see any changes where I was standing, considering what had happened the last time we were here.

"Why am I here?" I asked out loud.

I had a feeling to take the key out of my pocket. But, as I took a closer look, I couldn't see any scripture or symbols.

"Why this key?"

No thoughts or voices echoed within my mind to answer my question.

I knew the answer had to be here. I just needed to find it before it was too late for the others.

I decided to find a comfortable place to sit down to meditate and pray for guidance. After a short while, peace began embracing me with a sense of mindfulness of the task at hand. I placed all my focus on needing to find a resolution to the predicament we had found ourselves in.

I soon felt the intensity of love as it embraced me, followed by the voice that echoed within my thoughts

"William".

On opening my eyes, I was no longer in the old ruins of the sanctuary. Instead, I was in a beautiful sacred place. I remembered how Suzy had relayed her father's description of the place. A lady in white stood before me. There was an iridescence light about her.

"Please stand, William – I am known here as Catherine".

"Thank you", I replied as I returned to my feet.

"We have been waiting for you, William".

Looking around at the splendour of the architectural design, I could see that we were not alone. I could see others like Catherine walking around.

Turning back to face Catherine, "Are you able to help?"

"The key".

"The key", I wondered as I started to analyse her response.

"Please follow me".

We started to walk down a long corridor.

"Where are we going?"

There was silence at first, and then she stopped to point to what I could see as a large, heavy golden door.

"What you are seeking is beyond this door".

I felt the warmth from her smile as if to reassure me.

"The key that you had recently retrieved from the lake, William, unlocks many gateways into many dimensions and will enable you to travel beyond and between them. It is what has brought you here. The consciousness that occupies Jane's father's mind is trapped in this world, in his body. They can move beyond the body and into this world with this key. This key must not be given to Jane's father".

"Is there a way I can save him?"

"There may be a way to save her father, and it will not be easy. It will be through her love for him and his for her. Remember what you have learned of the heart since your arrival at the start of your journey".

Retrieving the key from my pocket, I now knew the significance of the opportunities it presented to me and the responsibility of having it in my possession. Even though I knew the safest option was to destroy it, I had an inner feeling I should keep hold of it.

Catherine nodded in affirmation and then smiled.

"The choice has been made".

While trying to understand the concept of what she was saying, my attention was drawn to the key in my hand, as I felt a warmth generate within my palm. Placing the focus on the key, I soon became aware of its integration within my energy system as it evaporated before my eyes. Though it was no longer physically present, the essence of its power resided in me. This had given me food for thought.

I turned to face Catherine, who appeared to be observing me.

"Is this what you mean?"

"Yes, William"

"The key, how will I retrieve it?"

"There is no need".

"The key is what they are after. Would this not make the situation worse if it no longer exists?"

"The key had initially been integral to their plans until your arrival. Apart from the land, it is you they seek now".

"That wasn't reassuring to hear!"

"It is time. William, can you please enter the room?"

As the door slowly opened, I began to see into the room. At the opposite end of the large room was a golden statue.

Turning to face Catherine, I asked, "Why are we here?"

"The journey of your path was to bring about an understanding of oneness, uniting with others through a greater understanding of the heart, that of love. To share in your heart connection, to bring out the best in them. You have prepared them well, and they are now ready".

"Ready for what?"

"For the next part of their journey".

Catherine then pointed to the statue.

"The answer you seek, William, is here".

The statue depicted a hooded figure without a face, holding a holy Sceptre that glistened.

"Catherine, can you please tell me more about this statue?"

"As old as time, reflected throughout history, one who has many names but collectively is known by that which is known through their presence", she replied.

I started to move closer inside the room, unaware that the door was closing behind me. As I reached the place where the holy Sceptre was contained, I heard the closing of the door as it echoed throughout the room. Turning to face the area behind me, I checked to see if anyone had accompanied me, then to find that I was the only one within the room. I could see multiple tiny statues sculpted in the walls, side by side, in many rows, from top to bottom, on both sides of the room. Names were written underneath, identifying each statue. I wondered if these were all the lives this being was born into. I slowly reached out to the holy Sceptre, grasping it in my hand.

I could feel its power coursing through my veins, producing a familiarity of sensations felt throughout my body. My body started to unravel within its energy structure as a light shone from within me. I started to let go to welcome the becoming of the new self. As the intensity became overwhelming, I soon lost consciousness.

Waking up, I was back in the old ruins of the sanctuary with the Sceptre in my right hand. It seems I was still the young boy of seven.

As I left the sanctuary, I could see no one on the land as strange as it seemed. There were no men and no sign of Suzy and Beth. I wondered if I had returned to the same time reference as I had left. I started to walk back to the house. As I reached the front door, I noticed that it was unlocked. I gently opened the door, peering through the gap to see if anyone was about. Not seeing anyone, I decided to walk through.

A familiarity of an aroma filled the air as meatloaf came to mind. I felt drawn to the study and noticed that the door was ajar. I made my way to the study, being cautious with every step. The parcel caught my eye as it rested on the small table. I was intrigued by how it returned here. I felt the need to check to see if anything was different from how I remembered it to be with the room. Facing the window, thinking about Suzy and Beth, my thoughts were soon interrupted by a noise that was heard behind me, as if someone had entered the room. As I turned around, I could see myself appearing in my direction, trying to work out who I was. It occurred to me that I had returned to the moment in time of my first interaction with the parcel. It wasn't long before Jane started to walk into the room. Focusing on the Sceptre, I knew it was time for me to leave.

With that thought, I found myself standing outside the café, looking through the window. Seeing myself as I observed Jane while she was demonstrating the art of singing. I could see her passion for the art of singing and her wanting to provide me with an understanding. It was a way of expressing emotion and feelings through the art of harmonising the voice. I noticed that Jane had reached a moment where she seemed to have paused to look my way.

I started to question why I was here, and then I caught a glimpse of Beth, the white layer of protection surrounding her auric energy field. The colour of her energy emitted a warmth, displaying varied shades of orange, pink and magenta. Realising that Beth may be integral to helping me to deal with what waited ahead, I placed my focus on the Sceptre to take me where I needed to be.

I soon found myself at the village fayre. Looking around, I could see no sign of the others, so I must have arrived before them.

I felt a presence within the fayre that was dark in its nature. I soon became aware of a man in a suit. Curious, I started to monitor his movements as he appeared to be looking for someone.

It wasn't long before Jane and Alice arrived. I could see them make their way through the fayre to the main stand. With enthusiasm for seeing her grandmother, I could see Jane make her way to where she would be. I appeared to be invisible, slightly out of phase in this dimension from all the rest.

It wasn't long before I could see Beth and I had arrived on the scene. Thinking about the young boy, who became unwell, I felt the need for Mrs Emmet to be in the right place at the right time to observe us.

Making my way over to where I had previously seen her, I noticed she wasn't at the stall. Instead, a younger lady stood in her place. As an image of a meatloaf entered my mind, I could only guess that Mrs Emmet must be putting in her entry for the competition. As I arrived, I soon noticed Mrs Emmet checking out the competition by seeing what other meatloaves were on show.

With my intentions set, I transmitted the thoughts with images of the children playing. Then another with the boy child suffering. I could see she was receiving them as her attention turned her focus on her surroundings and those within her vicinity. I repeated transmitting the images within her mind once more. This seemed to agitate her as she soon left the area to look for the children.

Suddenly I heard a voice I recognised. Looking to my left, not far from where I stood, I could see Jane standing near one of the stalls, talking to her grandmother.

Just a few yards behind Jane, I could see the man in the suit observing her. I could see his energy envelop hers, trying to extract information from her thoughts. It wasn't long before I saw Jane react, as her energy started to withdraw and change in colours as darker shades were intruding, setting about confusion within her thoughts.

I knew I needed to intervene but not to draw attention.

I focused on the two of us being transported to another place, more secluded. With the Sceptre in my hand and my intention set, it was a matter of minutes before this was achieved.

Finding ourselves on top of a mountain, not far from a cliff's edge, I awaited his response.

"Where am I?" the man asked.

"Somewhere where you cannot cause harm to others".

"You have no business here, child".

I could see his energy started to expand and try to manipulate mine, but it had no effect.

"What is your business here? Why are you observing Jane?" I responded.

I was soon interrupted by the man, as he seemed agitated.

"You do not know what you are dealing with, child. Return me at once!"

Thoughts of the memories of Henry came to me. It was as though I could start to read the man's mind. Then, it occurred to me that he was trying to find out if Jane knew anything about the artefacts and their location.

As I observed his energy, I noticed another consciousness occupying the same body, similar to what I had seen with Jane's father. However, on this occasion, there was only one other consciousness with him, not a group one.

"I have what I need", I informed him.

I wondered if I released the invading presence, would the soul that remained survive? I knew I needed to act if there was any chance that I could save him. With the intention set, by focusing on the Sceptre and my intention, even though the invading presence fought to remain, it soon vanished from the body it occupied. The body of the man soon collapsed on the ground, unconscious.

I could feel myself getting stronger with the power of the Sceptre.

On checking the man, I found his life force was still present but lacked strength. Suddenly I became aware of angels surrounding us. Realising they must be here for him, I knew it was my time to leave.

I soon found myself somewhere else, focusing on returning to the place I had left. I was standing at the edge of the forest. I could see the military barracks at a distance from where I was standing. As I began to walk toward the barracks, I caught sight of the main building. There weren't many men to be seen at first. With the intention not to harm them but to confine them, using the Sceptre, I was able to teleport the men to the barracks, locking them inside. I then moved forward, closer to the main building,

I suddenly found myself back on Jane and Henry's land, not far from where Suzy was seated, resting against a tree. I could see the soldiers heading in her direction, closing in on her. Somehow, the Sceptre must have known that Suzy would be in danger.

I headed to intercept the men from reaching Suzy. Having the intention to clear the land of these men and send them back to their families, the men in front of me vanished within a few minutes.

I noticed that the Sceptre started to feel different in my hand. It seemed to be dissolving, integrating within my energy system. My thoughts took me to the time when Beth's bracelet integrated with her. Then, I could see no tattoo of any kind. I had a feeling that if required again, I just would need to call on it.

As I reached Suzy, by the expression on her face and the pattern of her breathing, I could see how she was trying to redirect the focus of her pain. She appeared to be in a fragile state. I noticed she had lost blood from the wound on her side.

Assessing Suzy's energy, the colours of her aura appeared to reflect a weakness more prominent in the area affected by the wound. As a result, darker shades of magenta, red, grey and pink could be seen in her aura, affecting the vibrant colours that were already established.

Needing to let her know I was here with her, I called out her name a couple of times. Finally, recognising my voice, she looked up. I could see that she had been crying.

"I am sorry, William!"

"Let me help you".

"I am worried about my baby!"

I started to scan the energy of her aura, as she was so early in the pregnancy. The baby she was carrying was still alive and strong.

"Your baby is safe, protected by a shield of energy", I replied to reassure her.

Crouching down next to Suzy, I placed my hand on her shoulder. Healing light started to flow into her from the palm of my hand.

We were soon joined by Beth, who appeared slightly out of breath.

"William, are you OK? Is Suzy OK?"

Realising I was giving Suzy healing, she waited patiently for my reply.

I could see the healing not only healed the wound but restored the energy of her aura, as the colours in her aura began to lighten, becoming more vibrant.

"Sorry, Beth, how are you feeling? I noticed you were also wounded".

"I am fine, William - the wound healed by itself".

"It is good to hear, but just to be sure, I will check your energy once I have helped Suzy".

"OK – Where did they go? They all just disappeared, even the trucks", responded Beth.

"Every one of them?" I asked.

"I was gathering my breath, crouching behind the wood-chopping hut. One moment I could hear men shouting, and then suddenly, it went quiet. I thought it was a bit strange at first, but when I appeared from behind the hut, the vehicles and the men were gone. I knew Suzy was resting back here, so I thought I would come and check to see if she was OK. I am so pleased to find you here".

As I finished with Suzy, Beth approached me to embrace me with a hug. Reciprocating her embrace, I could feel her love and relief to know I was with them. However, as we pulled away, I noticed a few tears trickling down her cheeks.

"William", I heard Suzy from behind call out to me.

Turning around to face her, I noticed her strength was returning as she started to get onto her feet. With a little assistance from Beth, she was able to accomplish this.

"So, what now? Did you manage to assist Auntie and Uncle?" asked Beth.

"Beth, Let me check your energy first".

As I started to scan Beth's energy, to my surprise, iridescent light energy had integrated into her aura, introducing a varied range of higher vibrational colours. The protected layer could still be seen. As clearly as it was being shown to me, with the increased light within her physical structure, I could see that Beth was evolving. This could explain how she was able to heal herself. I shared this with Beth but still asked her to be careful.

I spent the next twenty, twenty-five minutes explaining what had happened since I last spoke to them.

"So that's how I found myself with you both and why the soldiers are no longer here".

"That explains a lot. Where is the Sceptre now?" asked Beth.

"When I need it, it appears to me in my hand. It seems I am the only one who can wield its power, as it is a part of me. Similar to the crystal that was given to you, Suzy, and the bracelet you have, Beth. The Sceptre is an extension of me.

"Can we see it?" asked Suzy.

"I want to know more about your conversation with God?" Beth responded with excitement in her voice.

I smiled at them both as I was amused by their curiosity. Then, applying emotion and intention to wield the Sceptre, it soon appeared in my hand for a brief moment. It then vanished, retreating back into my energy system.

"Amazing, Wil did say that it had something to do with you", Suzy responded emotionally.

Turning to face her, "A possibility", I replied.

Turning to face Beth, I replied, "Maybe you will get an opportunity to have a similar conversation one day".

"I do hope so!" replied Beth.

"Before we venture into the house, this is what I can understand from what I have learned. The old tree of the forest appears to be the power source for the phenomena manifesting here. The sanctuary is a gateway that requires an activator, which is the key to its operation.

There has been a lot of spiritual activity on the land, especially within the house. This is where I feel several dimensions converge, interlacing each other. The military camp that we visited wasn't real. It's a parity of the mind manifested through the consciousness of its creator, existing not of this dimension but is somehow bound to this one. The dark cloud that looms over the house appears to be the creation of a portal between dimensions. We need to close this as soon as possible before it has been fully established. Lastly, Jane's father is no longer who he appears to be. A group consciousness not of this dimension has infiltrated his mind, speaking as one. The ring on his finger, I feel, establishes their hold to this dimension and over him".

"If the tree is the source of the power for all the phenomena, shouldn't that be our first focus?" Beth responded.

"There must be another key creating this portal", replied Suzy.

"You both are on to something. I feel that Henry is somehow connected to what is happening here. But we have to be careful!"

"You mention the ring. Could the ring be another key that is creating the portal?" Suzy asked as I could see it was her mind trying to unravel the clues presented to us.

"Yes, it sounds plausible. Are you OK with walking?" I asked Suzy.

"Yes, feeling a lot better now".

I could see Beth was on hand to support Suzy if she needed assistance.

"Let's see if we can pull the plug on the power of this phenomenon!" I voiced out to empower us.

As we set off on our task, knowing that time was against us, we headed further into the forest, making our way to the large old oak tree. It wasn't long before we started to see tiny lights surrounding us. For some reason, they became more forever present within our sight. The energy of the forest seemed to be more tangible than ever before.

Tingling sensations were felt, stimulating a reaction on the surface of my skin.

I could see both Beth and Suzy's energy of the aura becoming more vibrant, charged by the energy that welcomed them. They appeared to be both glowing in iridescent light.

As we got closer to the tree, a light was manifesting, radiating from the vicinity of where the tree stood. The energy manifesting was caused by a quickening of the energy of our vibration. I could see the other two looking at each other and then at me as we were getting closer. My presence seemed to cause a reaction, causing a vibration of sound to emit from the tree. I also noticed it reacted to Beth and Suzy's emotions and thoughts. Therefore, I felt it best that the other two remained where they were, keeping a short distance away from the tree.

"Beth, Suzy, can you please hold back? I need you both to harmonise the energy for me".

"How do we do that?" asked Beth.

"Find your inner peace. The energy is reacting to your emotions and thoughts. Your intentions need to be clear".

I could see them both close their eyes. To assist in focusing, I shared the following with them.

"Remember to breathe, focusing only on the breath. The tree will react to this".

As I walked closer to the space surrounding the tree, I knew I needed to contain its energy somehow. It was as if the tree was aware of my presence, as I could feel a connection with it. The closer I approached the tree, I could feel the vibration of the energy of my body starting to alter. As It did, I noticed that I no longer existed in the physical form but was presented in a spiritual body of divine light. I was soon welcomed by a clarity that soon embraced my thoughts, awakening a connection to universal consciousness. I felt a tranquillity and oneness which surpassed everything, even the chatter. My focus was soon redirected as the energy blueprint of the tree was revealed to me – I felt humbled by its offering. Once I was able to identify the power source, I was able to isolate the connection that was providing the power to the phenomenon taking place. It wasn't long before this was achieved.

I could feel a connection –

As I approached, the tree became pure light. I also began to feel a reaction within my own energy.

I became aware of Beth and Suzy emotionally reaching out to me, calling out my name, and anchoring me to their moment in time to where I needed to be. It wasn't long before I found myself back in the forest.

It was good to see the tree appearing in its natural passive state.

I still existed in a spiritual body of divine light. I could see the angels and the little lights that greeted us when we entered the forest encircled me. With their love and help, along with Beth and Suzy, they were able to contain my spiritual energy. Restoring the layers of protection that encased me to be present within this dimension. As I looked and observed my body in its current state, the light soon receded, finding myself back within a short period of time, within a physical state.

I looked to Beth and Suzy and thanked them for assisting me in returning.

"We thought we lost you at one point", replied Suzy.

"We heard a voice telling us to focus on you and call your name. For us to focus on being your anchor – We both were shouting your name in the end", replied Beth.

"It helped, thank you. It was sensing you both and hearing your voices that made the difference".

Observing the area, it was amazing to see the angels surrounding me as well as the little lights that accompanied them. I thanked them for assisting me.

Both Suzy and Beth approached me to embrace me in a group hug. During our release, I felt another presence observing us. Turning to look, I noticed Alice not far from where we had stood. I noticed the others could see her too.

"Who is the little girl?" Suzy asked.

"Auntie Jane's Alice", Beth replied.

"This is Alice!" Suzy responded.

"Yep", Beth replied.

I started to walk over to Alice to see if she was OK. It was good to see her.

We then made our way to the house. As we reached the edge of the forest, we noticed that the phenomenon above the house had cleared. It was good to know that our theory had worked. Now we needed to get back into the house to help Jane and Henry. Looking around the grounds, all appeared to be normal. As we reached the house's main door, we noticed it was open.

"Shall we go in?" Beth asked.

We looked at each other, and with me taking the lead, we entered the hallway. Alice decided to remain out on the porch.

As we continued to make our way into the house, checking all the rooms on the ground floor, we could see no one.

"That's strange …. Where are they?" Beth asked.

"Beth, could you please check to see if anyone is upstairs?" I asked.

"Will do, William".

As she made her way up the stairs, I heard Suzy call out, "Beth, hang on one sec. I'll come up with you".

While they were checking upstairs, I had a feeling to go into the study. As I entered the room, I quickly looked to see if there was anything that could provide the whereabouts of Jane and Henry. Looking around the room, I also needed to check the floor. From what I could see, one of Jane's earrings was just beneath the small table. Reaching down to pick it up, I became aware of a change in my energy. I knew that having the earring would provide me with a connection to her, one that may prove useful to us later. As I stood up, I had a feeling of going back into the hall.

At the other end of the hall stood a tall, dark shadowy figure. A whispery black smoke encircled and emitted from it.

I started to feel unnerved by the presence that stood opposite me. I felt a coldness in the air as the temperature dropped. My breath became like white smoke as I took a deep breath in and out to try and regulate my breathing.

I could still hear Beth and Suzy checking the rooms upstairs.

I did my best not to avert my eyes from the figure standing in front of me so as not to give it the advantage.

It wasn't long before I was joined by the other two as they made their way down the stairs.

On seeing them, the shadowy figure started to move towards us. As it was moving forward, darkness followed, darkening the space it travelled.

Invoking the Sceptre, it soon vanished as it got within a metre of where we were. The darkness disappeared with it, leaving an impression within our minds of the clearing we had previously entered earlier that led us to the other dimension.

"That was close", I heard Beth say.

"Do you feel that Jane and Henry are being held captive? Was this a warning?" asked Suzy.

"A possibility! We need to go back to the forest and enter the clearing, like before. When we enter the mist and then reach our destination, we must sever the connection, and the only way we are going to achieve this is to destroy the ring. It seems we will need to fight them on their terms and in a place of their choosing. We really don't have a choice, so we need to work together to accomplish this and ensure that we return with Jane and Henry".

We started to make our way into the forest, with Alice staying behind to keep watch on the house. We soon passed the old oak tree and were on to the path leading to the clearing at the forest's edge. As we approached the clearing, a mist appeared, waiting for us to enter through. By us entering, I knew we would be in their territory. Entering a dimension, another world that would be unfamiliar to us.

"Are you ready, Beth?" I asked.

"As ready as I am going to ever be. What are the chances?"

Not knowing what we were going up against or where we would end up, I couldn't really provide her with an answer. But at the same time, I needed to give words of optimism and encouragement.

"We make a great team, and we have each other in support. I believe in us and what we could achieve as a team, as well as what we are capable of individually".

"How about you, Suzy?" I asked.

"Well, we've come this far and survived", she replied.

"That's true".

I knew I needed to encourage and instil confidence within them before we went forward.

"Please remember, stay focused and be clear with your emotions and thoughts. I am not sure where we will end up and how many we are going to face when we step through. We have each other, and we are not alone. Have courage for what you are about to do. Know that you are of love and allow it to be your guiding force. Be empowered by what you have learned about yourself and by the new abilities you have attained. Let these be your driving force as we go forward".

I took a deep breath and then made the others clear about our goals for this mission.

"Just to be clear, we need to find Jane and Henry, defeat our enemy, and most importantly, we must sever the connection that binds that dimension to this place".

The time had come to continue with our quest. I took a deep breath and summoned the will to walk through, and as I was just about to step forward, I heard my name being called.

"William", I heard a voice call out.

Turning around, Alice and the angel Peter stood before me.

"Hello, William", said Peter.

"What are you doing here?" I asked.

"Well, we couldn't let you fight an army of shadow warriors by yourselves", Peter replied.

Suddenly I became aware of a vast army of angel warriors that accompanied him. Their presence and light intensity were breathtaking, overwhelming me with heartfelt emotion.

"Alice will stay here. The entrance will be guarded and temporarily closed from this end", Peter continued to advise us.

Knowing that a battle between light and darkness was ahead of us, I stepped through the mist in anticipation of the task. Beth and Suzy, along with Peter and the army of angels, followed shortly behind....

*Chapter XVIII*

## The Uncertainty

I t felt like I was in a dream, lost in a mist that seemed to consume the space surrounding me. The mental imagery that played out soon brought to my mind that of two women; one appeared younger than the other. I felt I knew them, but my memory did not seem to support and validate my claim. The more I tried to make sense of what was happening, the harder it became, and I felt exhausted from trying. It was as though I was observing the life of someone I once knew.

Suddenly I felt a jolt within my body, followed by a shudder. Glimpses of the younger woman appeared in my mind conveying words like a silent movie to me. All I could hear was a high-pitched sound. I soon lost the mental imagery as it went black, accompanied by silence. It was as though I was held as a prisoner within my own mind and often getting a glimpse of an outer world before the blackness occupied the space. It was as if I became mindful of the confusion within this state of mind and not the clarity.

Images of a cave appeared within my mind's eye clairvoyantly, one that felt familiar to a place that I may have visited before but had felt no association to.

I felt another jolt within my body, bringing on much pain and discomfort within my head and chest. It was shortly followed by a numbness down towards my left side. All I could do was be aware of these sensations as they were being felt. What was more prominent was the strange taste that was resident in my taste buds, along with the scent of something burning.

Glimpses then appeared within my mind of seeing the two women appearing in the distance, just out of my reach. I could hear them shouting but couldn't make out any words.

Why do I have trouble remembering? A question that tried to reason to what was happening.

I felt the time passed within the blackness of what I could see. Any light I once saw was slowly diminishing, and my consciousness drifted with it.

My consciousness was soon brought back to my body as it reacted to a cough response. I could feel liquid in my throat as I struggled to breathe. Not sure what was happening, but I wondered whether this was the end.

Just as I started to dwell on this thought, a glimmer of light entered my mind. I suddenly caught a glimpse of a vision as an old man appeared within it. His skin was slightly tanned and rugged, with long white hair and brown eyes. I noticed I could see a light of an aura surrounding him, and I had a feeling that this man was wise and somehow seemed important. He appeared to be seated, kept company by a small fire in an open space.

As the vision faded, my thoughts returned to the two women I had seen earlier within the imagery of my mind. I also felt, somehow, that they were also important to me and that there was something I needed to do that involved them both.

## Chapter XIX

## A Trodden Path

I started to hear a voice, and within that moment, it became recognisable. Then, as I began to focus to see who had welcomed me, my memory started to return, and crouched in front of me was Beth.

"That was close, as we thought we lost you then!" exclaimed Beth.

I could see Beth reach down to help me onto my feet.

"As we entered the mist, we were separated from the others. It seems that it is just us three", I heard Suzy say.

"I'm trying to remember how I ended up on the ground!"

"You didn't seem yourself since we entered the mist. First, we could hear you begin to say something, and then it became gibberish. Then, although we could barely see you, suddenly you just collapsed to the floor", replied Beth.

I explained to Beth and Suzy what I had experienced. I could see Suzy looking concerned. I didn't mention the old man within the vision I had seen, as I didn't feel it was relevant.

"You appeared to be having a seizure! So I did what I knew best and what I was medically trained for. I had to make you as comfortable as possible while manoeuvring your body to what we refer to as the recovery position", said Beth.

Gathering myself, I replied, "Thank you for being there for me".

"Remember what I told you back in the forest the other day when you died on me the first time! William, I meant it, and please don't ever do that again!"

"We should be going?" suggested Suzy.

As I looked around, we were still in the mist. I knew I needed to be careful as I knew the others depended on me, as I was on them.

As we started to walk, it wasn't long before the mist began to clear. We appeared to be standing in a wilderness, with mountains on either side. Just off in the distance, at a lower ground level from where we were standing, I could make out a beautiful turquoise lake amongst tall trees.

Turning to face Beth and Suzy, I could see they were conversing. Although I couldn't hear what they were saying, I could see that Suzy was pointing to the trees by the left side of the lake.

Looking back over my shoulder towards the mist and the forest from where we had come, it was different. Only the wilderness that had welcomed us remained.

"William", I heard Beth's voice call out to me.

Quickly turning back to face the other two, I waited to see what Beth had to say.

"We should make our way to find some shelter. I'm not comfortable with us being here in the open".

"William, do you reckon Peter and the others are here too?" asked Suzy.

"I hope so – I am sure that we will find out soon enough".

We started to make our way down towards the lower grounds, heading for the lake on the other side of the forest. As we moved closer, I realised what Suzy was pointing to. I could see smoke appearing on the horizon just beyond the trees. Though we were curious, we hoped to find an answer.

As we entered the forest, it felt that the energy around us had changed. It became more vibrant, more refined in its structure and felt welcoming. Yet, although we could hear different sounds that welcomed us, we knew we were in unknown territory. We were unaware of what awaited us, albeit friend or foe.

I soon became aware of seeing a layer of light and colour reflecting off the leaves of the trees and the forest shrubbery that presented themselves before me. It was as though I was being shown where to go. The acuteness of sounds caressing my ears had created a tingling sensation throughout my body.

I felt a presence, a consciousness, was trying to reach out to me. I wasn't sure who, but I kept alert, paying attention to the signs that were being offered.

I was soon distracted by the whispering of voices in my head, urging me to leave this place as something was amiss.

A cold shiver was then felt down the back of my spine, followed by pain and a throbbing in my right temple. Holding my right hand to where the pain was, I called Beth.

Stopping to check to see what was wrong, "William, are you OK?" Beth asked.

"We need to keep our wits about us, as my senses are forwarning me about something", I replied.

I could see Beth turn to Suzy to share what I had mentioned with her. Then, keeping me close, we continued with our journey.

It wasn't long before we could hear branches snapping with ease as if, within each minute, the sounds got louder and appeared closer to our direction. Not quite sure what it was, we knew it wouldn't be long before it caught up with us.

My gut started to flare up as if my intuition were trying to tell me something.

We then heard another branch break just beyond the trees in front of us.

I looked up at Beth and Suzy, and I could tell by the colour of the energy of their auras that they were unsettled. Their colours appeared less vibrant, introducing varied shades of brown, red, pink and silver. It was as though they were preparing for the worst.

The whisper of the voices started to continue, calling me to go forward, then revealing another path that I couldn't see until now. Finally, a way was made clear as if lit up by light through a gap between two trees. As I moved towards the opening, I noticed that the path that lay before us was trodden. It seemed we weren't the only ones who had taken the route offered. As I wondered if they had fallen to the same fate.

"Are we safe?" I heard Suzy ask.

"We'd better just focus on where we need to get to", I heard Beth reply to Suzy.

I suddenly felt uneasy, as if we were being observed. I didn't want to alarm the other two, but now we had to increase our pace to move more quickly.

"Will this path lead us to Jane and Henry?" Suzy asked.

"I am sure we will find out soon enough", said Beth.

We started to make our way off the track onto the new path to see where it would take us. Hopefully, furthering ourselves away from the potential harm that was ready to pounce.

With the quietening of the whispers within my thoughts, I turned to see if I could hear the other two in their discussion. But instead, my thoughts reflected on what Beth had said about the seizure. It was concerning how debilitating this was to me, especially knowing where it could lead. Was the pain a reminder?

Suddenly I received the vision of the old man sitting by the fire. I wasn't sure what this meant, but like I felt before, it was somehow important.

Waiting for a pause in their conversation, I called out to Beth and Suzy. I went on to tell them about my vision.

"Do you feel that we will meet him?" Suzy asked.

"A possibility! I am sure when the time is right".

"Maybe he is the one that caused the smoke", said Beth.

The pain was still resident in my head, although subdued. Was this a warning sign that we were possibly still in danger?

The path was still lit up for me as the route to take, so we continued hoping it would lead us out of the forest.

As time passed, I noticed that recently burnt wood could be seen piled in a small area on the ground, just off to the left of the path. From this point forward, the trodden path seemed fresh, as if three of four people had just walked the path before us.

I could hear Suzy comment to Beth about something. I tried to see if I could listen to what they were saying, but their words seemed to blend as one.

I began to feel a strange sensation of numbness around my forehead. Then, cold shivers started to appear, running across my shoulders and down to the bottom of my spine. It was as though my whole body was reacting to the predicament of our situation.

We were soon alerted to rustling noises in the trees. The noise appeared to be coming from either side as if following us.

I noticed the other two had stopped to turn to face me, and as I joined them, Suzy asked, "What do we do now?"

Suddenly the temperature dropped, and an icy mist appeared around our feet. The path ahead was no longer lit.

The pain in my head felt more intense, causing me a feeling of nausea and sensitivity. I felt as if I wanted to vomit.

"Let's run", Beth responded as she grabbed my hand.

The pain was debilitating, and I wasn't feeling at all well. It felt like something dark in nature had overshadowed me.

Holding myself together and with all my strength, we started to run as fast as we could. Hoping that we would soon reach the clearing. I could feel Beth's strength, and her energy helped sustain me.

No matter how fast we were running, I felt a presence, dark in nature, closing in on us.

"The clearing is ahead, and I can see it!" Suzy shouted out.

The whispers of the voices could be heard again, urging me to hurry.

The uneasy feeling about our situation that we were faced with became more intense. As we were getting closer to the clearing, we started to hear the sound of the snarling of a wild animal. As I briefly looked behind, I could see yellow eyes piercing through the woods on our trail, getting closer. At first, there was one pair, then more appeared to our left and right as if running alongside us to get in front.

I could start to feel my heart pound and my breathing becoming erratic. Finally, I began losing consciousness as my vision began to sway on me.

Looking up at Beth, I could see that her focus was on getting to the clearing as soon as possible. I knew I was holding her back, but deep down, I knew she wouldn't leave me behind.

As we reached the clearing, I lost my lower body strength. I soon felt my body go forward, then hit the ground with a thump before rolling over onto my back.

Lying face-up on the ground just beyond the clearing, even though I could barely see, I could hear a scream and then it was followed by a silence as everything went black.

## Chapter XX

# The Seeker

Finding myself opening my eyes, I slowly lifted my head to look round, only to find myself all alone.

Raising my upper body off the ground using my elbows, I wondered what had happened to Beth and Suzy. It took a little time for me to get back onto my feet before gradually standing, brushing off the dirt, to take in the surrounding area.

My arms felt bruised, and my hands were a little sore. As I looked down at my pants, I noticed they were a little torn, probably due to how I fell. I also noticed that the pain in my head had gone.

It was getting late as the sun was starting to set, and the temperature had fallen. Needing to be warm, I rubbed my arms up and down to cause friction to gain warmth.

"I do hope they are safe!" as my thoughts went to Beth and Suzy.

As I became conscious of my breathing, I noticed a white whisper of air leave my mouth.

I knew I needed to make a move, so I decided to continue to head toward the smoke that we had seen earlier. Every so often, glancing back to see if I was being followed.

I looked up at the stars above me as the night sky drew in, and I soon felt a connection, but to what extent? Was this home? I still didn't know. But, finding myself getting closer to the destination felt like my path was lit and guided by a heavenly presence. Bathing me in its glory, reassuring me through the silence and the beauty of my surroundings.

I started to reflect on the time I had spent with the others. How they had been a part of my learnings.

Now appreciating the time given to me as I ventured forward, the more I reflected on this part, the more I felt myself seeking out the truth. Thoughts started to turn into chatter as my mind preoccupied the space with reasoning and often doubt. I knew I needed to silence that chatter, and by taking a deep breath, I focused on finding my answer – the truth. I wasn't sure why we were brought here. Was this real? Is this all in my mind? Maybe there is a truth to all this! Was this where it all began? Is this about me? Or was it to do with our true goal or destination?

Not only was it to find Jane and Henry, but it was also to bring them home. But first, I needed to find Beth and Suzy – Where were they?

I knew I needed to be patient and prayed that an answer would be revealed soon. At least I was in an open space, and with the stars lighting my way, I could see the surrounding areas from the path I had trodden to the path that lay out in front of me.

I started to see a slight whisper of smoke just up ahead. As I walked closer, there was no one in sight. When I arrived, all that remained was some damp, burnt sticks that lay on the ground in a circular pattern.

"Great, I was hoping for some warmth!" I gently voiced with a bit of sarcasm humorously.

I turned around with my back towards the pile of damp, burnt sticks on the ground, looking to see if there was anything I could use to help me get warm. Not having much luck, I soon found myself heading closer to the lake, collecting small branches on the way. I kept an eye out for any potential danger that may lay in wait.

It wasn't long before I felt I had what I needed, and now, it was to find a way to start the fire. I wondered how I was going to achieve this! I noticed before back in the house that it was just a matter of pressing a button, but I knew this wouldn't be as straightforward. Sitting on the ground where the remains of the last fire had been, I piled what I had gathered on top.

Trying to figure out the next step to achieve this, I asked myself, "Now, what do I do?"

I felt the notion of looking around near the fire to see if anything stood out. I soon received thoughts of rubbing two dry pieces of wood together, causing friction to help start the fire – unfortunately, I was unsuccessful. Feeling cold and slightly sore from the fall, I looked up to see if there was any shelter that could provide warmth, but none could be seen.

I knew I couldn't stay here, as I needed to find the others.

With this intention in mind, I started to walk further ahead, following the edge of the lake. I prayed for help to show me the way, but with only the light from the stars to light my way, I soon started to feel tired. Exhausted by the journey, I knew I had to rest to allow my body to heal. Also, finding a resting place that would keep me safe from predators.

I travelled a little further, seeking a haven, somewhere safe to sleep for the night, but this was proving difficult.

It wasn't long before I could hear a rush of water. As I listened closely, it seemed close to where I was walking.

Feeling a little thirsty, I decided to see what refreshments could be nearby.

Following the sounds, just off to the left and a little further ahead, I found myself entering a clearing just after some forest shrubbery and large rocks. Presented before me, I could see a water spring merging from a flow coming from two different directions. The area seemed secluded and enriched in energy. Supported by little lights gathering in the area.

"This looks like a good place to rest!"

The water spring was slightly illuminated by the night sky. As I approached, the water looked clear and welcoming. Assessing the depth, it looked as if it would reach up to my chest. As nobody could see me, I decided to strip to my underwear and step in to replenish myself from the spring. The water felt lukewarm to the touch against my skin.

I could see little lights gather around me. I remember seeing these back in the forest on Jane and Henry's land. Knowing that they were present gave me reassurance that I was safe.

As I rested, I could see dark misty energy leave my body and rise upwards before dissipating into the air. I felt rejuvenated as if all my ills and suffering had been removed.

Was this the shadowy figure that darted towards me in the house before we left to seek Jane and Henry? Had his consciousness attached itself to me? Was this the reason I had the seizure? Like Jane's father, was its intention to possess this body of mine? So many questions had entered my mind.

As I closed my eyes, I soon felt I wasn't alone. Not sure what was in the spring with me, I carefully opened my eyes, only to see a sphere of energy appear iridescent in colour and hovering above the water. Was this the guardian of the springs? As it spoke to me, the voice could be heard within my mind.

"Hello, William"

Not sure how to answer, I responded, "Hello, can I ask for your name?"

"I am known within this form as Selinah".

The sphere then raised from its position and hovered over an area of the ground to my left. Taking on a human form as its energy started to alter. As its vibration changed, it slowly harmonised to a new frequency. Standing before me, I could see the figure of a young woman dressed in white.

"Selinah... where am I?" I asked.

"This space we are in is only temporary. I'm able to reach out to you because of where you are".

"How do you know my name?"

"I have been observing you!"

"Was it you that was helping me earlier?" I asked.

"Yes, as it always has been".

"Are we the same, Selinah?"

"Yes...".

"What happened to Beth and Suzy?" as I was concerned for their life, I queried further.

"They are fine and are waiting for you as we speak".

"Where are they?" I queried.

"The time will come when you will be back with them".

"So, if this is temporary, how did I get here?" I asked.

"William, through your need to know, and for what you seek, please know that you are dreaming – It is through your dreams that I can reach out to you".

"So... then I... suppose none of this is real!"

I could see Selinah smile.

"I must say, William, since you have taken to human form, you have developed an enquiring mind – I can see why you had chosen this path. When fully conscious of what you truly are, you will no longer require asking these questions".

"I feel a lot better having rested", remembering how I felt before arriving here.

"Sometimes the illness is within the mind, William, battling for survival, needing to be the victor of its inherent domain. The mind is fragile and can be easily influenced, governed by beliefs and stigma of oneself and others who you choose to have empowerment over you. The path you are on can be clear only if you choose it. The illness that once took residence in you has left you now".

"Thank you, Selinah...".

"It is time for you to return to the others", replied Selinah.

"Will I see you again?" I asked.

Selinah became energy once more, light and iridescent in colour. Although I did not hear a response from her, it was as though there was no need for one.

Suddenly I was aware of light entering my mind. Finding myself gradually opening my eyes, lifting my head to look around, I soon found myself resting by a campfire. As I raised myself off the ground, resting on my elbows, I could see the shadowy figure of a man. Seeing that I was awake, he began to walk toward me. His face was mostly hidden, apart from the little light that had reflected upon his face.

"It must have been a dream, as Selinah had advised me", as the thought occupied my mind.

I wasn't sure what was happening as things seemed a little hazy, returning from the rest I had.

As the man stood over me, I could still only see part of his face, the part that was revealed by the light from the fire. I wasn't sure what his intentions were and wondered did I have time to react. I could feel his eyes see right through me. As he started reaching down towards me, I wasn't sure if I had time to escape.

## Chapter XXI

# The Trial

A friendly voice could be heard from the direction of the fire, calling out my name. As I turned to face to see who it was, I could see Suzy. From what I could see, she did not look harmed or held against her will.

I felt relieved, and as I looked up, the man's face was partly lit by the fire as he turned to her. It was just enough for me to recognise that it was the old man in my vision.

Realising that he was reaching down to help me up, I accepted his gesture and was surprised that my strength had returned.

"William, please come and join us by the fire?" the old man asked as he greeted me with a smile.

Seeing that I was awake, Suzy then ran over to me and briefly embraced me in a hug. I could see that she was pleased to know that I was OK.

"Where is Beth?" I asked Suzy.

"She is just collecting some water".

I asked the man who stood before me, "May I know your name?"

"I have been known by many, but what and how would you choose to identify me?"

I wasn't quite sure how to answer this one.

Although I couldn't see his energy, I felt at ease in his presence. I felt intrigued and wanted to see what I could learn from him.

"A name to identify you", I replied.

I could see the man smile and then reply, "When you choose a name for someone, ensure you are wise to capture the true essence of what defines them. So, when we talk of them, we know we are speaking a truth".

"What would you like to be called?" I asked.

The old man laughed and then replied, "You have a good sense of humour, William. When you have chosen a name for me, then we shall use it".

I could see Beth and Suzy heading my way, curious to see what had made the old man laugh.

The old man walked back to the campfire, chuckling along the way.

I could see that Beth was also pleased to see me as I was welcomed by another warm embrace.

"So, what was with the laughter?" Beth asked.

"A name", I replied.

"Oh... OK! Whose name and what did you decide on?" Beth responded.

"We didn't .... He wanted me to give him a name".

"Oh - I see!" Beth smiled.

"Earlier, when I fell, I heard a scream!"

Beth went on to tell me that once we had left the forest and entered the clearing, we were no longer being followed. Although the silence had fallen around them, they still felt on edge. With a feeling of unease in their emotions, they knew they were somehow safe but were concerned for me as I had taken a fall. I also learned that the scream was Suzy's reaction to the old man's presence.

I thought about what Beth had said and questioned if the chase had been one of survival. Could it have been a product of induced fear that resulted from the darkness surrounding us? Something I felt inside told me otherwise.

"The old man?" I asked Beth.

"He just appeared! as though he was waiting for us", Beth replied.

Somehow, I felt that the old man was to guide us on the next part of our journey.

I followed Beth to the campfire to find a place to sit. I could feel the warmth that welcomed me from the flames.

The old man started to talk about some of his past, beginning with the stories of his people. I could see that Beth and Suzy were mesmerised by his storytelling.

As I observed them, I soon became aware of Beth and Suzy's aura, as whispery energy of gold and bright yellow could be seen. But, curious, I couldn't see the old man's aura.

I wanted to listen to the old man's memories but felt a calling to the flames of the fire that bathed the camp in its warmth.

As my focus was gently placed on the flames of the fire, I soon found my thoughts drifting to the memories of earlier at the water springs. I was reminded of Selinah as she appeared by the water, smiling at me in iridescent light. It felt like a repeating dream, of a memory from a long time ago. I could feel the warmth of her love envelop me, reminding me of our connection. Curious, I realised now how familiar she appeared to me... My thoughts shifted as I became aware of another appearing on the other side of the springs. This was new, I thought! I was made aware that the other was a visitor for someone in the camp. Although I couldn't determine who they were, I felt their visit was essential to one of us. I began to feel myself return from my memories, opening my eyes. I was again facing the flames of the fire. I could feel the warmth, the cleansing, and the purification of its offering. It wasn't long before I took a rest, closing my eyes.

As I opened my eyes, I was welcomed by the sunrise of a new day.

Turning to face the others, I noticed Suzy had gone. I could see that Beth was restless in her sleep, so I thought I would check to see if I could help her.

Carefully, I moved closer to Beth, where she was lying, and gently placed my right hand over her forehead. I could start to feel tingling sensations within the palm of my hand. Interestingly, there was no heat or light I could feel or see at this time. Closing my eyes, I appeared to be taken to a moment within her life.

Beth was sitting by the bed where her mother was resting. Although she was clear to me, her mother appeared slightly out of focus. I could see Beth was trying to hold it together, as I could tell she was emotionally exhausted.

I began to realise that Beth was revisiting her last memories of the moments of her mother's life.

As I watched her in her dream, there wasn't anything I could do to reassure her that she wasn't alone in her suffering with her mother. I wanted to hug her, but I was only an observer at this time. It was as though history was repeating itself as I started to reflect on the time in the village fayre. I was soon alerted by an alarm that began to sound within the dream, bringing me back.

Feeling a presence hovering over us, I moved back a little and looked up to see what it was.

Standing in front of me, I could make out an apparition of a lady, slim in build with similar facial features to Beth. There was a smile on her face as she looked lovingly down at Beth while she slept.

As I looked at Beth, I noticed that her restlessness had settled. Although she looked contented, I noticed a couple of tears appeared, rolling down her cheeks. I then heard my name resonate in my mind. Looking up, I could see the lady watching me.

"William, thank you for looking after my daughter. Please can you continue to keep her safe? We will see each other again when the time is right. Oh, and tell her that her answer which she seeks can be found in Camarierhn".

The lady, now known to be Beth's mother, faded from view. From what I had learnt from Jane, Beth's mother's name was Emma. She looked so different to the frail lady I had seen in Beth's dream.

I didn't want to wake Beth, so I left her to continue with her sleep. I was pleased that she had the opportunity to speak with her mother.

Looking around, I couldn't see the old man and wondered if he was with Suzy.

Although the day was welcoming, I couldn't help but wonder if this was all a dream, as memories were being revisited. It was as if, within this place, we could build a special connection to those of our past. The more I thought about it, I was curious to see how the day would unfold.

It was easy to be caught up in the moment, sharing in the beauty surrounding me. But, being here with Suzy and Beth, I forgot about Jane and Henry. It wasn't until I made my way down to the lake that random images of Jane appeared in my mind. It felt like Jane was reaching out to me.

As much as this was the place to dwell in, I knew we had to leave. But I first needed to find Suzy and then go back to camp to get Beth.

As I continued to walk past some trees and then past some rocks nearer to the edge of the lake, it wasn't long before I could see Suzy just off in the distance. She appeared to be bathing in the water.

I could see that she couldn't hear me calling out to her. As I approached the water's edge, I received an uneasy feeling. I wasn't sure what I was sensing, but I knew I needed to bring Suzy back to camp.

As I walked around the lake to where she must have entered, I suddenly felt a gut-wrenching pain in my stomach as if my intuition were picking up on something.

"Maybe I should listen to my gut... but what about Suzy" I voiced to myself.

I then heard my name being called, and as I turned to look in Suzy's direction, I tried to make out what she was shouting about. The words seemed to blend as one.

I started to cough without reason as I felt it difficult to breathe.

"What was it that I am not seeing?" I queried.

I paused in my tracks, trying to catch my breath, "It doesn't make sense!"

I began to wonder if what I saw was just an illusion or if this was a place of memories - a hidden side of my memories that I had chosen to forget. Sometimes, fears of our past can be suppressed within our memories.

A voice was soon heard, calling my name from behind me. Turning around, I could see the old man.

"What are you doing here?" the old man asked.

"You had startled me! I have come for Suzy", I replied.

"William, Suzy is not here!"

"But she is ... she is in the water", I responded while turning around to point to Suzy in the water.

As I turned around, Suzy couldn't be seen.

"But she was in there!"

"William, time is getting on. Go back to the camp and be with the others, as it is not safe here!" I heard the old man say.

As I turned round to face the old man, he had disappeared.

I felt a cold shiver run down my spine.

Taking his advice, I quickened my pace to leave the area, heading back to the camp at great speed...

Arriving at the camp, I returned to find Suzy and Beth keeping warm by the fire. It was getting late, and I noticed the old man wasn't anywhere to be seen.

"Where is the old man?" I asked them.

"We haven't seen him", Suzy replied.

"William, are you OK?" Beth asked.

I nodded as to respond to Beth's question

"Where did you go earlier?" I asked Suzy.

"Why?" Suzy replied.

"Just curious, that's all".

"While I went for a stroll earlier, I came across a water spring... not far from here. So I decided to have a short bath in the water and found it refreshing", she replied.

"Did you notice anything strange?" I asked.

"At one point, when I was bathing, I felt I was being watched. When I looked around, I could see no one. This made me feel uncomfortable... I quickly got dressed and soon left, ensuring that I wasn't followed", Suzy replied.

I went on to tell them about what I had felt and seen down by the lake, and I noticed they were unsettled by what I said, especially Suzy.

"Beth, you seem to be preoccupied", as I made her aware of my observation.

"Were you with me earlier, William, at any point this morning? I mean, before you went looking for Suzy".

"Briefly, why?"

"I somehow revisited a dream about my mother. I am sure I felt you close by, within it as if you were watching me".

As this was personal to her, reliving a moment with her mother... I mentioned that I sat with her as she looked restless in her sleep, sending her healing.

I could see that she had somewhat accepted my answer.

It was as if I could reach into their memories, whether of the past or current times. What was intriguing was that the memories that were being manifested were blending into our reality in this place. As I had begun to experience this, I had wondered how long Suzy and Beth would too. I was curious to see if any of my past that I wasn't awakened to would manifest to reveal something about me.

I knew I needed to pass the message to Beth about what her mother had said and where she would find her answers.

"Beth, one other thing that I would like to share with what I heard earlier, I heard the word Camarierhn. Does this mean anything to you?"

"Only that I would overhear stories of it when I was a child".

I could see her ponder within her thoughts that something that had been mentioned in her past could possibly have something to do with her future.

"We need to go", I suggested.

Even though the day was bright, I began to think about what possible dangers may lie waiting for us.

As we started to prepare to leave, we checked that we had everything we came with.

"What about the old man?" said Suzy.

"We had better make a move, Suzy, as the longer we leave it, the less chance we may have in finding and rescuing Auntie Jane and Uncle Henry", suggested Beth.

We knew we couldn't head back in the direction we had come from, as it meant going back into the forest.

As we were contemplating a new direction, I suddenly saw a vision of the path we needed to take.

As per the dream I first had on my arrival at this place, I urged the others to follow and started to walk to the water springs. Beth and Suzy soon caught up, walking beside me.

Our initial destination seemed longer than I initially thought, as the path I had originally taken seemed to be thwarted by obstructions as if to deter us.

"Are we on the right path William?" Beth queried.

"I am sure of it!" I replied.

The temperature seemed to have dropped, and I could feel a coldness of a breeze encircling us. As I looked towards the sky, dark clouds started to appear. Knowing we needed to find shelter from a potential downfall of rain... We looked for the best place to protect the three of us.

Slightly wet, we soon found sanctuary under a large tree, then rested to dry off and gather strength while we waited for the weather to settle. Huddled with the other two, I felt warm and soon closed my eyes.

I started to hear voices, and as I tried to work out who they could be, it was made difficult by a humming noise in my right ear. I tried to open my eyes, but for some unknown reason, it proved impossible. The only companion available to me were the thoughts and voices in my head.

I seemed to be present in my mind again. All I could do now was listen, hoping to find a way to break me from this episode I was now going through.

Remembering that I still had the earring, I held it in my hand to help me establish a connection.

The voices became more apparent, and I could recognise one of the voices to be Jane. I couldn't hear Henry and felt they were somehow separated. Strange as it seems, Jane's presence felt natural as if she had shared in the occupancy of my mind.

"Jane!" I called out to reach her emotionally.

It seemed that even though we weren't together, we were still linked through the connection we had established back when we were at the house.

As I couldn't feel or hear a response, I wondered if this was a one-way channel!

"Jane, it's William... Where are you?"

Still, I waited for a response, but none was received.

"Maybe she's not here", I silently voiced to myself.

I tried a couple more times, but still, I couldn't hear any response. I then realised that maybe I was putting in too much effort. So I decided to relax a little, to see what else could be revealed to me in this state of consciousness. As I settled, I began to see a small, tiny light within the darkness of my mind. The light expanded, revealing the old man sitting by the campfire. The old man seemed to be the key. Could the answer to finding Jane and Henry have been with him the whole time? Is he the keeper of this place? So many questions had populated my thoughts, and It all seemed coincidental by how we ended up with him.

The light started to diminish into total darkness. As I became aware of my body, I could feel the ebb and flow of my life force as I inhabited it. Still waiting patiently, I waited to see where the next part of this awareness was taking me.

Silence soon occupied the space, as my attention was drawn to a memory of when we entered the forest. It was as if I was watching a rerun of the event. This time it started with Beth, Suzy and me sitting around a small campfire in the woods. Beth and Suzy appeared motionless, while I seemed to be waiting for something to happen as if I were an observer of events that were to take place.

Suddenly I could see the three of us walking past us, with myself glancing their way.

Confusing as this was, with the feeling of unease about the prospects of what was chasing us back then, what I was dreading was to soon pass us by.

I could then hear the howls. Although I was just an observer, it was still real for me. All I could do was wait. A short time passed, and still, I couldn't see what was chasing us.

I wondered why I was still here!

As I turned to face the three of us sitting around the campfire, I could only see Beth and Suzy as they sat motionlessly. Where did the other one of me go?

Turning back to face the path, I gasped! Fiercely staring in my direction was a pair of yellow eyes piercing my soul, with not much to its form that I could see, as it was mainly shrouded in darkness. But, all the same, it appeared large and menacing. I became unsettled by the whites of its teeth, and what I could hear as its snarling was directed at me.

I suddenly felt an emotion that I hadn't experienced before. My heart rate increased, and my breathing became erratic. The temperature in my body had also changed. What was more frightening was that my ability to defend myself was absent.

All I could do was face whatever I was confronted with. Every time I temporarily shifted my focus, it appeared closer, every so often snarling. Its yellow eyes grew brighter and more piercing by the moment, and I could feel it was ready to pounce at any given minute. I felt more like prey on its way to being slaughtered, and it reminded me of the time we were back in the other realm.

All I could do was pray! As I did, I could hear gentle voices silently harmonising in tune. I took a deep breath and could feel the love emanating from the single voice, which reminded me of Selinah. I knew I couldn't give in. Trying not to expect the worse, I stood proud in preparation for battle. I could feel clarity enter my mind, and I felt acceptance to embrace the representation of the fear that stood before me.

As the creature drew close, it started to change to human form. It then revealed itself to be the old man who stood before me with his eyes still yellow.

I looked for Beth and Suzy and noticed that they were gone, and then I wondered if they were truly here in the first place.

Facing back to the old man, I could see that his eyes were no longer yellow but brown, as when I first met him.

I felt a little shaken but, all the same, relieved!

"Why?" I asked him.

"This place you have found yourself in is a place we had created for you. To test the three of you to see if you were ready! Your imagination and your memories will be used against you. Be aware that the battle you are facing will play with your mind. Your emotions can highlight your weakness to your enemy, and again, they will be used against you. Both Beth and Suzy need you as their anchor to enable them to help you succeed. Little warrior, deep within you lies something great and powerful", the old man replied.

"Is that why Peter and the others are not with us?" I asked.

"They have gone ahead...".

"William, it's time to return back to the others".

Feeling better, I wondered, "If I had chosen to react differently, would I have failed!"

Before I returned, I asked, "Thank you ... have I earnt the right to know your name?"

I could hear the old man laugh one final time, and then I could see him as he faded from view.

Darkness started to appear and just before the light completely went, in my mind's eye, in front of me stood a wolf reflected in the colour of my hair. I soon had received thoughts that once he was a chieftain warrior, a peacemaker and a respected elder amongst his people.

As the image faded, I soon felt my eyes open. Although finding myself standing in a mist, I noticed that Beth and Suzy were resting, seated on the ground.

I gently rocked their shoulders to wake them both up, first Beth and then Suzy.

"William, how did we get here?" I heard Suzy ask.

Assisting them both as best as I could, I first gently helped them to their feet. I then went on to tell them about what I had seen and had learnt from the old man, who I now know as 'Yellow Wolf'.

"I'm glad I didn't have to go through what you had to!" exclaimed Suzy.

I could tell that Suzy was unnerved by my experience. Once she had settled, we began to walk forward through the mist, hoping that we were finally prepared for what awaited us.

*Chapter XXII*

# The Vantage Point

T he mist started to clear, and we soon found ourselves standing not far from a cliff's edge.

Looking at Beth and Suzy, I could see they were slightly concerned about the way forward.

I decided to take a closer look, to check to see what was lying beyond the edge.

"William, please be careful!" I heard Beth alarmingly voice out.

"I will!" I replied calmly and assuredly to set Beth at ease.

I noticed a slight gust of wind, and knowing I had a small frame, I wasn't ready to be taken over the cliff's edge. So as I got closer, I decided to take the rest of the way on my hands and knees.

As I peered over the edge, the drop to the bottom appeared to be at a great distance from the height where we were. I could see valleys and rivers. Unfortunately, my viewing was somewhat restricted by the onset of dark clouds hovering above some of the lands below.

I turned to Beth and Suzy and informed them of what I could see, and it wasn't long before they joined me, kneeling on either side to see for themselves.

I could see Suzy wiping off the dirt from her hands, voicing a few words of dissatisfaction about two of her fingernails.

"Are we supposed to be down there?" I heard Beth ask.

"I guess so", I heard Suzy respond.

I looked around to see if there was a route that could lead us to the valleys below. As I looked back at where we had come from, I felt that the path we needed to take would be revealed to us – We just needed to be patient.

"Maybe Peter or one of the other angels could fly us down to the bottom", I heard Suzy say.

I smiled and replied, "I am sure a path will be revealed to us".

I took another look below, and from what I could see, Jane and Henry's house could be seen as it would have been laid out on their land. Getting their attention, I then pointed it out to Beth and Suzy.

"Yes... I can see it", responded Beth.

Leaving them both to see what else could be seen, I moved away from the cliff's edge carefully, and when there was a little distance from the edge of the cliff, I returned to my feet.

Looking around from where I now stood, I still couldn't see an entrance that would have led to a path to the valleys below.

I started to question where we were. Why were we seeing Jane and Henry's house within the valleys at the bottom of this cliff?

This made me more curious as to what else we may find here.

I sat down to meditate, and then closing my eyes, I focused on receiving direction and seeing what could be shown.

I suddenly received a vision of Peter. I could see a battle between the angels and the dark forces, represented by warriors cloaked in a black mist that seemed to shapeshift as they fought.

Thinking about what I had just witnessed from the cliff's edge, I couldn't remember seeing any battle being fought below.

As the images of the battle between the angels and the dark forces continued, my emotions began to react with unsettling feelings and thoughts of anxiety.

I knew I needed to focus and breathe deeply to steady myself.

I soon was able to place my focus directly on Peter. He appeared much older and taller than I had initially seen him.

I could hear voices cry out in anguish, pain, and continual suffering of those who fell before my eyes within the vision!

Feeling helpless, I knew that there wasn't much I could do to help them. With that thought alone, the vision faded, and my eyes were opened again.

I noticed that Beth and Suzy were walking toward me, and as they arrived, I told them about my vision.

"I was hoping to get a ride… you know… on the back of an angel", I heard Suzy comment.

Beth smiled at Suzy, "The way your mind works!"

Considering our situation, it was good to see that Suzy still had her sense of humour.

"How are we going to get down to the bottom?" Beth asked.

Suddenly the ground we were standing on started to rumble. I could feel a change occur within the atmosphere around us. It was beginning to be difficult to remain on our feet as the ground beneath us started to give way.

"Look at the cliff's edge… It's coming away!" Suzy voiced out, as she was concerned about our safety.

I began to feel a dull ache on the right side of my temple, and it wasn't long before I could feel the sensation intensify. Trying not to worry the others, I began to focus on my breath to try and ease it.

"We need to get out of here!" Suzy voiced out, again in concern.

They both looked at me as if I had the answer.

"We are here for a reason!" I responded to their concern.

I noticed that Beth was focused on the crumbling edge as it broke away. Although it was getting harder to stand, we moved slightly further back to try to keep a safe distance. We soon noticed that the land was breaking away around us, not just at the cliff's edge.

"We are going to die!" I heard Suzy cry out while holding her stomach.

"Suzy, please breathe... take some deep breaths!" I heard Beth suggest to her.

The rumbling started to ease slightly, allowing us to balance on our two feet.

The dull ache in my right temple increased in intensity, and I started to feel sick... I then received a vision within my mind's eye; this time, I could see Jane.

As I looked at Beth, I noticed she had felt that something wasn't right with me.

"William, are you OK?"

As I was just about to reply, I started to feel dizzy, as everything started to sway. The pain soon became overwhelming, to the point that I felt my eyes had closed, to losing consciousness.

*Chapter XXIII*

# Strange Encounter

As I opened my eyes, and after a short period of being unconscious, I noticed that Beth and Suzy were not with me. Unaware of where I was, I brought myself to my feet and began to take note of my surroundings.

I was no longer on the cliff but appeared to be standing in a wheat field.

I wondered how I had arrived here. Trying not to dwell on it, I knew I needed to continue.

Maybe Beth and Suzy had gone ahead of me!

I could smell the scent of bread as if it were baked nearby. Yet when I checked the area, there were no buildings or villages within sight.

Whispers then started to caress my ears, as I could hear children laughing and playing. Although I couldn't quite make out what was being said, I could feel the emotions supporting the words being relayed between them.

Other sensations began to be felt, stimulated by a breeze that soon encircled and embraced me. As my senses became overloaded with information, I began to see and feel the electricity within the air surrounding me.

Suddenly, I was shown a small village within my mind's eye, then an image of what I had seen from the cliff's edge. Lastly, I was aware of energy, as it appeared to surround me, connecting me to all I could see. The only way I could describe it, the sensation reminded me of ... a spider web with threads linking all aspects of life.

I started to question what I was seeing.

Although I could feel the stimulation of the electricity, my senses returned to their normal state.

I knew that through the vision, I needed to find this village. So I began to make my way forward through the fields of wheat.

From what I remembered, it all appeared much smaller from the cliff's edge, but I knew it was just a matter of appearance and of my perception.

"Where am I?" as I did not recognise where I was, and it looked different from what I had seen from the cliff's edge – I felt slightly confused.

I continued my journey, hoping to find Beth and Suzy along the way.

I was soon alerted to children playing nearby, so I headed towards where the sounds were coming from. It wasn't long before the children were in my sight; a boy and two girls. They looked to be having fun, playing together just outside in a clearing by some trees near a small stream. Manoeuvring myself behind a tree, I tried to see if I could learn anything from them before I approached. Then, as I couldn't establish anything, I decided to step out from behind the tree and walk over to the children.

"Hello", I voiced out, slightly keeping my distance.

One of the girls, who appeared to be the eldest and looked similar to my age, replied, "Hello".

The other two continued to play.

"Where are we?" I asked.

"Don't you know where you are?" she replied.

I shook my head.

"Are you lost?" the boy replied as he joined us.

"I appear to be... I thought I knew where I was!"

"Where are your parents?" the girl asked.

I looked around and noticed that the youngest girl was making circles, creating ripples in the stream's water. But, strange that it seemed, she was also talking to what I could assume to be her reflection in the water.

"I am not sure!" I replied.

"My name is Charlotte. This is Henry, and my little sister over there is Emma. What is yours?"

"Nice to meet you, Charlotte, my name is William".

I now knew their names. It took a couple of minutes to sink in, but it became clear to me! Henry had two sisters, Charlotte and Emma. Although I wondered if I were a part of Henry's memories, this was different, as this felt more real.

"Where do you live, William?" Charlotte asked.

Again, I replied, "I am not sure!"

"You're not sure of a lot of things, William", she replied in response.

I could see Charlotte was trying to understand me and help in her own little way.

"Can he play with us?" Emma replied as she made her way over.

"We'd better get back", suggested Charlotte.

Charlotte seemed older in her years

"Goodbye, William", said Henry.

"Goodbye", said Emma.

Even though it was good to meet them at this age, I wasn't sure if I was transported back in time or what I thought earlier, that I was somehow in Henry's memories.

I started to wave goodbye but noticed Charlotte hadn't moved.

"Would you like to come with us?" asked Charlotte.

"Come with you?" I replied.

"William, It is not safe to be out on your own", responded Charlotte.

I noticed Charlotte extending her left hand to me as an offering to welcome me to join her. I could feel her intentions were honest and genuine.

As I reached out to hold her hand, I felt myself sway and started to lose consciousness.

I soon found myself sitting at an old wooden table. I appeared to be dressed differently, more suitable to the times. In front of me sat Charlotte, and to my right was Henry. Opposite him was Emma. I could hear a lady's voice as she appeared to be talking to someone else from within what I can assume to be the kitchen. Images started to come to mind, from the scent of baked bread to seeing it rise in an oven. I could then see vegetables being picked from a garden and stewed in a pot. The aroma of the food cooking smelled amazing... I could feel myself needing nourishment, accompanied by the slight gurgling sounds that could be heard from my stomach.

"Where are we?" I asked Charlotte.

"At Aunties", she replied.

"Where are your parents?" I asked.

"Ma is in the kitchen with Auntie... Pa is away".

"Is this your home?"

"No... we are staying with our Auntie for a little while".

I wondered what I was to learn from being here.

Turning to face Henry, I noticed there was something different about him, even at this young age. I tried to see if I could learn something from the energy of his aura, but my vision appeared to be limited. As I became aware of his emotions, I could feel his emotional connection to what I could assume to be his father. All were accompanied by his thoughts of having his father back home with him one day.

Turning to face Charlotte, "Charlotte!" I called to catch her attention as she appeared to be in thought, kept amused by something.

"William", she replied.

"Where is your pa?"

"Ma says he's fighting for our country".

I thought about what Charlotte had mentioned. Then, looking back at Henry, I soon became aware of another conscious presence with him. I wasn't sure who this could be, but I noticed a strong bond between them.

I felt a pull towards the kitchen and knew I needed to leave the table. As I started to get down, Charlotte called out, "William, what are you doing?"

"Going to the kitchen to fetch some water".

"Auntie and Ma will be back soon!"

"OK!"

I wondered who could be with Henry. As I looked at him, he appeared to be acknowledging them.

When Charlotte had turned her gaze towards Emma, I managed to get down from the chair at the table. Then, trying not to draw her attention, I made my way to the kitchen.

Standing by the kitchen entrance, I quietly listened to see what I could learn from the adult's conversation. I could just about pick up some words.

"… a while. There is no … him. What are we …? I'm … children … stay".

A different voice was then heard saying, "… dear … stay with…".

The conversation went on, but there wasn't much else that I could gather from the broken words.

Deciding to head back to the table, and as I arrived, I noticed Henry wasn't seated. Looking around for him, I noticed that the main door was open. I felt I needed to follow him.

As I approached the main door, I felt a cold breeze, followed by a shiver down my spine. It was as though someone had walked through me. Suddenly I felt myself lose consciousness.

Opening my eyes, I found myself sitting on a rock next to Henry, overlooking another small stream of water. Losing consciousness added more mystery to what was happening to me.

Henry appeared to be a few years older than he was a moment ago. Had I travelled in time? Hence my blackout! Or was this related to the place I now find myself in?

I noticed Henry appeared to be daydreaming, his thoughts elsewhere and possibly reminiscing on times gone by.

"Henry?" I asked.

There seemed to be no response.

It wasn't long before I felt the same presence I had earlier with him, like before at the table.

I couldn't see who it was but felt it was somehow protecting him.

The sun was bright, basking us from above. We appeared to be sheltered by some trees, just off to our left, which cooled us down from the heat.

My thoughts soon went to the stream, where I was welcomed by a state of solace, which brought about a self-healing to comfort the suffering I had witnessed. One that I had just realised that I had absorbed into my being and surprisingly had not acknowledged.

My thoughts then were taken back to when I first met Charlotte, Henry and Emma.

"The stream where I met them must somehow flow into this one – What was the connection? Why here?" I gently voiced and tried to unlock this mystery.

I began to walk around the area, and there wasn't anything that I could see that stood out. Maybe Henry needed to be the focus of my attention. Moving closer to where he was seated, I waved my hand in front of his face to catch his attention. As there was no reaction from him, I wondered if Henry couldn't see me.

My thoughts went to Beth and Suzy, and then I wondered where they were. I prayed that they were safe!"

A feeling of sadness came over me as Henry came to mind. As I looked at him, I noticed that he was watching me.

"Henry, can you see me?" I asked.

"Henry, it is time to go, as your mother is waiting for you", a voice could be heard from my left.

As I turned round to see who it was, a tall man dressed in a uniform was standing, holding his hand out to Henry.

"Yes, Papa", Henry responded.

Henry then briefly turned to face me as he walked over to the man and softly whispered, "Bye, William".

With Henry taking the man's hand, they started walking back to the house.

It was interesting to realise that the man couldn't see me. I tried to see the family resemblance between them, but there was none. Although he called him Papa, it didn't feel right. I needed to keep focused on what was being unfolded and revealed to me.

I started to follow them. It wasn't long before we arrived back at the house, where a black car was waiting outside. I could see Charlotte and Emma waiting in the car.

I could see Emma waving to me. She looked older, as did Charlotte. I returned the gesture and waved back to her.

As I turned to face the door to the house, I noticed someone watching me. An apparition of a figure of a man in a whispery form. As I acknowledged it, I felt a cold shiver go down my spine.

I then heard my name being called from behind me. As I turned around, I could see no one.

Turning back to face the house's entrance, the apparition had gone. Although some time had passed, it wasn't long before Henry and his mother appeared at the door to the house to make their way to the black car. They were shortly followed by the man carrying some luggage.

"Look after yourself, Mary!" Henry's mother shouted back to the auntie.

Tears could be seen on the auntie's face as she made her way back into the house.

Turning to face the black car, I could see Henry's mother sitting with Henry in the back seat. As the car started to move away. I then started to notice someone else appear between them. As I tried to see who it was, I recognised it to be the apparition of the man I saw watching me from the house. I could see him looking back at me and then nodding to acknowledge me somehow. I wasn't quite sure where this was leading.

I soon heard my name being called out from behind. As I turned around, I couldn't see anyone there. I decided to go back and sit on the rock by the stream to see if I could learn anything else I may have missed from earlier.

Closing my eyes, I took a couple of deep breaths.

I noticed a shadow begin to parade my eyelids, dimming any light that was present. Opening my eyes, I saw the day had turned to night, and the temperature had dropped. I felt the cold embrace me as a slight wind encircled me.

I was sure I could hear whispers, voices calling out to me in the dark. I suddenly heard a noise just off to my right, then quickly turned to see what it was. I could just about see the shrubbery of the woods, gently swaying from the stirring breeze.

As I got back onto my feet, I turned and circled the spot I was on. I couldn't see anything standing out to me. Strangely though, I could feel Henry's presence. It was as if he was occupying the same space.

When I saw him sitting here, was this what he had experienced? Was he seeing what I had just witnessed?

Then it occurred to me that my surroundings had changed. A tree that was on my left was now on my right. Other shrubbery had moved. I began to get a feeling of unease, and I knew I needed to leave. It felt that something or someone was closing in on me as the space around me started to lessen. I felt my breathing change, followed by an overwhelming sense of panic as it began to creep in. Needing to deal with this quickly, I began focusing back on my breath as I could feel myself starting to hyperventilate. Coupling my hands over my mouth, I kept on with the deep breaths. It wasn't long before I could feel my body return to its normal rational state.

"What is it I need to do?"

My thoughts were soon redirected back to the stream. So little could I see before me as the darkness became all-consuming? So, I decided to just head to where I knew where it could be.

The whispers were still resident, slightly more intense than before.

I started to quicken the pace, careful not to fall or catch myself on any shrubbery or a branch that may have fallen to the ground.

The pain that I had experienced earlier in my right temple started to return, causing a feeling of nausea. In addition, my mouth was dry, and my breathing became erratic.

It wasn't long before I had to stop to catch my breath.

I started to feel pain in the right-hand side of my chest, just above the rib cage.

Questions soon appeared in my mind, but the questions were from someone else this time.

"Why are you running? Where are you going?"

I looked around to see who could have said that! I took a few more deep breaths as I couldn't see anyone else in view. Feeling tired, slightly bruised, and worn from the throbbing headache. I knew I needed to rest and looked for a place where I could sit.

"What about the stream?" I thought to myself.

It was at a stream where I first met Henry, Charlotte and Emma, and again Henry was by a small stream before he left with the others.

The whispers in my head slowly started to fade, along with the pain in my temple. As it did, I noticed that I could start to see clearer in the dark.

I started to wonder who had spoken to me.

"William", a voice called out from the dark.

"Who's there?" I responded.

As no response could be heard. I voiced out, "Who are you? Who is calling me?"

"Who are you running from?" the voice once again asked.

The voice then moved from within my thoughts to outside of me, a short distance within the woods.

"What are you seeking?" the voice called out.

As I looked, I could see a shadow of a man watching me, partially blended with the darkness of the woods surrounding me. There was a familiarity about him.

"Who are you?" I asked.

"Henry", I could hear in response.

"Your name is Henry?" I asked.

"My son", I heard in response.

Was he the real father of Henry, Charlotte and Emma?

"William, You have your answer. I am the reason why he did not die that day in the laboratory. He is his father's son".

"What about Charlotte and Emma? Are they like Henry?" I asked.

"Not quite... Henry is special – He needs your help!"

"Is Beth special like Henry?"

I still couldn't see his likeness, as he still stood in shadow, as he continued to respond to my curiosity.

"The bracelet that was gifted to her was from me – It was meant for her... it is her destiny to awaken what was dormant".

"Just one other question! Was it you in the back of the black vehicle as it drove off?"

"Yes".

"So, how are you here with me?"

There was no response at first. Then suddenly, I saw Henry's father split in two.

"Oh, I see... I am still trying to fathom out where I am – I am also concerned for Beth and Suzy".

"My granddaughter and her friend are well and searching for you".

"How do I find them?" I asked.

"Simply open your eyes".

I wondered if his response was symbolic in some way, or was it literally on how he put it?

I looked back toward where I had come from and thought, "This feels so real!"

I turn back to face the father, only to see the shadowy figure dissipate slowly into the stream.

I thought about what he had said about Beth and wondered if he was with us at the time with the village fayre!

Taking a couple of deep breaths, I closed my eyes and thought about where I had initially sat before finding myself here. On opening them, I found myself sitting back on the rock by the stream.

Beth and Suzy were standing before me, calling my name to catch my attention.

"Beth, Suzy, how long have you been here?"

"About 10 minutes", Suzy replied.

"How did you find me?" I asked them.

Beth went on to tell me that soon after I had lost consciousness, the mist had returned. However, it only lasted for a short while. When the mist cleared, not only was I not with them, but they were also standing in a wheat field. She was led to my location by a voice she heard whispering in her left ear.

"How are you both doing?" I asked them.

"I am fine, just need to get on with the rescue", said Suzy.

"I am pleased you are back with us!" exclaimed Beth.

"So, where were you?" Beth asked.

I wasn't sure how to answer this question about how she would take it, but it was only fair for her to learn the truth about her heritage and the bracelet.

Just as I was about to tell her, a gunshot could be heard just off to our right; the bullet had just missed us.

Without delay, we took shelter beside a tree, in between some shrubbery.

"That was close...!" exclaimed Beth.

More shots could be heard .... We could then hear men shouting, heading in our direction.

"We need to get out of here!" I could hear Suzy as she voiced her concern.

"We need to remain calm!" exclaimed Beth.

I noticed a clearing not far from where we were. Strange though it seemed, I was sure it wasn't there before and that it only just appeared recently.

Just before I could inform the others, I received a vision within my mind's eye of an outline of a small person. There was a familiarity, taking my memory back to my dream when I first arrived at Jane and Henry's house. Also, again when I came back from the city. As I looked to the clearing, standing waiting was a young boy, beckoning with his hands for us to follow him.

I turned to Beth and Suzy, only to realise they could also see him.

"Do we follow him?" Suzy asked.

I looked at Beth and could see a smile appear on her face as she became slightly overwhelmed.

"I know who he is!" I heard her say, as I could hear the excitement in her voice.

I felt a cold shiver going down my spine. Who was this boy? What purpose did he serve?

*Chapter XXIV*

# The Chase

We carefully made our way to the clearing as soon as it was safe. When we arrived, focusing on getting to where we needed to be, we noticed that the other boy wasn't there to greet us.

"Where did he go?" asked Suzy.

"I am not sure, but I have a feeling he will show up again", Beth replied.

We knew we needed to remove ourselves from this place and gain a greater distance from the men with the guns.

I suddenly felt drawn to a narrow path that was just off to the left and in front of us. I then made the other two aware.

Quickening our pace, we made our way. The path led us down to a stream, sheltered on either side by trees and kept company by varying-sized rocks.

As I glanced at the stream, which now lay to our right, the water flowed fast and away from us, towards the direction I felt we needed to go.

A slight breeze gently caressed my face and brushed against my hair as we approached.

At this time, we seemed to be alone. It would seem to appear that the men that were after us could no longer be heard.

Stopping to take a breather, I noticed Beth walk over to the stream. She appeared to be looking down at something.

"Beth", I called over to her. "Are you OK?"

It was as though Beth couldn't hear me.

"Beth", I called over again to her.

I could see Beth lower herself down to rest on her knees. Shortly after, she leant forward to touch the water with her fingers.

Curious, I went over to see what she was looking at. As I got closer, I noticed Beth began to hum a tune.

"Beth, are you OK?"

Beth appeared to be totally unaware I was there, standing by her.

I noticed Suzy had then walked over to where we were to see what was happening.

As I looked at the surface of the water. Not only could I see Beth, but I could also see the image of a little girl's face. Recognising it to be Emma, Beth's mother.

I knew I needed to bring Beth out of this state she was in, but I felt at the same time I had to be careful.

"Beth, it's William! Listen to my voice... it's time to come back".

My memory returned to when I first met the children by the stream. Then, I could remember seeing Emma talking to someone. Was she reaching out to Beth?

I felt the need to gently place my hand on Beth's shoulder. With that thought alone, I noticed Beth was consciously returning to us.

"Sorry, William... I was with my mother".

Looking at Suzy, I could see she was intrigued and, at the same time, a little unsettled by what had just happened.

My thoughts then went back to the stream, and I wondered if there had been more to it!

I could see that both Suzy and Beth were smiling at me as I was trying to get into the stream. Although it looked safe enough to enter on the first appearance, I also knew I needed to be careful.

"William, would you like some help?" Suzy asked. "Do you not want to take your shoes off and roll up your pants?" she suggested.

"I'm OK", I replied.

I could see Beth take off her shoes, raise her dress above her knees, and then make her way into the water.

Thinking I might do as Suzy suggested, I fell backwards into the stream as I tried to take my shoe off.

I was pleased it was just a shallow stream, but all the same, I was now drenched. I also seemed to have escaped any injury.

As I pulled myself together and got to my feet, noticing the water was up to my knees, I could see both Suzy and Beth laughing.

"William, are you OK?" Suzy asked as she approached me.

"A little bruised, but I'm fine".

As Suzy entered the water, Beth went back to be with her. I could see them both having fun in the water as there was a lot of splashing between them. It was good to see that they were making the most of it.

The water had a lukewarm feel to its touch. Yet, it felt refreshing, and I felt energised standing within it.

I could feel the energy increase within my body as it rose to my head from my feet.

As I watched Beth and Suzy, it was as if time was slowing down. Not only were they moving very slowly, but everything else around me gradually reduced in movement until it had all stopped.

Suddenly I was shown a vision similar to what I had seen before. I found myself in a wheat field. I could see a web of energy interconnecting where the streams flowed into each other, and it was beautiful to see. I felt the stream was an entry point, leading to other aspects of time and places. I was then shown a waterfall; hidden behind it was the entrance to a tunnel that led to a cave. It wasn't long before I found myself returning, being brought back by Beth calling my name.

"Where did you go?" Beth asked.

I told them about what I had seen.

I noticed a physical reaction from Suzy as her body gave a little upper body shake and a lower body wiggle.

"What was that?" Beth asked her as she started to smile at Suzy's reaction.

"I am not sure... it was as if something had just walked straight through me", Suzy responded.

Listening to Suzy, I was a little concerned. I could see it unsettled her.

"I suggest we return to the path to get dry!" I heard Beth suggest out of concern.

With Beth's help and the sun still basking on us, it wasn't long before we returned to the path, and with her help, I was soon dry.

"Beth, who was the boy?" I asked.

"When I was young like you, he would often appear. Especially when I needed a friend".

I could see Suzy was listening to our conversation. Then, wanting to know more, she approached and asked, "Tell us more? Does he have a name?"

"He would often visit regularly... it was when we moved to another house that was the last I saw him".

"Does he have a name?" Suzy asked a second time.

There was a pause from Beth as I could see she thought back to the time of her childhood.

Just as Beth was about to respond, the weather started to change as clouds began to appear and raindrops started to fall. I could tell that a storm was brewing.

"We'd best find shelter fast!" Beth exclaimed.

We hurried along the path in the direction of where the flow of the stream was heading.

"Look up ahead... A waterfall! William, Didn't you mention a cave behind a waterfall?" Suzy queried.

"Yes, that's right!" Beth confirmed.

I could see that they both were concerned, not just for their own well-being but also for mine.

As we approached the waterfall, Beth told us to wait while she went behind the waterfall to check to see if there were indeed an entrance to a cave.

Both Suzy and I tried to find shelter under a ledge from a rock face that extended outwards. As we waited, we started to be concerned as the time was getting on, and Beth had not returned to us.

"Where is she?" Suzy asked out of concern.

"I am not sure!"

"Shall we go in and find her?" Suzy went on to ask.

I noticed a glow appear on her chest.

"Suzy, what are you sensing?"

"I'm not sure, as I can't feel her! We need to go and find her!"

I could see that Suzy was getting emotional, and seeing her concerns for Beth unsettled her, we decided to go and find her.

As we arrived at the waterfall, we noticed a small entrance leading to a path behind the waterfall. Although dark on the other side, I soon felt a shift in energy as we entered a cave.

"Are you OK, Suzy?"

I could see her nod in her response to my question.

"Do you remember how we created the inner light of the spectral mind?"

"Yes"

Watching Suzy, I could see it wasn't long before she achieved it, responding with a nod. Furthermore, I could see that the glow around her chest was still prominent, ready to guide her through this.

After achieving it myself, we started to make our way further into the cave.

"Like old times!" I mentioned to Suzy with a smile as I was trying to lighten the situation.

As we made our way, the tunnels were short, and it wasn't long before the light of day appeared to us as we reached the end of the cave.

A cry of voices could be heard just beyond, followed by loud noises. Peering out from just inside the entrance, we looked to see if we could see anything, but all looked peaceful.

It reminded me of the battles that others can often go through. A struggle for survival for self-preservation that is often hidden from the eyes of others.

I could see Suzy was shivering, concerned about our situation and the whereabouts of Beth.

My thoughts then went to Beth. Although she wasn't with us, I felt that I did not need to worry. It was as if someone was reassuring me.

"I am sure Beth is safe, Suzy. She is strong enough and is capable of looking after herself!"

Although I could see her smile, something did not feel right. I felt a misplacement of her energy, and I knew I needed to do something.

I looked to see if I could see the energy of her aura, the light around her body. Although the colours were faded and barely visible, the colours red, orange and brown seemed to stand out to me. From this, I knew she was still strong and determined to continue the fight and strengthen our cause.

I wrapped my arms around her to embrace her. It wasn't long before I could feel her energy change as light passed through me to her, creating warmth and an emotional lifting of her spirits. The energy of her aura began to appear brighter.

I took another look outside to see if any movement could be seen, and as I did, I could hear Suzy respond, "Thanks, William, I feel much better!"

Turning around to face her, I could see she was ready for what awaited us, so we moved forward into the clearing.

As we left the cave, the energy of the place changed again to one of conflict, preservation, and survival – We were now standing in a war zone. We could see the light fight against the darkness as souls collided, and warriors fought.

I felt the need to turn around to face the cave, and as I did, I noticed it was gone. We found ourselves on a battlefield.

"Watch out!" I heard someone shout behind us.

From out of nowhere, the angel Peter flew down to fend off, for what we could try to explain was a creature of shadow about to attack us.

"Phew! That was close", I heard Suzy say in relief at what might have been.

"Suzy, William, you both need to come with me, as we need to get you both to a safe place!"

Without question, we kept as close as we could to him as Peter directed us to where we needed to be. Other angels would join us, helping us to reach our destination.

As I looked within the midst of the warzone, dark forces could be seen, materialising from the dark areas on the ground, behind rocks, and in every direction. It could be seen as being in their territory, with the dark forces having the upper hand. As I wondered if we had a chance, I noticed we had help from the Reihasiem. As they could be seen bringing light where darkness fell. It was interesting to see them also shapeshift to counterattack the creatures from the shadows that appeared before them.

I became so absorbed in witnessing what was happening around me that my attention was taken away from Suzy.

I heard my name being called, and as I looked around to see who it was, I noticed something different about Suzy. The energy surrounding her seemed to be protecting her like a force field, a shield of some kind – Maybe it was the pendant. It was like the Suzy I had seen back at the house as she started to fend off the dark warriors with her mind.

"William, we need to hurry!" Peter exclaimed.

I could hear a loud noise, which sounded like shots being fired.

"Go, William, I will catch you up!" exclaimed Suzy.

"I am not leaving you, Suzy!"

"Please, William!" Suzy responded.

Another loud noise could be heard.

"She will be fine!" Peter could be heard as his voice was raised over the noise.

Looking around, I could see the casualties of the war lay near where I trod on the ground around me.

I knew I wanted to stay and fight, but there was little I could do as I appeared powerless, unable to call upon the Sceptre at will.

As we made our way, I kept looking back at Suzy every so often until she was no longer in sight.

As quick as we could, with Peter and the support of a few angels, we made it to an old building.

My thoughts went back to Suzy. I prayed in my thoughts that she would be safe.

As we entered the old building, it appeared larger inside than I initially thought, going by what I could see before entering.

I could see that many were injured and receiving treatment.

"Have you seen Beth?"

"No, she never arrived".

"We have to find her!"

With Suzy outside fighting in the battle, and Beth missing, I began to wonder if we would succeed in our quest.

With that thought alone, I started to feel pain in my right temple. Then, images began to appear of Jane within my mind, seeing her in her home, sitting motionless in the family room. Images then could be seen of Suzy.

"William, your priorities are to find Jane and Henry", emphasised Peter.

"What happened to the Sceptre, to my abilities?"

"We don't know! We just know we can't come with you where you are going – We will continue the fight from here".

I soon heard my name being called from the entrance. It was Suzy... she appeared to be partially injured. There were other angels with her.

"Suzy, you're injured!"

"It's just a slight graze. It will heal".

"You need to rest for a short while to allow the healing to mend your wound", Peter suggested to Suzy.

I turned to face Peter.

"How am I to fight?"

"William, it is not with a weapon that you will win this battle!"

I realised what he was saying. I thought about my battle with the apparition on the bridge back in the village. I needed to rescue Jane and Henry, and I now must apply this wisdom to achieve this.

I could see that Suzy was healing fast, but at the same time, I pondered why they were holding the fort here. What was so important about this place? What was this building we were in?

As I looked around one last time before Suzy and I left, I looked at Peter and thought about putting the questions to him. As the thought entered my mind, I was handed a small water bowl.

"What's this?" I asked.

"A drink before your journey ahead", replied Peter.

As I started to drink, a refreshing feeling came over me. I could begin to feel my eyelids closing. Then, closing my eyes, I soon lost consciousness.

A bright light appeared in my mind, and I wondered if I was experiencing a dream. I could see the old man from earlier, the one we now know to be Yellow Wolf. He appeared to be calling me, but I couldn't understand what he was saying. He was soon joined by the boy whom Beth had known from her childhood. Suddenly images of Beth's face came to mind overriding the vision.

"William", I heard my name being called out to me.

As I gradually started to open my eyes, and with the sun bright in the sky, I could begin to make out the outline of Suzy looking down at me. I found myself propped up by a tree trunk in the wilderness. There appeared to be another standing with her, and as I tried to focus to see who it was, I noticed they had the appearance of Jane.

"Jane, is that you?" I called out while trying to fully open my eyes.

## Chapter XXV

## Within the Shadows

"No, it's me, Suzy...".

I soon felt pain in my right temple again; this time, my eyes became sensitive to the light. To help relieve the pain and the sensitivity, which caused the surface of my eyes much discomfort, I closed my eyes. Then covered them with my right hand to help keep out any residue of light. Shortly after, the pain gradually left. As I removed my hand and opened my eyes, I could only see Suzy standing before me.

"Where is Jane?"

"Jane is not here, William".

"She was standing there beside you!"

"There is only me here".

Suzy went on to explain to me that the water that we had drunk was required to help us with the next part of the journey. She wasn't sure how we got here but felt we were where we needed to be.

I could feel the pain subside, and as I looked around, I couldn't see Peter or the angels. Along with the building, it was all gone. All I could see were trees and the rest of the wilderness keeping us company.

Suzy was able to help me stand and to get to my feet.

"How are you feeling?" I asked.

"I feel great! after drinking whatever was in that bowl – I'll have to get it on tap!" Suzy light-heartedly replied.

It was nice to see her smile as it brought a warmth within me... a little optimism.

"Where do we go from here, William?" Suzy asked.

I knew that we needed to find the path that would lead us to the house I had seen from the viewpoint of the cliff. Taking in the area, I could see two open-trodden paths and another untrodden path that looked as if it could lead us further into the woods. I wondered if the third would provide a shortcut to where we needed to be.

I had no inkling or a feeling of how to move on from here – I felt I was somehow being held back.

"William, any ideas?" Suzy asked.

I thought she had the idea, and maybe Suzy was to take the lead at this time. But then, just as I was about to suggest this to her, I could see her turn to face the woods and then point the way.

Suzy then said, "We need to go this way. The boy who helped us earlier... is there waiting for us. He is signalling for us to follow him into the woods! Can you see him?"

I couldn't see the boy in the direction that Suzy had pointed. As I wasn't sure if what Suzy had mentioned was right, not wanting to cause her self-doubt, I replied, "I can't see him!"

"What do you mean?" she replied.

Suzy turned back to face me. "William, what is happening? Is something wrong?"

"I'm not sure... possibly. When I arrived here, something felt wrong... I feel different to before".

Thinking back to what Peter had mentioned, I pondered to find a reason behind this for a minute! The more I tried and broke down each moment of this quest, the more questions were highlighted. All I could do was go with it and proceed forward with what I knew within my heart.

With this understanding, I began feeling an emotional warmth, followed by a rush of energy. It felt like electricity, similar to what I have witnessed earlier. However, it also reminded me of the clarity I had felt during the last moments I had experienced the other day in the village's cave.

Not noticing, as my thoughts were directed to myself, I looked up and noticed Suzy looking at me with tears flowing down her cheeks. I could feel her emotion as if it had reached out and touched me. Her eyes were glistening as reflecting light.

"Why are you crying?" I asked.

As I began to step to move forward to embrace her to hopefully comfort her, Suzy stepped back.

"Are you sad?" I asked.

Suzy, by this time, was looking at the ground with her hands covering her eyes.

"Suzy... what's wrong?"

Suzy removed her hands away from her face. Then, with tears still flowing, she walked up to me, knelt, and embraced me in a hug. The embrace felt strong.

"I'm sorry, William!"

"What's wrong?"

"Looking at you just then, a bright light appeared around you. I could feel and see it all... in the representation of my life in all its entirety... It felt all too deeply emotional! I stepped back because I realised that you, somehow, are the key to all this! I now understand why Peter placed so much importance on your path".

"Suzy!" I tried to reach out to comfort her.

Suzy moved away, stepping backwards, then wiping the tears from her face.

"In all that has happened. It has always come back to you, William... It's what defines you. It isn't a power or a weapon; it's a truth that will set others free".

Suddenly, we could hear voices calling out to us. Although we couldn't see anyone. We couldn't establish whether they were friends or foes either.

"We can't take a chance, William. We need to head further into the woods! At least we can hide. Even though time is not on our side".

I began to follow Suzy further into the woods. As we moved further, it was getting harder to pass through the gaps between the shrubbery and trees. Making it slightly more difficult for Suzy as she was much taller than me. A coldness started to settle all around us, more noticeable by the whispery white air that could be seen as we breathed out.

I could see that Suzy was tired but determined to get us where we needed to be.

"Suzy, we need to rest!"

"We can't, as it's not safe!"

"I'm concerned about you!"

"William, we are not far! Just a little longer, and then we can rest".

I needed to stop to catch my breath. Then, finding a log, I decided to sit down. I could feel my feet and legs ache from the walking.

I noticed her chest was glowing and wondered if the pendant was alerting her to something!

My attention was then drawn to some rustling to the right of us. Looking over, although not noticeable at first, I noticed as darkness started to move within the shadows.

"They're here!" I could hear her voice out alarmingly.

My hand was soon grabbed by Suzy. I then felt a tug of my body as she pulled me forward to get me to run with her. Although getting tired, weakness started to encompass the frame of my body. I knew I would only hold her back.

The rustling sounds seemed to keep up with us, as whatever was in the shadows was still chasing.

After a short distance, I called out to Suzy, "I'm tired – I can't do this!"

It wasn't long, and due to the lack of strength in the lower part of my body, my leg was caught on a broken branch that protruded out from the shrubbery. Toppling forwards onto the ground, I fell into some shrubbery. I noticed my left elbow was wet as it partly lay in a small hidden stream. The first thing I felt was a pain in my left leg. Looking down, apart from the dirt that stained my clothes, I noticed my pants on the left leg were torn and could see a little blood seeping from the area.

"William, you're hurt? Can you move? I shouldn't have rushed you – this is all my fault!" Suzy called out alarmingly.

Closing my eyes for a brief moment, and on opening them, I noticed Suzy was by my side, checking me over to see what other damage may have been done.

"A little – It's not your fault!" I replied to reassure her and not to lay blame.

While Suzy was checking, I had the feeling to look up and could see a shadow standing over us.

"Hello William – we meet again", a voice came from the darkness.

I then noticed the darkness began to conceal the light around us. A slight tightness was felt around the throat, with gasping of little air. I found myself making a wheezing sound with each in-breath.

Hearing the voice, I noticed Suzy look up and then around us and then back to me.

I could see the fear on her face as the realisation sank in.

I noticed the glow on her chest, and with each second, it grew brighter. It was as if it were reacting to her emotions about our situation. I could then see Suzy rise to her feet, extending her left arm out and to the left, slightly behind her, and with her hand open. Her body was facing me to somehow cover and protect me. Then, a light began to emit from her hand, creating a protective shield that encircled us. Any shadows within its reach were dispelled and no longer present in our view.

I soon found breathing easy, taking a deep breath in and then out again.

"William, are you OK?"

I noticed Suzy seemed to be struggling while trying to keep out the darkness, as it proved to be strong and increasing in strength with each moment that passed.

Surprisingly I started to regenerate, my wounds began to self-heal, and the bleeding stopped.

"Yes, I feel much better!"

"William, I can't hold them at bay for long – If we can try and make it a little further, maybe we can get to the clearing – I need you to be safe".

My attention was drawn back to the stream beneath us. I felt the need to place my hand into the water.

"William, I'm here to help!" as thoughts populated my mind.

"How?" I responded back.

"Hold Suzy's hand, and don't let go!"

"Can I trust you?"

Images of Henry came to mind.

"Suzy, please come close and hold my hand?"

"I'm not sure that will help!"

"Please, Suzy!"

With that, Suzy reached down with her right hand while trying to keep the shield in place.

Trusting the voice within my thoughts, I took hold of Suzy's right hand with my other hand.

"What now!" I voiced out in my mind.

Suddenly, the water absorbed my hand within the stream. I could see Suzy's face as she started to panic.

"Suzy, go with it. I feel Henry's father is trying to help us!"

"How!" she exclaimed.

It wasn't long before we both lost consciousness for a brief moment, only to find ourselves floating in a dark space surrounded by many doorways of light.

"Where are we?" Suzy asked.

"I'm not sure!" I responded.

"Did we die?" Suzy then went on to ask.

"No... I am sure there is a valid explanation for this!"

"William and Suzy, I presume?" a voice we could hear just off to my right.

We both turned round to look. Appearing before us, we could see Henry's father.

"Where are we?" being curious, I asked him.

"You are standing between portals that lead to many dimensions, many worlds. Here, we use thought".

"Are you a ghost?" I heard Suzy ask.

I could see Henry's father smile and then reply, "You see, your dimension is just one of many realities. There is so much for humans to learn! As you can see, a form does not have to be as dense as humans wear it. Many people in your history have evolved beyond the physical as you see it. They now exist to serve humanity within a particular cause. You may reference them as 'ascended masters' or 'ascension beings'. It is often governed by what you define as the 'personality'".

"What about Charlotte, Henry, and Emma?" I responded

"My time on Earth was cut short, in that I agree... it was through circumstances out of my control that had caused me to leave. However, I had never forgotten about them, as I often appeared in their dreams. Although the girls wouldn't often remember their dreams in detail, Henry, on the other hand, would. Henry is somewhat different from the others, which is why both Henry and Jane have been brought here. It was never about the house!"

I could feel Suzy's curiosity directed to Henry's father, wondering who he was. Her thoughts couldn't be clearer.

As if on cue, I could see Henry's father turn to face Suzy solely and respond, "I am Elijah, Henry's father".

"What do they want with them?" I asked.

"They're keeping them captive to keep Henry from discovering the truth about who he really is and the power that's been bestowed upon him – I am pleased they have help in you both".

I noticed that he didn't respond to Suzy's question, but he did give valuable information about Henry.

"So, what now?" I asked him.

"The reason you are here… to help rescue Henry and Jane – William, they know you are here and are looking for Beth and the both of you!"

"Could they be anywhere?" Suzy asked.

"They can't see you now – Hide and blend within the shadows until it's no longer required".

"Is that where we are?" I responded.

"The shadows are a vehicle and, in one way, a means. Use them to your advantage".

"How?" I asked.

"When you stand within a shadow, call upon it, and then the emergence process will commence. You will find yourself in control, manipulating it with your intentions".

"Is that all we have to do?" Suzy replied.

"Thoughts, along with your intentions, are the driving force to manipulate the shadows – Also, use the water streams to teleport yourselves from place to place. Just think of where you need to be, and then the portal will open for you. Remember to be standing in the stream when you do this".

"So, you are saying as long as we stay within the shadows and blend, we will be able to do what they are doing?" Suzy asked.

"That's all you have to do, and you'll need all the help you can get – It will give you the upper hand. That was how I managed to pull you through. It is often called 'shadow emergence'".

Remembering laying partially in the stream, it all made sense now!

"Will they not see or sense us?" I asked Elijah.

"Let's just say that it is one place they will not think to try and search for you!"

"I now feel even much better than I did before!" Suzy responded.

"Only use 'shadow emergence' as less frequently as you can, as otherwise, you will lose yourself to it. It is a bit like your earthly addiction. If you need to remove yourself from the shadow, simply just will it so. Set your intention and allow the process to commence".

"Thank you, Elijah!"

"It is time for me to go. I will be observing from afar so as not to be seen".

"How did you manage to save us? Were you not seen?" I thought I'll ask out of concern.

"It was because of Suzy's protective shield. The shield gave me enough time to bring you here without being noticed. Thank you, Suzy!"

Just as I was about to say goodbye, we soon found ourselves beside some shrubbery near the house of Henry and Jane - the one we'd seen from the cliff's edge.

"Sorry, William, I thought I would try and see if it worked!" I heard Suzy say.

"That's OK... I hope we get the opportunity to meet with Elijah again".

"I wonder where Beth is?" I heard Suzy say quietly.

"Hopefully, she will join us soon", I replied.

Scouting the area with our eyes, it wasn't long before we heard a commotion coming from the wood-chopping area. As we looked carefully to see what was going on, we could see Beth being retained, with her hands tied in front of her. She looked harassed with bruising to the left cheek, accompanied by a cut on her lip.

I noticed that she was pulled along with a soldier on either side, holding her upper arms as she struggled to get free. They seemed to be heading towards the main door of the house. Interestingly to get there, they would need to pass near we were hiding.

"What should we do?" I heard Suzy ask. "We could use the shadows to our advantage to rescue Beth?"

There appeared to be a light source in the sky, lighting up the ground. To ensure this would work for us, I began looking at the route the soldiers closest to us potentially would have walked through. Also, we needed to consider the other soldiers patrolling the area, as we did not want to make a scene to draw attention to us.

"Well, do you think it is a good idea?" I heard Suzy ask.

Knowing that they would pass near where we were, it may draw the soldiers' attention if we could rustle some shrubbery. Then maybe Suzy could put them to sleep, as she did at that time by the conservatory. We could then rescue Beth from her captives.

I decided to share my idea with Suzy.

"That's plausible!" she responded.

Our attention was drawn back to Beth as she was shouting at the soldiers. We couldn't quite hear what she was saying, but I could guess it wasn't pleasing to their ears.

"It isn't going to be easy, as we will need to be careful, just as Yellow Wolf had said", I reminded Suzy.

"I suppose so, William!"

I could feel her anxiousness as her emotions started to stir, knowing we were so close to saving her friend Jane, whom she so dearly loved like a sister.

It was also interesting to feel my emotions heightened as empathy became more at the forefront of my intuition.

"They are getting nearer, William... I will get into position", Suzy went on to say.

Knowing I needed to blend within the shadows, I started to step back to locate a darker space where a larger area of the shadows could be seen.

I could hear the voices get louder as they came closer.

Just as I was about to invoke 'shadow emergence', I became aware that we were being observed by someone or something a short distance from behind us. In that recognition, everything then went black, and I lost consciousness.

*Chapter XXVI*

# Finding the Way

It was as if time had stood still, as the boy that befriended Beth was standing in front of me. He appeared to be looking over my shoulder for some reason and pointing in the direction of his gaze.

I thought about what I would see if I turned around. Should I? Would I like what would be shown to me?

Turning around slowly, Suzy was no longer where I thought she would be. The soldiers and Beth had also disappeared, looking to where Beth was. The other soldiers were still patrolling the grounds but appeared motionless.

I wondered what was going on!

"William", the boy called out.

Turning back to face him, I could feel that he wanted to reveal something to me.

"Who are you, and why are you here?" I asked.

"I am Cole. It's not too late to save them!" he replied.

I thought about what he had said and wondered if he was talking about Henry and Jane or Beth and Suzy.

"So, who are you referring to?"

"William, both Beth and Suzy have been captured and are being kept guarded in the living room. Jane and Henry are somewhere else in the house...".

"Why, how comes, as Suzy was only there a second ago!"

"William... a few hours have passed – Somehow, when you blended, there was a reaction to the emergence process".

I wasn't quite sure where he was going with this one.

"What are you saying?"

"Unfortunately… I am unable to say or even guess at this moment. With all the changes taking place with you… I haven't seen anything like this before. I am trying to say that it will be impossible for you to invoke shadow emergence".

"Are you able to help me get into the house?" I asked.

"Sorry, this is as far as I can go".

Taking a deep breath, I began to analyse my position to see what options were available to me.

I soon realised that Cole was nowhere to be seen, leaving me solely to continue with this last part of the journey. I had a feeling that he had somehow been involved with me not being captured, and I am thankful for this. However, I also felt this would not be the last I would see of him.

I decided to try and observe and learn the pattern and direction of each group of soldiers as they walked on the grounds. This way, a clear path will be revealed, hopefully providing a safe route for me to get to the back of the house. To first rescue Suzy and Beth and then to find Jane and Henry.

As time went on, after establishing where the five groups of soldiers would patrol, I learnt that I could utilise the small building within the grounds and the shrubbery and trees. Being small enough, I hoped to play this to my advantage. However, as it was getting darker and the grounds were slightly lit, I still needed to be careful.

I made my way as far as I could to a point nearest to the wood-chopping area. I knew a patrol of soldiers would pass by soon, so I waited patiently.

It wasn't long before I could hear voices getting closer to where I was waiting. Keeping hidden so as not to be seen. I happened to notice hearing one of them coughing, which seemed louder than the general conversation they were having. As they passed, I checked to ensure that there wasn't anyone following shortly behind them.

Carefully I started to make my way. Just as I did, a torchlight shone in my direction. I managed to quickly lower myself to the ground and kept still. I noticed that I was partially buried in some grass, covering parts of my body. As no voices could be heard, I waited, and soon enough, the torchlight had gone. As quickly as possible, I made my way to the wood chopping area, where I could keep partially hidden by the logs. I knew that apart from the patrols of soldiers, I needed to keep hidden from those who shone torches.

This is going to be much harder than I thought it would be!

Looking in the direction of where the cows would have been, stood in the way was another patrol. It looked like three soldiers were discussing something that had happened earlier. Trying to listen, I could only make about ten words from their conversation.

I heard, "... can be persuasive... trouble... Jane... shoot on sight... those two".

I wasn't sure who they were talking about, but I knew it wasn't safe to be for any of us.

I searched for any small rocks I could find to create a distraction. But first, I had to make sure that after creating my distraction, no other attention was being drawn my way.

After a few minutes, it went quiet. With no other soldiers in sight, I could see it would be safe to continue. I soon identified a tree stump that was situated in close proximity to where the soldiers stood.

"Here goes nothing!" as the thought entered my mind.

I threw a rock as close to the tree stump as I could - I just missed it. Still, though, no reaction from the soldiers. So again, I threw another rock, a slightly smaller one. On this occasion, not only did it hit the tree stump, but it also bounced closer to where they were standing.

The men turned around to see what the noise was. I could see one of them walk towards the rock.

This allowed me to quickly get to the shrubbery and fencing where the cows would have been. I knew I needed to be quiet. Carefully making my way, crouching down, and giving them a wide birth around them. I was about a third of the way to where I needed to be when I noticed one of them appearing in my direction. Although it wasn't lit and darkness was probably sheltering me, I thought I would surely be caught if I did not run at this point.

Realising that I still had one more small rock in my pocket, I took it out and then carefully threw it in the direction of one of the soldiers. Clipping the soldier's leg, it then travelled a little distance from where he had stood. I could see the soldier reach down to see what had hit his leg, and I noticed the others had turned to see what he was doing.

I then quickly continued, making my way to where I needed to be.

"That was close", I quietly whispered to myself.

I then made my way through the shrubbery to the other side of the fence. This would put me halfway to where I needed to be. Although slightly out of breath, I knew I needed to continue. As dark as it was getting, I knew I needed to be calm, taking in deep breaths to help alleviate any reactions within my emotions.

As the next lot of soldiers had gone past, and it could be seen as a clear path for me to take the opportunity to run and to get where I next needed to be, I decided to take a chance.

Sprinting across the field, I could feel and hear my heart thump louder.

"I hope I make it!" as thoughts occupied my mind.

Suddenly I could hear a shot, which seemed to hit the ground just off to my right. I could hear shouting, followed by barking as if directed at me. Every so often, the torchlight would light up my clothing. All I could do was run, changing direction to escape the light and hopefully avoid the sight of the soldiers.

I managed to reach the trees and the shrubbery at the other end of the field. I knew I could probably be sheltered by what surrounded me from the soldiers as I was in the thick of the shrubbery, but I wasn't sure about the dogs.

Having to keep my breath, I wondered if this was all too much for me. Feeling tired and worn out, I could feel the pressure on my eyelids. Struggling to keep them open, I soon found myself drifting off, losing consciousness.

Flickering images of my time with Jane and Henry appeared within my mind as if watching moments captured since being on earth. Each second, I felt a pull on my emotions. It felt strange, as I didn't feel alone, and it was as if I had an audience with me. My thoughts went back to the village fayre. Remembering the angels that surrounded Beth at that time. Were they with me now?

As the images faded, I could hear the voices of Beth and Suzy of our discussions together of times past. Of the humour and banter that we had shared. It was as if I could feel them with me.

Without warning, I felt my soul leave my body, soon finding myself looking down. Laying on the ground was me.

Suddenly I heard a voice to my left, and as I turned around to see who it could be, I could see Cole.

"William, be strong, as help is on its way!"

Suddenly, I felt as if I was thrust back into my body. The jolt had caused my eyes to open. Looking up into the night sky, I felt slightly paralysed as I lay in the shrubbery. I knew I needed to move, and even though help was coming, time was an issue.

At first, I found it a little difficult to move. Then, as I started to raise my upper body, I felt discomfort as I began to ache. I could feel tears flow down my cheeks, accompanied by a feeling of relief. Carefully getting to my feet and brushing down my clothes from the dirt, I started wiping away the tears.

With some effort, trying to get my focus together, and taking it easy, I began establishing my position with those who gave me chase. I noticed that the soldiers and the dogs were no longer chasing me. It was then I noticed something. I could get a glimpse of what could possibly be Cole. He appeared to be distracting their attention. At that moment, I felt gratitude and appreciation for the kindest of actions supporting my endeavour.

Knowing that all the soldiers were at the other end, it was easy for me to make my way to the shrubbery by the patio door.

With a slight headache gradually making itself present, I felt the need to close my eyes. As I did, I could see Jane, within my mind's eye, appear before me.

"It's a trap, William. Please don't go in! They're waiting for you. Run while you can!"

I began to open my eyes, partially wanting to see Jane stand before me.

Slightly confused and alarmed by what I had just experienced, I wondered if this was true or if what I had just witnessed was merely a deception to deter me.

Remembering what Yellow Wolf had mentioned, I knew I needed clarity and focus right now!

The headache started to ease, and as soon as it did, little voices popped into my mind, creating doubt and confusion. They soon adapted to charge me with fear, attacking my self-worth and what potentially could be any failures on my part. As they persisted, the voices became one voice, being of mine. Continued to dominate every area, overriding any other thought.

Taking a deep breath, as breathing became shallow and irregular, I knew I needed to clear my mind of this clutter and eliminate the conflict within my own mind.

I began to imagine that the voices and the thoughts that supported them had gathered. Bringing them together as one entity and centred within a small area within my mind. They were not my creation, so I saw them as independent of my thought process. I then began to place my focus on creating peace and love within the core they represented. From there, I imagined a small ball of universal divine light in my mind occupying that space. With the ball growing in intensity, I could feel the peace and harmony return as the unwanted voices and thoughts gradually disappeared. I continued this exercise until my mind was free and the clarity had returned.

I found that breathing became much easier after carrying out this exercise. I just needed to remind myself to breathe, as focusing too much on the task at hand will often shift the focus away from the self and the need to regulate the breath correctly.

Looking through the patio door windows from where I was standing, there wasn't much I could see – the only thing I noticed was that the room appeared empty.

I thought about what Cole had mentioned, about the help - do I wait!

I started to wonder if this was a test of my character, strength, and, more importantly, self-preservation. It felt like I was kept in the dark, and considering what was happening, I started reflecting on the situation.

What would happen next? I wasn't sure!

Looking at the reflection in the patio door windows and with what I could see of the landscape behind me, there wasn't any movement that could be seen or heard. Instead, it became very quiet, as if everyone and even nature surrounding me had retired for the night.

At first, the door appeared to be locked as I tried to open it. After the fourth attempt, the door became loose and began to move. Peering into the family room and to my relief, I could see no one, especially anyone, that would want to cause me harm.

"Now, to find the others!" I quietly voiced.

As I entered the house into the family room, it felt empty. There wasn't any emotional warmth or association to welcome me. I felt disconnected, yet it somehow brought me closer to Jane and Henry.

As I looked around, there wasn't anything that was out of place. Although dark, with little light and a little cold, I could as well have been back at home instead of this version of it.

I decided to take a quick peek into the hall to see if I could see anything. As I moved closer, a little thud could suddenly be heard behind me. Quickly turning around to see what or who it was, I noticed the patio doors had closed without any intervention.

I felt my heart had missed a beat. Having to steady my breath, I then focused on keeping calm. I tried to justify with logical reasoning, making sense of what was and could potentially manifest within this house.

I couldn't hear any voices from where I stood by the door that would lead into the hallway.

Moving from the family room through into the hallway, I decided to make my way up the stairs, first heading towards Jane and Henry's bedroom. As quietly and carefully as I could as to not make any noise.

As I was halfway up, I had a feeling that I was being observed from more than one location. Turning to look to the ground floor hallway, I caught a glimpse of a shadow quickly gliding low along the floor and then disappearing into the darkness within the study. Turning away briefly and returning my gaze back to the hallway, I caught a glimpse of another entering the family room. It seemed that every time I averted my gaze, there was movement.

"Could they see me?" I quietly voiced.

On that note, I quickly made my way to the door that led to Jane and Henry's bedroom. As the door closed, I placed my ear as close as possible to see if I could hear anything coming from it.

I soon felt another presence from behind, as if making its way up the stairs. A cold shiver could be felt down my spine.

"What do I do?" I thought to myself.

Suddenly I felt someone close, standing behind me.

I could feel the hairs on the back of my neck stand up! Then, moving my head away from the door, I slowly turned around to see who it could be.

Standing before me were Suzy and Beth, and at this time, I felt confused.

"Where did you disappear to?" asked Suzy.

"I am so pleased to see you both. I thought you were captured!"

"We were initially, but remembering what Elijah had taught us, we were able to escape", Suzy replied.

"So, how did you know I was here?" I asked.

"Cole was able to point you out to us. We then could see you enter the house", Beth replied.

"Once we were in, we checked out the other rooms – We noticed you on the stairs".

Had they been the shadows I had seen! It was a relief to have them back with me.

"So, where did you go?" I asked.

"It's a long story, one to share when we get out of here!" Beth replied.

"Did you learn anything of Jane and Henry?" I asked.

"All the answers led to here! I did, though, meet my grandfather... he informed me that he had also spoken with you, William. He approves of you", Beth replied.

"He seemed nice", I responded.

Thinking about what Beth had mentioned... All the answers were here, but where do we go next?

Beth then moved beside me to open the door to Jane and Henry's room. As she gently opened the door, I could see her look in to see if anyone was in the room.

"The room is empty", I heard Beth say.

"Where can they be? With the soldiers guarding the house outside... it doesn't make sense!" I heard Suzy exclaim.

Although I could hear the anxiety in her voice, I knew the best way to help her was to help bring clarity to our situation in its most logical sense.

I then heard myself replying, as if overshadowed, "You both have shown tremendous strength and courage... Just need to finish what has been started. There will be a door of some sort that will need to be found. It may not be what would normally be seen as a door, but all the same, you will need to look at all representations, whether tangible or not!"

"Could they be hidden in plain sight? Say, for instance, within the shadows?" I heard Beth respond.

Thinking about those words that came out of my mouth, remembering how it happened before, back in the city with Jane, I replied, "A possibility!"

Going over where to look first, the thoughts of the parcel we had dealt with earlier came to mind. I then wondered if there were more to the object inside the parcel than we first thought. I thought it would be best to mention it to Beth and Suzy to see if they can add any reason or logic behind it.

"Do you think it is back in the house, William?" Beth asked.

"I'm not sure! The only way to find out is to check downstairs, within the rooms where the parcel was last seen".

Suddenly we could hear a noise coming from one of the rooms on the ground floor.

"We'd best go and check to see who is downstairs", I heard Suzy say.

"Be careful, though!" Beth quietly responded.

With Suzy taking the lead, followed by Beth, we crept to the top of the stairs. We were then trying to look down to see who or what could be seen on the ground floor.

Although we noticed we weren't alone, we could make out someone or something checking the rooms.

"Can you see who it is?" Beth whispered.

"It looks like a child!" Suzy replied in a soft voice.

Suddenly we could hear Beth's name being called.

I had a feeling Beth wanted to see who it could be before she responded, just in case it was a trap.

Beth's name was called again, as whoever it was, was making its way into the dining room.

"Who could be looking for you?" I heard Suzy ask Beth.

I suddenly felt a hand gently touch my shoulder, which sent a cold shiver of energy down my spine. There was a familiarity about it, and knowing Beth and Suzy were in front of me, I carefully began to turn around to see who it was!

I couldn't see anyone, only the door to the room that led into Jane and Henry's bedroom.

Noticing Beth and Suzy being quiet, as I turned back to face them, they appeared to have vanished!

I wasn't quite sure what was happening and soon became unsettled by the notion, as I appeared to be alone again – Were Beth and Suzy really here? I queried as I started to question my sanity.

I knew I needed to focus, despite losing sight of the other two. The house was quiet again, and thinking about the parcel, I thought it best to check out the rooms downstairs, starting with the study.

As I made my way down the stairs as carefully as possible, I looked out for any movement within the dim-lit hallway. I thought about the hand that gently touched my shoulder... Then, with thoughts turning to Jane, I wondered if she was trying to reach out to me.

I soon arrived at the door to the study and noticed that it was slightly open. I tried to see if I could hear voices, but there were none that I could hear. As I opened the door enough to see inside, I looked in, and the room appeared empty. Checking the table, the parcel did not seem to be there. Also, there wasn't anything else that was out of place.

Thoughts soon appeared to me of the living room. Receiving them, I wondered if the parcel would be in there. Leaving the study, I carefully made my way to the living room.

As I turned the handle, the door to the room appeared to be locked. Could the parcel be in there? I tried the handle again, but still no luck. Voices could be heard from inside the room. There was a familiarity about them, and as I listened closely, I could hear my voice and soon recognised both the voices of Henry and Jane.

I couldn't remember talking to anyone in this room and wondered if this was my voice, or if it was, could this be happening in the future?

As I tried to listen, the words appeared to be distorted.

I tried to open the door once more with a little more force, as I was curious to see what was happening in this room. Still no luck!

Looking around, I soon realised that the only partially lit space in the hallway was where I was standing.

"This had to be it – I need to get through this door!" I quietly voiced with self-accomplishment, having found the door that would lead me to Jane and Henry. With even a possibility that Beth and Suzy could also be in there.

I looked around to see if I could try and find something to assist me in getting the door open. Still, I couldn't see anything of use.

Thoughts of the parcel returned to my mind. Turning to face the direction of the study, I felt an overwhelming emotional pull to it.

"Could the key to open the living room door be in the study?" I quietly voiced to myself.

I tried to open the door one more time, but still, it wouldn't open. With the attempt from my end, it was interesting that no one responded from inside the room.

With the study being the only option available, I started to walk back.

As I passed the family room and was just about to reach the study door, I could hear a loud click from behind me. Turning around, I noticed that the living room door was slightly open.

Do I continue to see what draws and awaits me in the study, or do I head back to the living room? It felt like someone was playing not only with my emotions but also with my mind! Remembering what Yellow Wolf had mentioned, I knew I needed to keep focus. Taking a deep breath, I felt an emotional urge to make my way to the study.

Looking back towards the living room, and contemplating returning, suddenly visibility was reduced as darkness started to occupy the space before me.

Had I gone into the living room, would it have been a trap?

Quickly, I stepped into the study, closing the door behind me.

Slowly stepping backwards away from the door and briefly closing my eyes, I soon found the touch of a hand on my left shoulder. Feeling the quickening and deepening of my breath, along with a rapid heartbeat, I wondered what my fate would be. Turning around and opening my eyes, I was back on the first floor, crouched next to Beth.

"Are you OK, William? You look very pale!" asked a concerned Beth.

I could feel a tear being brought on from the relief of seeing Beth and Suzy.

I wasn't quite sure what had then just happened but wondered what to have taken from it. It also seemed that I just witnessed either an insight for an answer or a possible warning that we were out of our depth. It also reiterated to me first-hand the fragility of human life, especially relating to that of emotion and mind.

I was soon embraced with a loving smile and a brief hug from Beth.

"We are here now and will not leave your side!" Beth then reassured me.

I could also see Suzy looking my way with a concerned look on her face.

"I will be fine, knowing you are both here!" I responded to try and reassure them both, considering what was happening.

With Suzy leading the way, we made our way down the stairs to the dim-lit hallway.

"What are your feelings about where to go from here, William?" I heard Suzy ask.

"I feel we should make our way to the living room".

"The living room it then is", I heard Suzy respond.

As we approached, I noticed the door to the room was ajar. Although there were no voices, or sounds coming from the room, I felt emotionally slightly uneased by what we were heading into.

As Suzy opened the door, the room was dark, with very little light to entertain.

"Shall we go in?" I heard Suzy ask.

"What can you see within the room?" I heard Beth ask Suzy.

"Not much, but it feels cold in there!"

I suddenly heard a whisper in my left ear, "It will be OK. For within the darkness, a light will shine, and what is hidden will soon be revealed. This is where you will find an answer".

I informed the other two of what I had heard.

"We'd best go in!" Beth responded.

I could see that they were both unsettled by the notion of entering a dark room with a below-zero temperature, considering what they were wearing.

Suzy entered first, followed by Beth.

Before I entered, thoughts of what I had witnessed earlier in this room started to populate my mind. I knew it was something I had to overcome and take that step. If I didn't, I felt that I would be separated from Suzy and Beth again. It was as though something or someone was still trying to prevent me from reaching Jane and Henry.

As I stepped through, the door closed shut behind me. The three of us stood very close in each other's company within a room saturated in darkness.

"What do we do now?" I heard Suzy ask.

As if on cue, we heard a voice calling out to us.

At this time, I could feel that all our emotions were heightened and on alert.

"It sounds like Cole!" I heard Beth respond.

The environment of the room started to feel different, as we were soon welcomed by a light that embraced us. As the light receded, we soon found ourselves standing in the forest.

"Where are we?" I heard Beth ask.

Taking in the environment, I didn't recognise where we were standing.

Looking into the sky, I could see two moons over to my right and a smaller one to my left. The sky had a tint of mauve and yellow. I could hear the sounds of life echoing through the trees and on the cusp of a cool breeze caressing my ears.

We appeared to be standing by a large tree that seemed to be circled by others. It appeared similar to the one back on Jane and Henry's land.

In response to Beth's question, we soon heard an answer from another who stood out from one of the surrounding trees. With the light shining from his direction, it was difficult to see who it was. It wasn't long before the light receded, and appearing before us was Elijah.

"I am pleased you made it!"

I noticed Beth then quickly approached him and embraced him in a hug.

"Welcome home, Beth!"

*Chapter XXVII*

## The House of Hibahrous

It was all starting to make sense, as realities can become confusing. What is the norm for one life form can be alien, so to speak, for another! Invoking confusion and misunderstanding, and often fear if the clarity has not been revealed.

"The last I checked, we only had one moon in the sky! Where are we?" I heard Suzy ask with a little apprehension.

"This is our home world – Welcome to Camarierhn", responded Elijah.

"So, we're not on earth?" Suzy asked.

"You are far from earth. We exist and resonate in different realities of dimensions than your own – with a different set of laws".

Both Beth and I looked at each other as we recalled our conversation back when we were in the camp with Yellow Wolf. The mention of this place, Camarierhn.

"Are we safe?" Beth asked.

"We need to get you out of those clothes so that you will not be seen as an outsider to our people", Elijah responded.

As Elijah was speaking, I noticed two others join us. One looked to be male, and the other female, carrying clothing for us. They were tall and slender in build.

"Suzhareehen and Jarahanee will assist you", Elijah went on to say.

With a little privacy provided, it wasn't long before we were dressed in the attire of the people who lived here.

"So why are we here? Where are Jane and Henry?" I asked Elijah.

"When you stepped into the room when you were back in the house, you entered a portal to this world. This is the last part of your journey – You will find Henry and Jane in the hidden city of Camarierhn, deep within the forest. When you arrive, head for the House of Hibahrous. They are kept in two separate rooms on the second floor on the south side".

"Are there any guards?" Beth asked.

"There are… We do have help from the inside, ready to support us", Elijah responded.

Curious, I asked, "The living room?"

I could see Elijah knew what I was trying to ask.

"It was the only space that contained a portal that was bridged to this world", Elijah replied.

My thoughts then went back to when I was in the living room the other day at Jane and Henry's home. When I had travelled back into Jane and Henry's past, I discovered more about Jane… before she had lost the baby and what I had learnt about her father. The room was significant then, as it is now from where we had just come from.

"Unfortunately, I am unable to come with you. As you are aware, William, for when we had spoken earlier, I am still to remain hidden, out of sight until the time is right", said Elijah.

"How will we find the House of Hibahrous?" I heard Beth ask Elijah.

"Jarahanee will be your guide. Once you're in the city, he will show you where you need to go. After that, you will be met by another that will help you get into the House of Hibahrous. Once you're in, the rest will be up to you three", Elijah replied.

With Beth by his side, Elijah turned to face Beth, took her hands, and said, "Beth, let your senses guide you. It is your birthright that others will recognise you, especially with the bracelet you wear on your wrist. Once they know who you are, they will assist. Also, there are places within the House of Hibahrous that you will be able to enter where others cannot".

"What about Suzy and William?" I heard Beth reply out of concern.

"They will not have the need to enter, as there is something I need you to see".

I then noticed Elijah had whispered something in Beth's ear.

Turning to face Suzy and me, Elijah said, "It was nice to see you both again".

Elijah and Suzhareehen soon left the area, disappearing back into the forest.

"What did he say?" I heard Suzy ask Beth out of curiosity.

"I will tell you later!" I heard Beth reply to Suzy with a smile. She then turned to me and then winked.

I wondered if it had something to do with me. I was still concerned that there was little I could do due to my size and not having any ability to use any power under my control at this time. I took comfort in knowing that Beth and Suzy still had their bracelet and pendant that was given to them.

Following Jarahanee's lead, we started to head to the city. A little time had passed, and we were still in the forest. I wondered how long it would take!

"Jarahanee, how far now?" I asked.

There was no response to my question. Could Jarahanee hear or even understand me?

While walking, I noticed we were passing some old stones with scriptures on some of them, partially hidden by the shrubbery and trees surrounding them. Curious, I shared my findings with the others. Jarahanee did not appear to be interested – he just waved to move us on. Needing to check, as I felt somehow they were important, I walked over to see what I could see. I could see Beth and Suzy standing patiently while Jarahanee was doing his best to keep us moving towards the city.

The standing stones were part of some structure, similar to the sanctuary on Jane and Henry's land. This one would have been larger in size. Looking at the scripture, it seemed familiar. I could also see images of a figure with light around its head, with others circling him. I knew I had to be careful in wiping away some of the dirt so as not to destroy what could be seen. As I started to try and make sense of the scripture, the language seemed to become clear. I could start to read what was being written.

From what I could see, the scripture referred to a visitor from the skies. They mentioned an understanding of new technologies and advancements within their culture. After what I could gather was two years, he had returned to the skies. There was a lot more text, but that was all I could read, as most writings were worn away. Looking at the figure drawing of the visitor within the images, I could see that he was holding a staff in his right hand. This reminded me of the scriptures back on earth.

I found the scriptures interesting and wanted to know more, but I knew I needed to get back to the others. Just as I was about to leave, something glistened on the ground, reflecting light from the sun. As I bent down to pick up what looked like a gemstone, many flashing images appeared in my mind. Although the light was bright, the images came in fast and went as soon as they appeared - I could only interpret a few. All of which seemed to resemble moments of a time that, although seemed familiar, had reflected moments in history. I felt they had triggered something within me. For that, I knew I was to discover later. I decided to keep the gemstone for what it had shown me and stored it away in a pocket I found on the clothes I was wearing.

I could hear Beth calling out for me to return.

As I started to make my way back over to them, I received a notion that the gemstone would be of valuable use when we reached the city.

"What did you find?" Beth asked.

I quietly shared with Beth and Suzy what I had learned. But, for now, I kept the finding of the gemstone to myself.

"That sounds familiar! I wonder if we would learn more about the visitor when we reach the city", Suzy responded.

It wasn't long before we could see a tall spire reaching upwards from the trees ahead. Ensuring we kept as close to Jarahanee as possible, we soon found ourselves entering through the city's gates. It must have been hidden by an energy-cloaking field of some kind. It wasn't until we entered that we realised how vast and advanced it was, especially how it integrated with nature. Yet, looking from the outside, we couldn't see much.

"I can live here!" I heard Beth comment with a smile.

Each one of us could give a different description of our perception of the place. For me, it was to see how nature was the core component that dressed the buildings and formed the bases of the city. I could see the other two were taken by the beauty of the place.

"Beth", a woman's voice could be heard.

Turning around to see who called her, I noticed it was someone who had her face partially hidden by a cloth.

"Come, please follow me", she requested.

I wasn't sure as a feeling of uncertainty came over me.

"Please follow me, as we must hurry", asked the woman.

I could see Beth and Suzy move over in her direction. As I started to follow, I felt as if I was being held back.

"William, come with us!" Beth called over to me.

"I can't! I am not sure what it is!"

"We must hurry, " the woman reiterated her plea to Beth.

There was something about her that I couldn't put my finger on.

We suddenly started to hear a commotion coming from someone in a crowd of people not far behind the woman. I could see that Beth was torn on what to do.

With Suzy turning to Beth, I could hear her say, "I'd better stay with William. We will catch up with you later!"

"Keep safe!" I heard Beth reply.

After receiving a heartfelt hug from Beth, she soon disappeared out of sight with the others, leaving only Suzy, who soon stood by my side. I noticed the feeling had gradually left me.

"What do we do now?" Suzy asked.

"We just need to find the House of Hibahrous", I replied.

"How?" Suzy asked.

I realised that Suzy was looking to me for guidance within a strange land. I wasn't sure how to answer her but replied, "Our path will be made clear to us. I have a feeling that others will show us the way!"

With no initial guidance, we ventured further into the city, taking in the sights and avoiding anyone that could look official.

"I wonder if we can get any food to eat, I am getting a little peckish", I heard Suzy say.

I deeply admired Suzy and her journey over the last few days.

I could suddenly feel a slight vibration coming from my pocket. As I reached in and took out the gemstone, I noticed it was pulsating coloured light, and I could feel the warmth it was generating.

Turning to face Suzy, I could see that she hadn't noticed what I was doing, as her sight was fixed on trying to see if there was a place that offered food.

The gemstone soon returned to its normal state. I returned it to the pocket to keep it safe, leaving me to wonder why it had reacted that way.

My thoughts went to Beth; I had hoped she would be safe and find her way to where she needed to be. With thoughts turning to the conversation between her and Elijah.

Looking at Suzy, I could see she was looking a little pale and needed a little food and drink to keep her going.

"Are you ready, William? We'd best get going and find this House of Hibahrous".

Not seeing any recognisable faces, I prayed in my mind, calling for assistance.

"William!" prompted Suzy.

As we headed into a busy city area, we started making our way, asking for directions to the building we were seeking. We found it wasn't easy as the response from the locals was either they couldn't understand us or weren't interested. A few were kind enough to assist but were suspicious of us. We were to look for a glass building with a spire that stood opposite a fountain.

A couple of hours soon passed, and I could see that Suzy looked tired.

"Suzy, we should rest!" I called out to her.

"You're probably right!" she responded.

I could see it was starting to get late in the day. Not knowing who we would be coming upon as it was getting dark or who would be lurking in the shadows, I wanted to ensure we were somewhere safe.

As we sat to rest for a short while, sheltered in a small outbuilding, my thoughts returned to the gemstone and how it pulsated with colourful lights. I decided to take another look. As I put my hand in the pocket, I noticed it had gone. It must have fallen out somehow, so I looked to the ground where I was resting. The gemstone couldn't be seen.

Looking at Suzy, I could see she was scouting the area and appeared unsettled by something. Then, turning to face me, she went on to say, "William, I have a feeling we are being watched!"

Acknowledging what Suzy had mentioned, I carefully and slowly circled my spot to see if I could see anyone observing us. Not seeing anyone, I thought it would be best to trust Suzy's intuition, given our circumstances.

Following Suzy's lead, we began to head further in, using the spire to guide us. My concern at this stage was ensuring Suzy was OK.

I could feel the weather change as the day was retreating and bringing a drop in temperature. I noticed that my body was reacting under strain, as I could feel the discomfort creeping in and my feet and legs began to feel sore.

"William, you're shivering", responded Suzy.

I could see that she was also feeling cold.

"We need to find somewhere warm to rest and get out of this cold!" I heard Suzy exclaim.

I could feel my eyelids getting heavy, and not having the strength to fight them, I soon found myself briefly closing them.

"William!" I could hear Suzy calling out my name.

As I pulled the strength to open my eyes, I could see Suzy's eyes were transfixed, observing me. Then, I started to see a glow around her body ... as the colours began to flow to build up her aura. It seemed that the ability to see energies had returned.

"William, you're glowing!"

My attention was suddenly drawn to two men not far from where we were standing. I could see that they were approaching us, and within the darkening of the day, I wasn't sure if they were friendly.

I felt the need to reach out and hold Suzy, placing my arms around her waist, and I was pleased that Suzy reciprocated. Being in this embrace, I soon found myself again closing my eyes in the comfort of Suzy's arms.

Opening my eyes, I was no longer in Suzy's embrace. Instead, I appeared to be lying in a bed in a large ornamental room. The room was decorated in glass and of a rich and regal design. I wondered how I got here .... There was no one else present, not even Suzy!

"Where am I?" as the thoughts entered my mind.

The door to the room appeared to be closed, and sunlight lit up the space through large windows that seemed to extend from the ceiling to the floor where one wall would be.

I felt different somehow as if I was reborn. Looking at my body and checking my hands and face, I was still William but different in some way. I appeared briefly semi-translucent with a slight iridescence of colour emanating from me.

As I lifted myself off the bed, I noticed that I was dressed in clothing that, in one way, seemed familiar, but in another, I felt I had not worn it before.

I decided to walk towards the window to take a look outside. As I did, I saw my reflection and noticed I appeared much taller. I was no longer a child but a young man.

"Am I still in Camarierhn?" I quietly voiced to myself.

I noticed my voice appeared slightly deeper but was also soft to the listening ear.

"Is this my true form?" I again quietly voiced to myself.

As I felt no reaction to the acknowledgement of my reasoning, I wondered if this was another form that gave my essence shelter.

By this time, I could hear voices outside the room, on the other side of the door.

With the uncertainty of this place, I looked for a place where I could hide. I noticed a portable partition which provided an area for the ritual of privacy when changing clothes. Without any delay, I quickly hid behind it.

I could hear footsteps enter the room. Whoever they were, had then walked across to the bed.

"William!" I heard a voice exclaim.

Taking a quick glance, I could see Beth seated on the bed, crying. Suzy was standing next to her. I could also see a couple of men guarding the room entrance.

It was interesting, as I could see the energy of their auras and how they interacted and permeated with the others that joined them.

I knew I had to reveal myself without getting caught. I needed to wait to listen and to have an understanding of the situation here.

"Is there anything else you could remember?" I heard Beth ask Suzy.

"As I said before, only that light started to come from him, and then he collapsed. If it wasn't for the help of those two outside, I wasn't sure what would have happened to us!"

One of the men approached Beth. I heard her instruct him to search for me.

As he left, a lady entered the room and approached Beth with attentiveness. Sitting by her and holding Beth's head on her shoulder, I heard her say, "Dry those tears, dear. If he is wandering, he can't be far".

I could see Beth nod in response.

As I was trying to recollect my thoughts on the lady's identity, I found it difficult as I was still adjusting.

"I need to be by myself! Can you please give me some time?" I heard Beth quietly voice to the lady.

"Of course!"

The lady soon left the room. Just as Suzy was about to leave, Beth asked her not to go. Suzy soon joined her, sitting on the bed with her.

Once the door was closed, I thought it was a good opportunity to somehow reveal myself to them. Removing myself from behind the changing clothes screen, I softly walked up to Beth and Suzy. After trying to catch their attention, I noticed that they couldn't see or hear me.

"Was that your mother?" I heard Suzy ask Beth.

"Yes, I guess!"

"That's it! I knew I had seen her before", I thought to myself.

"I thought you said she died?"

"I thought so too, but there is a lot I am discovering about my family here!"

"Is it true that you are a princess?"

"It would seem so!"

"Who would have thought that I would be mixing with royalty!" Suzy responded.

I could see that she was amused by the mere fact of what she thought she knew of the family, as in the light of this new revelation.

"If your mother is hiding us from your great uncle, how will we rescue Jane and Henry without your great uncle knowing that you are here?" Suzy asked Beth.

"My Grandfather mentioned a hidden chamber with artefacts within. The room held items from times past – One of the items belonging to Gulielmus, the protector".

"Gulielmus, the protector?" Suzy queried.

"It was said by my mother that a long time ago, a ball of light appeared in the sky – A great warrior and peacemaker appeared to our people. No one knew where he came from, but we are where we are today because of him. He was shortly joined by another called Selinah. Between them, they became our saviours for our people during a great war. It is said that within our scriptures, the prophecy speaks of his return within the coming days. How exciting does this sound!" Beth exclaimed.

"Gulielmus! – I wonder who he is?" Suzy replied.

"In the meantime, we will need to find William", I heard Beth say to Suzy.

"I agree, but it is worth knowing where we need to look for him", Beth responded.

"Why does Gulielmus sound familiar!" the thought entertained my mind.

Not paying any more time to this thought, as they both couldn't hear or see me, I decided to follow and observe them until a time I would be able to return to my human state.

"Now we just need to get past the guard", I heard Beth mention to Suzy.

I remembered how we escaped the family room back within the house. It was getting Suzy to put the soldiers to sleep. Somehow, I just need to make Suzy aware of this.

Looking at the energy of her aura, colours of yellow, gold, red and mauve could be seen. With the supporting colours that permeated the initial ones, I could see that Suzy was already planning what to do and having the courage to go through with it.

Extending my hand to touch her energy, to provide answers, I started to transmit thoughts to Suzy of putting the guard to sleep. As the energy of her thoughts became stimulated, I could start to see aspects of gold, white, and yellow, with the support of a metallic blue, emanating around her head. I then noticed orange, varied shades of pink and mauve could be seen fusing within the emotional aspects of her energy. It was as though I had triggered a change that somehow awakened her to other possibilities.

"William is that you!" I heard Suzy exclaim.

"Suzy, what's happening?" I heard Beth ask her.

"I felt William was standing close to us, trying to reach out to me!"

I could see tears flow down from Suzy's cheeks.

"It was as though I felt him reach out to me, but it was different from before!"

"What are you saying? Is he dead?"

"I don't think so...".

"William, can you hear us?" Beth called out.

Knowing that my presence was the only way to provide an answer, I again reached out to both of their energies and projected my image onto their thoughts. I could see that they were starting to be aware of my presence. Something was happening, but I wasn't sure what, as I could feel myself getting stronger, blending with their energies. It wasn't long before I could see them both looking in my direction. I could feel their emotions as they tried to visually comprehend how my form now presented itself.

"William, is that you? You... you look different!" I could hear Beth say as she adjusted her vision to my current form.

I could see that they were both pleased to see me. It was also noted within the colour of both Beth and Suzy's auras, as greater shades of pink and red appeared. I also noticed brown and blue colours shortly introduced into the emotional aspect of Beth's aura.

We were soon interrupted by the guard who made his way into the room.

"What is going on?" I could hear him say. Looking to Beth and Suzy, "Who were you talking to?"

It seemed that only Beth and Suzy could see me.

After I shared my thoughts with Suzy to put the guard to sleep, the guard was soon lying on the floor, unconscious.

It wasn't long before Beth and Suzy lost sight of me, but at least they knew I was there with them.

The soldier was placed on the bed and laid to rest while he slept.

I soon started to follow them as they both made their way out of the room.

"Where do we go from here?" I heard Suzy ask Beth.

"Follow me, but we must be careful. My mother mentioned that the guards were unsavoury and our mission would be jeopardised if we were caught. Especially with great Uncle being alerted of our presence here", I heard Beth reply.

"Your grandfather had mentioned looking for Henry and Jane on the second floor on the south side of the building. I just hope there weren't too many rooms for us to search in", I heard Suzy say.

I followed behind as they dealt with the guards. It wasn't long before they found a route that led to the second floor, as stairs were soon offered through an open archway.

I could see Beth look around to see if anyone had followed them.

I suddenly felt a pull of my energy from Beth as if to seek my emotional support. I could see strands of light move between us, introducing varied colours of red and yellow, supported by slight variations of pink and brown within her aura.

I could also see the exchange of colours between Suzy and Beth as they relied on each other to succeed.

I knew I needed to reassure Beth, to reassure them both. So I extended my energy to embrace both of theirs. Suzy had shivered in acknowledgement of her sensitivity, as confidence was expressed in her smile. As with Beth, I could see her change her posture in how she held herself, as she was ready to lead the way.

"Whatever awaits us on the second floor, we will deal with it together. As we have done before!" I heard Beth exclaim to Suzy.

I became aware of a change in the rhythm of their hearts and their blood pressure.

I could see tiny lights, like the ones I had seen in the forest, which had surrounded me. I then began to feel tingling sensations …. Looking at both Suzy and Beth's energies, they seemed to be more vibrant.

I then heard a voice enter my thoughts, "William, it's Jane… if you can hear me… I can feel you close by – please be careful!"

I wondered if this was really Jane or if it was something else! If this was true, then I needed to let the others know.

As I turned to Beth, I realised our emotional bond had strengthened, as if a deeper inner connection with her had been revealed. Looking into her eyes, I noticed it had caused a change in her energy. It was as though she had also picked up something that had confirmed this.

My energy seemed to provide a cloak of protection for them both, slightly altering the frequency of vibration of their energy to match mine.

"William!" Suzy exclaimed.

I wondered if they could now be seen by the guards. Beth and Suzy looked somewhat relieved and reassured of seeing me.

I was soon embraced by Beth. As she released her embrace, I could see her wipe some tears from her face.

"Beth, are you OK?" I asked her with concern.

"I'm not sure! I have been experiencing these feelings that I am trying to understand!"

We could suddenly hear voices from the stairwell as if they came from the floor above. After hearing a voice that sounded familiar, curiously, we started to make our way to see who it could be!

As we entered through the second floor from the stairwell, we saw Henry, accompanied by three guards. They soon entered one of the rooms.

A memory of the time in the warehouse from the other day came to mind. It felt like I was reliving a moment in time! This I found interesting.

Standing at the stairwell exit that led into the hallway, and although present, we were still invisible to anyone else due to the frequency we were vibrating at.

As we were focused on what was happening, we hadn't noticed two men walking past us, heading to the room that Henry was in. One of them felt familiar! A strong feeling came upon me that this was Bethany's great uncle.

Was this the man who manipulated, overshadowing Jane's father on earth? I wondered.

I could see him turn round in our direction as if being alerted somehow of our presence. As he turned to face the other man, I could see him whisper something to him. As he did, the man left him and walked further down the hallway to enter another room. Bethany's great-uncle entered the room that Henry was taken into.

Turning to face Suzy and Beth, I noticed Beth had gone.

"Where is Beth?" I asked Suzy.

"She had to go. There was something that she needed to do!"

I felt a slight pull of my emotions as if to indicate something was amiss.

"Can I ask you a question?" Suzy asked.

"I will do my best to answer!"

I wasn't sure if the feeling I was getting was related to this question or what we might find in the room!

"How is this possible! Once a child and now a young man?"

"I'm not sure... I get little snippets of memories, but I am sure I will find out in time".

"It is though there is a hidden depth with you that I can't fathom out. It's bugging me as it feels and goes beyond anything I have ever felt!"

"I can't give you an explanation at this time".

Although it wasn't the answer she was looking for, Suzy somewhat accepted it. I felt I would be able to offer a better one once I understood more. I could see that this questioning had affected her energy, as it started losing its frequency of vibration, becoming denser in its form than before.

Thinking about what Suzy had mentioned about how they felt around me gave me food for thought about how I felt about them.

## Chapter XXVIII

# Gulielmus

As Suzy started to make her way to the room. I began to follow her, keeping as close to her as I could. As I did, I began to feel different. The frequency of my energy vibration started to alter in density to match Suzy's.

Turning around having hearing footsteps behind her and seeing me, she whispered, "What has happened! If I can see you, then others will be able to".

I was still the age of a young man and was no longer a child. I tried not to question this as I was sure that there would be a valid reason for why this was happening.

"A possibility, but at least we can rescue Jane together", I replied.

Although I could see Suzy's smile, I wasn't convinced by the expression on her face that she was happy with what I suggested.

As we reached the room where the man had entered, I gently placed my ear to the door, hoping to hear any conversation that had maybe given a clue to what was happening inside.

There wasn't much I could hear, and with time against us, I knew we needed to act. I removed myself away from the door to face Suzy.

From what I could see within the energy of her aura, her thoughts were reacting to her emotions. I could see the colours of metallic blue and varied shades of pink and yellow entwined and merged around the areas of the head and chest region. White shards of light intermittently appeared between the colours as if there was a spiritual influence guiding her. Mauve and brown became the supporting colours to what was already resident within a beautiful display of colours that was represented before me.

I noticed Suzy was observing me.

"It's coming back to you, William, isn't it?"

I replied with a smile.

"When?"

"Only recently... it comes and goes!"

"We might need it!" Suzy replied.

I could see that she was somewhat relieved.

My thoughts went back to Beth having mutual concerns about her safety.

"William, what should we do now!" I could hear Suzy ask quietly, bringing my attention back to our situation.

I noticed that the energy of her aura was no longer visible. Still, remembering what I had seen, I knew that whatever was to happen next, it would be the act of Suzy.

Suddenly I could feel Jane, as her thoughts soon were imposed on mine, or could it be that I was suddenly engaged with the thoughts of her mind? It was as though I was being made aware of what she saw within the room. This reminded me of the moment I first experienced this with Jane on the first day I met her, learning of her dream and that of her brother.

I shared with Suzy what I had learnt and what I had seen within the energy of her aura. I noticed that this had given her the encouragement that she needed to empower her to act. This brought a different side to her, one that I hadn't seen in her before. It was as though she no longer required or needed to seek reassurance. That her confidence and self-reassurance had stepped up to another level.

My thoughts were soon distracted as I could hear an audible voice calling my name within my mind. It sounded like Beth. Turning around to see if I could see her, but there was no one there.

Turning back to face Suzy, I noticed she was no longer standing next to me.

Curious, seeing the door to the room open, I decided to look inside. Walking in, I could see Suzy talking to Jane. The men guarding

Jane were unconscious on the floor, and it was good to see they were still alive.

"William!"

Hearing my name being called, I turned to face Suzy and Jane. I could see that they both were watching me as I observed the men's condition.

Suddenly I felt slightly in a state of unease, a little lightheaded as the room became visually distorted for a brief moment. I found myself soon placing my right hand over the right side of my temple, covering my eye to try to relieve the sensation. At that moment, I could hear Beth's voice in my head, as if she was trying to reach out to me, calling my name.

"William!" I could hear within the room.

I soon felt the presence of two others, one close by and the other embracing me in a hug.

Again, I could hear, "William!" and this time, I recognised the voice to be that of Jane.

As I focused on her voice, I was soon able to stabilise myself. Then, on opening my eyes and not realising that I had closed them, I could see Jane stepping back to stand next to Suzy.

Taking a deep breath, I smiled, as I was so pleased to see her again.

"William, you seemed to disappear and reappear before us!" Suzy exclaimed.

I noticed Jane had been crying. I could see that she was relieved to be with us again.

"You've grown since the last time I saw you! It's something I am going to have to get used to", I heard Jane comment. She then continued to ask, "How are you feeling?"

"Not quite sure, but hopefully, it will all make sense".

I could still feel Beth's presence with me.

"We need to find Henry!" I heard Jane exclaim.

I soon felt a warm, tingling sensation across the palm of my hands. Looking at them, they appeared to be vibrating, with shimmering white energy surrounding them. I then could feel my whole body gently vibrate as though something was occurring. Suddenly my senses were filled with light, blinding me to what I could see. I then found myself in a large hall, where I could see statues and artefacts shimmering with light. It felt like a dream. I could see Beth standing next to one of the statues. As I focused on her, I could see the light etched like a field of energy around her. She appeared to be telling me something, but I couldn't hear her. I noticed her pointing to the statue and then to me. Trying to grasp what she was trying to reveal, I soon found myself drawn to the staff held in its right hand. It seemed to stand out from the statue. This also rekindled memories of the time in the cathedral. Turning to face the statue, the face seemed familiar. The reality I found myself in was becoming more real by the second. Turning back to face Beth, I found I was starting to hear her, from a whisper to her natural voice.

"William, it's you! You're Gulielmus".

Hearing her say those words, a rush of energy could soon be felt throughout my body at every level. I found myself experiencing a cold shiver, as though shaking off the remaining excess energy to stabilise myself.

There was something different about Beth. Most likely to do with the newfound realisation of what she had learnt of this place and the artefacts. The knowledge would have added to her own personal discovery.

Turning to face the statue, I decided to examine the Sceptre. As I briefly touched it, the statue dissipated to iridescent dust and then evaporated. Suddenly I was embathed in light and soon found myself wearing the clothes of the statue that once was. The Sceptre could now be felt, held in my right hand. I could feel the power within the Sceptre run through me, bestowing upon me the powers contained within it.

Looking at Beth, I noticed she was now wearing an emerald robe. With her eyes glistening, she carried a beautiful smile. I could feel my memories starting to return of times past, and I wondered if Beth was a part of it!

"We need to talk, but now is not the time!" I could hear Beth say.

I could feel something stir within me as a feeling of emotional intensity began to build. Wanting to learn more about these newfound feelings, I felt Beth was the only person I could ask.

Walking up to me and briefly placing her finger on my lips, she said quietly, as if she were reading my thoughts, "Another time".

Taking my hands, standing opposite me, she went on to say, "It is time to join the others...". Then, with a smile and a pause, she said, "Gulielmus!"

Light started to surround us both, and as the room began to fade, I could still feel Beth with her hands in mine. Then, closing my eyes briefly, in the realisation of my truth, all memories reflected in images of the past as Gulielmus was shown to me in short sections from a film reel. This fuelled my curiosity even more.

As the light started to fade, we appeared in the hallway, outside the room where I once stood with Jane and Suzy. As we looked into the room, we noticed that Jane and Suzy weren't there.

Suddenly we could hear a commotion coming from the other room, which I had seen Beth's great-uncle enter earlier. The door from the room was suddenly ripped from its hinges and then thrown into the hallway.

As we made our way to the door that led into the room and then carefully appeared within, what we saw, wasn't what we expected to see.

Inside was a portal, iridescent within its colour and structure. What lay beyond it, we had no idea! Our only chance was to step through.

"This shouldn't have happened!" I heard Beth exclaim.

Wanting to understand more, I asked, "What are you trying to say?"

"From what I had learnt from my mother, the city is protected by the Ecriyin magical stones of Emlkuyh. They were brought here to prevent a certain type of magic or phenomena. However, they also had another purpose: to keep the city hidden".

"Emlkuyh, why does that sound familiar?"

"I'm not sure, Gulielmus, but Emlkuyh, according to mother, is a mystical place that very few have visited!"

I wondered if the awakening of my presence here, in the discovery of self, deactivated the protection placed upon the city!

"Are you ready, Gulielmus?"

It was strange that she called me Gulielmus, knowing she knew me as William. I guess it was out of respect for the being that first graced this city and the people contained within.

The last thought that entered my mind was out of curiosity. I wondered if this portal differed from the rest and if our destination would be where all the other discoveries would lead us to!

After acknowledging her request and taking my hand, we entered the portal together.

## Chapter XXIX

## The Enchanted Isle of Emlkuyh

An overwhelming sense of emotion rested upon me as we stepped through. When I tried to understand these feelings, I tried not to over analyse what I was starting to become aware of. It felt like I had come home. The sights were pleasant and refreshing for the eyes to see.

"When mother had spoken of this place, I never thought I would have seen it for myself!" I heard Beth comment as I took in the sights and the sounds of the world presented before us.

I could see that Beth was getting emotional as the beauty of the place was overwhelming her.

Emlkuyh was a place of wonder where the very life force was in touch with every living being. It was both magical and breathtaking. With the vibrancy of nature surrounding us, a spring of water was not far from where we stood. The water springs had a harmony of sound that felt energising and uplifting. There was so much I began to remember of the place, of times I had spent here, that I wanted to share with Beth. I could see she was mesmerised by the colour of the energy that permeated around us. We soon had visitors, varied small life forms that we found welcoming, which shortly encircled Beth. She found them interesting, so it was mutual for the life forms gathered with the fascination of her reactions and her ability to love and laugh.

I soon felt that another presence had joined us. As I turned around to see where my intuition had directed me, I could see Selinah.

"How did you find me?" I asked.

"I have always been with you", she replied and smiled.

"It's good to see!"

"Who are you speaking to?" I heard Beth ask.

Turning to face her, I replied, "Can you not see Selinah?"

"It is only you that can see me", I heard Selinah respond.

"Who is Selinah?" Beth went on to ask.

"Can you remember when I fell as we were trying to outrun the wolves back in the forest? Selinah appeared to me during a dream I had when I lost consciousness?"

I could see Beth's energy had altered slightly, as I could feel her wanting to know more about who she was and our relationship.

Turning to face Selinah, I asked, "Is there any chance she will be able to see you?"

"She will only be able to see me through your eyes".

I knew I needed to play a part by helping Beth raise her consciousness to match mine. Then, calling Beth over to stand to my left. When she arrived, I then gently held her right hand.

"Beth, if you now take a look over to the water springs ahead of us, you may need to look to the right a little".

It took a couple of minutes before Beth responded.

"I can just about see a small sphere of light, like a whispery white iridescent orb appearing just ahead of me".

Knowing that we carry no form within our true essence, I asked her to relax a bit more and have no expectation of what should be. I could feel an energy pass through me to her and wondered if this had helped. It wasn't long before she responded.

"I see her!" Beth exclaimed.

I noticed Beth was getting emotional, for what she witnessed was again overwhelming.

"She's beautiful! Why had you not mentioned this to me before now!"

Looking at Beth, I noticed that her energy was changing, becoming more passive with an acceptance of a truth that Selinah was empathically sharing with her.

As with the truth being shared, all I could gather at this time was that it wasn't for my ears.

Although I was present, my thoughts returned to the café where I first met Beth. At that time, I knew she was different but didn't realise just how important she would be, especially to me.

I soon heard my name being called. I felt myself consciously return to the here and now. As I turned to face Selinah, I noticed they were both looking at me.

"For those you seek can be located within the cavern just off to your north, near the Ecriyin stones. Now that I have imparted this to you, it's time for me to take my leave. But, before I go, I am to tell you that Peter has won the battle and is waiting for you back on the land, back in the house".

After thanking Selinah for her message, she gradually faded before our eyes. Although Selinah was only with us briefly, it was nice to know she was close by, watching over us. It was also good to know that the only battle left to fight is the one that awaits us within the cavern.

Turning to face Beth, she was again enjoying the company of her new friends. As I admired her, my feelings for her were unconditional. I wasn't sure if these feelings could be matched, as they went beyond any depth of emotion and surpassed anything that, within my knowledge, I had felt before. I wasn't sure if she felt the same. I knew I had to put my feelings to one side for now, as I had to focus on what lay ahead of us.

We started to make our way on the winding and rocky path ahead of us. With our minds reflecting on the conversation that we had recently, silence accompanied us.

As my thoughts turned to the Ecriyin stones, I wondered how much they had changed since my last visit. Going by the memories of this place, the stones were magnificent in size and depth of colour – Varied depths of green, orange, and yellow. I could remember how I felt in their presence, as I had felt a resonance of energy that hummed, causing a tingling sensation throughout my body. It was told that when the inquirer was ready and the time was right, it would reveal your true self within the reflection of the central stone that the other stones encircled. In my memory of the times when I had visited, I couldn't see my reflection, only the surface that glistened from the light in the sky. It may just be that my time was never right. It would be interesting to see if Beth had a reflection!

"Do you think the others will be OK?" I could hear Beth ask.

Turning to face Beth, "I am sure, as he will need them".

As we ventured further, we found ourselves walking alongside a little stream that lay to the right of the path we were travelling on. The sound of the water rushing and passing us by in the stream felt revitalising and refreshing to my ears, causing me to relax more. Often, I could feel a sprinkle of the water spray in my direction, as felt on my face and hands. Being in a relaxed state, I soon found my attention focused on the movement of our new little friends. I could see them hovering around Beth as they accompanied us at this point on our journey. It wasn't long before they behaved differently to inform us of something we needed to be aware of. Paying close attention, I could see that the path ahead was blocked. Although it would mean a temporary change in our direction, I needed to ensure that we were safe, as other rocks could be unstable.

Turning to Beth, she seemed to be preoccupied with thought. Wanting to inform her of our predicament, it took a couple of times before she responded to her name. I told her about the insight from our new little friends. Listening to me, I could see that she wasn't herself.

"Something doesn't feel right!" Beth replied hesitantly as to conceal what she was truly feeling inside.

Wanting to try and reassure her, I held her close in my arms. I could hear her breath quicken, along with the pace of her heart rate. I knew then that my thoughts about her emotional state had been confirmed. Taking a deep breath, a feeling of warmth encircled us both. The feeling brought a welcoming sensation of oneness. My thoughts returned to the beach from when I first arrived on earth. First, witnessing the feeling of connection and one of relationship. Initially, it was with self and then with others. Then I remembered the feeling of loss and the desperation of being alone within my own suffering back when I was in the cave. All these feelings were now coming together. Although overwhelming, I could feel them being mutually shared. Not only had we acknowledged them, but it was also accepting the truth they had imparted to us.

With Beth's head slightly resting on my shoulders, I gently expressed a heartfelt reassurance that all would be OK and that she would need to remain strong.

I could feel her heartbeat lessen slightly, along with her breath, as if my words carried the reasoning she needed. Although I could feel her relax, she soon gently raised her head to then align her eyes with mine. I could see that she was crying, with her face wet from the gentle tears that flowed. It looked as if the embrace was lightening her burden, and although I could see that she was upset, along with the tears, I knew that there was more to it. The little knowledge she held from me was causing her to still hurt within. Although I wanted to ask, I knew she couldn't reveal it to me, and I hoped she would share what was troubling her with me later.

"Beth, I would like to ask you something. About these feelings I have?"

Beth had stepped away from our embrace and stood wiping away her tears.

"Not now, please, Gulielmus!"

"But when!"

Beth shook her head to reject the enquiry about my feelings and then started to walk away from me. Ensuring her safety, I soon caught up with her to walk by her side. We remained silent until we had reached the stream where we could cross over.

The stream was shallow at this point, and we were mindful of our steps as we crossed. As we reached the other side, to begin with, we were met by uneven rocks beneath our feet. It wasn't long before we found ourselves on another path. One that we'd hoped would take us also in the direction of the Ecriyin stones.

"Sorry, Gulielmus, it's just me. I'm feeling slightly emotional at the moment!"

"I understand – I think I am falling... I mean to say I am".

Before I could finish the sentence, Beth interrupted as she started to briefly say, "Gulielmus – I".

A loud explosion could be heard just off in the distance.

"What was that!" Beth voiced out loud, seeing her hands covering her ears.

Whoever they were, they didn't sound friendly, and the explosion seemed to be coming from the direction of the Ecriyin stones. Then, as the smoke in the distance started to clear, we could hear the faint distant voices of men. I knew we needed to move forward, knowing we must be close. If the others were in the cavern, this must be a party sent out to find us and prevent us from reaching it.

Taking Beth's hand, we cautiously hurried along the path, trying to avoid being seen in the open. However, it wasn't long before we could hear voices close to our position.

To avoid capture, we knew we had to alter our direction and find a path that would allow us to go around the men. It wasn't long before we managed to find a route that enabled us to climb to a position that would see us above the land and the soldiers that lay in wait. As time passed and the night drew in, we took some time to rest to gather our energy for the journey ahead. Glancing over some smaller rocks by the edge near the rock face, I noticed I was overlooking the party of men in uniforms. Some were resting by a handmade fire, while I could see others were trying to cause damage to the Ecriyin stones. It was as if they were trying to get fragments but were unsuccessful in doing so. As the light of day left us, the night had fully arrived. I noticed that the temperature had dropped. Apart from the handmade fires lit below, the only light provided was from the stars in the skies and the moons that accompanied us in the night sky.

Knowing we had to wait for the right opportunity to arrive for us to then make our move, we knew we had to be patient. The right opportune moment would be just before the first light.

It wasn't long before the temperature was getting to Beth. Being back with her, I could see she was feeling the cold, seeing her shiver. I knew we needed to get some sleep and offered that she could cuddle beside me to keep warm. Although I had received little response from her, I knew I couldn't say anything more other than just to pray for warmth. As I lay with my back against the rock, I soon felt the need to close my eyes as I rested.

Upon opening my eyes, I could gather that some time must have passed. As I could see the sun rising in the sky, I noticed that Beth was gone. Although she was no longer present, I could hear her voice. She appeared to be talking to someone. As I listened, the male appeared to be older and vocal about Beth's journey. The more I tried to make out what he was saying, the more I found it challenging. It was as though I was overcompensating for the emphasis of each word being spoken. I knew I had to be careful not to misinterpret what was being conveyed. I wondered who she was talking to and thought it would be best to check – Especially knowing what we needed to achieve.

Lifting myself to my feet, with the rocks supporting me, I began to see where the voices would lead me. I soon came upon Beth with an elderly man. Standing not too far from them, I remained out of sight. I thought it would be best to catch a glimpse of their conversation.

Although I wanted to call over to her, the conversation between them, I felt, was one to be had, and I also knew this would be good for her. I could see the light of the energy of her aura expand as the discussions went on.

I happened to have heard one part of the conversation with Beth taking her own path. So maybe the last part of the journey was for me alone to take!

I had a lot to say to her! It had never been the right time to understand my feelings when I was around her. I knew they were different from how I felt about the others!

Carefully stepping back, I tried applying reasoning and logic, although this was becoming intense. Still, I couldn't find any to describe what was happening to me.

Listening to their conversation, all I could think of was Beth and making the right choice. I knew I had to go ahead alone to keep her safe!

Like the bird on the beach and with the feeling of loss I had felt then. Even though I was pleased for it to fly and begin a new life. As with Beth, she was where she needed to be, and I knew it wasn't right for me to hold her back.

As I arrived back where we had rested for the night, appearing over the edge of the rock, I noticed that most of the soldiers were asleep. Knowing that Selinah was close by, it was time for me to head down past the soldiers, pass the Ecriyin stones, and then make my way into the cavern.

I found the route I had chosen wasn't easy, as the ground was uneven. Passing through between narrow parts of large rocks, I often found myself misplacing my feet on the ground and losing my grip when holding on to the walls for balance. With the time against me, I knew I had to hurry, which didn't help. About a third of the way down, I could feel that my feet had welcomed a new pain. As the day was becoming full light, I could see my right ankle had carried a little swelling. As I examined the skin further, I noticed a slight reddish-blue discolouration. Feeling tired and finding it difficult to walk, I was soon relieved as I reached the lower ground. Even though I could call on the Sceptre, I had a feeling that using the power to heal me wouldn't work. I wasn't sure why I felt this, but I knew there would be a reason, and it would be best to just go with it. Especially knowing that the Ecriyin stones were close by!

Although there were voices that could be heard, and with the close proximity of soldiers carrying weapons, I knew I would have to make a move to confront them at some point. I felt more assured of my success, knowing I had the Sceptre.

The Ecriyin stones from where I stood were only a stone's throw away. I could feel myself being pulled by the force that resonated within them. I was becoming aware that something was amiss as I started to feel lightheaded, followed by a feeling of nausea. I then began to feel myself sway a little. As much as I could do to try to steady myself, my balance soon left me. I fell forward onto a large rock, just in front and to the left. It must have been a minute or two before I lost consciousness.

I could start to hear a faint whisper of my name being called. Then, focusing on the voice, the words seemed to get louder. Finally, as I opened my eyes, I noticed Beth was beside me.

"Do you feel any discomfort or pain, Gulielmus?" Beth softly enquired.

There was an emotional fragility about her, especially in her voice – I could see that she was worried about my state of health.

Beth continued to examine me to see if any other damage, other than what was noticeably visible, had been inflicted. Being with Beth, I couldn't take my eyes off her, as every part of her was perfect. It felt as if time had slowed down. I could feel the beat of my heart quicken with the tenderness of her touch. I found myself observing her breath, the way her lips moved, which were soft and moist with a hint of red, as she spoke to me. The way her eyes carried depth, like the ocean – They were spellbinding, especially as her eyes met mine. I wasn't sure what was happening to me, but I knew I needed to relax and control these new symptoms causing me to react this way in her presence.

"How did you find me?" I asked.

"It was Selinah! She appeared to me and told me where to find you".

Although I hadn't noticed it before, as my focus shifted to becoming more aware of my body, I could begin to feel a pain in the right side of my forehead. As I touched where the pain could be felt, I noticed my fingers were moist with blood on further observation of my hand. I was pleased that Beth was on hand to treat me. After treating the injury to the side of my forehead and treating my ankle, Beth then helped me get to my feet.

"So why did you leave without me?" asked Beth.

Not having to tell her about the conversation I was aware she was having or how I felt at the time, I replied, "I thought you had gone ahead!"

"Is that the best answer you have!"

Being around her brought out a weakness within me, which I was trying to comprehend! Another side of me that I thought didn't exist until now. Hearing her response, I could tell she wasn't happy with the answer I had given her.

Gathering myself, and with no soldiers in sight, we made our way over to the stones, being careful as trying not to be seen or find ourselves in the line of fire.

I was soon standing next to the stone in the centre, encircled by the others. As I looked around, there wasn't anyone else other than us. I had wondered if they were in waiting, ready to deal with us once we were out in the open.

"What happened to the soldiers we had seen earlier?" asked Beth.

"I'm not sure, but we better be on the lookout".

After scouting the area, Beth walked up to me. Standing close in front, she reached out to gently touch the right side of my face, near the injury, with her left hand. Her hand then began to caress the side of my face. I then noticed the way she was lovingly looking at me.

The feelings I had felt earlier came rushing back, more intense than before.

I could see her lean into me and could feel my heart quicken.

Unaware of what was to happen, anything that had been of discomfort and pain simply went away.

I soon felt her lips softly press against and then gently caress mine. It was like she had triggered certain emotions and sensations that were not known to me before now. On releasing her lips, Beth then embraced me in her arms, with her body pressed to mine. As she relaxed, I could feel her gently place the right side of her head on my chest. All I could do to fully embrace the moment was to reciprocate by embracing my arms around her. It felt warm, and we were one. Fully immersed with our hearts beating as one, I wanted to remain this way forever. As we further embraced, my thoughts returned to the kiss. As I reminisced, it was breathtaking... I was so pleased Beth had acknowledged my feelings for her.

"I love you!" I could hear these three words expressed by Beth.

I knew I had to then respond by acknowledging my feelings for her.

"I love you too!"

"I know..." I could hear Beth respond.

Beth then gently released her arms from the embrace and slowly moved her upper body away from me. Then, turning to face me, she leaned in for another short kiss before stepping back.

"There will be more where that came from later ... but for now, we need to save the others!" Beth continued to say.

"What about the soldiers?" I responded.

"When I checked the area, the soldiers were nowhere to be seen".

Without realising it, the moment we embraced, I suddenly became healed. The wound to the head had gone, and my ankle was no longer bruised or swollen.

In reflection, from the moment I arrived on earth, I began to realise that love, especially how it's expressed through relationships, made me realise the importance of those in my life. We should have mutual respect in all relationships, whether family, friends, lovers, or partners. Being selfless and one without condition, where all parties give to that connection that binds us. It's having that understanding of what we can learn from each other. Learning from our responses and reactions to what is being asked or the situations we find ourselves in. It's how we can feed into our relationship that will bring out the best in one another. So, with my last thought, we need to be mindful of the moment, as every second counts.

It wasn't long before we could hear voices surrounding our space. The voices appeared to be not only those in the present but also of the past and possibly the future! I could only describe it by seeing many apparitions roaming the grounds. Some seemed lost, while others came and went.

"What's going on?" I could hear Beth ask as she was witnessing this too.

"It looks like somehow we are not where we thought we were".

"What do you mean?"

"Earlier, before I fell, I felt a shift, as if something was amiss. It could've been the Ecriyin stones! What if we both had shifted from one vibration to another and didn't realise it!"

"That makes sense, as it was interesting how it was easy for me to find you!"

Thinking back to the church and holding the energy, we had to keep our emotions intact.

"We'd best hurry to the cavern to rescue the others!" I heard Beth respond anxiously.

Taking Beth's advice, we made our way promptly to the cavern and soon found ourselves near the entrance. Looking back, we no longer could we see the apparitions. The soldiers had returned and continued as before, unbeknown that we had been there.

Turning to look at Beth as she was observing and assessing the path ahead, all the questions and conflicted feelings I had felt before our embrace had gone. I felt at peace from the clarity of what I had gained and had learnt of the heart – I was in love.

Beth must have realised that I was reflecting on our moment together, as when she turned to face me, she smiled and then approached. Caressing my face again with her hand, she leaned in to bless me with another kiss and then took a couple of steps back. Although I knew we needed to find the others, I liked how I felt when she did this. I could also sense that Beth also enjoyed the intimacy.

Taking my lead, we began to head into the cavern. At first, there was an eeriness of silence that filled the air. We must have been travelling for over an hour in the tunnels' dim-lit and sometimes dark regions. It reminded me of when I was in the cave near the village. Keeping close, we both ventured further in. We had to go by our inner sense of direction, hoping it would lead us to Jane, Henry, and Suzy. As I looked at Beth, I could see that she remained calm but alert with every step we took. The darkness of the tunnels seemed to have an essence of pretence about them. It was as if they were keeping a secret, causing us both to harbour thoughts that could be detrimental to our mental health and well-being. We needed to focus on the right outcome, seeing our end goals come to fruition. Although I felt we were being watched somehow, it felt different. It was as though another presence within these walls dwelled within this cavern, observing our every move.

*Chapter XXX*

# The Enchanted Isle of Emlkuyh – The Cavern Part I

"I need to rest for a moment!" I could hear Beth say.

Looking for a good place to sit, a flat rock that supported both of us, we then sat to rest. I placed my arm around her to keep her warm and hopefully give her the energy to recover. I could feel the warmth build, feeling her adjust her seating position to make herself more comfortable.

With the Sceptre in hand, I knew we would be safe, especially to what may lay in wait as we moved forward.

A cold chill could be felt from a small breeze from one of the tunnels ahead of us. It wasn't long before a whisper of wailing noises could be heard from one of the other tunnels.

"What do you think it is?" I heard Beth ask.

"I'm not sure!"

Suddenly we could hear scurrying noises, first to our right and then behind.

Beth stood up, unnerved by the situation. In support, I stood up to stand beside her. As I could see with Beth, we both noticed the temperature had dropped, as it felt like someone was breathing down our necks. As we started to circle the spot we were on, we became more alert to anything that would move within our view of the area. Although nothing had made itself known, we remained vigilant.

Was it waiting for us to make the first move? I wondered.

Beth whispered, "Shall we run for it?"

As there wasn't much to see on the path ahead, I knew we needed more light. So, calling upon the Sceptre, I raised it in the air. I then set the intention to light the way ahead, blinding others who wish us harm and preventing them from following us.

Suddenly a bright light pierced the space within the cavern we were in. As it did, we could see multiple shadows diminish from sight. There was also something large, which was impossible to describe because it was partially hidden. To avoid the light, we noticed it had hidden behind the rocks just off to our right.

"Oh my god! What was that!" I could hear Beth exclaim.

Without wasting any more time and while we had the chance, we headed down the tunnel that the light had revealed to us. We needed to gain a greater distance from the creature, as we didn't know whether it was a friend or foe.

It wasn't long before the light had faded, although we knew we were close, as we could hear voices just ahead of us. We assessed our choices as we appeared to be at a junction on our path. We had the option of two tunnels, one steered off to the left, and the other was straight ahead. The only way that felt comfortable was the route ahead. Knowing what else had accompanied us in the cavern, we had to be careful. Not always backtracking our steps would be healthy in some situations. Still, it could also be detrimental to our health and well-being, especially involving others.

I soon felt a sense of echolocation as my senses became fine-tuned by our environment. Closing my eyes, I then allowed my senses to scan the tunnels ahead, hopefully revealing a route that would lead us to the others.

"Gulielmus, are you OK?" I could hear Beth ask.

Although I was still working on the route to take, in response to Beth, I gestured a nod. Still, with my eyes closed, I shared with her what was happening. I could feel her grip strengthen as she held my hand.

Focusing on the voices, it wasn't long before I could single out Jane's voice. As I did, it was as if I was there with them. Jane, Henry, and Suzy had their hands tied and were guarded by five soldiers. I noticed Beth's great-uncle wasn't with them. As I ventured slightly further into the tunnel, I could see two large statues guarding a doorway that was partially buried in rock. I could see scriptures written on tablets around it. Here was where Beth's great uncle could be found, accompanied by four others as they were examining the scriptures. Intrigued, I wanted to try and see who the statues had portrayed.

I soon could hear my name being called by Beth to bring me back.

"Gulielmus, I'm not comfortable here. Can we please go?"

"Of course, we need to head down the tunnel on the left, and shortly there will be an opening to a larger part of the cavern. We will find a hole at the far end that will lead us into another open area. That is where we will find the others".

The scurrying noises could be heard again, not far from where we had stood.

I could see Beth was unsettled. Taking her hand, we both headed through the tunnel, increasing our speed as we headed to our destination. We were soon in a large open area of the cavern. As we reached the centre, I felt the need to stop.

"Why are we stopping?" I could hear Beth ask.

Suddenly we could see the floor a short distance from where we stood, which had encircled the spot we were standing in, had filled with dark mist.

"What are we going to do?" I could hear Beth prompt me.

Suddenly out of the mist came tormented soulless shadowy creatures.

Although considering our predicament, I could see a resilience to her strength when I turned to face Beth. A sense of focus, bravery and courage had empowered her, and I could tell she was ready. Remembering what happened at the village fayre, I had a feeling and a possible insight into what would happen next.

Suddenly with her arm raised outwards, a thrust of energy was pushed forward from all sides, wiping those caught in its path from the area. However, it wasn't long before the mist and the soulless creatures reappeared. They seemed to come from everywhere.

Looking at Beth, I could see she was ready to do it again.

This time we noticed that the mist was denser than before, and the creatures had multiplied.

I knew this time I needed to help her. As I began raising the Sceptre, we suddenly heard a large thump behind us. Feeling our balance misplaced, the ground we stood on started to rumble. Turning around, we could see the creature that we had seen earlier. It was huge, larger than we first thought. I found it interesting how the mist reacted to its presence. We were surprised to see that the soulless creatures from the mist appeared to be more focused on the larger creature that joined us.

As the battle was in play, we could hear the larger creature give out a loud wailing sound as if to cry out for help.

"What's happening" I heard Beth voice out, concerned for the larger creature.

"I'm not sure!"

"Shouldn't we help it!" Beth exclaimed.

Suddenly we could hear another loud wailing. Lifting my Sceptre, I started to set my intention, to destroy the soulless creatures attacking the larger creature. As I began, further wailings could be heard coming from different directions around the cavern. From nowhere, we were soon in the company of a number of these large creatures, appearing from different entrances. Again, with the intention set, suddenly, a piercing light appeared, mainly focusing on the ground. We could see the light clear the mist. The light remained for a further period until every ounce of it was entirely eliminated to prevent the soulless smaller creatures from appearing. Any of the smaller soulless creatures that had remained were confronted and dealt with by the larger creatures.

With the mist gone, for now, we were soon encircled by the larger creatures. Not sure what would happen next, we noticed that a smaller of their kind appeared from an opening of the others, as they parted to one side to allow it through. We could then see it walk towards us.

"Gulielmus, it is good to meet you again, as it has been a long time, my friend!"

Looking at Beth, I could see how she looked at me in wonderment, as she couldn't believe what was happening.

"There were rumours that you had returned. I'm sorry that we had to meet again under these circumstances. However, now that you have returned, the time has come for us to act!"

I could recognise the tone of the voice was feminine, but the voice wasn't familiar.

"Don't worry if your memory has left you! We are here also to help you remember".

Suddenly as she walked a few more steps toward us, she transmogrified into a human.

"You're shapeshifters!" I heard Beth say.

"My name is L'Aisrell, and I represent the Caserhien people".

L'Aisrell looked elegant, beautiful, and serene. She went on to say that she first met me when she was a child. That one day, like with Beth's people, I had disappeared. That it was an honour and privilege to stand amongst my kind.

"What do you know of my kind L'Aisrell?" I asked.

"You come from a race that exists from one of the highest dimensions of consciousness to set out to explore the lower realms. The form you wear now satisfies us, and we find it pleasing to our eyes. Your kind has graced our dreams for a millennium. Through a sequence unbeknown to us, you and another had appeared to us. It was our honour and gratitude to have you both in our presence. Through Selinah, we gained the power and knowledge on how to take another form. You, yourself, wanted to experience the matters of the heart. It was through your curiosity to experience love in its most tangible and broken form, even with its frailties. From then, you decided to incarnate. To experiment further by continuing to lower your vibrational density of self. To experience raw emotion within one of the densest forms that could be offered within this universe. This was when you decided to further discover relationships and the true essence of exploring and knowing love. You can operate at this level because of Selinah and now Beth".

There was a pause before L'Aisrell went on to say, "The Sceptre is only an extension of you - but you know this already!"

As I started to listen, the words began to trigger memories and awaken me to a truth of a life that I once was sheltered from.

"What is she saying, Gulielmus?" I could hear Beth enquire.

Suddenly we could hear an explosion coming from the direction from where the others were kept that I had seen in the vision

"Although there is more to be told, we must go!" L'Aisrell responded.

L'Aisrell turned to her people, and as she started to walk toward them, she began to transform back into the creature. Within minutes they had all disappeared from our sight.

"You haven't responded to my question!" Beth went on to say.

"I'm still discovering and learning about who I am – There is still so much I don't know. For instance, my relationship with Jane and Henry. You know where I'm trying to go with this, don't you?"

"Yes, I do, and you can depend on me", replied Beth.

"Shall we find the..." Beth soon interrupted me as she placed her finger on my lips to quieten me.

"Just one thing!" she went on to say.

Beth then embraced me, holding me tight as if to claim some sort of reassurance and comfort. I can only assume it was the uncertainty of what we were leading ourselves into. What seemed a long time was only minutes. Beth then released her hold, and as she did, she then leant in for another kiss. As we parted lips, she smiled and said, "Just in case!" This was followed by a short giggle as she stepped back a few steps. I could see she was observing me for my reaction. I could feel the excitement as my heart filled with joy in response to her attention. Seeing that she added a little light playfulness to tease me a little to help lighten our situation was good. Although we were heading into a battle, all I could do now was think of Beth on how I enjoyed her company and her banter, especially the way she teased me!

"You know we can stay here a little longer!" I responded and then smiled.

"Although that is tempting, we need to go!" she smiled and then winked.

As we made our way, my focus and eyes were on Beth as she took the lead, especially in the way she held herself as she walked – I was captivated by her! At moments, I could even feel my heart flutter. It was as though she was sending me little signals to let me know she was there, that I needed to know it.

We soon reached the hole I remembered seeing in the visual exercise earlier. As we looked through, the place where I had seen the others was empty.

"So where are they?" I heard Beth enquire as my focus was checking the area on the other side of the wall.

After assessing the area, it wasn't long before we began to enter through the hole. We then found ourselves in another large opening space of the cavern. I decided to walk over to where Jane, Henry, and Suzy were last seen. As I reached down to touch the ground and see if they had left anything behind, I suddenly started to receive a visual insight. I could see Henry with his hands tied together behind his back. He was being pulled away from Jane. A short struggle could be seen with Henry as he tried to fight them off. With a little heavy hand, it wasn't long before they could remove him from the area into another tunnel. I noticed Jane and Suzy's hands were tied in front of them instead of behind them. Although I couldn't make out what she was saying, I noticed Jane was emotionally voicing something out loud to one of the soldiers – It looked a bit intense. It wasn't long before they began to be removed from the area. It was only when they had taken six to seven steps that the explosion we had heard earlier had occurred. At this moment, both Jane and Suzy were on the floor. The vision then stopped after that.

As Beth wasn't near me, I called over to her and shared what I had seen.

Shortly the ground began to rumble, causing a shift in my balance as I tried my best to keep standing upright. Then, turning around, I could see Beth on her left knee and her right hand supporting her upper body as it lay flat to keep her from falling onto the ground.

"Are you OK?" I asked as I went over to help her stand.

"I will be fine; just give me a second!"

While I waited, Beth started to wipe away any dirt from her left knee and then wipe away the dirt from her right hand.

As soon as she was ready, we made our way into the tunnel I had seen Henry being taken into. As we ventured further in, we were careful not to make any noise so as not to draw any attention to us. With myself in front, avoiding contact, we soon found ourselves overlooking the area where we had a good position to see what was happening. It was cosy enough to keep each other warm. Considering where we were placed, we could pick up the conversations of those below.

As I started to assess, apart from Henry, Jane, and Suzy, I could see eleven soldiers with weapons. I could also see Beth's great-uncle with four other men. I also had a closer view of the statues as they were unveiled from the controlled blasts on the rocks that encased them.

The statues were of two figurines guarding a doorway that was closed shut. On closer inspection, I noticed the one on the left was me, as I am now. The other was of Selinah.

"Do you see what I see? – Isn't that you and Selinah!" I heard Beth ask.

Suddenly we could hear a commotion coming from below.

I could then see Henry as he was forced to approach a platform in front of the doorway. I noticed they had untied his right hand to place it on one of two plinths.

I could then see Jane, again like Henry, being forced to approach the platform.

"What are they doing with them?" asked Beth.

"I'm not sure, but I feel the result will be detrimental for them!"

"We should help them!" I heard Beth, out of concern, suggest.

Suddenly I received a soft whisper in my left ear, "Gulielmus, it's Selinah. They will be safe! Stay where you are, as help is on its way!"

Turning to Beth, I relayed to her the message I had just been given.

I could see that Beth was getting anxious.

As I looked below again, I noticed Henry and Jane were on the ground.

"Please, let's help them; they could be dying!"

I could start to see tears appear and then flow from Beth's eyes.

Another soft whisper could be heard, "Remember, you are not the emotion, but the intelligence and the facilitator for its use".

Seeing Beth in this state, I needed her to somehow be at one to reconnect with her true higher self. I needed her to glimpse the bigger picture. Gently taking her hands, then passively looking into her eyes, I started to look deep to reach into her inner soul. Once I could connect, I asked her to close her eyes. I soon felt something pass through me into her. I could then see Beth was in a deep state of relaxation, and I was pleased she could achieve this. It wasn't long before I felt my own eyes close.

I soon began to hear another soft whisper, "The eyes can deceive, as not what all you see is the truth but an illusion to lead you away from which you seek. So believe and trust in what you know. Not just of the mind, but one that involves the heart".

I was soon distracted by hearing raised voices, higher than normal. I wasn't sure how I left Beth, but I found myself looking over the ledge to see what was happening below. As I tried to see what was happening to Henry or Jane, they were nowhere to be seen. Instead, seven soldiers were lying on the ground with three other men who had accompanied Beth's great-uncle. Curious, I noticed he wasn't there.

Wanting to go and investigate, I knew that Selinah had asked me to stay where I was. I knew it would be for a good reason if she asked me.

I soon noticed a portal as it began to appear in front of the doorway. As I kept my eyes on the portal, curious to see who would come through, I hadn't realised the men on the ground had vanished. It wasn't long before Selinah appeared from the portal, and I could see she was waiting for someone. After what seemed five minutes, Beth's great-uncle appeared.

Questions started populating my mind to understand the truth of what I could see. It didn't make sense to see Selinah with Beth's great-uncle.

Taking a deep breath, I began recalling the messages imparted to me recently. Especially the message about what the eyes can perceive.

Suddenly I could see Beth's great uncle thrush a sharp-pointed object into Selinah's back while her back was turned. Selinah soon fell to the floor with blood saturating her clothes. It was then I saw the portal close.

I then noticed the dark mist as it saturated the ground and consumed Selinah.

I wanted to first shout, but there was no voice as my emotions began to build. I started to feel anger and suffering for the loss of Selinah, and I so wanted to carry out justice on her behalf. However, my thoughts became clouded as I became judgemental towards myself, redirecting the blame inwardly.

I soon felt a passiveness welcome me, realising that my eyes were opening as if awakening from a dream. I noticed that I was still holding Beth's hands. Gently releasing them, I looked over the ledge and noticed that everyone was still there. It was a relief and felt good to see that Jane and Henry had recovered and were being brought to their feet.

I wasn't sure what had happened or what I had just experienced. But, it made me realise how emotions, if not dealt with intelligently, can dictate and incorrectly direct energy to cause harm. To not just only affect others but potentially also self. I also realised that if we allow our emotions to influence our perceptions, we find ourselves being the judge and jury. We will then live under the dictatorship of our own emotional creations.

Now that I understood this, I felt it was time for us to rescue the others.

Reconnecting back with Beth and holding her hands, she opened her eyes. As she did, she leaned over to kiss me gently but briefly on the lips and then said, "Thank you".

I soon heard another soft whisper of words, "Hi Gulielmus, it's Selinah, thank you for listening to me. It is time".

I thought about what I would consider a warning of a potential outcome. But even though it was a vision of some sort, I couldn't dismiss what I had seen. Also, when Selinah mentioned time, what was she actually referring to?

I needed to start with the dream and wondered what Selinah was trying to show me. Did she know more about what was going on? Was she even keeping something back from us?

Looking below, I could see that whatever they were trying to achieve wasn't working. As I observed further, the men appeared to struggle to understand the writings on the base of the statues and tablets.

Helping Beth off the ground, we decided to carefully make our move to rescue Jane, Henry, and Suzy.

We soon found ourselves within close distance of Suzy. We had noticed that the soldiers, apart from one, appeared to be more focused on Jane and Henry. They were near the plinths, next to Beth's great uncle.

Hiding behind a rock, we needed to catch Suzy's attention. Although a soldier was standing next to her, forcibly holding her forearm, it was a good place to start.

Taking some small stones from the ground, we threw them one at a time, as close as we could get to Suzy. It was on the fourth attempt that we managed to achieve this. Once we had her attention, we needed Suzy to try and lure the soldier away from the others.

With Suzy looking our way and seeing us, I noticed that she tried to warn us off carefully and quietly. We could then see her silently whisper, "Go, it's not safe!"

Seeing her react this way, we wondered why she wasn't using the powers bestowed upon her by the necklace.

Suzy then again silently whispered, "Go, go now!"

Although the soldier couldn't see what she was saying, he noticed that she kept looking in one direction. Pulling on her arm, we could see her turn back to him. The soldier turned to face our direction, scouting the area where we stood. Fortunately, we managed to avoid being detected. Quickly and carefully, we lowered ourselves further behind the rock.

"What's wrong with her?" asked Beth.

Remembering when we first entered the cavern, I asked, "What aren't we seeing? I mean, we had encountered L'Aisrell and her people, who, from memory, I'm still trying to recollect!"

"She did know a lot about your past!" Beth commented in reply.

"We also encountered the mist and the shadowy creatures that came from it", I added to Beth's observation.

"In which I would prefer to keep my distance from!" Beth responded.

There was a moment of silence between us, taking note of everything we had seen and felt since entering the cavern.

"Gulielmus", I heard Beth whisper to me to catch my attention as my thoughts were analysing the dream I had.

As I turned to face Beth, I realised that a possible answer was facing me all the time – Was she the missing link?

Choosing to be mindful of her, I listened to what she had to say, which I had found easy.

"If this is the illusion, we don't appear to be getting closer to the battle. What I mean to say is that everything to me appears to be an observation. If you take your memory back to when we were fighting the creatures, did that really go down the way we thought it did? Even to the point, to what we could see while observing from above. The cavern could be a test for us both. Challenging our thoughts and taking advantage of how we feel. Not only about each other, but those we know - our family and friends!"

Even though everything felt very real, there was still an element of truth to her words.

As we both looked at each other, I wondered what would happen next. I could see by the expression on Beth's face that she was also thinking the same. Taking her left hand with my right, we then made our way to the statues.

"Where have they all gone" I heard Beth enquire.

"I'm not sure", I replied.

Noticing that the area had been untouched, Beth began to check the area near the statues, including the tablets and the plinths.

"It as though no one has been here!" Beth voiced out.

"Maybe we had gone back in time before the others had arrived", I replied.

"Even if this is true, surely there must be a reason to support this!"

Hearing Beth's response, if we were in the past, maybe we had to preserve and protect the statues from any abuse or misuse in the future.

Seeing Beth over by the plinths, I had the feeling to join her, as I felt it could be significant.

"What do you need me to do?" she asked.

As I arrived to be with her, it was as if I had received the answer, "I need you to help me activate the portal".

"Do you know where this portal, when activated, will take us to?"

As I tried to recollect, the memories started to return.

"Yes, I remember now! It would enable us to travel to a destination known only to our kind. From there, we would be able to reach the higher realms, where great universal power and knowledge would be bestowed upon those that would venture on this path. It was there that both Selinah and I were able to gain access to reach across and establish a presence in this world. Selinah and I regularly travelled through this portal, using this gateway. Sadly, Selinah had trusted another that took advantage of her physical form while here. From that day, she had closed the portal. Selinah decided to no longer enter this realm within a body that matched this vibration and density".

I could see deeper colours of red and pink around her mental and emotional regions appear within Beth's aura. It can only be by how she felt from hearing what I had conveyed about Selinah's betrayal. I also started to recognise something new, a particular signature of energy that could only be found with my kind.

"Do we know who it was?" asked Beth.

"Yes, I do now – It was your great uncle! He was young at the time, and although he had shown great enthusiasm, there was a darkness within him that Selinah wanted to help him with – From time to time, she still looks out for him".

"But why!"

"As I took on the challenge of understanding love, Selinah made it her goal to bring light, along with compassion, to save the souls where darkness dwells!"

"So why doesn't she challenge him!"

"She will, but when she feels it's time".

I had wondered what had been passed on to Beth back when she first met Selinah. I remember seeing a change within Beth at the time.

But, because I was infatuated with her, I hadn't really paid much attention. As with L'Aisrell, Selinah must have altered her DNA by adding her own to Beth's – This is why particular layers of energy can be seen within her aura.

Facing me and taking her left hand within my right, I asked her to place her other hand on one of the plinths to her right. Then, with my hand on the other, we waited to see if my theory had worked and, between us, if we were able to open the portal.

As I faced Beth, I could still see the playfulness in her facial expression, and although loving, she wore a cheeky smile.

Something was urging me to move closer to Beth, and as I did, she leaned over to kiss me. As our lips embraced, suddenly, we were both in light. Standing not far from us was Selinah.

"Congratulations to you both on your relationship, it took a little while, but you both soon got there in the end – You both have my approval!"

I could see Beth rush up to her to give her an emotional embrace.

As Beth stood back from her embrace with Selinah, Selinah then said, "Beth, you have been chosen to stand in my place alongside Gulielmus. This decision wasn't taken lightly, as some would disagree. However, seeing how you have blossomed recently has gone in your favour. Great responsibility comes to those who hold this position. Gulielmus loves you dearly, and we know there is much you both can achieve together. I ask you to look after him, as he is special to me and important to our people".

As Beth and I moved closer, Selinah said, "Soon, you will be returning to the future. This is where you will complete your journey to rescue the others".

I then noticed Selinah walk up to Beth. Taking her to one side, I could hear Selinah ask, "Are you sure about this? Once done, there is no going back!"

"I love him and...".

I couldn't grasp the rest of Beth's response as her voice became muffled, directed for Selinah's ears only.

I could see Selinah step away from Beth. As she did, whispery white iridescent energy began to appear, encircling Beth.

Selinah smiled at me to acknowledge my feelings and said, "It is time for me to go, and I will see you both soon!"

Selinah began to gradually fade from sight. As she did, I then found myself slowly and unwillingly returning, hoping to delay the experience of seeing Selinah leave us.

"Wow, that was something!" I heard Beth express with delight.

Hearing Beth, as my eyes started to open, I could now see she was waiting for me to return. I could also see the energy building around her with my eyes open.

"I'm only just getting started!" I replied and then smiled.

Beth then started to laugh at my response.

"So, what do you suggest we do next, as we are all alone?" asked Beth. She then winked at me to continue with the banter.

I could see she was waiting for me to respond. Although I liked where the conversations were heading, and I could feel the excitement of the energy between us, I knew we needed to focus. But I felt something inside required me to let this continue, so I thought I would meet her halfway.

Smiling, I responded, "Where do you want to take it!"

"Our meeting with Selinah had stirred something within me, and I can't explain or even describe to you how I am feeling right now. Especially without embarrassing myself", Beth went on to say.

I had a feeling she was aroused by the creative energy building with her. Stimulating parts that would normally be pleasurable when performing certain exercises.

Her eyes were now closed, and as the iridescent energy increased, it wasn't long before she began to rise slightly up from the ground.

"I'm here, Beth!" I voiced out to her, so she could hear me. Just in case the transformation was interfering with her hearing.

I could feel the intensity increase within her and noticed the expression on her face as she was trying to deal with it. Although I could begin to see her breathing had changed, I needed to somehow pacify her.

"Gulielmus!" Beth voiced out.

I could hear the tone of her voice change, followed by her inhaling deeply and then exhaling with deep short breaths.

"I am here with you!" again, raising my voice to provide her with some reassurance.

I noticed that she was perspiring from the heat her body was producing, accompanied by the colour tone of her cheeks as they appeared to blush a rosy red.

"It's just too hot!" expressed Beth.

I could then see her using her tongue to moisten her lips, slowly circling from top to bottom. This was followed by her briefly tugging a few times on her top to cool herself down. I knew I couldn't help her at this stage, as she was going through a change that would raise her energy to the point that her abilities to manifest would be enhanced. Apart from wanting to help, if I intervened, it could be detrimental to her health at this stage of the transformation.

I could see Selinah briefly appear in a spiritual form next to Beth.

"Selinah is with you. Try and reach out to her. Try not to focus on me, as it will not help".

"I can see her – This isn't easy!" I heard her exclaim as she then was biting her bottom lip while slightly raising her head.

I could then see Beth as she was slightly trying to adjust her body, as she was somehow trying to pacify the urges that she felt. While simultaneously trying to keep her dignity intact without too much embarrassment.

"Beth, what you feel is integral to a change within you. This will help you to manifest to your fullest potential!"

Looking at the tablets containing the writings, I could feel a presence altering the energy within them. It was as if someone was reprogramming them. I also noticed the writings soon told of another story not relating to this place, and the information on the portal was removed.

"Gulielmus, this is Selinah", the words could be heard as a soft whisper in my ear.

"I can hear you", I replied out loud.

Selinah said, "I have now finished reprogramming the portal, restricting its use".

Her words began to fade at this point, and the transformation had been completed as if on cue. As Beth started to be lowered to the ground with the energy that encircled her, I could see she was about to collapse. I managed to capture her in my arms and then gently lowered her to a seated position on the ground. Beth was unconscious when she sat with her body embraced in my arms and her head resting on my shoulders.

I knew Beth needed to rest, and I was happy to be her cushion while she recovered.

While I waited, I started to reflect on what I knew. All I could manage to focus on was how I felt, and Beth was central to it. It was interesting to see how she reacted to the transformation. I'm sure this will be a talking point with her later, amongst other things! Reflecting on what conversations we could potentially have, made me smile and chuckle a little.

It wasn't long before my eyelids started to get heavy. Knowing that we were safe within this period, I let them slowly close. After a short time, I found myself awakening, and as I opened my eyes, I could see Beth was looking at me.

"Thank you for not taking advantage of me earlier!"

"I could never do that to you!"

Beth then leant over to gently caress the left side of my face with her right hand. As she looked lovingly into my eyes, she then leaned further in to kiss me, caressing my lips with hers.

As we parted lips, my heart rate increased, resulting in the comfort and joy the kiss had given me.

"Gulielmus, with what went on with me while I was going through the transformation, it stays between us, as no one, I do mean no one, else needs to know, do you promise!" Beth went on to say with a smile.

I could see where she was coming from and how embarrassing this would be for her. Although it was a natural process, I respected her wishes.

"Yes, I promise".

"Thank you".

Adjusting my position, I managed to get back on my feet. To help Beth, I then reached down with my right hand. Grabbing my hand, Beth was able to pull herself up to get to her feet, and as she did, I felt her brush up against me.

Although I wasn't sure of the intention, I couldn't help the feeling in the way it was received. My attention then went directly to Beth, observing her while she was brushing herself down and then wiping away any dirt. It was as though she was teasing me again.

"Can I ask, are you still feeling, you know, the urges? From the transformation process?" I asked.

I could see Beth look at me with an expression as if butter couldn't melt in her mouth, and then she replied, "I can't help how my body is reacting - it... it just needs a little bit of TLC!"

I couldn't help but smile in her attempt to, in her way to seduce me.

"Although tempting, Beth, you will need to control your desires. Your energy needs to be contained, for now anyway, as the transformation process is still in its early stages.

"I understand, but it isn't easy to pacify these urges – I can't help it!"

I needed her to fully understand how important it was that she could, in no terms, release the creative energy that was channelled to her.

"I know what you are trying to say! I will do my best to control my urges – Just keep your distance from me, as being close to you is not helping!"

Realising her dilemma, I did what she had asked until she was ready to continue.

A little time had passed, and I could see Beth was looking my way, observing me from where she had rested. She didn't seem overly pleased, as I could imagine her thoughts and emotions were conflicted.

I decided to approach her, as I felt it was time we had left.

"How are you feeling?"

"I feel... It's not my finest hour!"

"Are you ready to continue?"

I could then see Beth nod to indicate that she was ready.

Taking her hand, we walked back to the part of the cave where we had previously stood, behind the large rock near where Suzy was standing captive. Although we were standing close to each other, it was good to see Beth could temporarily restrain herself.

As we closed our eyes and held hands, we focused on returning to the point in time in the future after we had left.

I could soon feel a jolt within my body, and on opening my eyes, I could see that we had returned, back within our future from where we had left. Not feeling myself, I commented to Beth that something had changed, but not quite sure what had!

"I felt it too!" Beth replied as she looked a little out of sorts.

## Chapter XXXI

## The Enchanted Isle of Emlkuyh – The Cavern Part II

As I appeared behind the rock, I could see more soldiers with weapons. Dark mists were coming out of the crevices within the walls. I could see Beth's great-uncle standing near Henry, but there was no sign of Jane or Suzy.

"Who were they fighting?" I could hear Beth enquire.

I wasn't sure where to start, as there appeared to be a lot going on, and the view was also restricted from where I had positioned myself. We could hear someone shouting out to Beth from above. As I looked up, I could see Suzy waving at us.

Surely, we hadn't changed the future that much.

The dark mist was everywhere, and it wasn't long before I realised what was happening. As I moved a little further, I could see L'Aisrell and her people were in the battle. They must have rescued the others!

Suddenly we heard a voice behind us. Turning around, we could see Suzy.

Thinking about how she had managed to get down here in such a short time, I remembered that she could teleport.

"Where did you both go?" asked Suzy.

"A little bit of time travelling", Beth replied.

"We had to put events into motion – We need to get everyone that matters out of here as soon as", adding to what Beth had said.

"Good luck with that!" exclaimed Suzy. She then went on to say, "Henry is still with him, and he's not himself. There is stuff coming out of him that I had a feeling that is somewhat the cause of all this. I did, though, manage to get Jane to safety – Then, they just appeared, these huge creatures. I was pleased that they appeared to be fighting on our behalf".

"How are you feeling, Suzy!" I heard Beth ask.

"I feel better now that you both are here!"

It was good to know that Suzy was still on top, gaining strength within each encounter and the challenges that were put to her.

Turning away, I needed to assess and see how the battle was fairing.

"So, what have you really been up to - don't go telling me any little white lies now. I know something needs to be aired!" I heard Suzy enquire with Beth.

"I thought this would be interesting to hear!"

Turning back to face them, I noticed Beth whispering something in Suzy's ear.

I could then see Suzy turn to face Beth as she went on to say, "Oh, I'm sorry, Beth! Honestly, I can't believe you had to endure all that by yourself. Look, I know you love him...".

I could then see Beth interrupt her to whisper something else into her ear.

Suzy then replied, "Oh, I see!"

They both looked at me as if expecting a response or a reaction.

I could understand that girls would like to talk, but time was crucial to what we had learnt, and we needed to bring everyone together.

"Suzy, can you please teleport Jane here, and once returned, can you both wait for the portal that will open here soon? Could you then please help Jane through to the other side of the portal? We will follow shortly after we have collected Henry".

"I will ensure that she gets through. Please ensure you follow; otherwise, I will return to get you!"

After Suzy left, I turned to face Beth and said, "I thought we weren't to discuss this with anyone!"

I could tell by the expression on her face that her emotions and thoughts were still conflicted, and even though I thought she had control of it, I was wrong. I could see that her health was deteriorating with each minute that passed us by. It wasn't long before Beth started to feel sick, as her complexion turned pale. I was also wondering if the jolt had triggered her body to react this way.

"Please, Gulielmus – I can't do this!" Beth exclaimed while trying to compose herself.

I could see Beth lean over to release the build-up of sick.

Thinking back to my previous conversations with Selinah and with Beth's transformation, I felt I had misplaced my focus. Although I still needed to be here, I knew that Beth's condition also deserved my full attention. There wasn't any doubt in my mind that she needed to leave with the other two. Her health and even her life could be at risk. I knew that the only viable option was the Ecriyin stones and that they would be able to heal her. If she went back to the city, there wouldn't be much that the local physician would be able to do.

It wasn't long before the portal appeared, shortly followed by Suzy with Jane.

By this time, I could see Beth was crying, holding herself for self-preservation.

Turning briefly back to face the direction of the battle, the situation didn't look as if it was improving.

As I returned my focus back to Beth, although I could see that Jane was attending to her, I could see that she was doing her best to try and keep it together.

Turning to face Suzy, I informed her that the portal was the only way out. As I had the feeling the portal was somewhat reacting to my needs, I advised her that the exit to the portal would appear near the Ecriyin stones. When they arrive, they must head to the stone in the centre. It would benefit them all to receive the healing that the stones would offer them. Although Suzy had queried about the soldiers, I had a feeling that they all were in the cavern, fighting alongside Beth's great uncle. I then shared this with her. With the assistance of Jane and Suzy, it wasn't long before the three of them entered the portal.

Any efforts now were to rescue Henry. Although, I did find it hard to focus, as my thoughts of concern were with Beth and her health.

With my attention set on getting to Henry, suddenly, time began to slow down to the point where it had stopped. I was then able to walk to where Henry was kept. But, as eerie and uncomfortable as it looked, darkness could be seen to materialise from the facial orifices of his body.

I could see that Henry was frozen in time like the others. From the expression on his face, I could see that he was in pain. His face was pale, supported by piercing pitch-black eyes.

Turning to face Henry's uncle, I could see he was wielding a black crystal in his right hand. I wondered if the crystal I could see him with had been a part of the crystal I had seen on the ring in General Hammond's possession back on earth. Were the two crystals one and the same?

With the intention set to restore time, time soon returned to normal.

"Where did you come from? Who are you?"

I could see that he was unsettled by my sudden appearance.

"Destroy him!"

It was as if no one had heard his command, as no one else could see me apart from him and Henry.

"It's no good, as you could voice as many commands as you like, they will not be able to see me or even sense my presence".

Seeing the statue behind and just off to his right, I asked him to take a look and went on to say, "As you can see, it is a pretty good likeness!"

As he did and realised who I was, turning to face me, I could see the panic on his face.

"It's not me who you have to be concerned about", as I had the feeling that Selinah would be arriving soon.

Suddenly a portal of light began to appear behind him. I could see him turn to face the portal and then place his focus back on me.

"You must really respect your elders", I called out to him.

As he turned his head slightly to face the portal, I could see his eyes fixed in anticipation.

Suddenly the crystal that he was holding had vapourised within his hand. Then, realising it had gone, I could see him look Henry's way.

Turning to face Henry, I could see him starting to recover. As he did, I noticed that he was looking my way. Interestingly I could see him nod to acknowledge who I was. Once I knew he was OK, I gave him the location of where the portal would be. With this information, Henry soon left us, hurrying to the portal to find his way to be with Jane. Shortly after he had entered, I felt the portal had closed from this side.

Looking around and seeing the battle, I knew I had to prevent any further unnecessary losses of life, especially that of L'Aisrell's people. I felt it was time to bring this fight to an end. Calling upon my Sceptre, I slightly raised it in front of me, just above my head. Again, setting the intention for this to happen, a great light appeared as before. It was good to see only L'Aisrell people had remained.

I could see that Beth's great-uncle was starting to feel unsettled with the predicament he was now finding himself in. Suddenly, to try and better his situation, I noticed that his physical structure began to slightly alter as if it was trying to take another form. Although as it began, I could see the process fluctuate back and forth slightly.

Back to his human form, I heard him exclaim, "Why can't I transform!"

Suddenly a voice could be heard behind him, as Selinah had appeared from the portal.

"Why do you continue to travel on this troubled path Ethan? I had forgiven you of your betrayal, but you never learn from that of suffering. Even with the many opportunities I had given you to correct this path to right-a-wrong, you still disappoint me and again cause disappointment for yourself. As I had given you the power to transform, I have now taken it away, along with every other power I had bestowed upon you".

Although I knew only of his relationship with Beth until this point, I now knew of his name!

"I'm sorry, Selinah!" I could hear Ethan exclaim, knowing the seriousness of his situation as it confronted him now.

Selinah then walked from behind Ethan to the front of him. I could see his head turn as his eyes followed her. As she stood next to me, she went on to say, "I have corrected a wrong, one that I should have done many years ago. However, I'm not going to give up on you, as I now need you to prove to me that you are willing to change. I will, though, be watching over you. I know it isn't going to be easy, especially with what you have put your people through, but you need to learn. Are you ready to be challenged physically, mentally, and emotionally? Do you understand me and accept what I am proposing?"

Looking at Ethan, I could see that he had no other choice, especially if he wanted redemption. With his powers stripped by Selinah, he was now defenceless and alone. I can only imagine all the enemies that he has built up over the years.

"If I choose this path of redemption, who will protect me?"

"If you choose this path, then I will see that you stay alive, but you will experience suffering", I heard Selinah reply to him.

"How long for!"

"Until those you have wronged find it in their hearts to forgive you – It can't be forced. You must prove that you are worthy of their forgiveness and love for you to be accepted in their hearts".

I knew that my time here was nearing its end. Turning to Selinah, I could see she could sense this.

"Thank you, Gulielmus".

"Until we meet again, Selinah".

"I accept your proposal!" we heard Ethan exclaim, feeling defeated in his efforts.

"Of course!" replied Selinah.

"I have notified your people of your return. You will undergo a trial for the crimes against your people, along with other charges. Those who had been supportive of your crimes will also undergo the same treatment".

We were soon joined by L'Aisrell, in her human form, as called upon by Selinah.

"L'Aisrell, could you please do the honour of escorting Ethan back to his world and his people, as they are ready to receive him?"

"It would be my honour Selinah!"

"Thank you, L'Aisrell!"

With that, another portal opened. L'Aisrell was joined by two of her people in human form.

Before L'Aisrell left, I expressed my thanks to her and her people. Not only for protecting this place but for helping to fight alongside the others. I also wanted to acknowledge their valour at these times and to accept my heartfelt apologies for the losses they had incurred.

"Thank you, Gulielmus! It means a lot to our people. They will always be remembered in our hearts and within our memories".

As I turned to face Ethan, I noticed his hands were tied together by an electronic device. I was advised by Selinah that this was to prevent him from escaping.

L'Aisrell soon left with her people as they escorted Ethan through the portal.

As the portal closed, Selinah told me that the portal that led us to this world was now closed permanently. She then enlightened me about my reasons for arriving on earth.

"You appeared as a child primarily to understand the needs and requirements of love and relationships. Beginning with understanding frailty, which could be offered to a human, especially at a young age. For you to fully embrace the part, any knowledge that proceeded you needed to be temporarily removed from your memory, including your abilities to manifest".

"Can I ask about Jane and Henry and how they fit into all this?"

"Jane was known to you and Beth before your life incarnations on Earth. Through a mutual agreement, she had agreed to help you with your learnings. It was also agreed that Beth would be a part of it! You were to arrive at a crucial time to help Jane elevate her understanding and perception of the world and others around her. In establishing the relationship with Jane as her niece, Beth was also to help her aunt surpass her own suffering. Especially with those around her, including Henry and Suzy".

"Is Beth known by any other name?"

"Like us, there are many, but she prefers this one".

I had a feeling that Selinah received some news that she needed to share with me.

As if on cue, Selinah shared, "Gulielmus, I have been informed that the crystal on the ring within General Hammond's possession had also vapourised. It had occurred at the same time as the crystal that Ethan had held".

I thanked Selinah for sharing this new information with me.

Finally, we had accomplished what we had set out to do.

Embracing Selinah as we said our goodbyes, a light soon encircled and embathed us both. Then, as the light receded, I soon found myself back on the streets within the city of Camarierhn.

Looking around, I hoped I would find the others arriving soon. As it was a beautiful day, I thought I would take a pleasant walk through the marketplace. It wasn't long before I noticed a little stall selling statues, necklaces, and bracelets. Intrigued, I thought I take a closer look. As I began to see what could be of interest, a voice could be heard from behind me,

"Have you found anything interesting?"

*Chapter XXXII*

# Camarierhn City

As I turned around, I noticed Elijah, Henry's father, was standing before me.

"As you are here, Elijah, I can gather you are back in residence?"

"Indeed, let me first thank you, William, or Gulielmus, as you are known around here, for rescuing my son and my granddaughter".

It was interesting that he hadn't mentioned Jane or Suzy!

"Have they arrived yet!" I asked.

"No, not yet, but let us continue to have a nice stroll, as we have been blessed with beautiful weather".

We began to walk, leaving the area of the marketplace. As we walked past others, I could see that they acknowledged Elijah with respect.

"You know, Gulielmus, I hear that you and my granddaughter are in a relationship!"

I began to wonder where this conversation was going.

"Beth has a beautiful soul and takes after her mother, and albeit I'm speaking to you, Gulielmus, I need to know that you have her best interest at heart".

"I understand!"

"Are you in love with her?"

"Very much so!"

"I am pleased, although, despite the age difference, you appear to look around the same age. What will happen to Beth when the years pass her by, as age changes her appearance? What will happen to you both then?"

"I will love her all the same...".

"Can you be sure of this?"

"With the alteration of her DNA, partly because of the bracelet, Beth had undergone a change. With this, with Selinah favouring her, she had chosen Beth to represent our people – Beth doesn't know the extent yet of what she is. She will never age beyond what she is now, and I hope to discuss this with her as soon as I get the chance".

"Did she get a choice? Was she aware of what she was signing up for?"

"It was her choice, her decision with Selinah! I... I had no part in it".

It then just occurred to me why she had been crying on the way to the cavern earlier. She must have known that the life she had, that one day, would only be a part of her past. They would soon become a memory for the family and the friends she loved and had known over the years.

If only I had known, I'm sure she had reasons to withhold it from me.

"I see... She has chosen you", Elijah had shared with me, and then went on to say, "You know, there is a home here for her, but we know she will want to be with you".

"I will honour her decision!"

"You could always base your home here and stay with us!" responded Elijah.

"I could... It is a conversation I will need to have with Beth".

"I can trust that even what I know of you and what you are capable of, you will do the right thing by her?"

"I will!"

"Good, I am pleased we are on the same page!"

I wasn't sure what I agreed with, but reading between the lines, I knew he was watching out for his granddaughter.

"What about your brother, Ethan?"

"My brother, as outlined by our laws, will pay for his crimes. I understand Selinah has asked that we keep him alive. Brother or no brother, we will make sure that the punishment fits".

I could then see him beckon others to join him.

"Gulielmus, this is where we part. Again, I would like to express my gratitude!"

I wasn't sure what to make of our conversation. Though I felt as if I was being interrogated.

As Elijah left, he was soon joined by his guards.

Intrigued by earlier, I turned around and went back to the stall in the marketplace, to the one that I had found of interest.

Surprisingly, I could see little statues of Selinah and me, which made me smile. I thought about buying Beth a little pendant necklace as a token of my love for her.

"Is there anything of interest, maybe something I could help you with!"

Looking up, although the voice sounded familiar, a scarf could be seen to partially cover her face. From what I could see, I was unable to recognise her.

"I was looking for a pendant for someone special!"

"Let's see what I could do to help. May I know the name of the lucky girl who has captured your heart?"

"Why do you ask?"

"Each name resonates to a certain vibration! I would like to ensure that the pendant fits the person".

"How does that work?" I asked out of curiosity.

"The young lady you were referring to".

The woman then revealed a bracelet similar to the one gifted to Beth at the village fayre.

"I have a matching pendant necklace".

"Where did you get the bracelet from?"

"I am sure Bethany would like the pendant to match", the woman suggested.

"I didn't mention her name. What game are you playing?" I asked.

"No game... I happen to hear your conversation with Elijah".

I wasn't sure what she was up to, but I am sure I didn't mention Beth's name in front of her.

"They are one and the same! As the bracelet is now part of her, so must be the pendant".

"Who are you?" I asked.

I could see that she placed the pendant on the table and then said, "Take it... please take it, as the pendant will be needed".

As I looked down at the pendant, for that split second, I could feel a breeze encircle me. Then, as I looked up, an old man looked at me and asked, "Can I help you, sir?"

Curious, I asked, "May I hold the pendant?"

"Where did that one come from? It's not one of mine!" replied the old man. "If you want it, and I am not sure why I am saying this, you can have it".

The old man soon handed me the pendant in a little bag and then continued with another customer

Feeling unsettled by the chance meeting earlier with the woman had presented many questions that populated my mind. This increased further piqued my curiosity about who the mysterious woman was. Though I felt a depth with her, I had a feeling we had spoken before. So why now, and what did this have to do with Beth?

As I walked away from the marketplace, I looked back a couple of times, wondering where I could have seen her from.

Feeling a little fatigued, I looked around for a seating area I could rest on. With the help of the locals, I was soon directed to what is generally referred to as a park. Finding a place to rest, I noticed I was kept company by a small lake. It was now just a matter of waiting for the others to arrive.

The recent conversation with Elijah had absorbed some of my energy. All I wanted to do, for now, was to close my eyes.

Flashes of images then populated my mind. I initially saw images of Beth with Jane and Henry but not Suzy. Then the bracelet, followed by the pendant that was shown to me. I saw the pendant on the stall and then saw Beth wearing it. Images of Suzy then appeared, first by herself and then with Beth. I could then see Beth waving goodbye to someone, followed by all four of them sitting around the dining room table back home. Lastly, I could see another image of the mysterious woman.

Although there wasn't much I could make of what I had seen, I was sure that it would all make sense soon.

I was soon awoken, as I could hear someone calling my name and tapping my right upper arm.

"Gulielmus, please wake up!"

Although it was a struggle at first, I achieved it on the second occasion of hearing my name called.

As I opened my eyes, I could see Suzy standing beside me. Seeing her made me smile.

"Gulielmus, we need to go?"

"Go where?" I replied as I was trying to establish where I was. I felt like I was recovering from a deep sleep.

"They're waiting for us!"

"Sorry... Sorry, Suzy... who's waiting?"

Suzy went on to say that she had been looking for me for the past couple of days and finally found me on the morning of the third day.

Listening to Suzy, I was trying to fathom out what had happened and where the last couple of days had gone!

She then went on to inform me that she was about to give up but then, as if guided, was drawn to this park.

It was lovely to see Suzy and that she had made an effort.

As I enquired more, I was told that others had been searching, but they were ordered to return as the day progressed. It was only through Beth's connection to me that she was adamant I was still out there. As Suzy continued, she mentioned that Beth hadn't been the same, as her body was still adjusting to the change. I learnt from Suzy that Beth had spent most of the time sleeping while recovering.

I felt there was more to be told. Although I could feel that Suzy was hesitant, she had been a witness to something and wasn't sure how to put it to me.

"So, what are you keeping from me?" I asked.

"I'm sorry, Gulielmus – How do I put this? On one occasion, Beth had called for me, and during that time, she asked about you. It could have been five minutes, and while I was talking, she had a seizure, and then blood started coming from her nostrils. It happened all so quick. A couple of the physicians rushed into the room, and I was told to leave. As I was being hurried out of the room, I wasn't sure what they were doing with what I could briefly see. It looked as if they were putting something in her ears. I noticed that they didn't take kindly to me being there... I know I don't practice medicine like Beth, but it didn't look conventional. I believe they're saying that I had something to do with the deterioration of her condition. I was informed that they would deal with me appropriately if I was to go near her again. I had to leave, and that is why I had to find you".

"Surely Elijah understands what is happening to her", I responded to her concern.

I then reflected on my conversation with Elijah. Thinking about it now, about his questioning, something didn't ring true with him.

"From what I have learnt, he does things by the book and is also against the plans to let Beth leave with you".

"It isn't his choice, as it is up to Beth!" I responded.

I then asked, "So, how is Jane coping?"

"Currently putting up with the in-laws. Sometimes she looks at me, and I can't put my finger on it, but certainly, she knows something is going on or is not happy with the situation. Also, it is as though the light has gone from her".

Thinking about what the mysterious woman at the stall had told me. I thought about the pendant. Taking it out of my pocket, I handed it carefully to Suzy.

"When we arrive at the House of Hibahrous, I need you to go to Beth's room. While Beth is resting, it is important that you place the pendant around her neck!"

"It's beautiful!"

"Could you do this for me, Suzy?"

"Of course! Is it magical like her bracelet?"

"Only that it will help her!"

"Would there be one for me?" Suzy replied and then smiled.

"We'll see".

I went on to tell her that if she heard any commotion from the main hall, she would stay with Beth, just in case I needed her to teleport Beth out of there.

"I have tried, but something in there is preventing me from using my abilities".

I felt a cool breeze gently caress my left ear. As it settled down, I could hear soft voices whispering to reassure me. Firstly, putting my mind at rest about Beth. Secondly, reminding me of the portal I had gone through earlier to arrive in Emlkuyh. The portal had been within the room where they had initially interrogated Henry. What if there were other tears in the fabric of the protective energy field? This could mean the protective shield was breaking down. Maybe there could be a chance that we could use this to our advantage. We would need to act fast, as this would be of concern for those who lived in the city. This would make the city vulnerable to attacks, especially from other realms. For now, everything seemed to be calm.

I shared with Suzy the whispers I had heard and what I had realised.

"How are we going to even know where to look!"

I shared with Suzy how the protective shield was first established.

"First of all, how old are you, and secondly, what is your secret for remaining young?" Suzy enquired.

"There is something that I will need to share with you later!"

"So, does it come in a bottle?" Suzy replied with a cheeky grin.

I laughed a little at her response, as I wasn't sure where this topic of conversation was going.

"Can I ask you something!"

I noticed the colours of the energy of her aura had changed, as varied shades of pink, red and brown appeared around the heart region.

"Of course!"

"I have had thoughts recently about my baby!"

Sorry, Suzy, I had forgotten! Looking at her, although I could see that she was barely showing, she indeed was pregnant.

As if on cue, I received a vision of the child that was yet to be born. It was still intact and healthy. I then shared with Suzy what I had seen.

I went on to say, "Your baby is still being protected".

I could see that she was relieved. Suzy then reached over to briefly embrace me in her arms.

"Thank you, Gulielmus!"

As she pulled back, she asked, "What about Jane and Henry?"

"I just need you to focus on Beth, for me".

"Leave her to me".

What I kept from Suzy was that my powers and even Selinah's weren't prohibited in their use, especially within the city. It was something Selinah, and I had agreed on in case of situations like these. So I just chose not to use them.

We started to make our way to the House of Hibahrous as quickly as possible, with Suzy taking the lead.

As we reached the gates, I informed Suzy I needed to take a breather.

As we waited, I could see she worried about the reception we would receive as we entered.

I could see that Suzy was scouting the area for guards. While she was distracted, this allowed me to restore the protective shield over the city. By doing this, it will then prevent any other magic or power from being manifested. With the recent rift within the energy field causing a disruption within the protective shield, I couldn't delay this any further. Also, others may take this opportunity as an advantage for control. I couldn't tell Suzy what I was about to do, but when this had finished, she would be one of the first. With my intentions set, I began to cast a chant that would restore the protective shield over the city. I could start to feel the Ecriyin mystical stones were being reset. It wasn't long before restoring the protective shield over the city was complete.

As I gathered myself, I asked Suzy to step to one side with me, saying that I needed to talk to her about something. That it was necessary to be in private, away from prying eyes.

"Oh Gulielmus, I'm flattered. What will Beth say!" she giggled and then winked at me.

I love her sense of humour, her banter, and especially her cheekiness.

"You had me there! Although there is something I truly need to share with you".

I could see Suzy flush and then respond, "It sounds exciting - will it take long?" She then continued to giggle.

It was good to see that she was still upbeat and making light-heartedness about the situation we were faced with by bantering with me. I could see why Beth and Suzy had gotten along.

With us both moving into a short alley, away from prying eyes, I went on to say, "Suzy, you are a good person and one who acts from the heart".

Asking for her hand, I placed it on her chest with my hand over hers.

Smiling, I softly said, receiving a short glimpse of her thoughts, "Suzy, honestly!"

"OK, what are you having me do?" enquired Suzy, as she was trying to understand what I was up to.

"You know we all love you. It is where your heart is, where your true power lies. When you need to act, it is here where you need to apply your focus to empower your strength and your abilities".

"Gulielmus!" I could hear her voice my name in such a way. It was as if I could read between the lines to enquire where I was going with this.

"Are you OK with me continuing?" I asked her.

Although there was a short silence, I could see her nod to confirm she was happy for me to proceed. I could feel her trust me, as I was sure she knew there would be a reasonable explanation for why I was getting her to do this.

I could then start to feel the centre of my palm tingle. Within minutes, a part of my soul energy, of my power, was channelled, passing through my hand into hers. As the intensity increased, warmth and light started to flow into the pendant. It then flowed into her heart and then around the rest of her body. I first noticed that Suzy's chest began to glow, and then it happened with her eyes. I could see her take a deep breath. As she released it, I felt the part of her that was holding her back had given way. She seemed a little shaky to start with, and I could see that her emotions began to react as tears began to flow from her eyes. Her cheeks had started to blush a rosy red. Removing my hand to release hers, I waited for the change to complete within her.

Seeing the way she was, I knew I had to help her. So I went on to say, "Breathe, as it will help with the process".

I could feel the heat radiate from her as she began to perspire and then wipe the tears from her eyes and the sweat from her brow.

Taking her hands with her palms facing down in front of me, I could see they were shaking.

With a heart like hers, I felt she had graciously earned the right to evolve to the next stage of her spiritual evolution and spiritual awakening. As for my gift to her, I had bestowed a greater power of manifestation. Therefore, Suzy now also has the right to use her newfound powers within the walls of this city.

With her hands in mine, I then focused on bringing the harmony back within her core self.

I could feel her body temperature drop back to normal as she brought her emotions back under control, which I was pleased to see.

"How are you feeling?" I asked.

"What did you do?"

"This is my gift to you!"

I then went on to explain to Suzy that she was now empowered with a power that was far greater than she had. Therefore, a great responsibility has been bestowed upon her to use the power wisely. I then mentioned how we, including Beth, now have a telepathic connection, irrespective of wherever we are. So, if she needed us, we were only a mental thought away.

"If ever you would like me to remove this power, then I will understand", I asked her.

"I am truly grateful! It was just unexpected, that's all".

"I understand!"

"So, as you have done this for me, I assume you are not without your powers?" Suzy asked.

I smiled at her question and replied, "We need to keep this between us for now. Elijah will probably think he has the upper hand".

"So, what will I be able to do?" Suzy went on to ask, as I could see her curiosity aroused.

"Let's keep it simple for now... Just the teleport. Remember to keep your emotions intact. Also, let's keep this between us for now!"

"You can count on me!"

We both then made our way to the gates of the house, with Suzy again taking the lead.

As we arrived, we were soon approached by two of the guards of the House of Hibahrous to escort us into the main hall.

I noticed that both Elijah and Henry weren't there to greet us, but it was good to see Jane, although I could see that she wasn't herself.

As I looked around the hall, I could count around seven guards. Some were guarding doors that led into other hallways or rooms.

Just as I was about to speak to Suzy, I noticed that she had quickly made her way to Jane. It was good to see that Jane had welcomed her with a brief emotional embrace. Suzy was quite the tonic, and if anyone was going to liven up Jane's mood, it would be her. I could see them talking, catching up on gossip. I also noticed the odd laugh too.

Wanting to know what was happening, I walked over to them both.

"William!" Jane exclaimed.

"If you prefer to still call me William, then that's fine... I honestly don't mind".

I could see that Jane wasn't sure how to approach me.

Looking at Suzy, I heard her say, "I have told Jane everything, summarizing where I could ...".

Moving closer to Jane, I reached out to hold her in an embrace. I whispered in her ear to reassure her that I was still her William, who had matured into a young man.

I felt her strengthen her grip to hold me even tighter, "I missed you!"

As we parted our embrace, I could see her wipe away some tears.

The guards appeared to be watching our every move and listening to our every word. I can only assume that this was for Elijah's benefit.

"I'm not happy here! I miss my home", Jane shared with us.

"So, what's keeping you here?" I asked.

"Partly Henry, but once his father found out I was pregnant, the idea to return home was squashed. I'm sure that his father has brainwashed him into staying!"

"So, have you spoken to Henry privately about your feelings on the matter?" Suzy asked Jane.

"I have, but he's still undecided at the moment!"

I thought about Henry, considering the circumstances he is presented with while being here. I suppose, learning that his father and sister were still alive, he needed to get his head around the notion of it being true. It was an opportunity that very few people get the chance to have. Knowing that when he was a child, he was told that his father had been a casualty of war. It was then later in life he presumed that he had lost his sister Emma to cancer. It was as though he was given a second chance, and I realised that this would be hard for him to give it a miss.

I shared my thoughts with Jane and Suzy to help them see it through Henry's eyes and possibly see how emotional this could be with him at this time.

"I do understand, and I am supportive of him. But I just can't be here, and the longer I stay, I know I will not be happy!"

I thought about what Jane had said. Going over it in my head, as thoughts populated my mind, "If Henry remains inside the city, then he can't be a danger to anyone or himself. But, If returning home with Jane by his side, there could be a possibility that she should be able to help him control his power. And within time, I'm sure that he will learn to master it".

We could soon hear Henry and Elijah's voices as they returned to the hall. Accompanied by Henry's sister and Beth's mother, Emma.

"Ah, Gulielmus, you finally have graced our house with your presence?"

I looked at Emma and could see she was keeping quiet.

Turning back to face Elijah, I replied, "Thank you for welcoming me".

"So, what can we do for our distinguished guest?"

"I have come to see Beth, especially knowing she has been unwell!"

As he was about to respond, I could see him addressing everyone within the hall before turning to face me.

"Beth is sleeping, and she's not to be disturbed".

"I would like to see her while she sleeps".

"As I said, she is resting, and, on this occasion, she will receive no visitors. Are we clear?"

I noticed some of the guards had left their posts by the doors to gather around to provide him additional support.

Turning to face Henry, "Surely, one visit will not hurt!"

I could see Henry turn to Jane and then back to me. I could see that he wasn't happy with the decision he was going to make, supporting his father.

"Can you please come back another day! She does need her rest".

I could feel my eyelids close for a brief moment, only to receive a vision of Beth coughing and looking a little pale. I knew she could feel my presence, as I could hear her telepathically call for my help.

As I opened my eyes, I casually turned my gaze to Suzy. I could see her nod to confirm she was also able to receive Beth's request telepathically.

"Henry, I understand you are only supporting your father. However, I feel Beth needs help, and I am sure you understand! If not for me, then how about doing it for Jane!"

I could then see Henry look at his father.

I went on to say, "Henry, she is your niece, and this is Beth we are talking about!"

Henry, along with Jane, left the room to check on Beth.

While we waited, all eyes were upon me, and I could see Suzy was waiting for my signal.

"Elijah, why are you doing this?" I asked.

Although what he offered was silence, from his emotional energy, I could sense a sadness within him.

"Elijah, I respect you, but you will only create misery within your own household".

It wasn't long before Henry returned. I noticed Jane wasn't with him.

"Father, Beth isn't improving; she's getting worse!"

"I must take my leave to be with Beth, Gulielmus please leave this house. My guards will escort you out".

I knew I needed to act! I then telepathically asked Suzy to put all the guards to sleep.

Testing the strength of her powers, the guards soon collapsed to the ground.

"What's going on!" I heard Elijah exclaim.

Turning to face Henry, "Jane really needs you right now!"

Knowing where this would leave him with his relationship with his father and sister if he left, I could see that Henry was torn.

"Henry, I promise this will not be the last time you'll see your father and sister".

Turning to Elijah and then to Emma, "Please don't make this difficult for them!"

I could see Emma nod in agreement.

Turning to face Elijah, I went on to say, "You will not lose sight of them, I promise! You must understand why I am doing this!"

He knew he had very little option but to let them go. With a slight nod from his father, Henry left the room to be with Jane and Beth.

I then asked Suzy telepathically to go and be with them and ensure that Beth got the pendant.

"Elijah, I'm slightly disappointed. Albeit for where we are, my powers are not restricted here. I helped to rescue your family and assisted in the capture of your brother. Please don't make this any harder for yourself or anyone else. Forcing your son and daughter-in-law to remain here, along with your granddaughter, would result in regret for all parties concerned. Build relationships with them based on trust and without any conditions. Be supportive and be happy for them, especially as you will become a grandfather to their newborn. You may even find that they will accept you more, allowing you to be an integral part of their lives".

I could feel a warmth build within my palm as I placed my right hand on his chest. Then, as the light started appearing, I could see it enter him. It wasn't long before his emotions had gotten the better of him, as I could see him break down emotionally in tears. I could only imagine the years he was deprived of his family and the burden he had kept deep inside. The anxiety, the stress of watching over them and the emotional longing to be with them. It must have been hard for him, for them not to know that he was there. Sometimes alone and often invisible, hiding in the shadows for their protection. All this I could sense, along with the pain that could be felt.

He was soon embraced by Emma, supporting her father.

"I'm sorry I wasn't a father to you, to Henry and Charlotte! It was hard for me to watch someone else bring you up. To miss out on your birthdays and where I couldn't be there for you when you needed me. But I did hear your prayers and laughed when you laughed. I was even in the background when your heart was breaking. This is why I find it so... so hard to let go, knowing that I am free to love you as I should have!"

"I knew you were watching over us! I always felt you close, father!" I heard Emma exclaim as tears appeared, flowing down her cheeks.

I felt for them both and thought about what I had learned. I then decided to share the following, "Whether you are the parent, the child, a friend, or a lover, each relationship is unique. From what I have learnt, with any age, with those in your life, the relationships are never forgotten; they are just often misplaced. Relationships are often delicate and even fragile – Subject to emotions and time. But, I will say, for the bonds that are made, especially... Especially the ones that were created out of love will last an eternity".

I noticed that the others, including Beth, were standing in the doorway listening to us.

I could see that Beth was wearing the pendant.

I could see the tears flowing as they stood there listening to us.

Emma soon released her embrace with her father to then stand by me.

It wasn't long before Beth, Jane, and Henry each had their turn to comfort Elijah.

"Emma"

"Yes, Gulielmus!"

I asked her to hold out her left hand, and as she did, I could see a bracelet materialise on her left wrist.

"This bracelet I am giving you will help you to travel great distances. Just within your mind, think about where you would like to be, and then a portal will appear. Please use this gift responsibly. This way, you and your father can visit Henry and Jane in their world and return to this one as often as you need to. It will only be visible to you and only activated by you".

Emma then threw her arms around me and kissed me quickly on my right cheek.

As she released herself from the embrace, she asked, "Will it allow me to visit my daughter!"

"Of course! Are you OK with us being in a relationship?"

I noticed that Beth was watching us.

Nodding her head, a gesture of confirmation, Emma then went on to say with an excitable tone in her voice, "Yes!"

I knew Beth wanted to get in on the act, so I stepped back from Emma.

It was good to see Beth and her mother happy, whispering and giggling together.

Turning to face Elijah, "Elijah, please adhere to Selinah's request about your brother! I know she will be observing from wherever she is".

"I will... I promise," responded Elijah.

It was time for us to go, and a portal soon appeared with this thought in mind.

As each of them said their goodbyes, Jane, Beth and Henry entered the portal. It left only me to step through.

As I waved goodbye to Emma and Elijah, I noticed Selinah standing not far from them as she presented herself in a spiritual energy form. I could see her smile, and then as she faded, she blew a kiss with her right hand in my direction.

Before I could respond, I found myself absorbed by the portal light.

## Chapter XXXIII

# Home Sweet Home

Arriving through the other end of the portal, I found myself in the old ruins of Jane and Henry's land. I could see it was light outside, so I started to make my way through the exit. As I left the building, I saw Charlie, our Labrador Retriever. He was lying on the ground, waiting for me. Although it was good to see him, I wondered why the others weren't with him.

Reaching down to pat him on the back of the neck and around the shoulders, I asked, "Where's mummy? Where's daddy... Charlie? Take me to them... Charlie, good boy!"

Then I could hear a voice behind me softly say, "You took your time! As soon as we knew you were arriving, we both came to welcome you home!"

Turning around, I could see Beth... although she appeared slightly differently! Noticeably Her hairstyle had changed, along with the colour.

"Beth, beautiful as ever... are you... what's... You look different from when I saw you just five minutes ago! Have you... Have you materialised this new dress... the hairstyle is new?"

I soon realised that someone else was standing in the old ruins I had just come from. Looking over Beth's right shoulder, I could see the spiritual energy of the mysterious woman I had seen at the marketplace.

"Gulielmus!" Beth called my name to bring my attention back to her.

"Gulielmus! Who are you looking at?"

A quick snippet of images flickered, appearing in my mind of children - like a reel of film as if I recalled memories. They seemed important, but to what extent, I wasn't sure. I could see myself lying in a bed amongst others, in a strangely familiar place in what appeared to be a hospital ward.

Beth's voice brought me back to the here and now. Seeing her waiting for an answer, I replied, "Sorry, what were you saying?"

"Gulielmus, it's been just over a year! When the portal closed without you coming through, we didn't know what to expect. Although I could feel your presence, you never returned. We had confirmation from Emma that you went through it, but fourteen months have passed by! Where have you been?"

## A Personal Thank You

*Dear Friend,*

*Through your truth, your love, and the insights you offer, it brings an understanding of who you are in your true self's identity. Let this be a blessing for others.*

*Share in the miracle of your life!*

*In the revelation of your wisdom!*

*Allow hope and faith to be your companion.*

*Lastly, I would like to thank you for taking the time to read my story. I look forward to you joining me on my next adventure from the new title of the series, "The Road to Recovery".*

*With love always,*

*William*

*(aka Gulielmus)*

# An Excerpt from "The Road to Recovery"

It felt that I was awakening from a deep slumber. I could hear faint voices echoing through the auditory space of my senses. I could feel my eyes gradually open, and as they did, my eyes began to grasp the sight before me. I found it strange, as the voices I could hear were no longer present. Apart from the silence, and within my initial observation, I appeared to be in a partially lit room with what I could make out to be a hospital ward. I could see eleven other beds. Six were placed against a wall to the left of the entrance, and another six were placed opposite. I was in a bed on the right, fourth from the entrance. Apart from one, every bed was occupied by a child. A few beds were accompanied by a respiratory system to monitor vital body organs. Before I could inspect further, I was soon drawn to two women in dark-coloured clothes. I could see the women move to the bottom of each bed and, from what I could assume, discuss the child's medical condition. Although I tried to hear, I couldn't make out their conversations.

I soon found myself in a seated position on the bed. I wasn't sure how, but it helped me get a better view of the ward.

It was then I could see another woman enter. From what I could see, she seemed to stand out more visually than the other two. Passing me by, I could see her walk over to a cabinet to my right, adjacent to the wall opposite the ward entrance. I noticed it was also adjacent to a large window, hidden by curtains. I could see her pull out a folded blanket and then place it onto a trolly just off to the right of the cabinet. Opening another cabinet door, one that was locked, I could see her retrieve other items but wasn't quite sure or could see what they were. I noticed that she then placed them under the blanket to conceal them. Once she had finished, she then closed and locked the cabinet door. Turning around to return to where she had entered, she walked past without even noticing I was watching her.

...

I started to hear a young boy's voice as he whispered a name in my left ear. Although I couldn't quite make out the name he was calling me, I could feel him gently push and pull me to wake me up. Then, not being successful, I could hear him call the name again.

...

Suddenly the lights in the ward had mysteriously switched off. I could feel a coldness envelop me. I felt unease and was soon unsettled as I felt something or someone was waiting for me in the darkness...